image comics presents

THE WALKING DEAD™

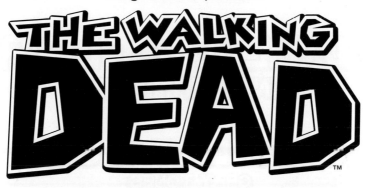

ROBERT KIRKMAN
CREATOR, WRITER

CHARLIE ADLARD
PENCILER, INKER

CLIFF RATHBURN
GRAY TONES

RUS WOOTON
LETTERER

TONY MOORE
COVER

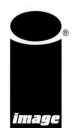

IMAGE COMICS, INC.

Robert Kirkman - chief operating officer
Erik Larsen - chief financial officer
Todd McFarlane - president
Marc Silvestri - chief executive officer
Jim Valentino - vice-president

Eric Stephenson - publisher
Joe Keatinge - sales & licensing coordinator
Betsy Gomez - pr & marketing coordinator
Branwyn Bigglestone - accounts manager
Sarah deLaine - administrative assistant
Tyler Shainline - production manager
Drew Gill - art director
Jonathan Chan - production artist
Monica Howard - production artist
Vincent Kukua - production artist

www.imagecomics.com

THE WALKING DEAD, VOL. 4: THE HEART'S DESIRE. Fifth Printing. Published by Image Comics, Inc. Office of publication: 2134 Allston Way, 2nd Floor, Berkeley, California 94704.

PRINTED IN CHINA

ISBN: 978-1-58240-530-8

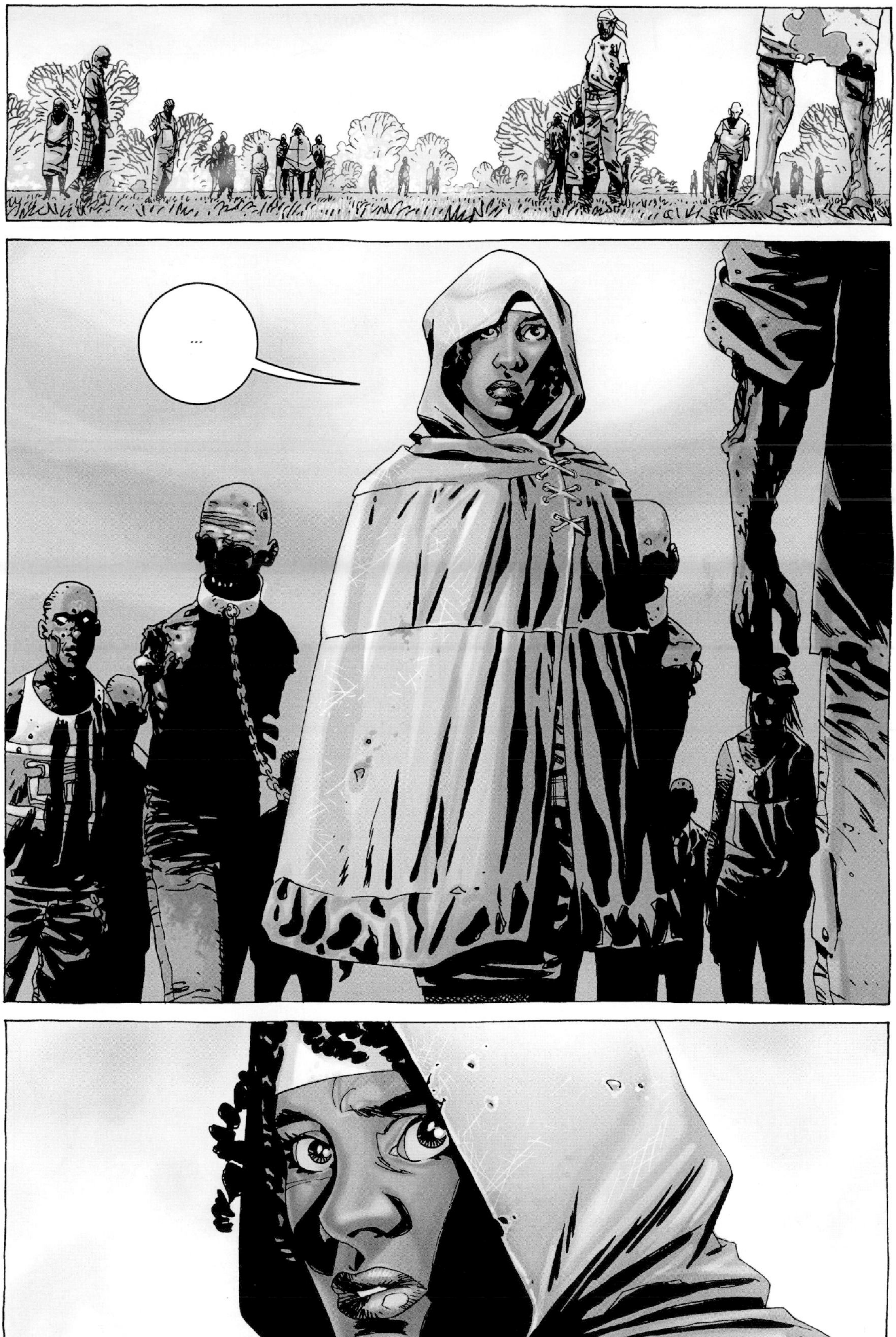
...

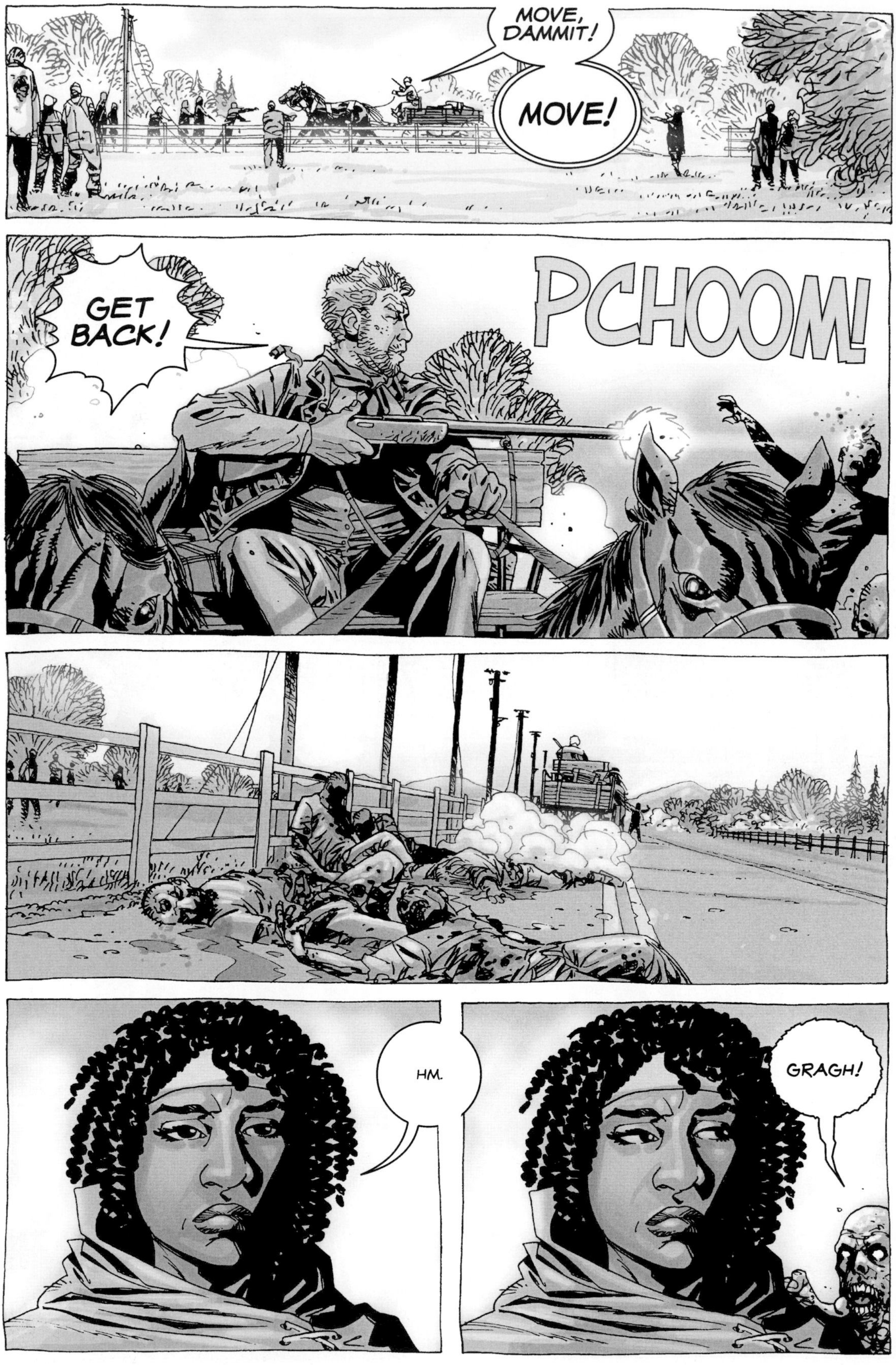
MOVE, DAMMIT!
MOVE!
GET BACK!
PCHOOM!
HM.
GRAGH!

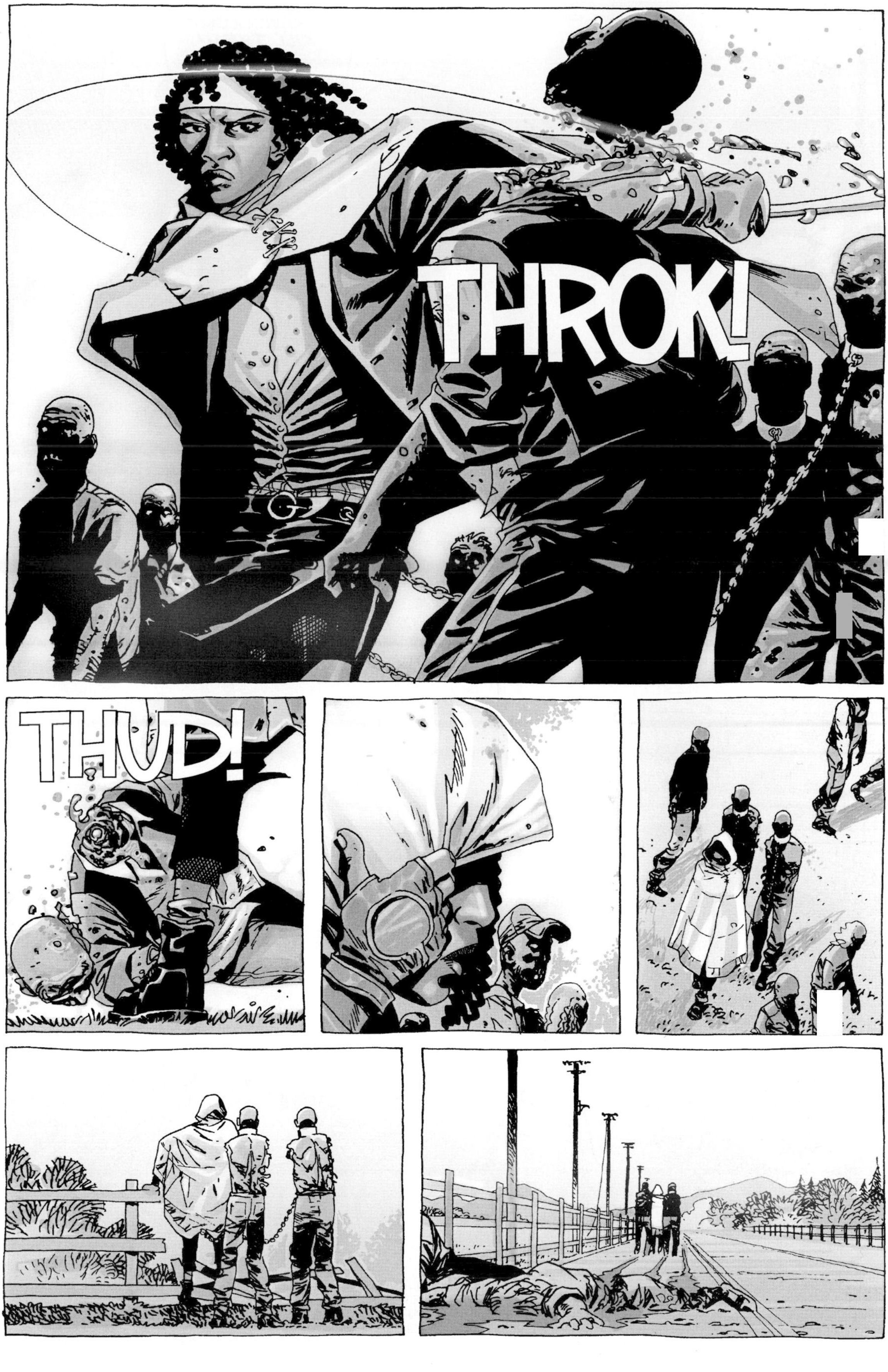
THROK!
THUD!

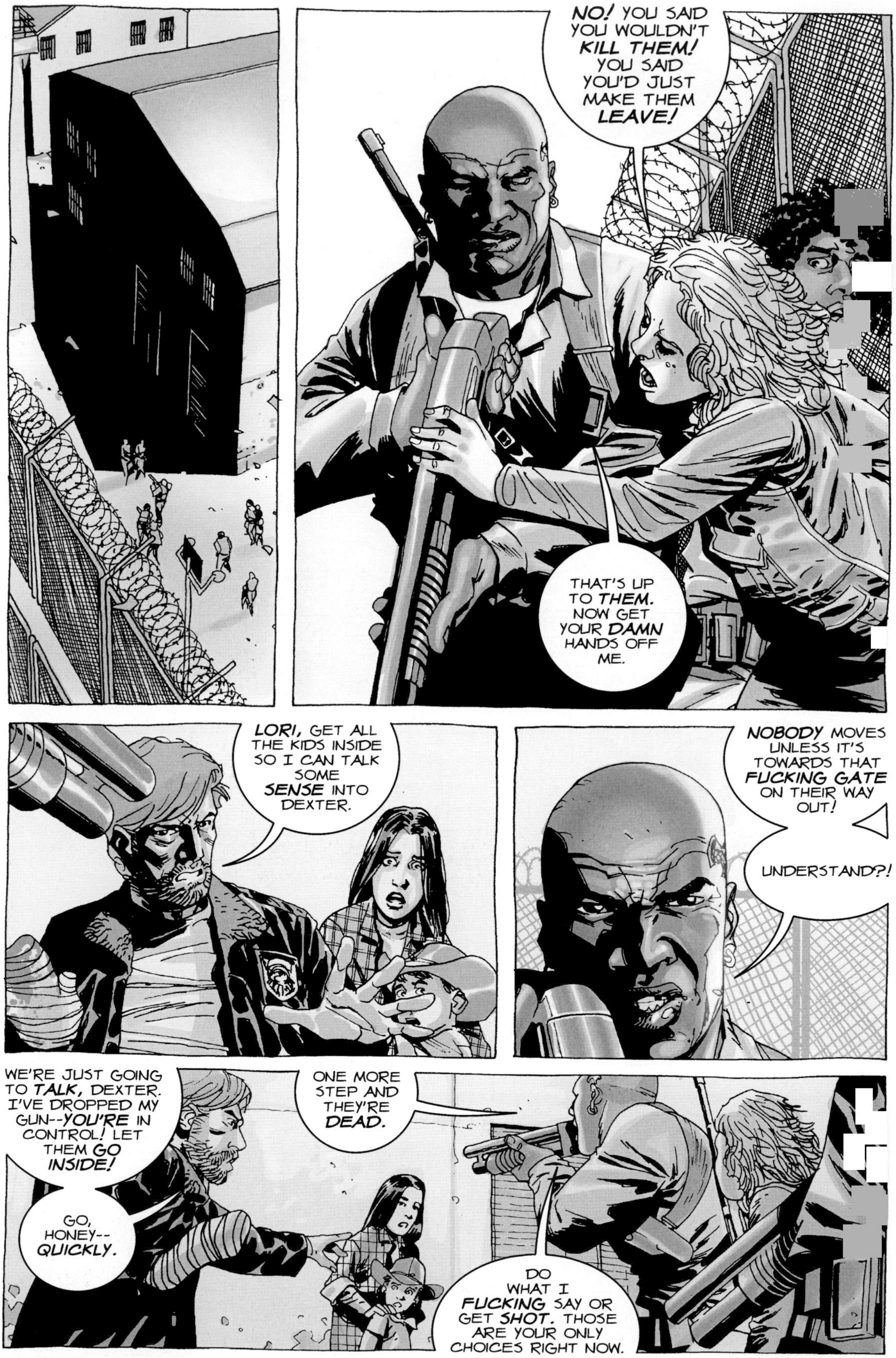
NO! YOU SAID YOU WOULDN'T KILL THEM! YOU SAID YOU'D JUST MAKE THEM LEAVE!
THAT'S UP TO THEM. NOW GET YOUR DAMN HANDS OFF ME.
LORI, GET ALL THE KIDS INSIDE SO I CAN TALK SOME SENSE INTO DEXTER.
NOBODY MOVES UNLESS IT'S TOWARDS THAT FUCKING GATE ON THEIR WAY OUT!
UNDERSTAND?!
WE'RE JUST GOING TO TALK, DEXTER. I'VE DROPPED MY GUN--YOU'RE IN CONTROL! LET THEM GO INSIDE!
GO, HONEY-- QUICKLY.
ONE MORE STEP AND THEY'RE DEAD.
DO WHAT I FUCKING SAY OR GET SHOT. THOSE ARE YOUR ONLY CHOICES RIGHT NOW.

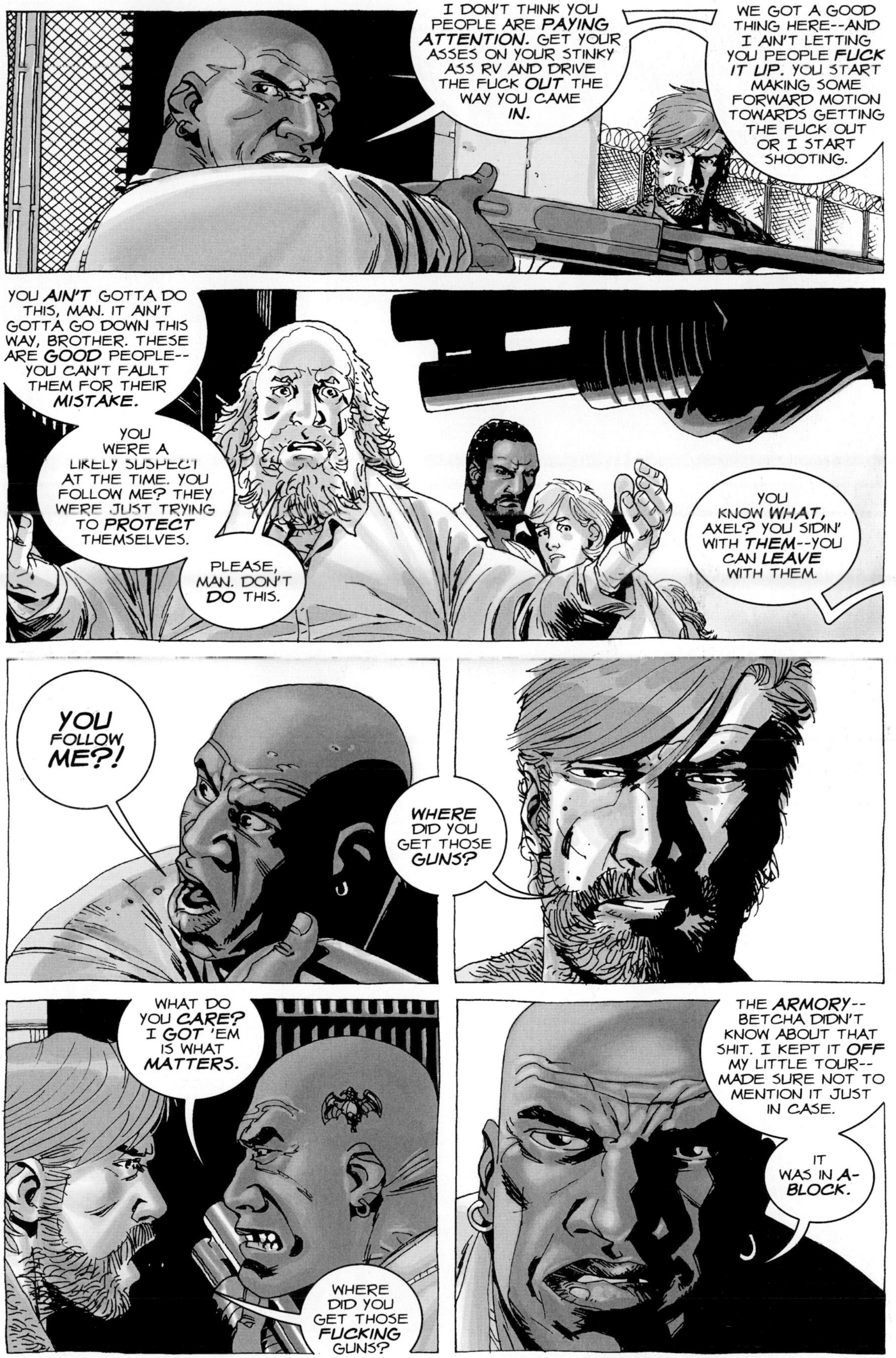
I DON'T THINK YOU PEOPLE ARE PAYING ATTENTION. GET YOUR ASSES ON YOUR STINKY ASS RV AND DRIVE THE FUCK OUT THE WAY YOU CAME IN.
WE GOT A GOOD THING HERE--AND I AIN'T LETTING YOU PEOPLE FUCK IT UP. YOU START MAKING SOME FORWARD MOTION TOWARDS GETTING THE FUCK OUT OR I START SHOOTING.
YOU AIN'T GOTTA DO THIS, MAN. IT AIN'T GOTTA GO DOWN THIS WAY, BROTHER. THESE ARE GOOD PEOPLE-- YOU CAN'T FAULT THEM FOR THEIR MISTAKE.
YOU WERE A LIKELY SUSPECT AT THE TIME. YOU FOLLOW ME? THEY WERE JUST TRYING TO PROTECT THEMSELVES.
PLEASE, MAN. DON'T DO THIS.
YOU KNOW WHAT, AXEL? YOU SIDIN' WITH THEM--YOU CAN LEAVE WITH THEM.
YOU FOLLOW ME?!
WHERE DID YOU GET THOSE GUNS?
WHAT DO YOU CARE? I GOT 'EM IS WHAT MATTERS.
WHERE DID YOU GET THOSE FUCKING GUNS?
THE ARMORY-- BETCHA DIDN'T KNOW ABOUT THAT SHIT. I KEPT IT OFF MY LITTLE TOUR-- MADE SURE NOT TO MENTION IT JUST IN CASE.
IT WAS IN A-BLOCK.

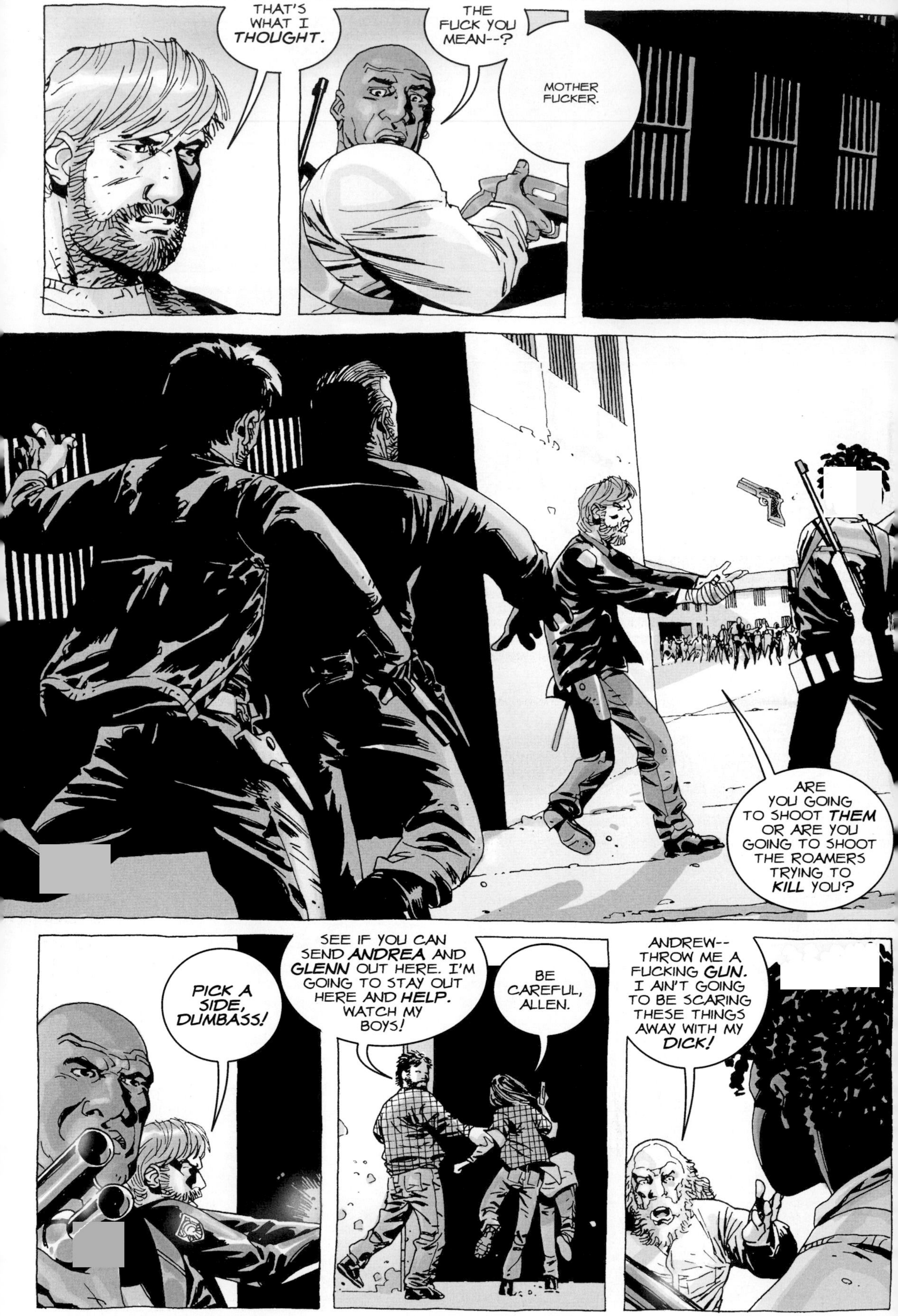
THAT'S WHAT I THOUGHT.
THE FUCK YOU MEAN--?
MOTHER FUCKER.
ARE YOU GOING TO SHOOT THEM OR ARE YOU GOING TO SHOOT THE ROAMERS TRYING TO KILL YOU?
PICK A SIDE, DUMBASS!
SEE IF YOU CAN SEND ANDREA AND GLENN OUT HERE. I'M GOING TO STAY OUT HERE AND HELP. WATCH MY BOYS!
BE CAREFUL, ALLEN.
ANDREW-- THROW ME A FUCKING GUN. I AIN'T GOING TO BE SCARING THESE THINGS AWAY WITH MY DICK!

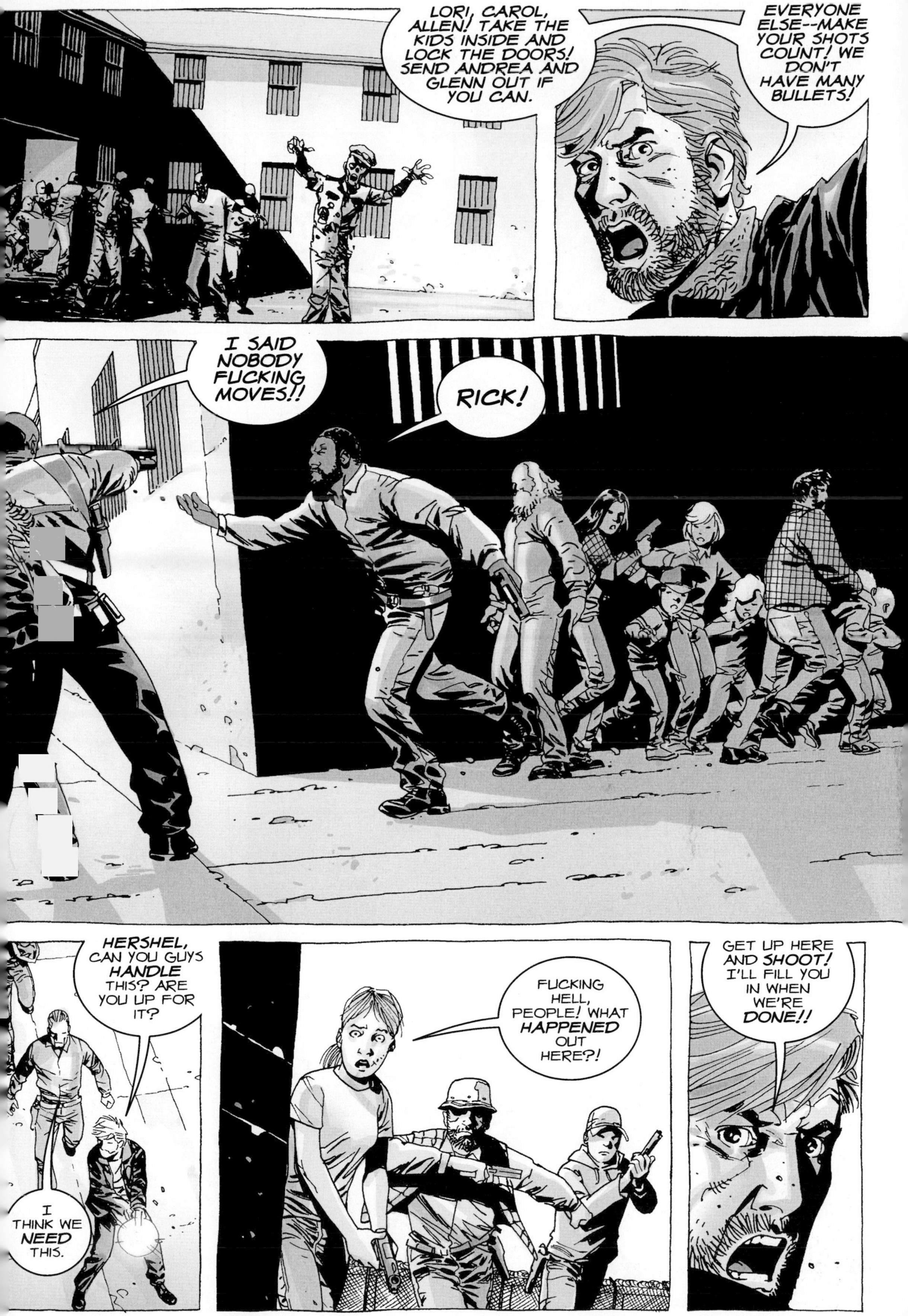
LORI, CAROL, ALLEN! TAKE THE KIDS INSIDE AND LOCK THE DOORS! SEND ANDREA AND GLENN OUT IF YOU CAN.
EVERYONE ELSE--MAKE YOUR SHOTS COUNT! WE DON'T HAVE MANY BULLETS!
I SAID NOBODY FUCKING MOVES!!
RICK!
HERSHEL, CAN YOU GUYS HANDLE THIS? ARE YOU UP FOR IT?
I THINK WE NEED THIS.
FUCKING HELL, PEOPLE! WHAT HAPPENED OUT HERE?!
GET UP HERE AND SHOOT! I'LL FILL YOU IN WHEN WE'RE DONE!!

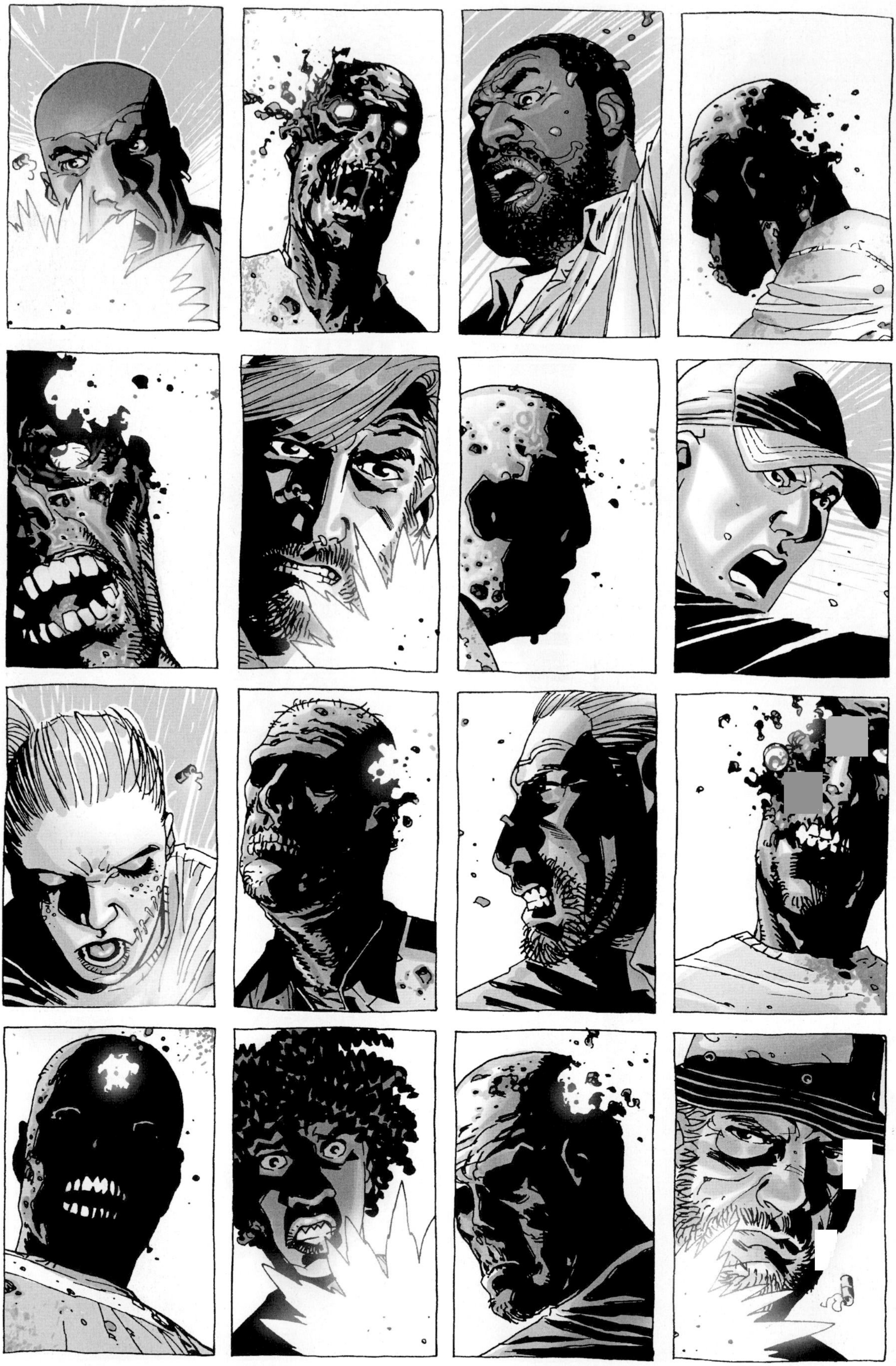

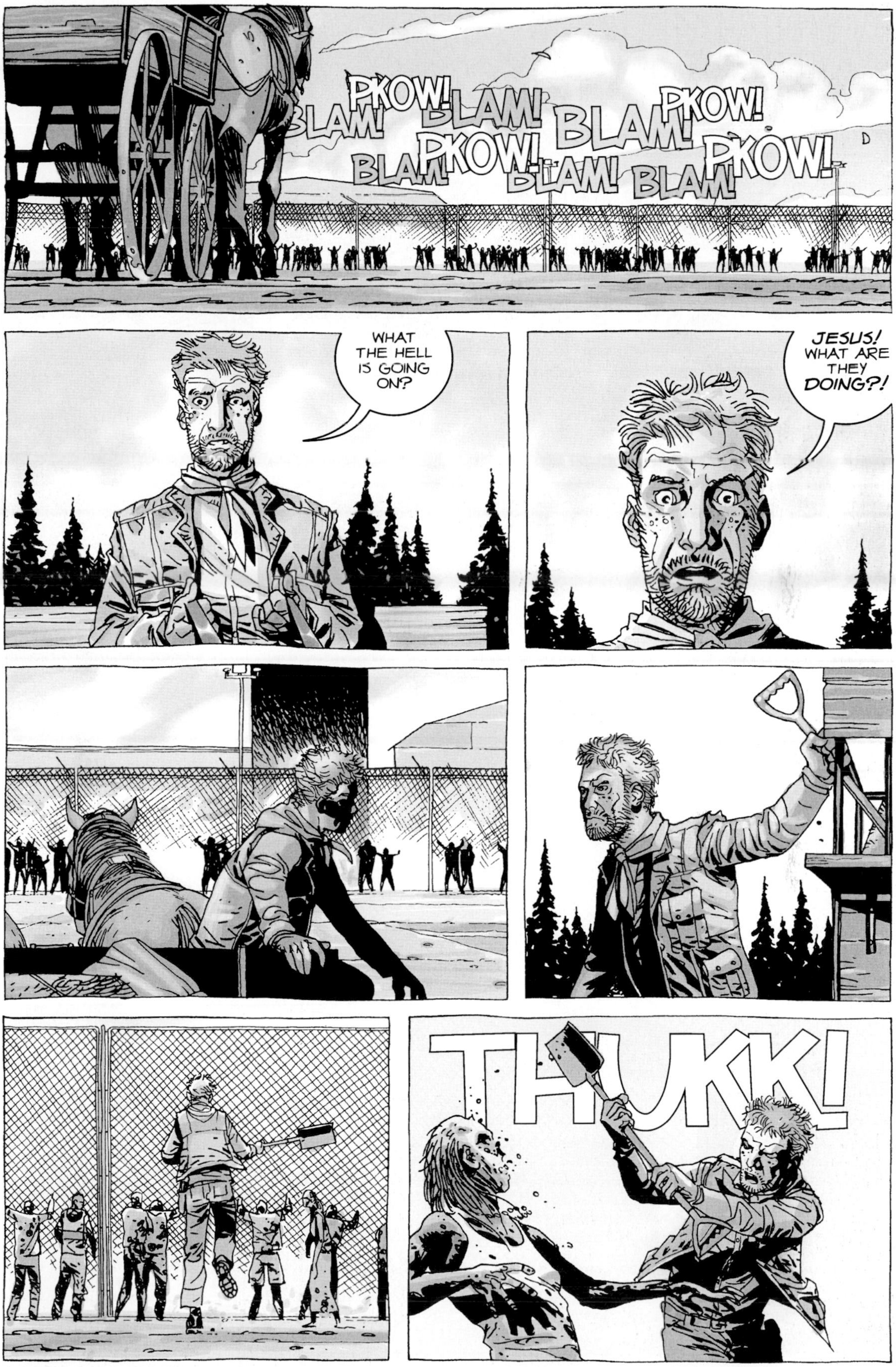
PKOW! BLAM! BLAM! BLAM! PKOW! BLAM! PKOW! BLAM! BLAM! PKOW!
WHAT THE HELL IS GOING ON?
JESUS! WHAT ARE THEY DOING?!
THUKK!

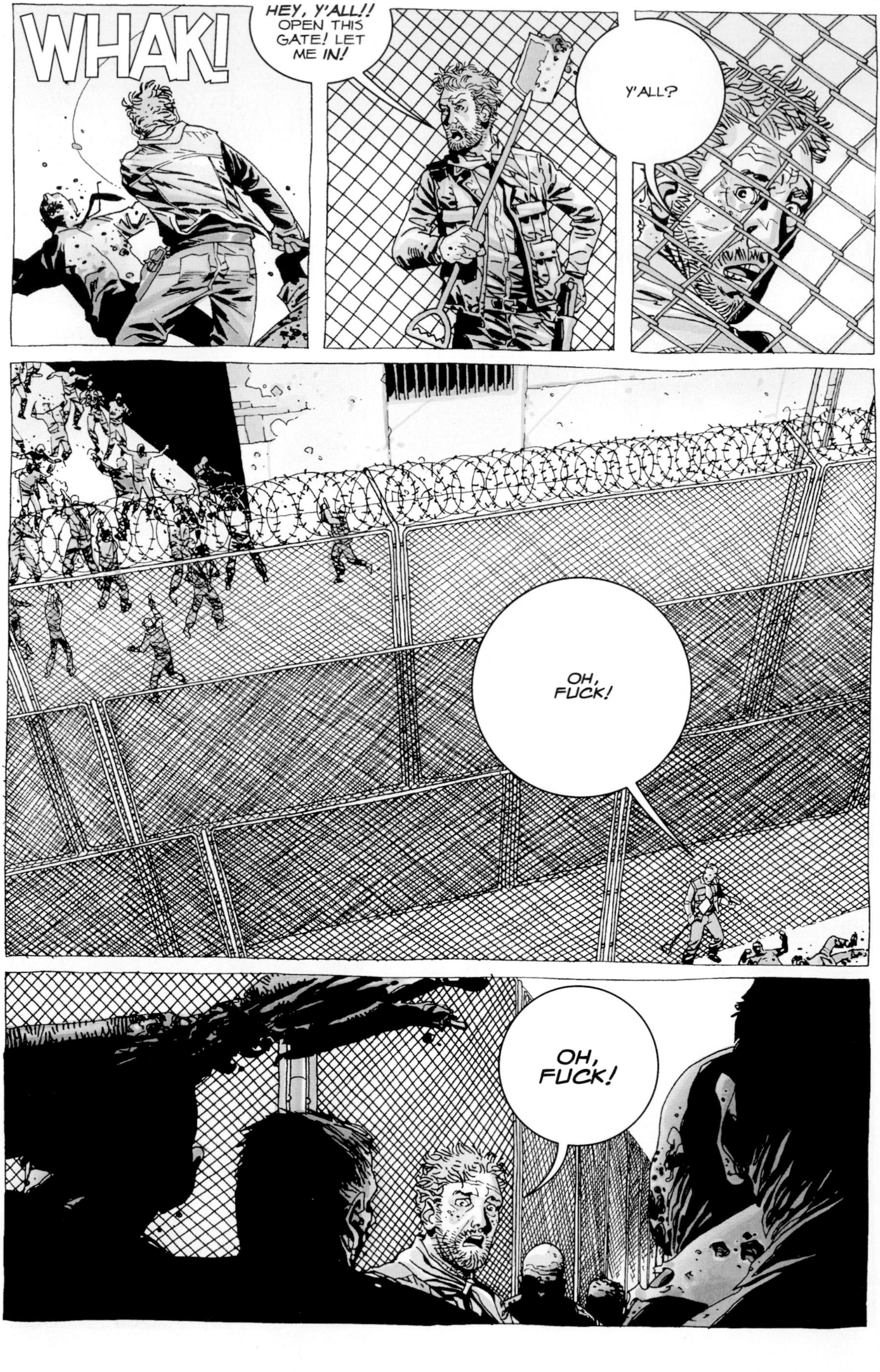
WHAK!
HEY, Y'ALL!! OPEN THIS GATE! LET ME IN!
Y'ALL?
OH, FUCK!
OH, FUCK!

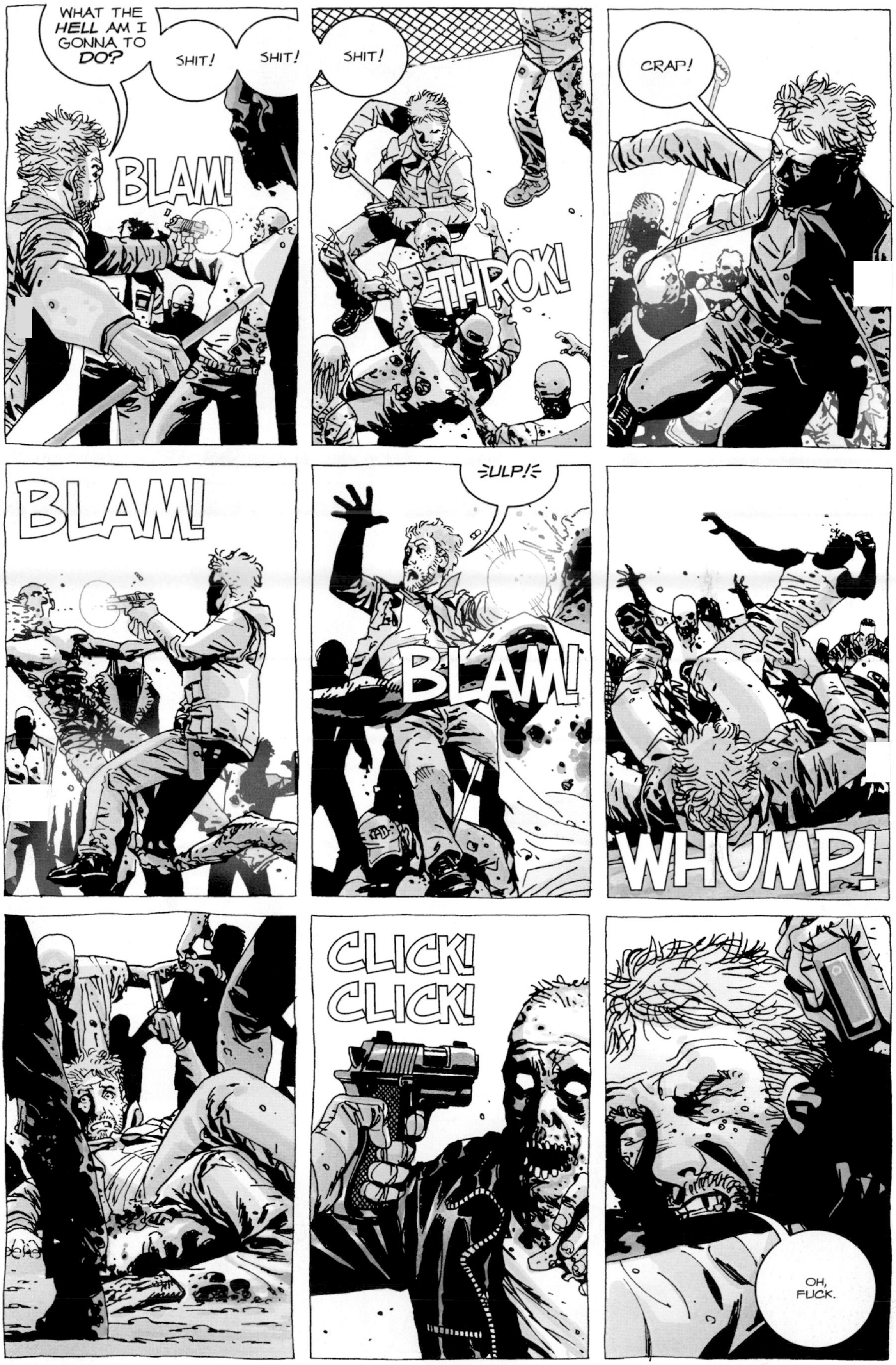
WHAT THE HELL AM I GONNA TO DO?
SHIT!
SHIT!
SHIT!
BLAM!
THROK!
CRAP!
BLAM!
ULP!
BLAM!
WHUMP!
CLICK! CLICK!
OH, FUCK.

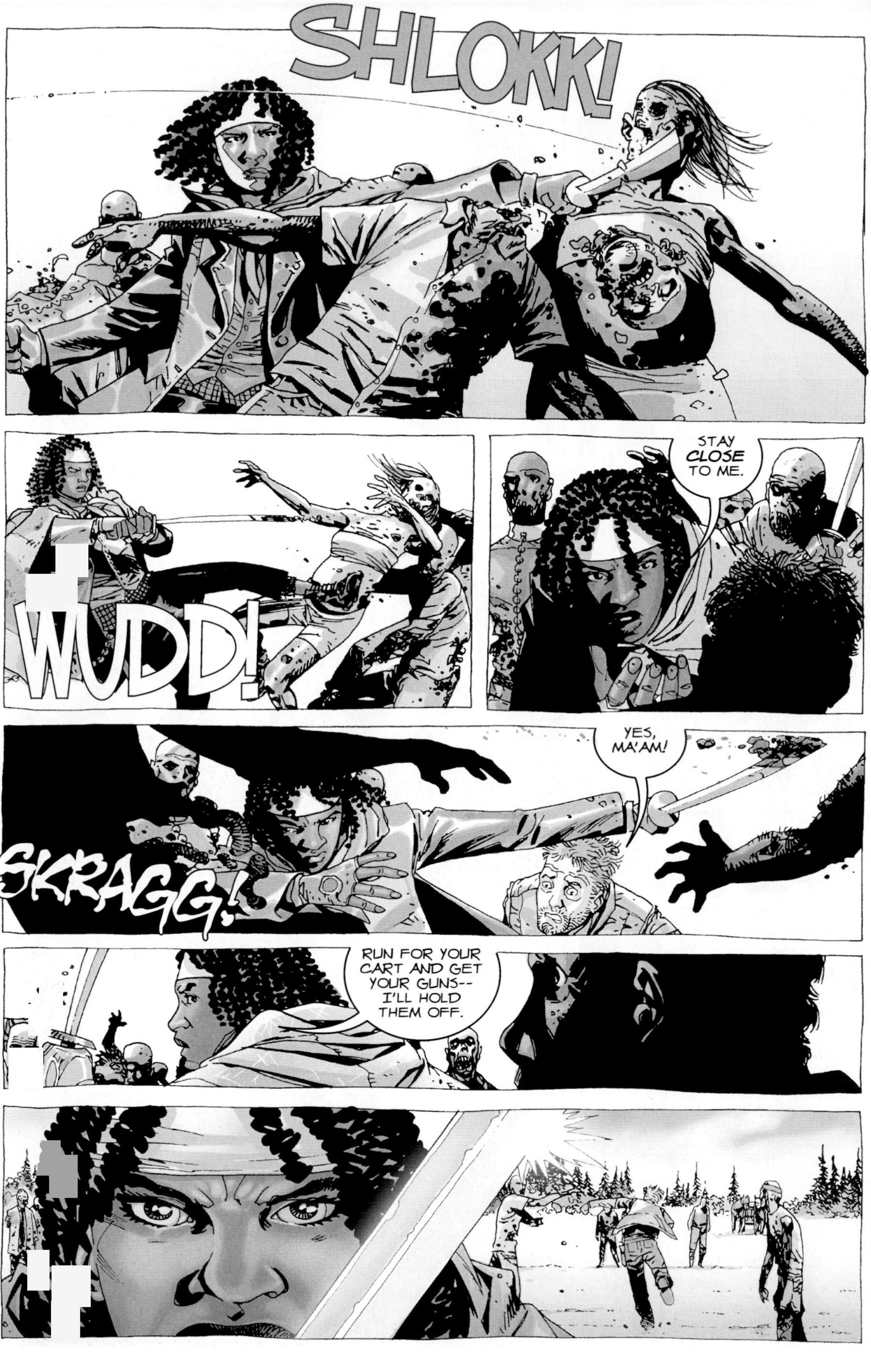
SHLOKK!
WUDD!
STAY CLOSE TO ME.
SKRAGG!
YES, MA'AM!
RUN FOR YOUR CART AND GET YOUR GUNS-- I'LL HOLD THEM OFF.

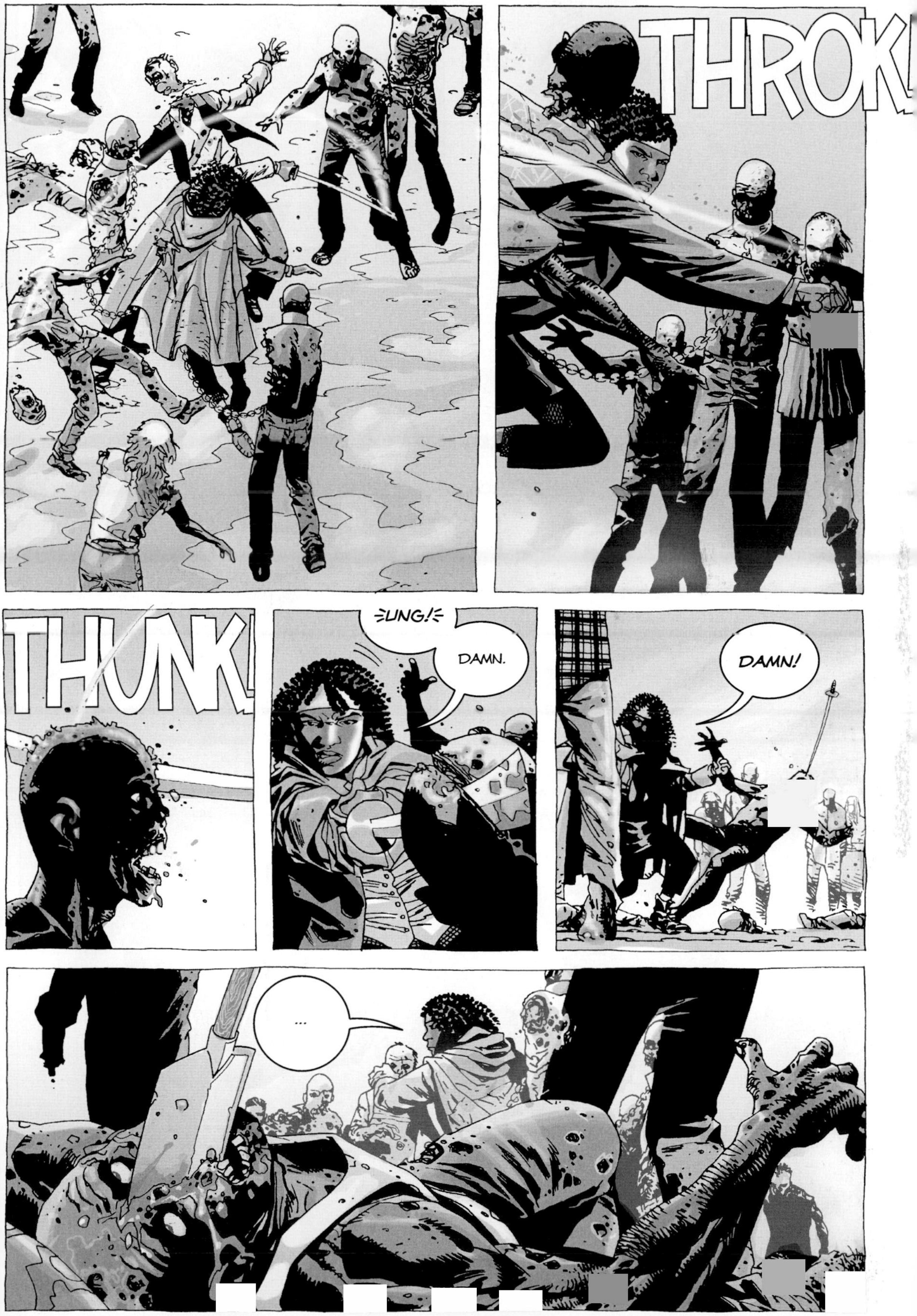
THROK!
THUNK!
UNG!
DAMN.
DAMN!
...

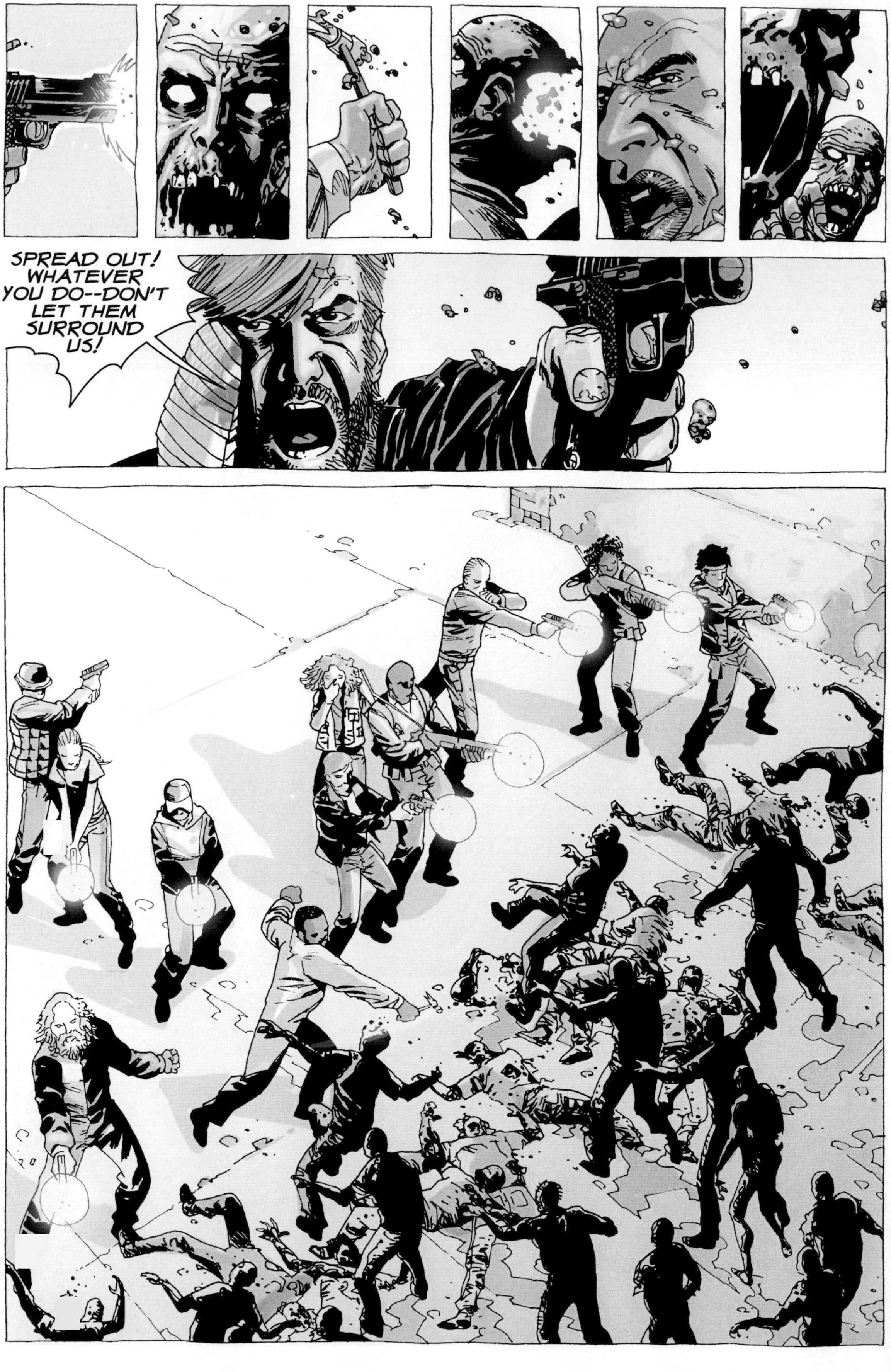
SPREAD OUT! WHATEVER YOU DO--DON'T LET THEM SURROUND US!

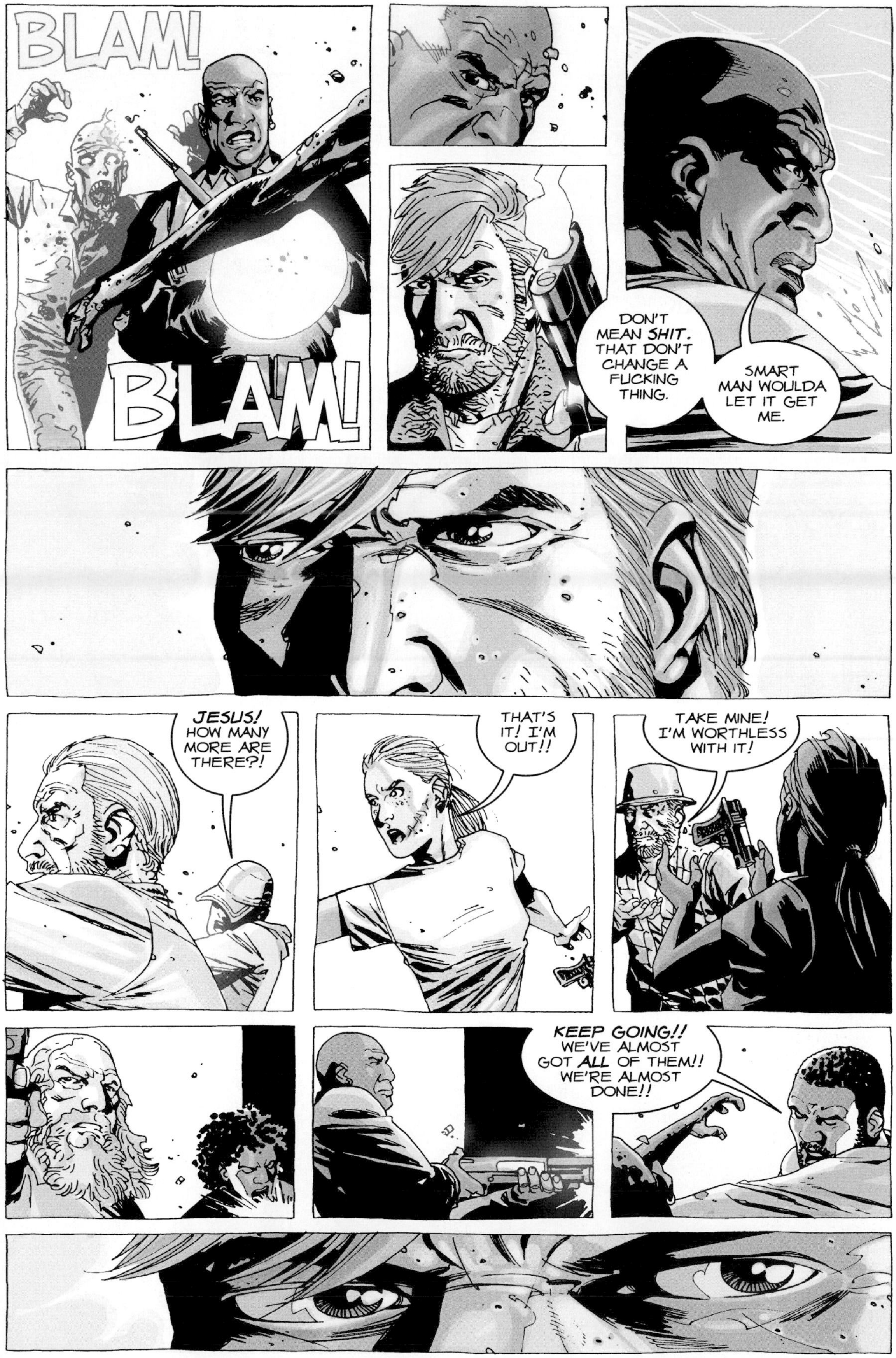
BLAM!
BLAM!
DON'T MEAN SHIT. THAT DON'T CHANGE A FUCKING THING.
SMART MAN WOULDA LET IT GET ME.
JESUS! HOW MANY MORE ARE THERE?!
THAT'S IT! I'M OUT!!
TAKE MINE! I'M WORTHLESS WITH IT!
KEEP GOING!! WE'VE ALMOST GOT ALL OF THEM!! WE'RE ALMOST DONE!!

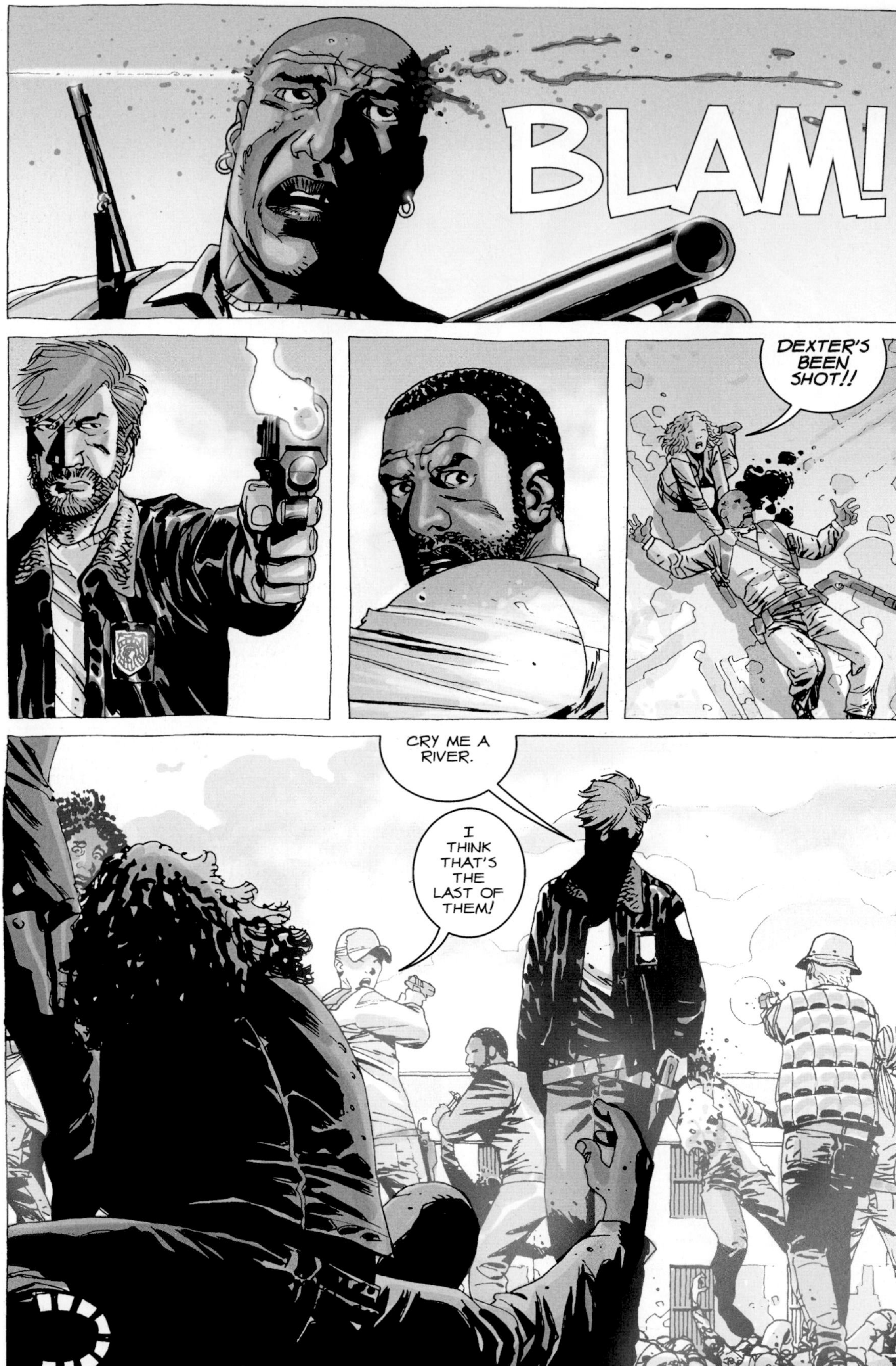
BLAM!
DEXTER'S BEEN SHOT!!
CRY ME A RIVER.
I THINK THAT'S THE LAST OF THEM!

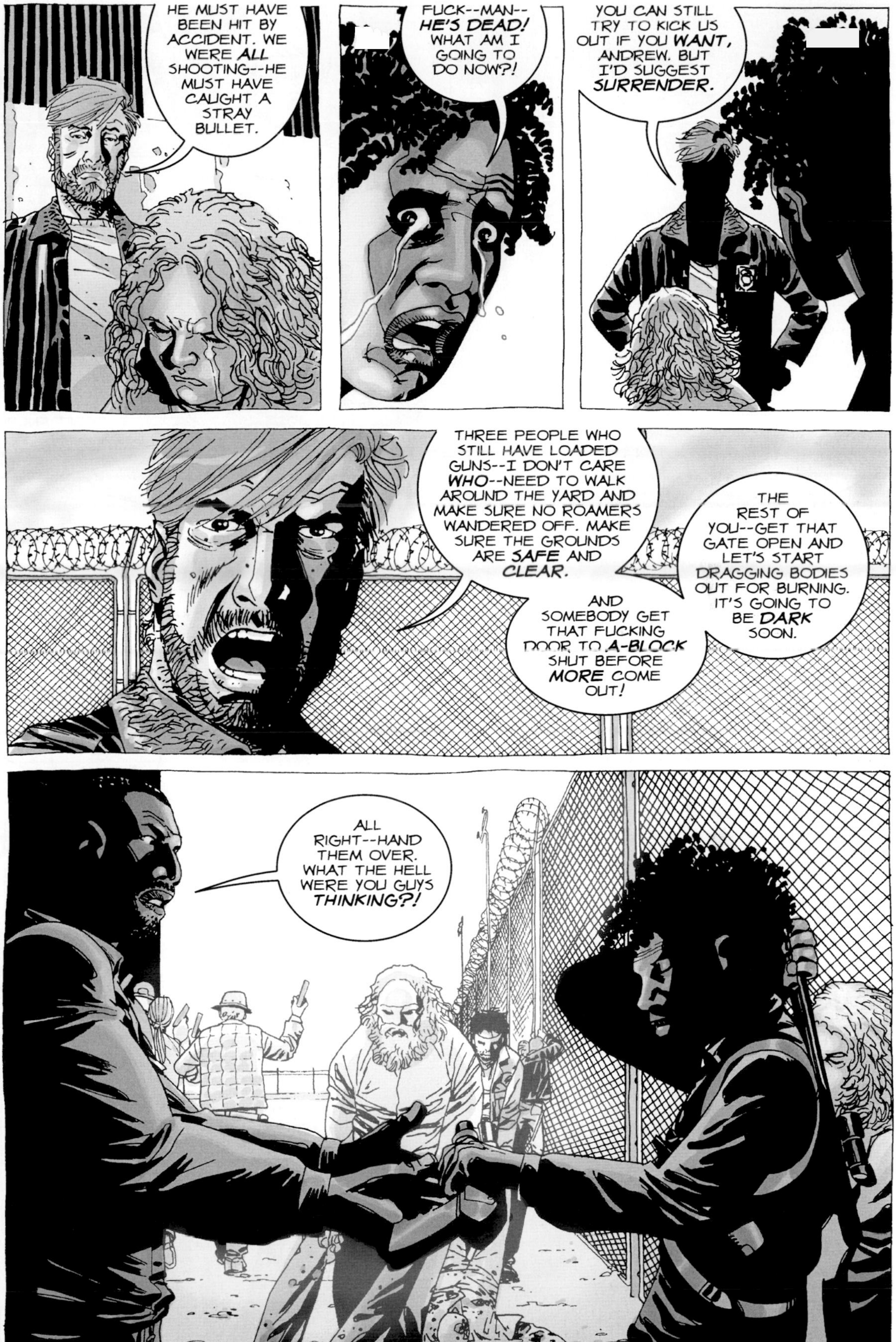
HE MUST HAVE BEEN HIT BY ACCIDENT. WE WERE ALL SHOOTING--HE MUST HAVE CAUGHT A STRAY BULLET.
FUCK--MAN-- HE'S DEAD! WHAT AM I GOING TO DO NOW?!
YOU CAN STILL TRY TO KICK US OUT IF YOU WANT, ANDREW. BUT I'D SUGGEST SURRENDER.
THREE PEOPLE WHO STILL HAVE LOADED GUNS--I DON'T CARE WHO--NEED TO WALK AROUND THE YARD AND MAKE SURE NO ROAMERS WANDERED OFF. MAKE SURE THE GROUNDS ARE SAFE AND CLEAR.
AND SOMEBODY GET THAT FUCKING DOOR TO A-BLOCK SHUT BEFORE MORE COME OUT!
THE REST OF YOU--GET THAT GATE OPEN AND LET'S START DRAGGING BODIES OUT FOR BURNING. IT'S GOING TO BE DARK SOON.
ALL RIGHT--HAND THEM OVER. WHAT THE HELL WERE YOU GUYS THINKING?!

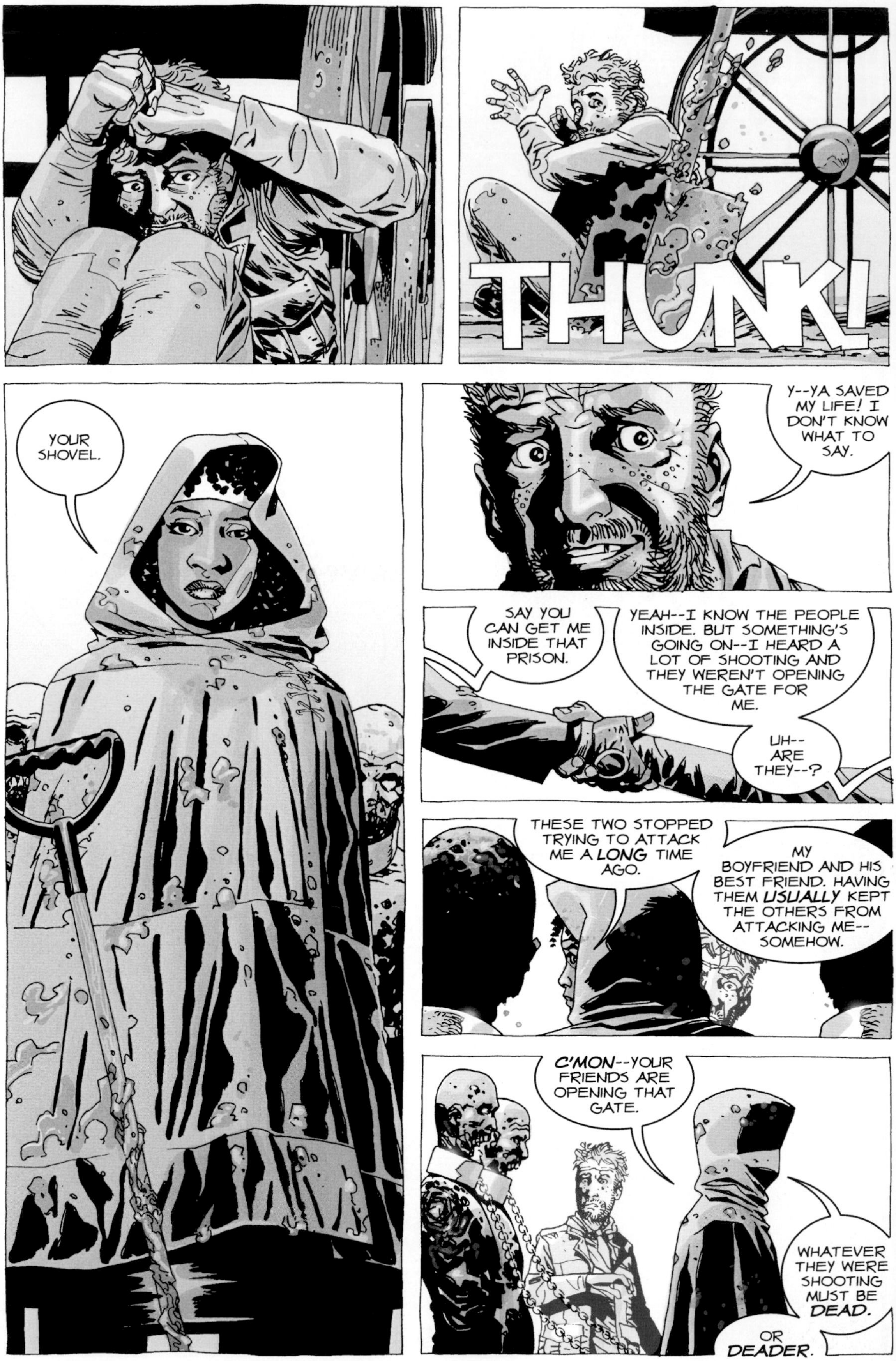
THUNK!
YOUR SHOVEL.
Y--YA SAVED MY LIFE! I DON'T KNOW WHAT TO SAY.
SAY YOU CAN GET ME INSIDE THAT PRISON.
YEAH--I KNOW THE PEOPLE INSIDE. BUT SOMETHING'S GOING ON--I HEARD A LOT OF SHOOTING AND THEY WEREN'T OPENING THE GATE FOR ME.
UH-- ARE THEY--?
THESE TWO STOPPED TRYING TO ATTACK ME A LONG TIME AGO.
MY BOYFRIEND AND HIS BEST FRIEND. HAVING THEM USUALLY KEPT THE OTHERS FROM ATTACKING ME-- SOMEHOW.
C'MON--YOUR FRIENDS ARE OPENING THAT GATE.
WHATEVER THEY WERE SHOOTING MUST BE DEAD.
OR DEADER.

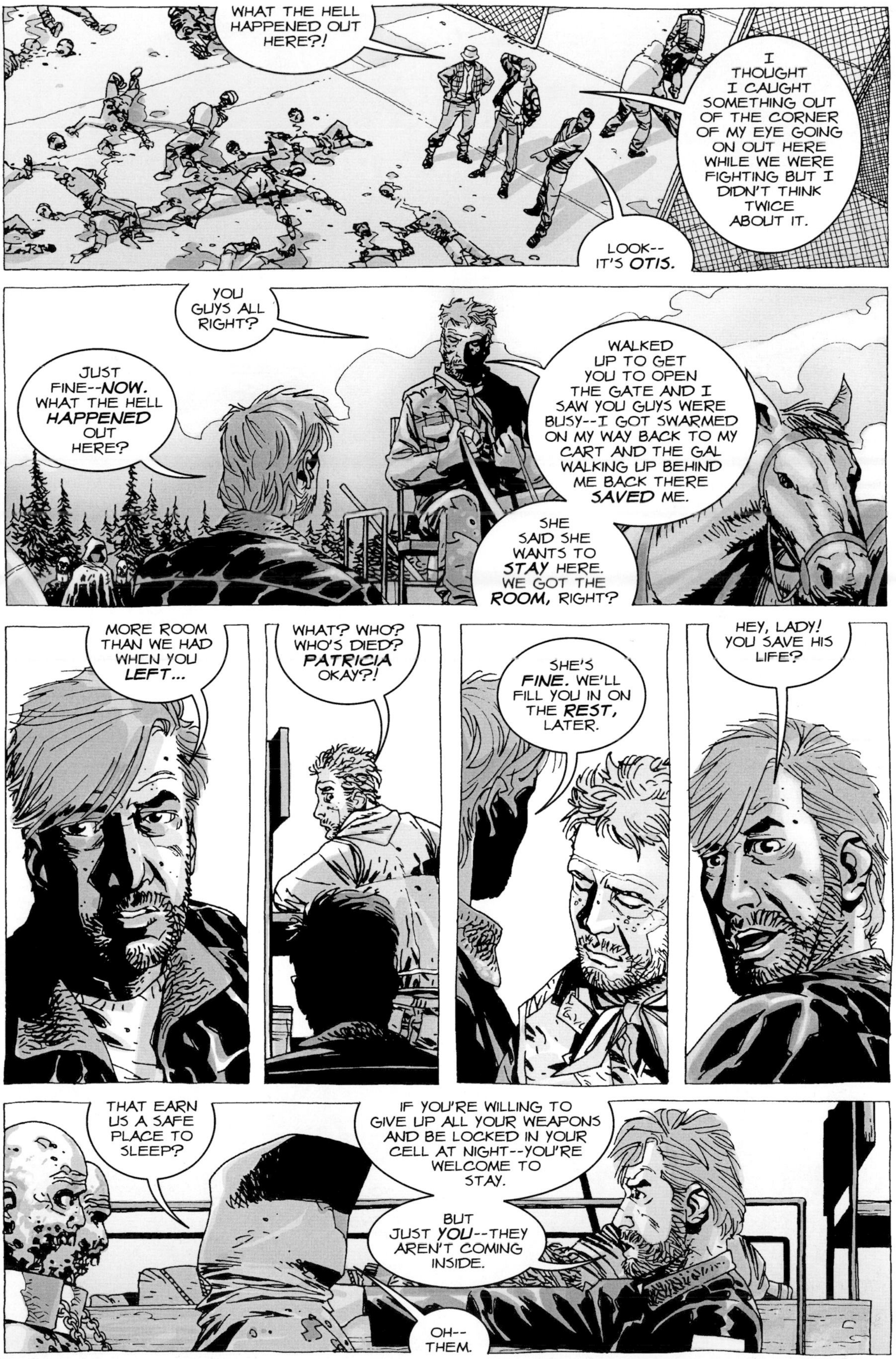
WHAT THE HELL HAPPENED OUT HERE?!
I THOUGHT I CAUGHT SOMETHING OUT OF THE CORNER OF MY EYE GOING ON OUT HERE WHILE WE WERE FIGHTING BUT I DIDN'T THINK TWICE ABOUT IT.
LOOK-- IT'S OTIS.
YOU GUYS ALL RIGHT?
JUST FINE--NOW. WHAT THE HELL HAPPENED OUT HERE?
WALKED UP TO GET YOU TO OPEN THE GATE AND I SAW YOU GUYS WERE BUSY--I GOT SWARMED ON MY WAY BACK TO MY CART AND THE GAL WALKING UP BEHIND ME BACK THERE SAVED ME.
SHE SAID SHE WANTS TO STAY HERE. WE GOT THE ROOM, RIGHT?
MORE ROOM THAN WE HAD WHEN YOU LEFT...
WHAT? WHO? WHO'S DIED? PATRICIA OKAY?!
SHE'S FINE. WE'LL FILL YOU IN ON THE REST, LATER.
HEY, LADY! YOU SAVE HIS LIFE?
THAT EARN US A SAFE PLACE TO SLEEP?
IF YOU'RE WILLING TO GIVE UP ALL YOUR WEAPONS AND BE LOCKED IN YOUR CELL AT NIGHT--YOU'RE WELCOME TO STAY.
BUT JUST YOU--THEY AREN'T COMING INSIDE.
OH-- THEM.

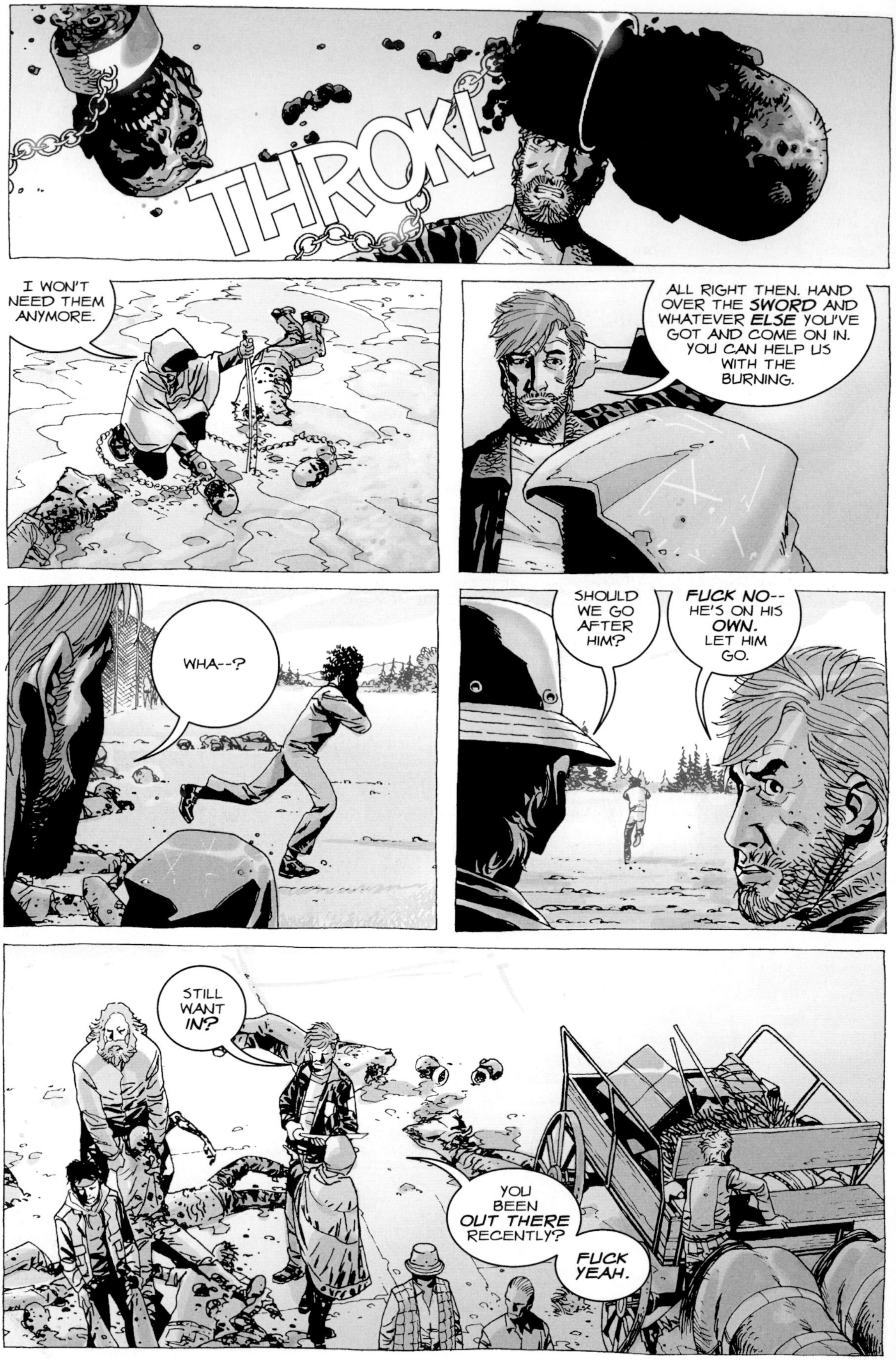
THROK!
I WON'T NEED THEM ANYMORE.
ALL RIGHT THEN. HAND OVER THE SWORD AND WHATEVER ELSE YOU'VE GOT AND COME ON IN. YOU CAN HELP US WITH THE BURNING.
WHA--?
SHOULD WE GO AFTER HIM?
FUCK NO-- HE'S ON HIS OWN. LET HIM GO.
STILL WANT IN?
YOU BEEN OUT THERE RECENTLY?
FUCK YEAH.

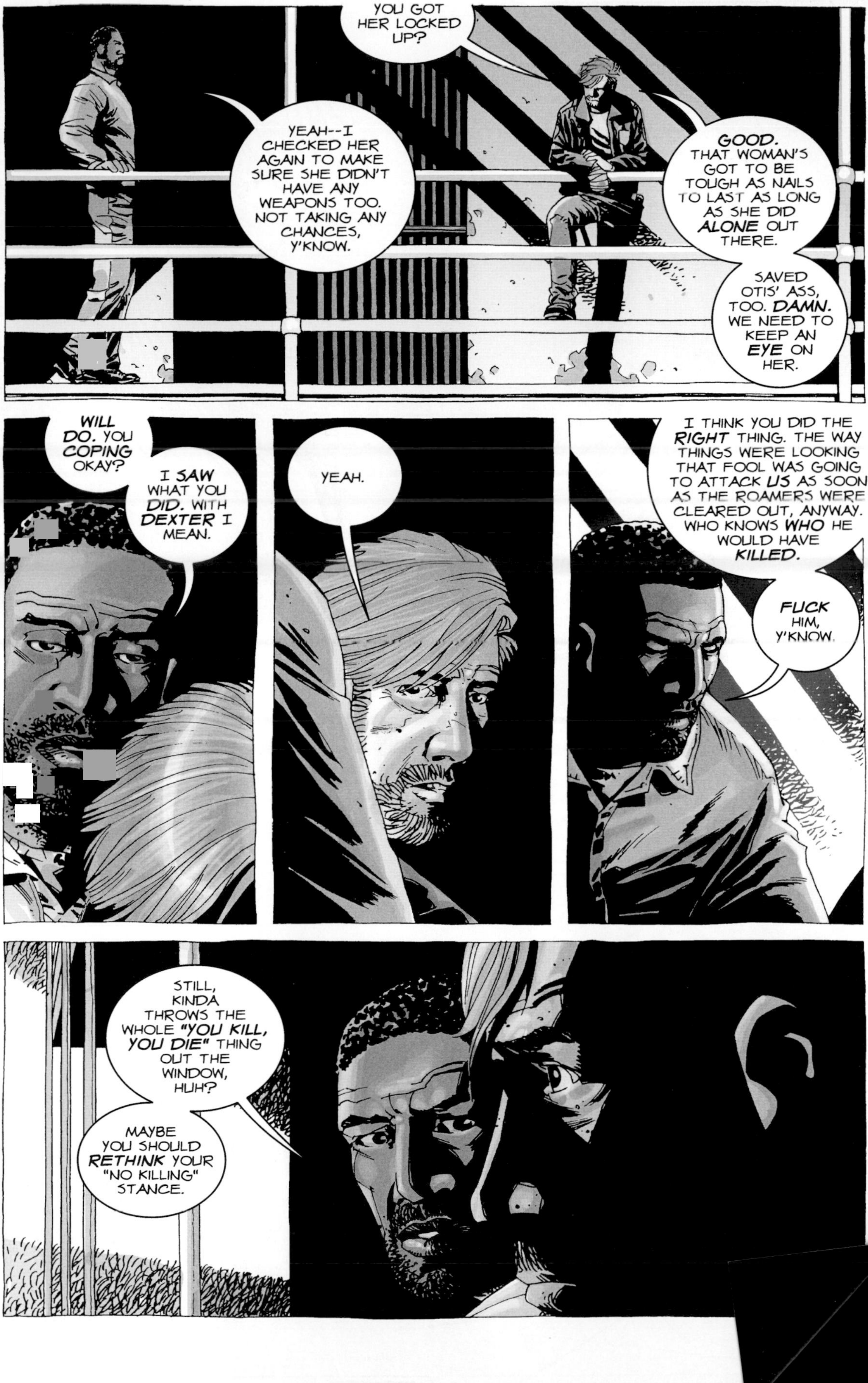
YOU GOT HER LOCKED UP?
YEAH--I CHECKED HER AGAIN TO MAKE SURE SHE DIDN'T HAVE ANY WEAPONS TOO. NOT TAKING ANY CHANCES, Y'KNOW.
GOOD. THAT WOMAN'S GOT TO BE TOUGH AS NAILS TO LAST AS LONG AS SHE DID ALONE OUT THERE.
SAVED OTIS' ASS, TOO. DAMN. WE NEED TO KEEP AN EYE ON HER.
WILL DO. YOU COPING OKAY?
I SAW WHAT YOU DID. WITH DEXTER I MEAN.
YEAH.
I THINK YOU DID THE RIGHT THING. THE WAY THINGS WERE LOOKING THAT FOOL WAS GOING TO ATTACK US AS SOON AS THE ROAMERS WERE CLEARED OUT, ANYWAY. WHO KNOWS WHO HE WOULD HAVE KILLED.
FUCK HIM, Y'KNOW.
STILL, KINDA THROWS THE WHOLE "YOU KILL, YOU DIE" THING OUT THE WINDOW, HUH?
MAYBE YOU SHOULD RETHINK YOUR "NO KILLING" STANCE.

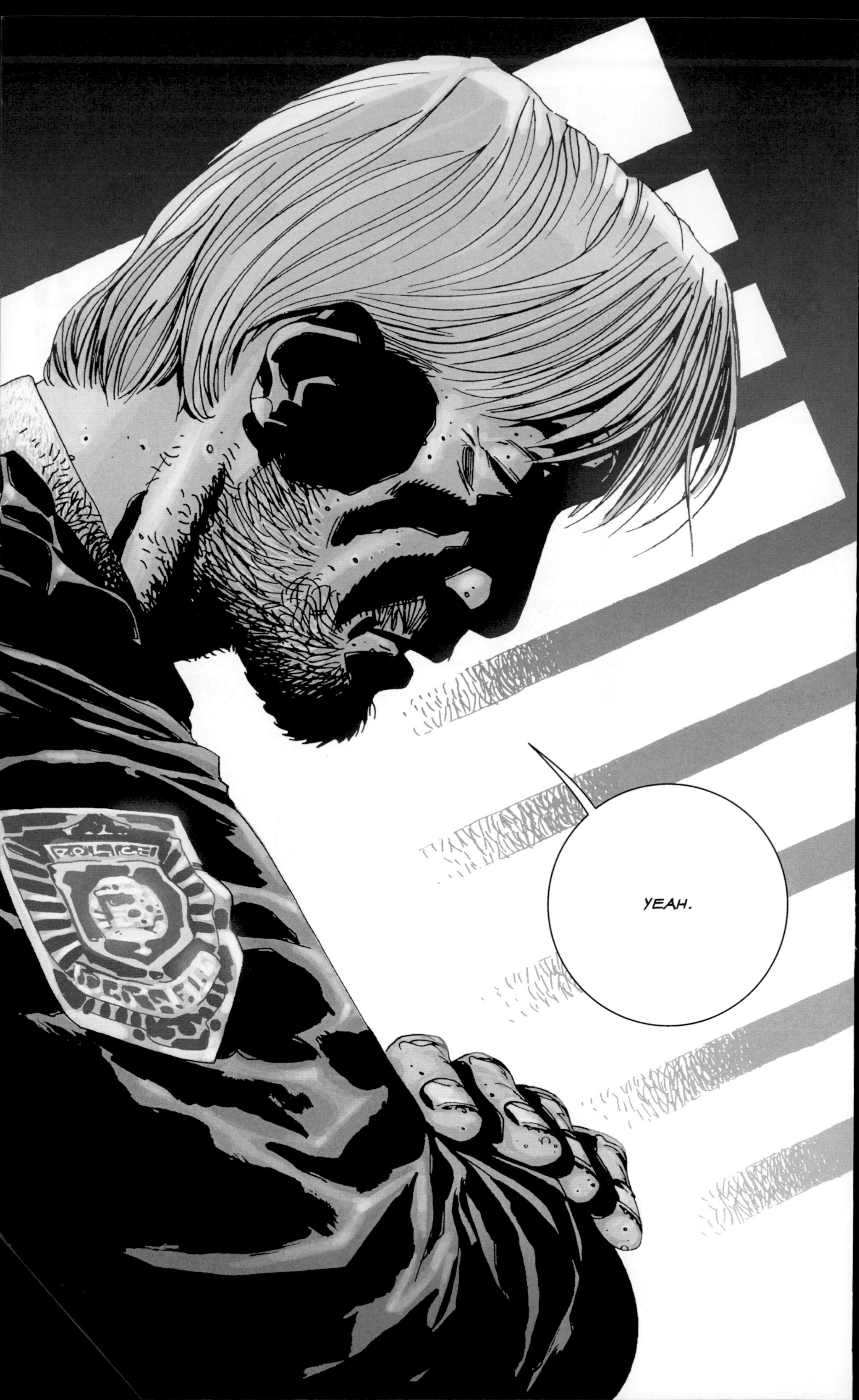
YEAH.

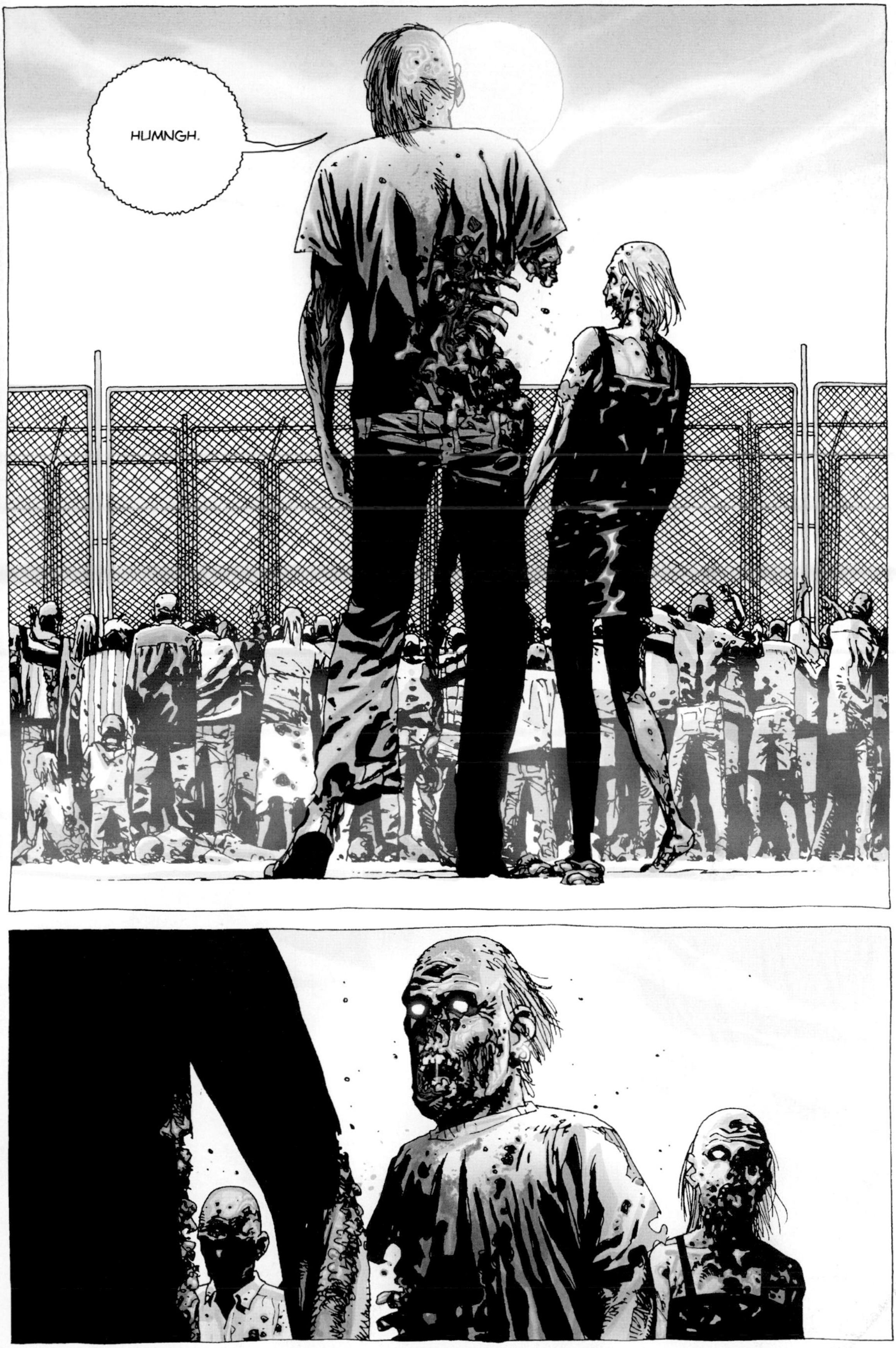
HUMNGH.

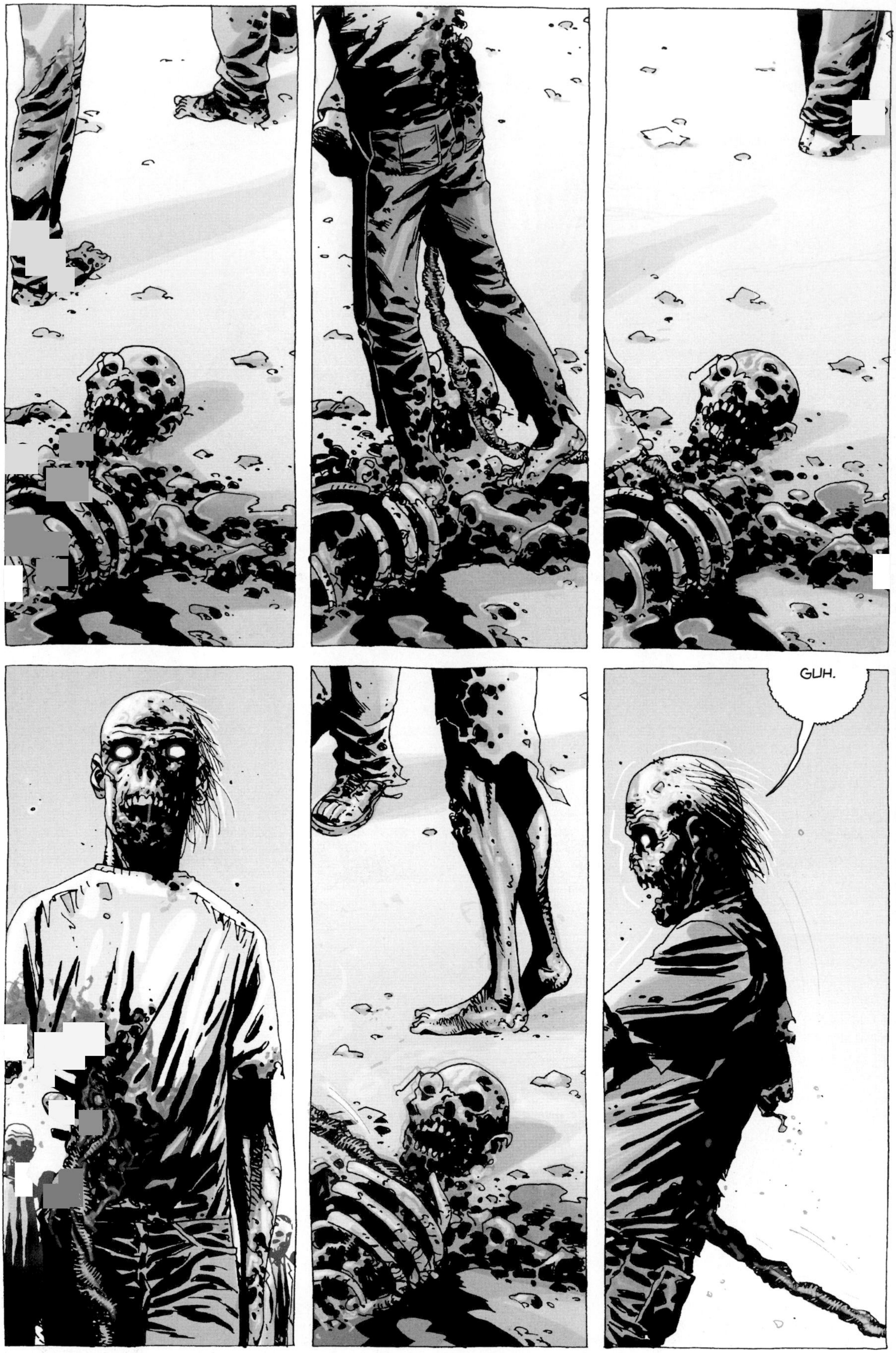
GUH.

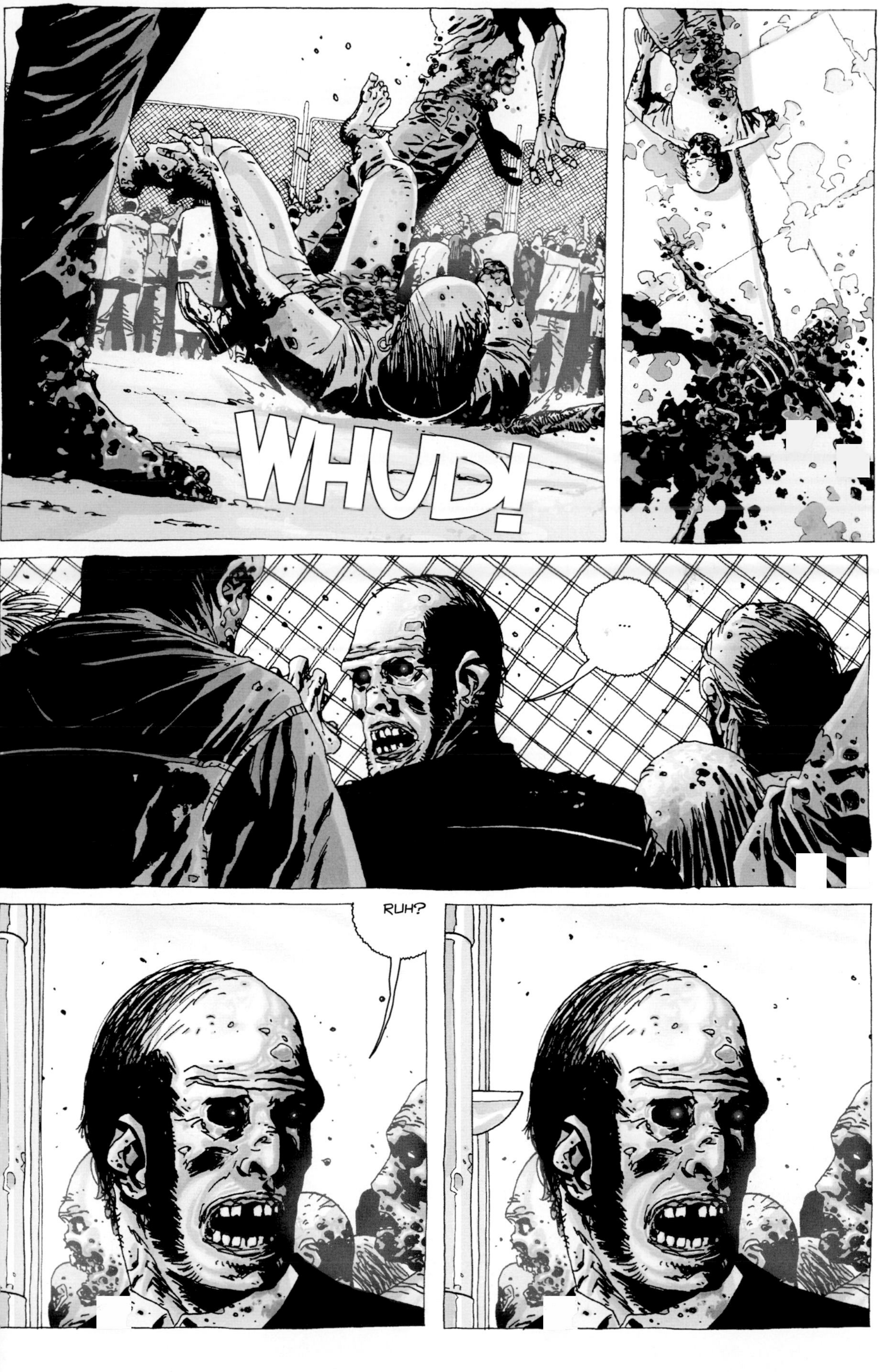
WHUD!
...
RUH?

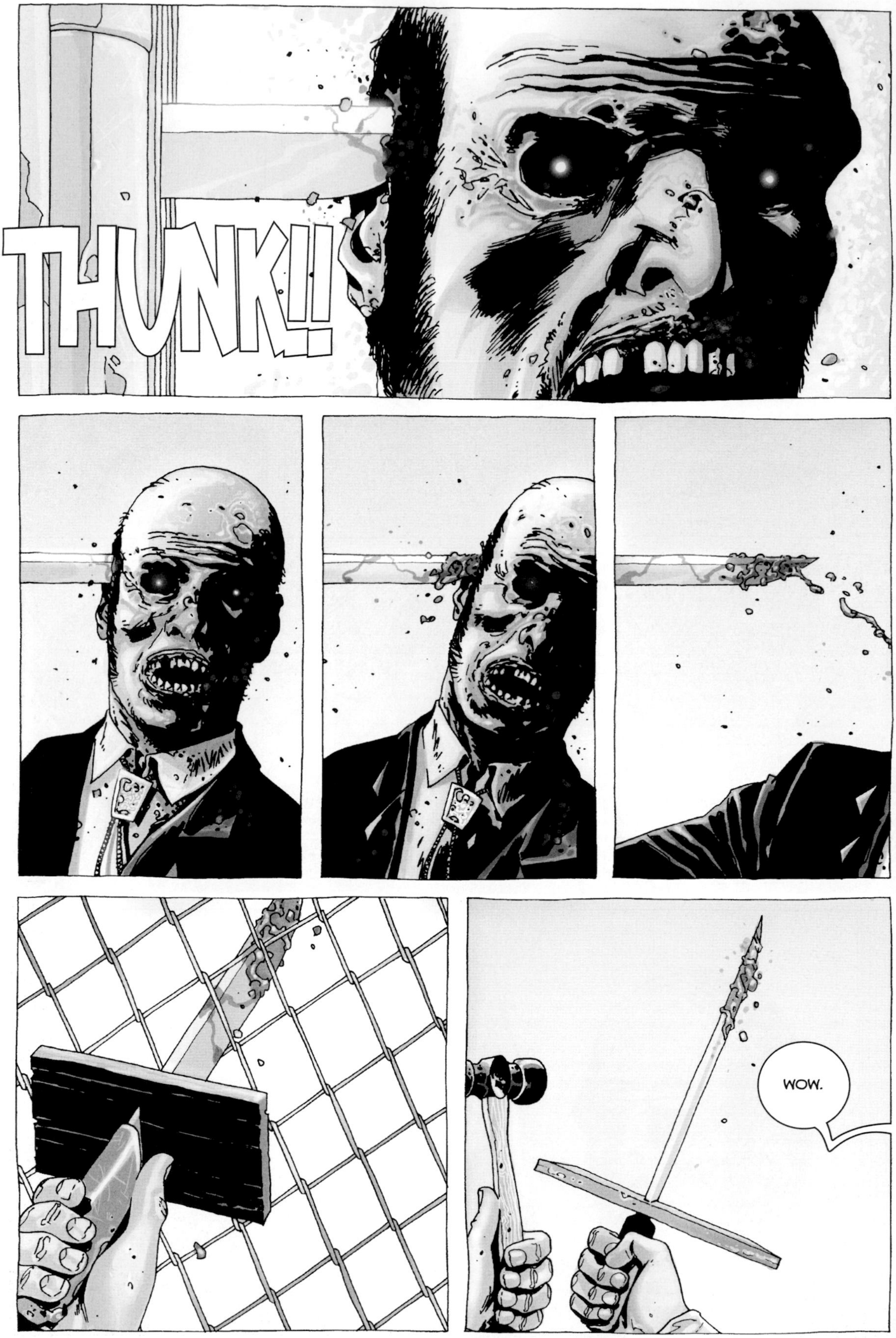
THUNK!!
WOW.

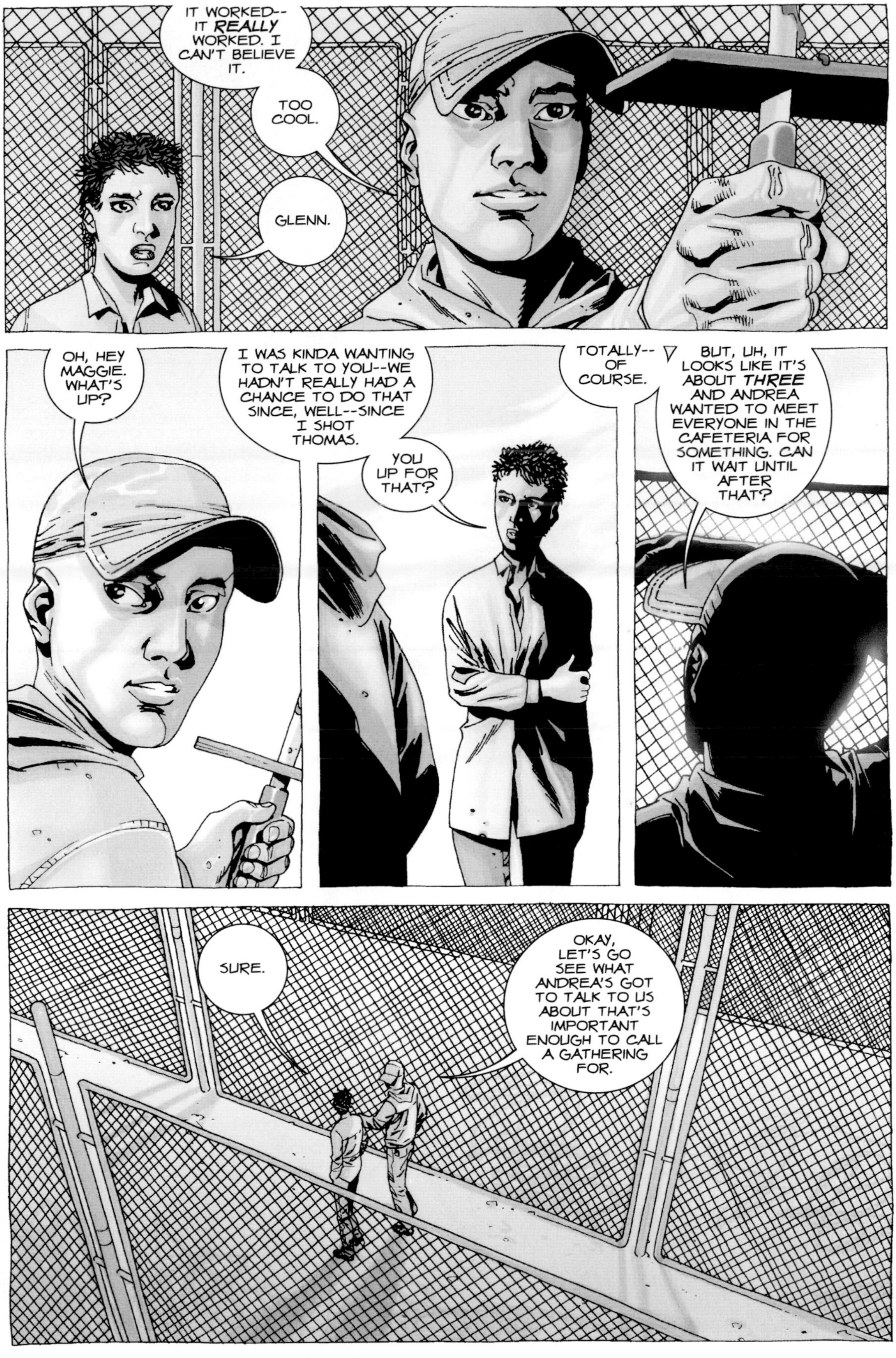
IT WORKED-- IT REALLY WORKED. I CAN'T BELIEVE IT.
TOO COOL.
GLENN.
OH, HEY MAGGIE. WHAT'S UP?
I WAS KINDA WANTING TO TALK TO YOU--WE HADN'T REALLY HAD A CHANCE TO DO THAT SINCE, WELL--SINCE I SHOT THOMAS.
YOU UP FOR THAT?
TOTALLY-- OF COURSE.
BUT, UH, IT LOOKS LIKE IT'S ABOUT THREE AND ANDREA WANTED TO MEET EVERYONE IN THE CAFETERIA FOR SOMETHING. CAN IT WAIT UNTIL AFTER THAT?
SURE.
OKAY, LET'S GO SEE WHAT ANDREA'S GOT TO TALK TO US ABOUT THAT'S IMPORTANT ENOUGH TO CALL A GATHERING FOR.

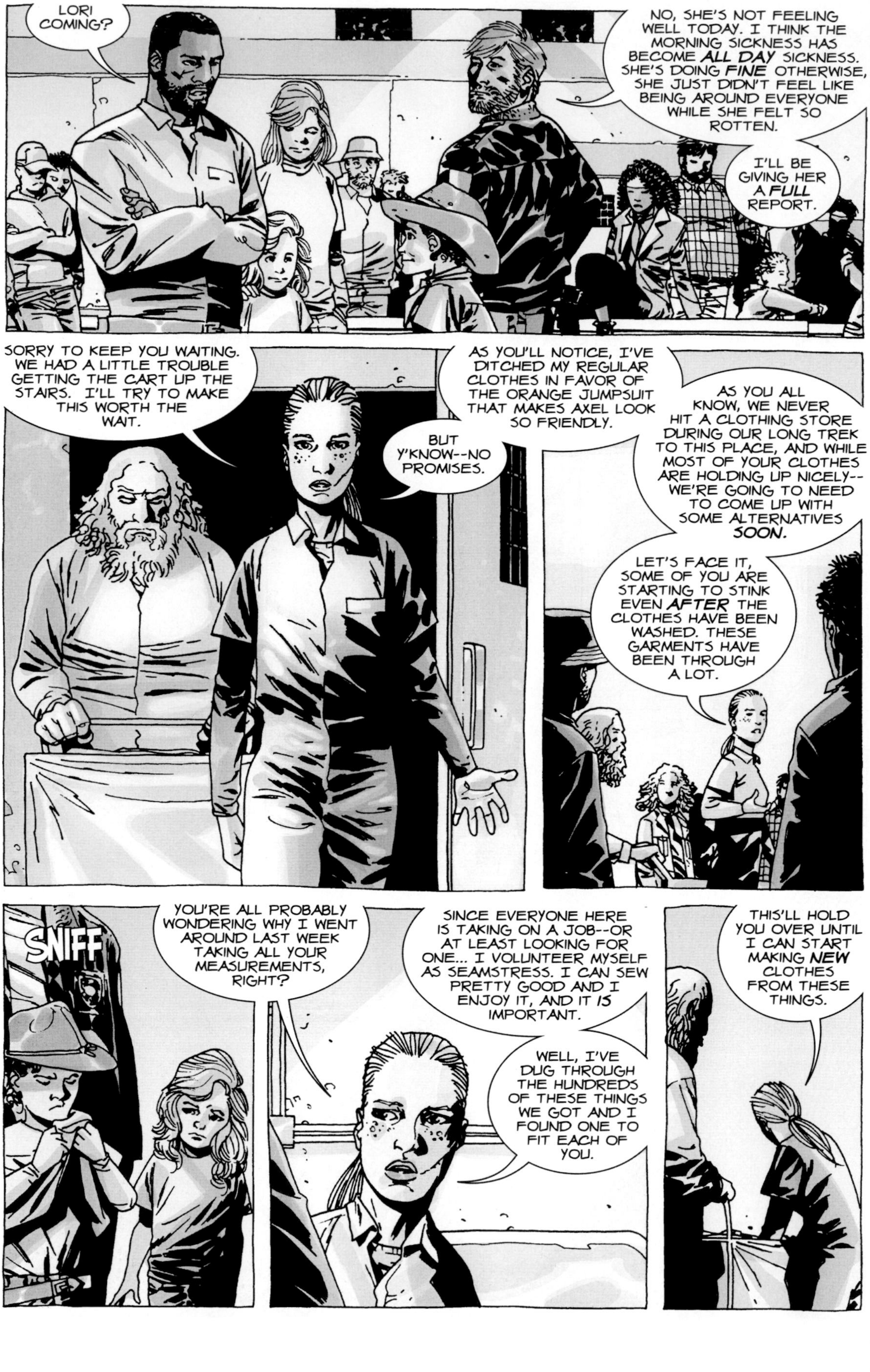
LORI COMING?
NO, SHE'S NOT FEELING WELL TODAY. I THINK THE MORNING SICKNESS HAS BECOME ALL DAY SICKNESS. SHE'S DOING FINE OTHERWISE, SHE JUST DIDN'T FEEL LIKE BEING AROUND EVERYONE WHILE SHE FELT SO ROTTEN.
I'LL BE GIVING HER A FULL REPORT.
SORRY TO KEEP YOU WAITING. WE HAD A LITTLE TROUBLE GETTING THE CART UP THE STAIRS. I'LL TRY TO MAKE THIS WORTH THE WAIT.
BUT Y'KNOW--NO PROMISES.
AS YOU'LL NOTICE, I'VE DITCHED MY REGULAR CLOTHES IN FAVOR OF THE ORANGE JUMPSUIT THAT MAKES AXEL LOOK SO FRIENDLY.
AS YOU ALL KNOW, WE NEVER HIT A CLOTHING STORE DURING OUR LONG TREK TO THIS PLACE, AND WHILE MOST OF YOUR CLOTHES ARE HOLDING UP NICELY-- WE'RE GOING TO NEED TO COME UP WITH SOME ALTERNATIVES SOON.
LET'S FACE IT, SOME OF YOU ARE STARTING TO STINK EVEN AFTER THE CLOTHES HAVE BEEN WASHED. THESE GARMENTS HAVE BEEN THROUGH A LOT.
SNIFF
YOU'RE ALL PROBABLY WONDERING WHY I WENT AROUND LAST WEEK TAKING ALL YOUR MEASUREMENTS, RIGHT?
SINCE EVERYONE HERE IS TAKING ON A JOB--OR AT LEAST LOOKING FOR ONE... I VOLUNTEER MYSELF AS SEAMSTRESS. I CAN SEW PRETTY GOOD AND I ENJOY IT, AND IT IS IMPORTANT.
WELL, I'VE DUG THROUGH THE HUNDREDS OF THESE THINGS WE GOT AND I FOUND ONE TO FIT EACH OF YOU.
THIS'LL HOLD YOU OVER UNTIL I CAN START MAKING NEW CLOTHES FROM THESE THINGS.

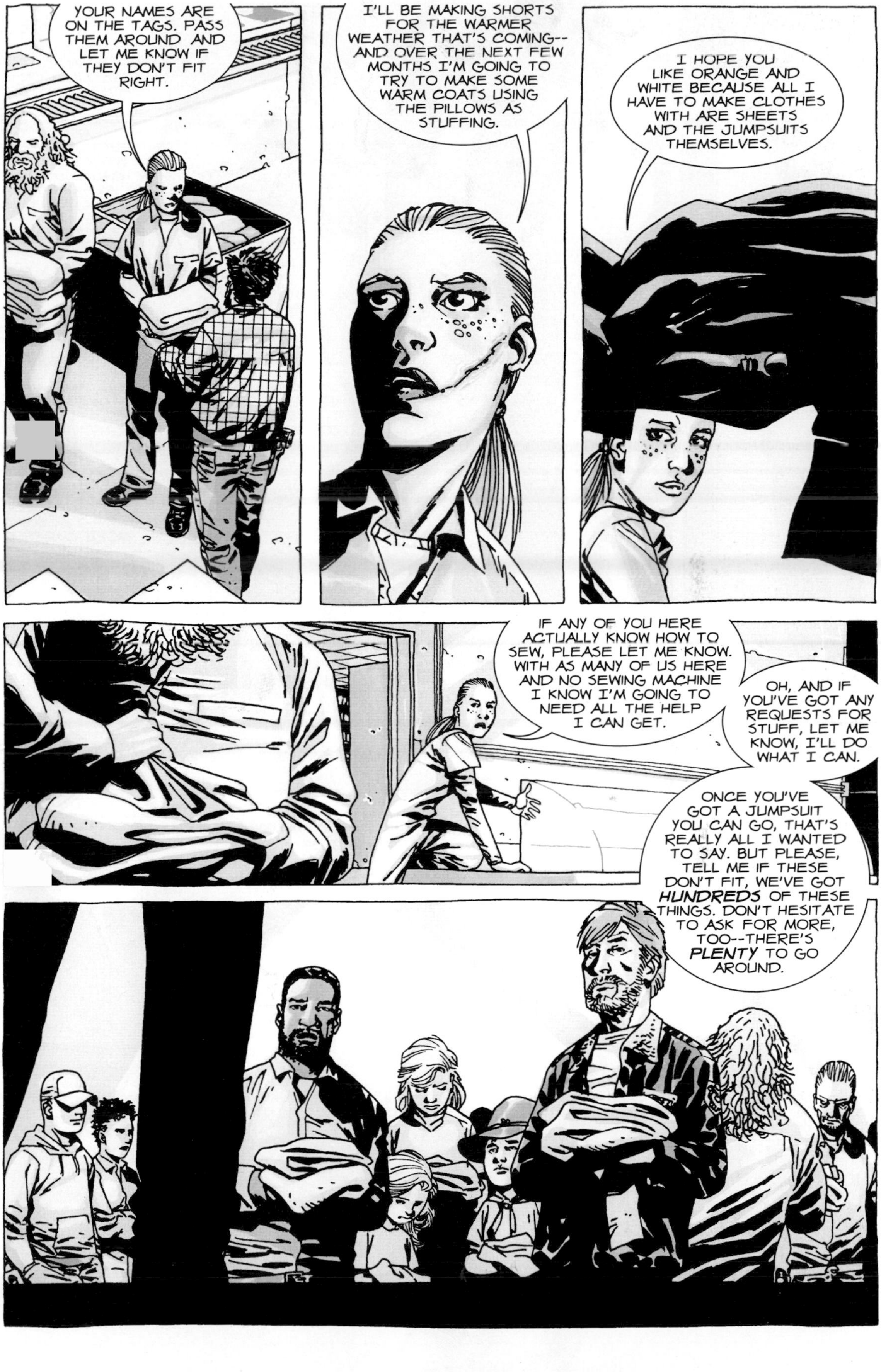
YOUR NAMES ARE ON THE TAGS. PASS THEM AROUND AND LET ME KNOW IF THEY DON'T FIT RIGHT.
I'LL BE MAKING SHORTS FOR THE WARMER WEATHER THAT'S COMING-- AND OVER THE NEXT FEW MONTHS I'M GOING TO TRY TO MAKE SOME WARM COATS USING THE PILLOWS AS STUFFING.
I HOPE YOU LIKE ORANGE AND WHITE BECAUSE ALL I HAVE TO MAKE CLOTHES WITH ARE SHEETS AND THE JUMPSUITS THEMSELVES.
IF ANY OF YOU HERE ACTUALLY KNOW HOW TO SEW, PLEASE LET ME KNOW. WITH AS MANY OF US HERE AND NO SEWING MACHINE I KNOW I'M GOING TO NEED ALL THE HELP I CAN GET.
OH, AND IF YOU'VE GOT ANY REQUESTS FOR STUFF, LET ME KNOW, I'LL DO WHAT I CAN.
ONCE YOU'VE GOT A JUMPSUIT YOU CAN GO, THAT'S REALLY ALL I WANTED TO SAY. BUT PLEASE, TELL ME IF THESE DON'T FIT, WE'VE GOT HUNDREDS OF THESE THINGS. DON'T HESITATE TO ASK FOR MORE, TOO--THERE'S PLENTY TO GO AROUND.

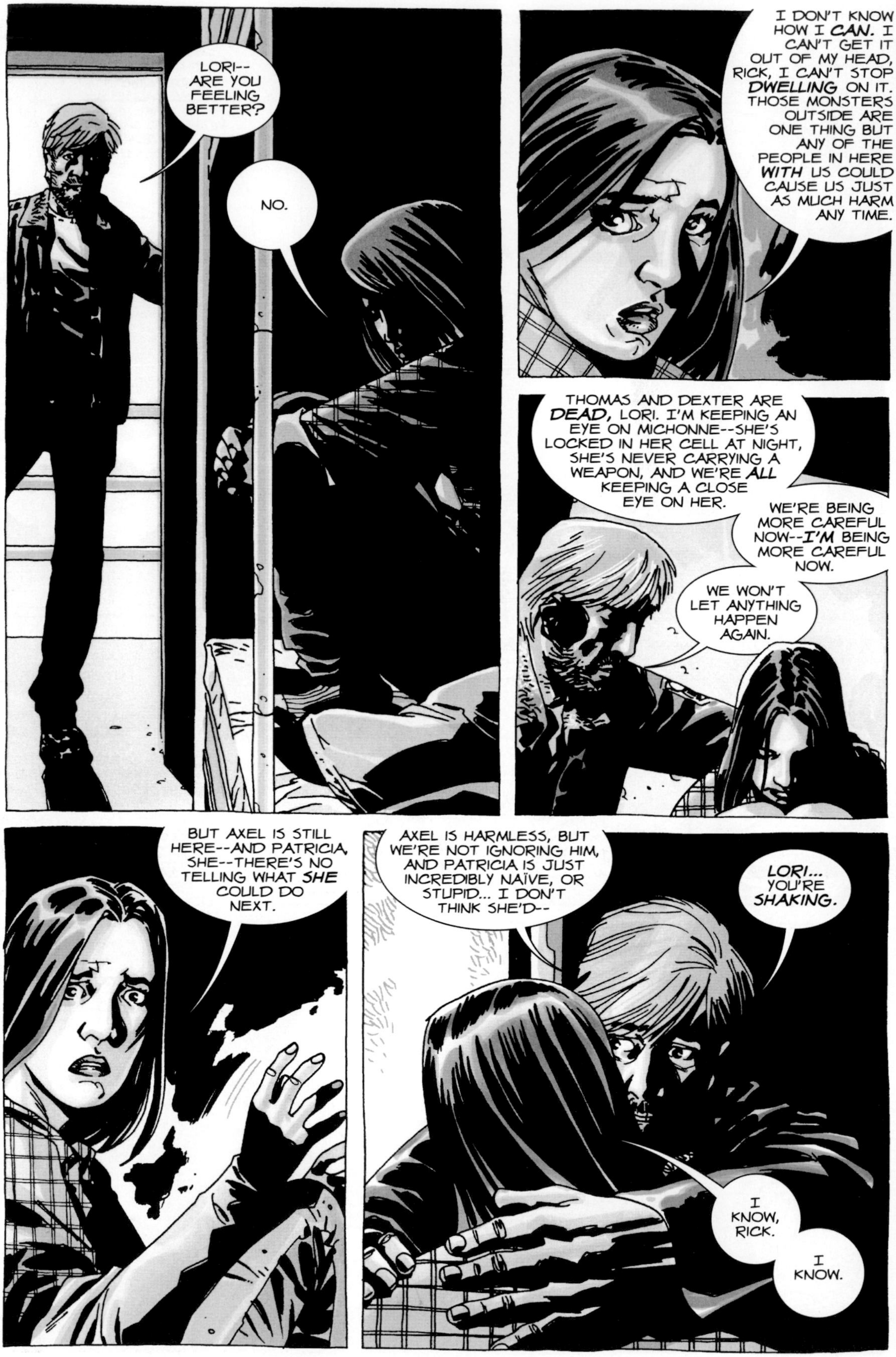
LORI-- ARE YOU FEELING BETTER?
NO.
I DON'T KNOW HOW I CAN. I CAN'T GET IT OUT OF MY HEAD, RICK, I CAN'T STOP DWELLING ON IT. THOSE MONSTERS OUTSIDE ARE ONE THING BUT ANY OF THE PEOPLE IN HERE WITH US COULD CAUSE US JUST AS MUCH HARM ANY TIME.
THOMAS AND DEXTER ARE DEAD, LORI. I'M KEEPING AN EYE ON MICHONNE--SHE'S LOCKED IN HER CELL AT NIGHT, SHE'S NEVER CARRYING A WEAPON, AND WE'RE ALL KEEPING A CLOSE EYE ON HER.
WE'RE BEING MORE CAREFUL NOW--I'M BEING MORE CAREFUL NOW.
WE WON'T LET ANYTHING HAPPEN AGAIN.
BUT AXEL IS STILL HERE--AND PATRICIA, SHE--THERE'S NO TELLING WHAT SHE COULD DO NEXT.
AXEL IS HARMLESS, BUT WE'RE NOT IGNORING HIM, AND PATRICIA IS JUST INCREDIBLY NAÏVE, OR STUPID... I DON'T THINK SHE'D--
LORI... YOU'RE SHAKING.
I KNOW, RICK.
I KNOW.

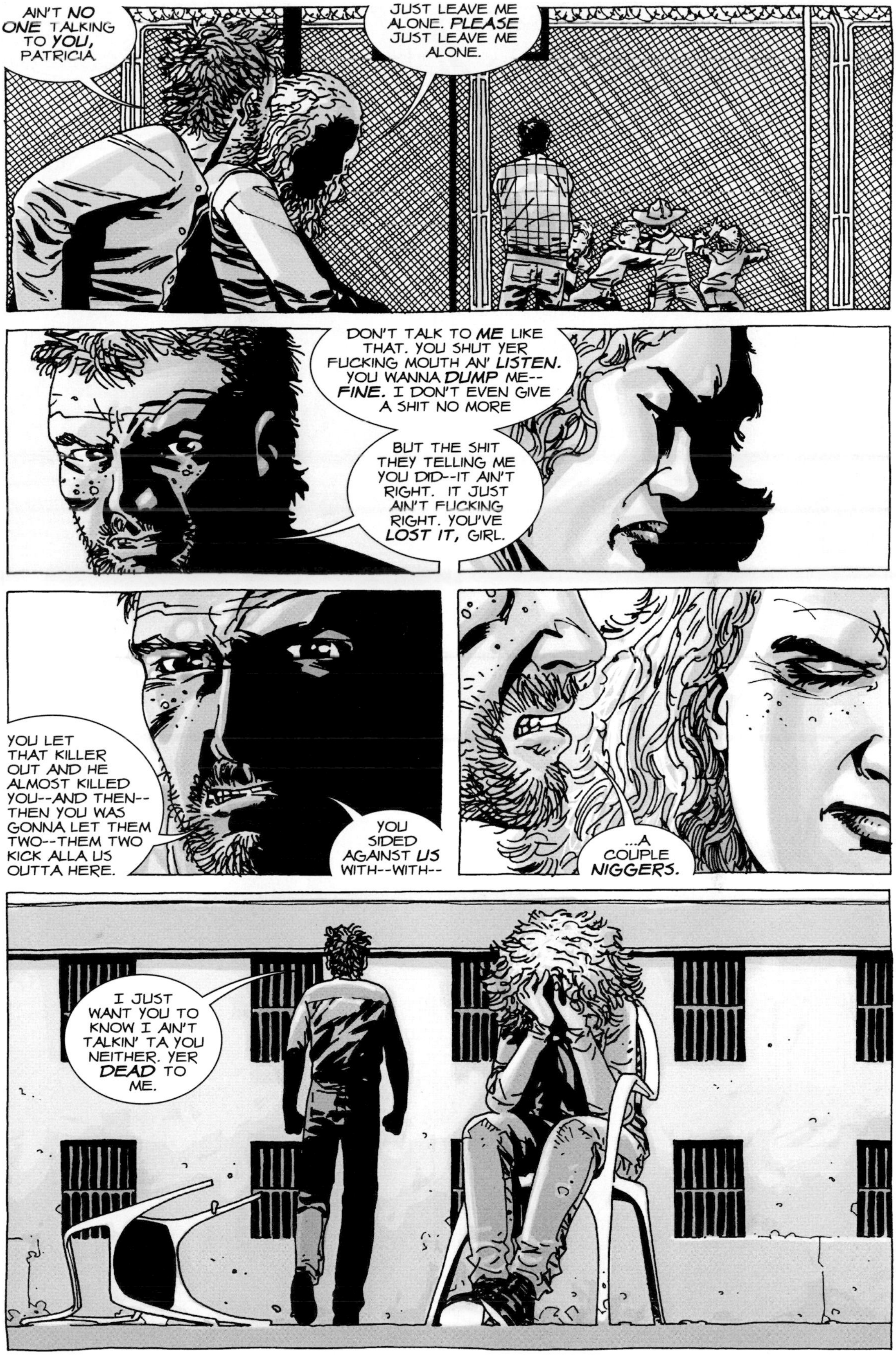
AIN'T NO ONE TALKING TO YOU, PATRICIA.
JUST LEAVE ME ALONE. PLEASE JUST LEAVE ME ALONE.
DON'T TALK TO ME LIKE THAT. YOU SHUT YER FUCKING MOUTH AN' LISTEN. YOU WANNA DUMP ME-- FINE. I DON'T EVEN GIVE A SHIT NO MORE
BUT THE SHIT THEY TELLING ME YOU DID--IT AIN'T RIGHT. IT JUST AIN'T FUCKING RIGHT. YOU'VE LOST IT, GIRL.
YOU LET THAT KILLER OUT AND HE ALMOST KILLED YOU--AND THEN-- THEN YOU WAS GONNA LET THEM TWO--THEM TWO KICK ALLA US OUTTA HERE.
YOU SIDED AGAINST US WITH--WITH--
...A COUPLE NIGGERS.
I JUST WANT YOU TO KNOW I AIN'T TALKIN' TA YOU NEITHER. YER DEAD TO ME.

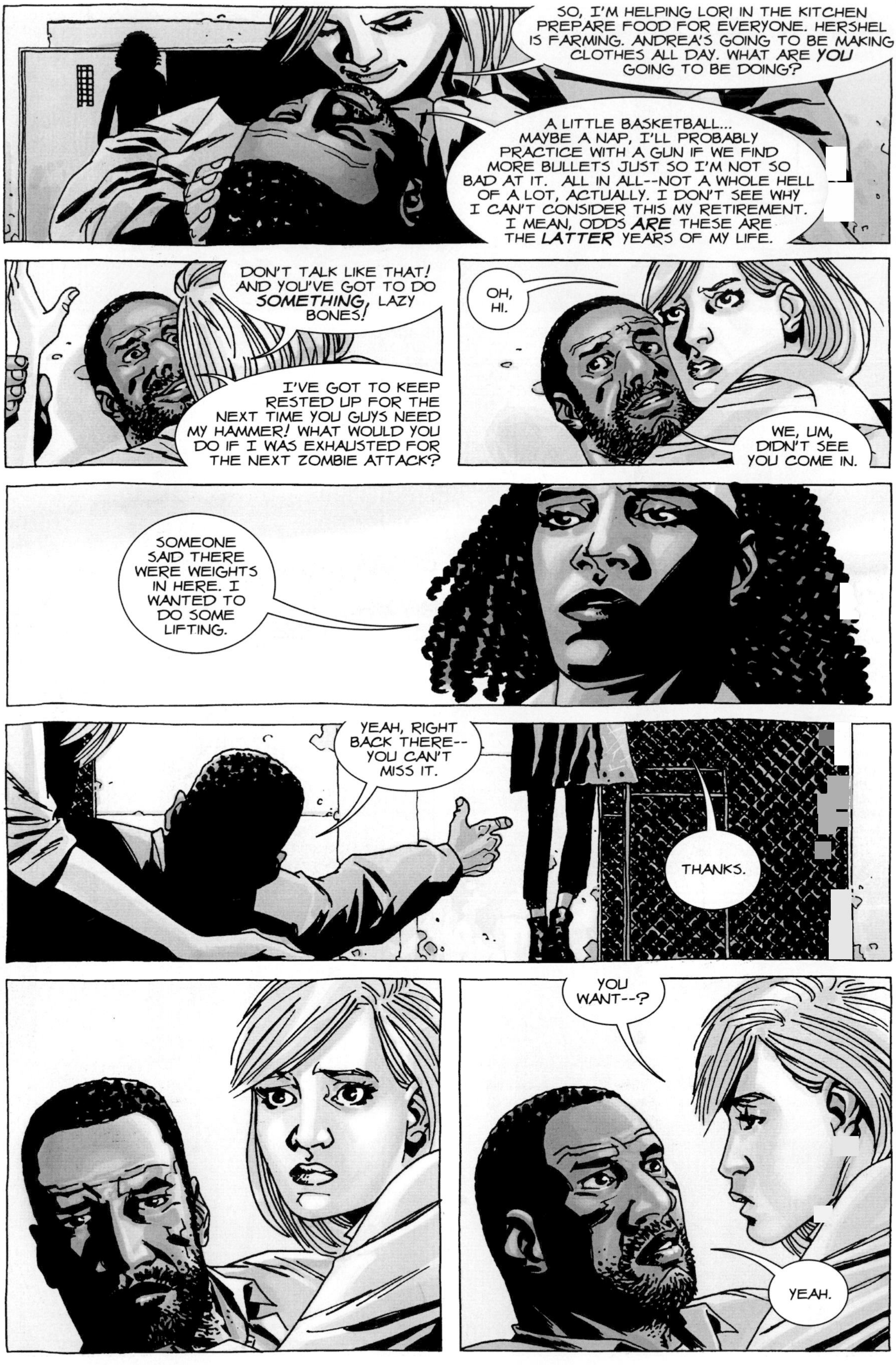
SO, I'M HELPING LORI IN THE KITCHEN PREPARE FOOD FOR EVERYONE. HERSHEL IS FARMING. ANDREA'S GOING TO BE MAKING CLOTHES ALL DAY. WHAT ARE *YOU* GOING TO BE DOING?
A LITTLE BASKETBALL... MAYBE A NAP, I'LL PROBABLY PRACTICE WITH A GUN IF WE FIND MORE BULLETS JUST SO I'M NOT SO BAD AT IT. ALL IN ALL--NOT A WHOLE HELL OF A LOT, ACTUALLY. I DON'T SEE WHY I CAN'T CONSIDER THIS MY RETIREMENT. I MEAN, ODDS *ARE* THESE ARE THE *LATTER* YEARS OF MY LIFE.
DON'T TALK LIKE THAT! AND YOU'VE GOT TO DO *SOMETHING*, LAZY BONES!
I'VE GOT TO KEEP RESTED UP FOR THE NEXT TIME YOU GUYS NEED MY HAMMER! WHAT WOULD YOU DO IF I WAS EXHAUSTED FOR THE NEXT ZOMBIE ATTACK?
OH, HI.
WE, UM, DIDN'T SEE YOU COME IN.
SOMEONE SAID THERE WERE WEIGHTS IN HERE. I WANTED TO DO SOME LIFTING.
YEAH, RIGHT BACK THERE-- YOU CAN'T MISS IT.
THANKS.
YOU WANT--?
YEAH.

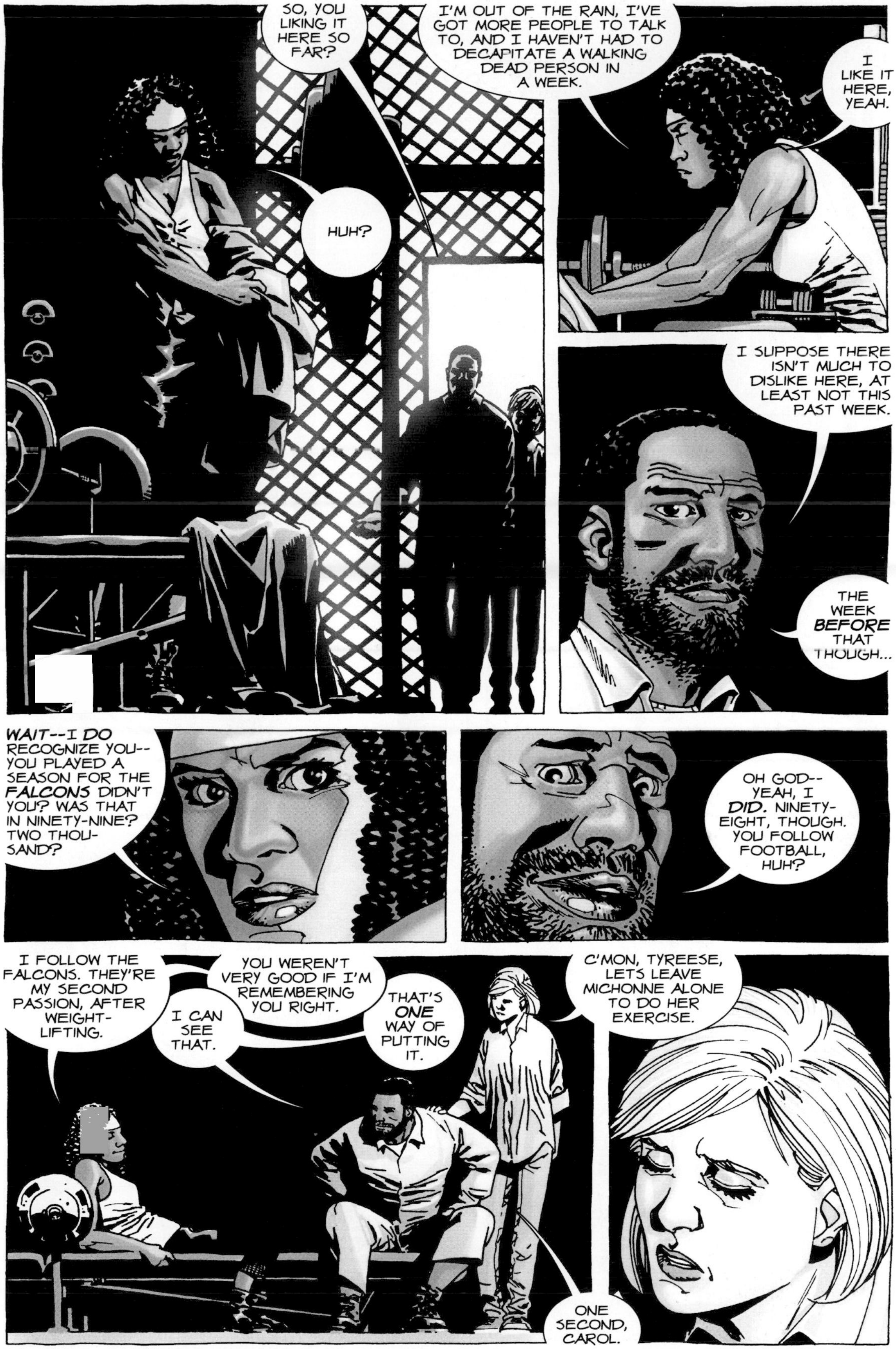
SO, YOU LIKING IT HERE SO FAR?
HUH?
I'M OUT OF THE RAIN, I'VE GOT MORE PEOPLE TO TALK TO, AND I HAVEN'T HAD TO DECAPITATE A WALKING DEAD PERSON IN A WEEK.
I LIKE IT HERE, YEAH.
I SUPPOSE THERE ISN'T MUCH TO DISLIKE HERE, AT LEAST NOT THIS PAST WEEK.
THE WEEK BEFORE THAT THOUGH...
WAIT--I DO RECOGNIZE YOU--YOU PLAYED A SEASON FOR THE FALCONS DIDN'T YOU? WAS THAT IN NINETY-NINE? TWO THOUSAND?
OH GOD--YEAH, I DID. NINETY-EIGHT, THOUGH. YOU FOLLOW FOOTBALL, HUH?
I FOLLOW THE FALCONS. THEY'RE MY SECOND PASSION, AFTER WEIGHT-LIFTING.
I CAN SEE THAT.
YOU WEREN'T VERY GOOD IF I'M REMEMBERING YOU RIGHT.
THAT'S ONE WAY OF PUTTING IT.
C'MON, TYREESE, LETS LEAVE MICHONNE ALONE TO DO HER EXERCISE.
ONE SECOND, CAROL.

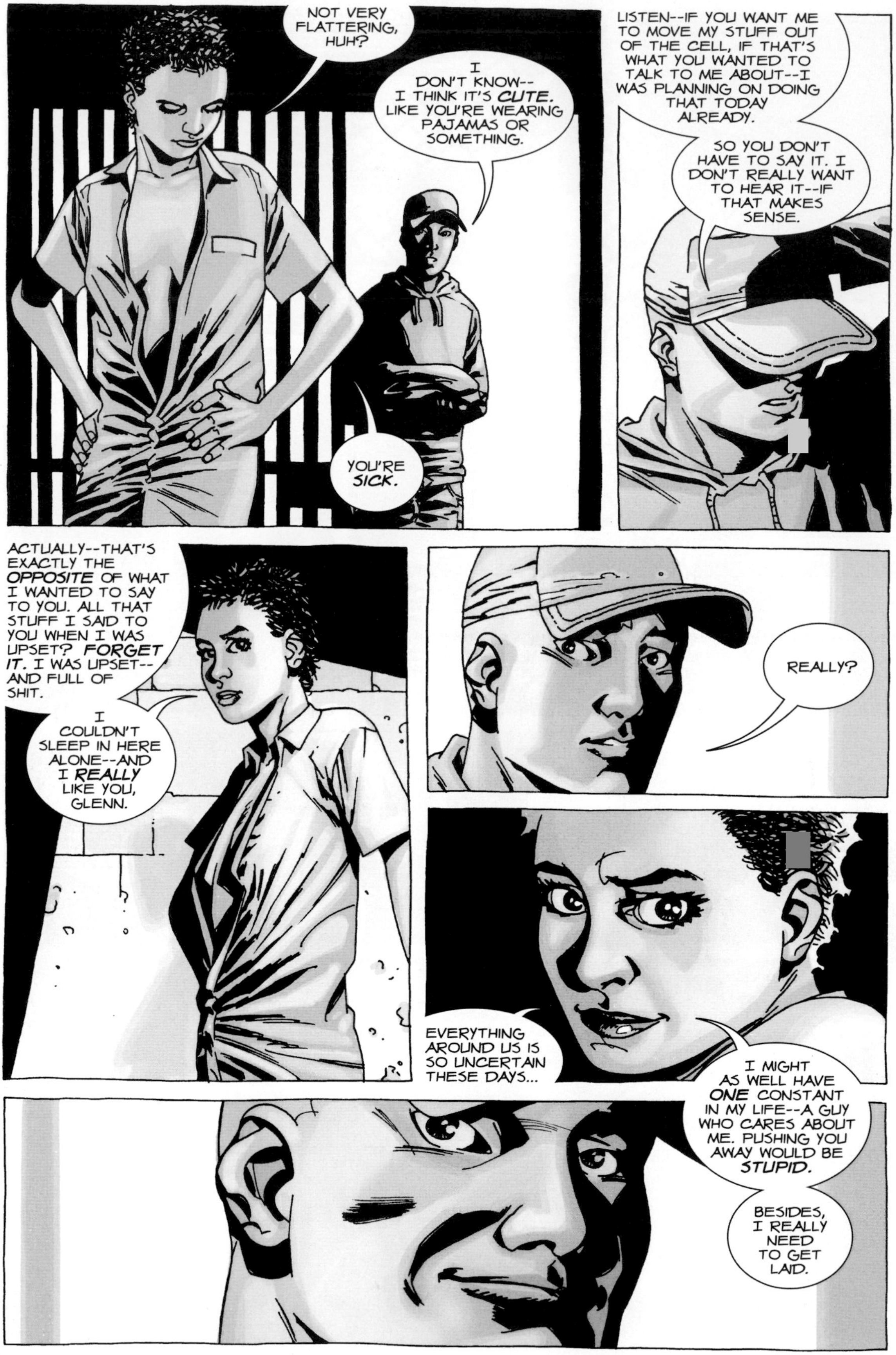
NOT VERY FLATTERING, HUH?
I DON'T KNOW-- I THINK IT'S CUTE. LIKE YOU'RE WEARING PAJAMAS OR SOMETHING.
YOU'RE SICK.
LISTEN--IF YOU WANT ME TO MOVE MY STUFF OUT OF THE CELL, IF THAT'S WHAT YOU WANTED TO TALK TO ME ABOUT--I WAS PLANNING ON DOING THAT TODAY ALREADY.
SO YOU DON'T HAVE TO SAY IT. I DON'T REALLY WANT TO HEAR IT--IF THAT MAKES SENSE.
ACTUALLY--THAT'S EXACTLY THE OPPOSITE OF WHAT I WANTED TO SAY TO YOU. ALL THAT STUFF I SAID TO YOU WHEN I WAS UPSET? FORGET IT. I WAS UPSET-- AND FULL OF SHIT.
I COULDN'T SLEEP IN HERE ALONE--AND I REALLY LIKE YOU, GLENN.
REALLY?
EVERYTHING AROUND US IS SO UNCERTAIN THESE DAYS...
I MIGHT AS WELL HAVE ONE CONSTANT IN MY LIFE--A GUY WHO CARES ABOUT ME. PUSHING YOU AWAY WOULD BE STUPID.
BESIDES, I REALLY NEED TO GET LAID.

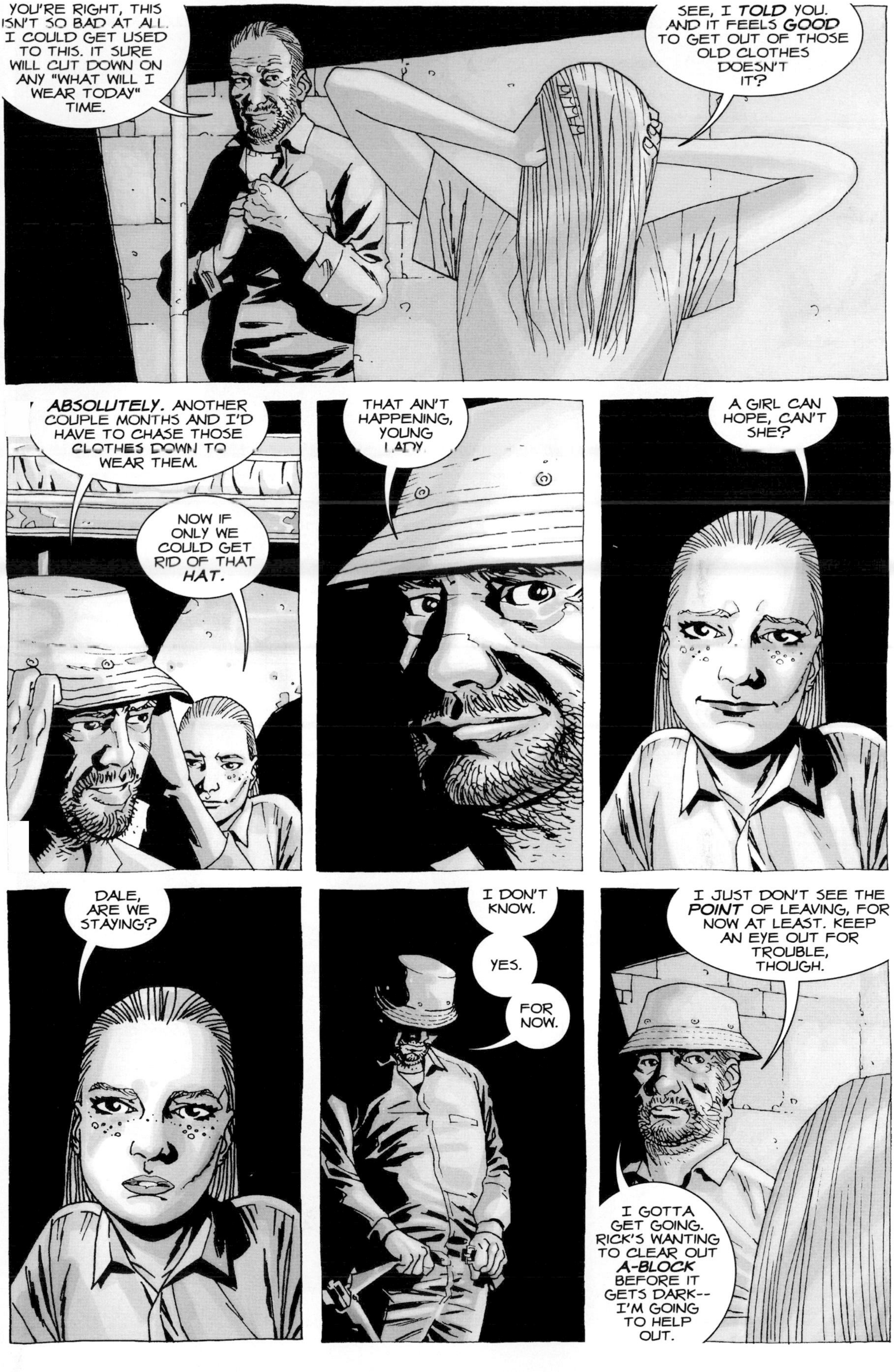
YOU'RE RIGHT, THIS ISN'T SO BAD AT ALL. I COULD GET USED TO THIS. IT SURE WILL CUT DOWN ON ANY "WHAT WILL I WEAR TODAY" TIME.
SEE, I TOLD YOU. AND IT FEELS GOOD TO GET OUT OF THOSE OLD CLOTHES DOESN'T IT?
ABSOLUTELY. ANOTHER COUPLE MONTHS AND I'D HAVE TO CHASE THOSE CLOTHES DOWN TO WEAR THEM.
NOW IF ONLY WE COULD GET RID OF THAT HAT.
THAT AIN'T HAPPENING, YOUNG LADY.
A GIRL CAN HOPE, CAN'T SHE?
DALE, ARE WE STAYING?
I DON'T KNOW.
YES.
FOR NOW.
I JUST DON'T SEE THE POINT OF LEAVING, FOR NOW AT LEAST. KEEP AN EYE OUT FOR TROUBLE, THOUGH.
I GOTTA GET GOING. RICK'S WANTING TO CLEAR OUT A-BLOCK BEFORE IT GETS DARK-- I'M GOING TO HELP OUT.

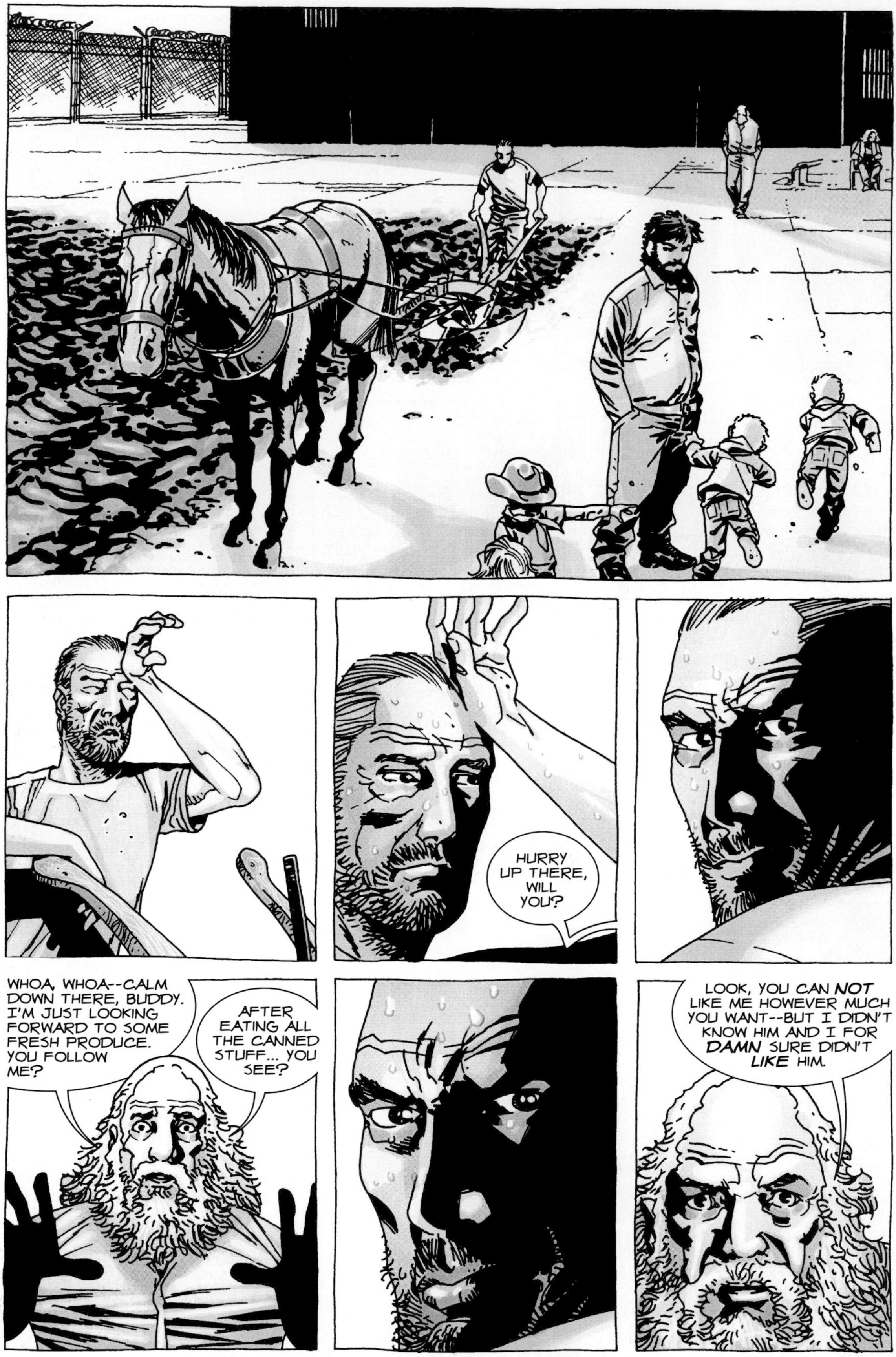

HURRY UP THERE, WILL YOU?
WHOA, WHOA--CALM DOWN THERE, BUDDY. I'M JUST LOOKING FORWARD TO SOME FRESH PRODUCE. YOU FOLLOW ME?
AFTER EATING ALL THE CANNED STUFF... YOU SEE?
LOOK, YOU CAN NOT LIKE ME HOWEVER MUCH YOU WANT--BUT I DIDN'T KNOW HIM AND I FOR DAMN SURE DIDN'T LIKE HIM.

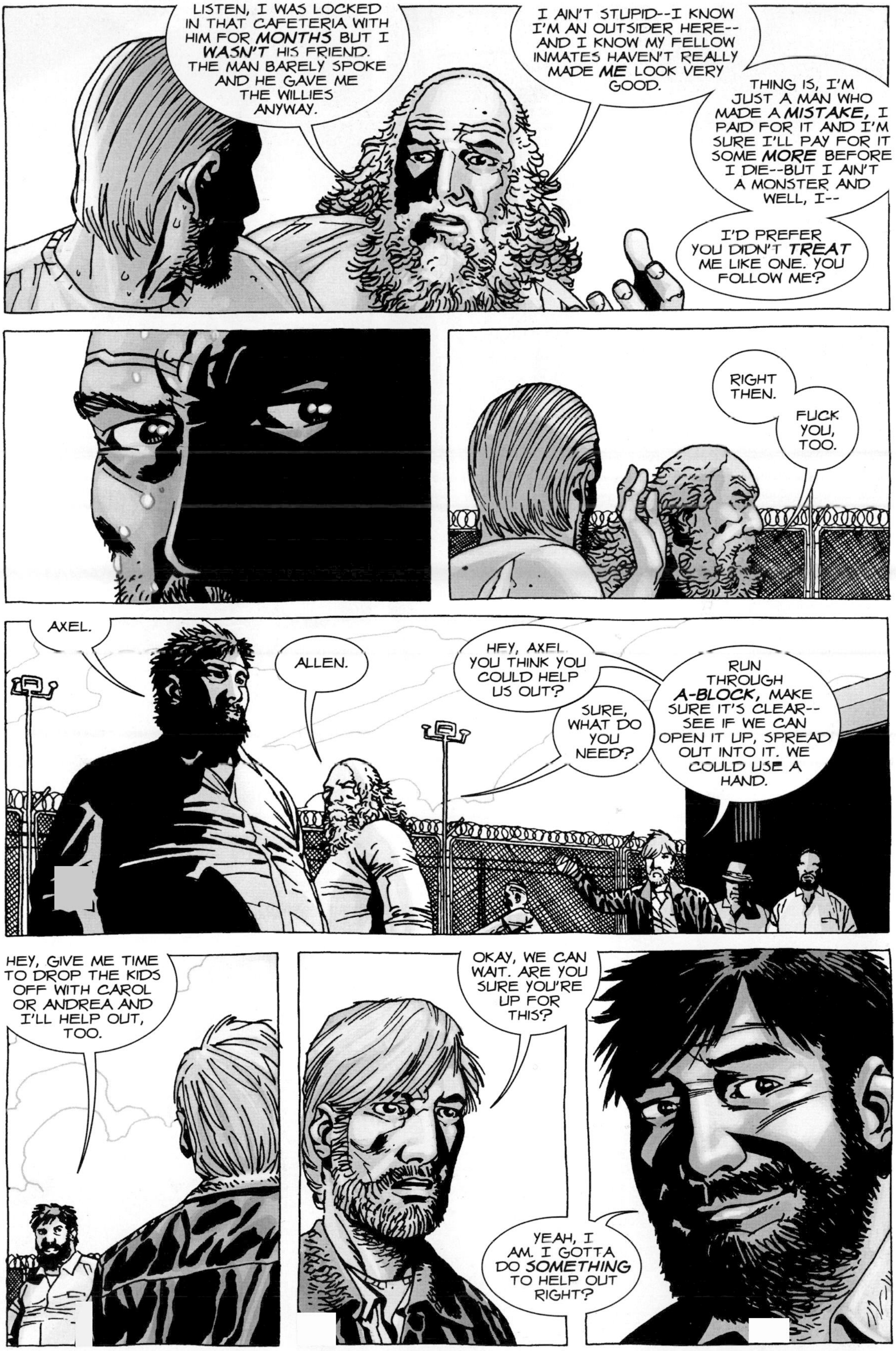
LISTEN, I WAS LOCKED IN THAT CAFETERIA WITH HIM FOR MONTHS BUT I WASN'T HIS FRIEND. THE MAN BARELY SPOKE AND HE GAVE ME THE WILLIES ANYWAY.
I AIN'T STUPID--I KNOW I'M AN OUTSIDER HERE--AND I KNOW MY FELLOW INMATES HAVEN'T REALLY MADE ME LOOK VERY GOOD.
THING IS, I'M JUST A MAN WHO MADE A MISTAKE, I PAID FOR IT AND I'M SURE I'LL PAY FOR IT SOME MORE BEFORE I DIE--BUT I AIN'T A MONSTER AND WELL, I--
I'D PREFER YOU DIDN'T TREAT ME LIKE ONE. YOU FOLLOW ME?
RIGHT THEN.
FUCK YOU, TOO.
AXEL.
ALLEN.
HEY, AXEL. YOU THINK YOU COULD HELP US OUT?
SURE, WHAT DO YOU NEED?
RUN THROUGH A-BLOCK, MAKE SURE IT'S CLEAR--SEE IF WE CAN OPEN IT UP, SPREAD OUT INTO IT. WE COULD USE A HAND.
HEY, GIVE ME TIME TO DROP THE KIDS OFF WITH CAROL OR ANDREA AND I'LL HELP OUT, TOO.
OKAY, WE CAN WAIT. ARE YOU SURE YOU'RE UP FOR THIS?
YEAH, I AM. I GOTTA DO SOMETHING TO HELP OUT RIGHT?

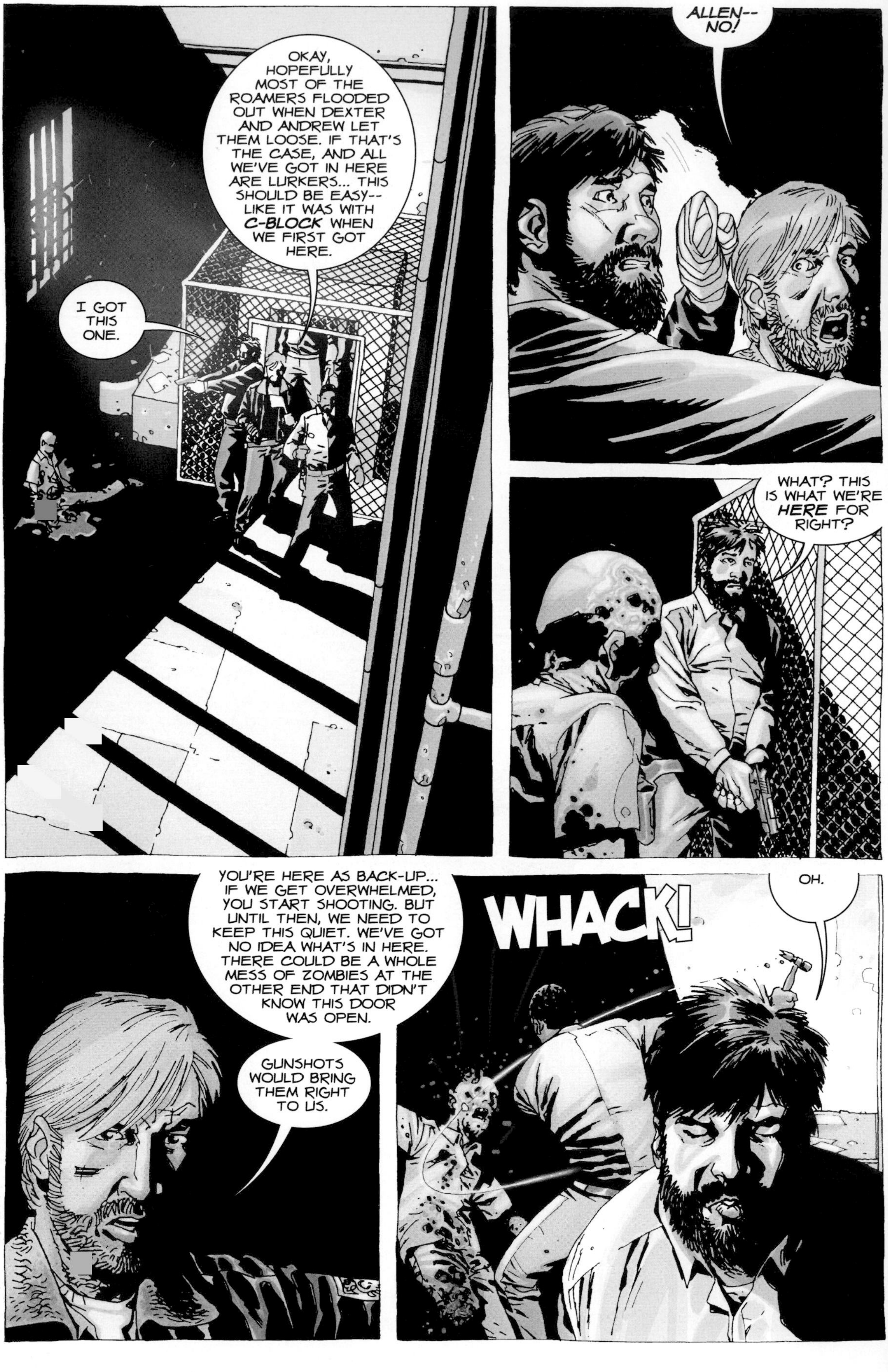
OKAY, HOPEFULLY MOST OF THE ROAMERS FLOODED OUT WHEN DEXTER AND ANDREW LET THEM LOOSE. IF THAT'S THE CASE, AND ALL WE'VE GOT IN HERE ARE LURKERS... THIS SHOULD BE EASY-- LIKE IT WAS WITH C-BLOCK WHEN WE FIRST GOT HERE.
I GOT THIS ONE.
ALLEN-- NO!
WHAT? THIS IS WHAT WE'RE HERE FOR RIGHT?
YOU'RE HERE AS BACK-UP... IF WE GET OVERWHELMED, YOU START SHOOTING. BUT UNTIL THEN, WE NEED TO KEEP THIS QUIET. WE'VE GOT NO IDEA WHAT'S IN HERE. THERE COULD BE A WHOLE MESS OF ZOMBIES AT THE OTHER END THAT DIDN'T KNOW THIS DOOR WAS OPEN.
GUNSHOTS WOULD BRING THEM RIGHT TO US.
WHACK!
OH.

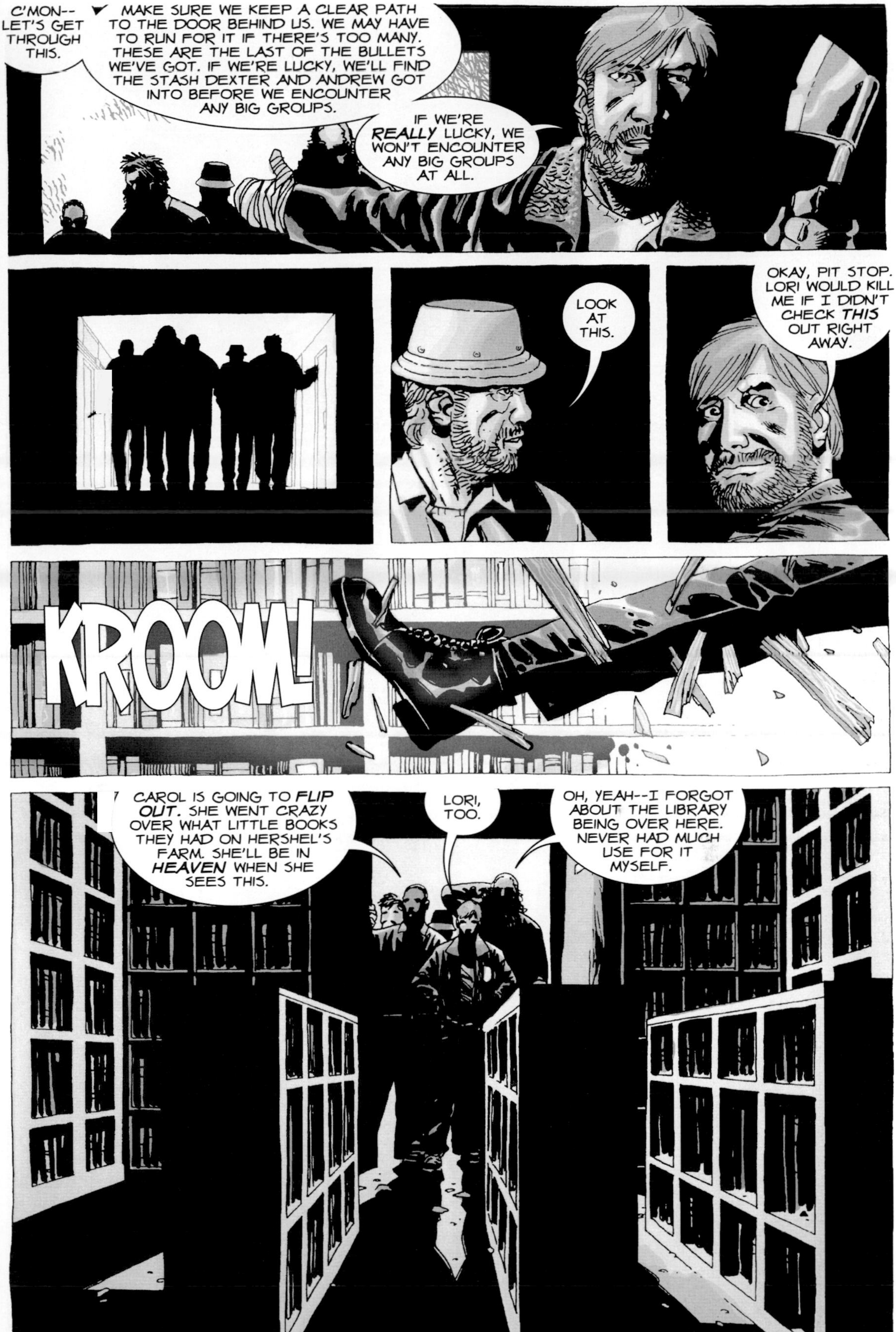

C'MON-- LET'S GET THROUGH THIS.
MAKE SURE WE KEEP A CLEAR PATH TO THE DOOR BEHIND US. WE MAY HAVE TO RUN FOR IT IF THERE'S TOO MANY. THESE ARE THE LAST OF THE BULLETS WE'VE GOT. IF WE'RE LUCKY, WE'LL FIND THE STASH DEXTER AND ANDREW GOT INTO BEFORE WE ENCOUNTER ANY BIG GROUPS.
IF WE'RE REALLY LUCKY, WE WON'T ENCOUNTER ANY BIG GROUPS AT ALL.
LOOK AT THIS.
OKAY, PIT STOP. LORI WOULD KILL ME IF I DIDN'T CHECK THIS OUT RIGHT AWAY.
KROOM!
CAROL IS GOING TO FLIP OUT. SHE WENT CRAZY OVER WHAT LITTLE BOOKS THEY HAD ON HERSHEL'S FARM. SHE'LL BE IN HEAVEN WHEN SHE SEES THIS.
LORI, TOO.
OH, YEAH--I FORGOT ABOUT THE LIBRARY BEING OVER HERE. NEVER HAD MUCH USE FOR IT MYSELF.

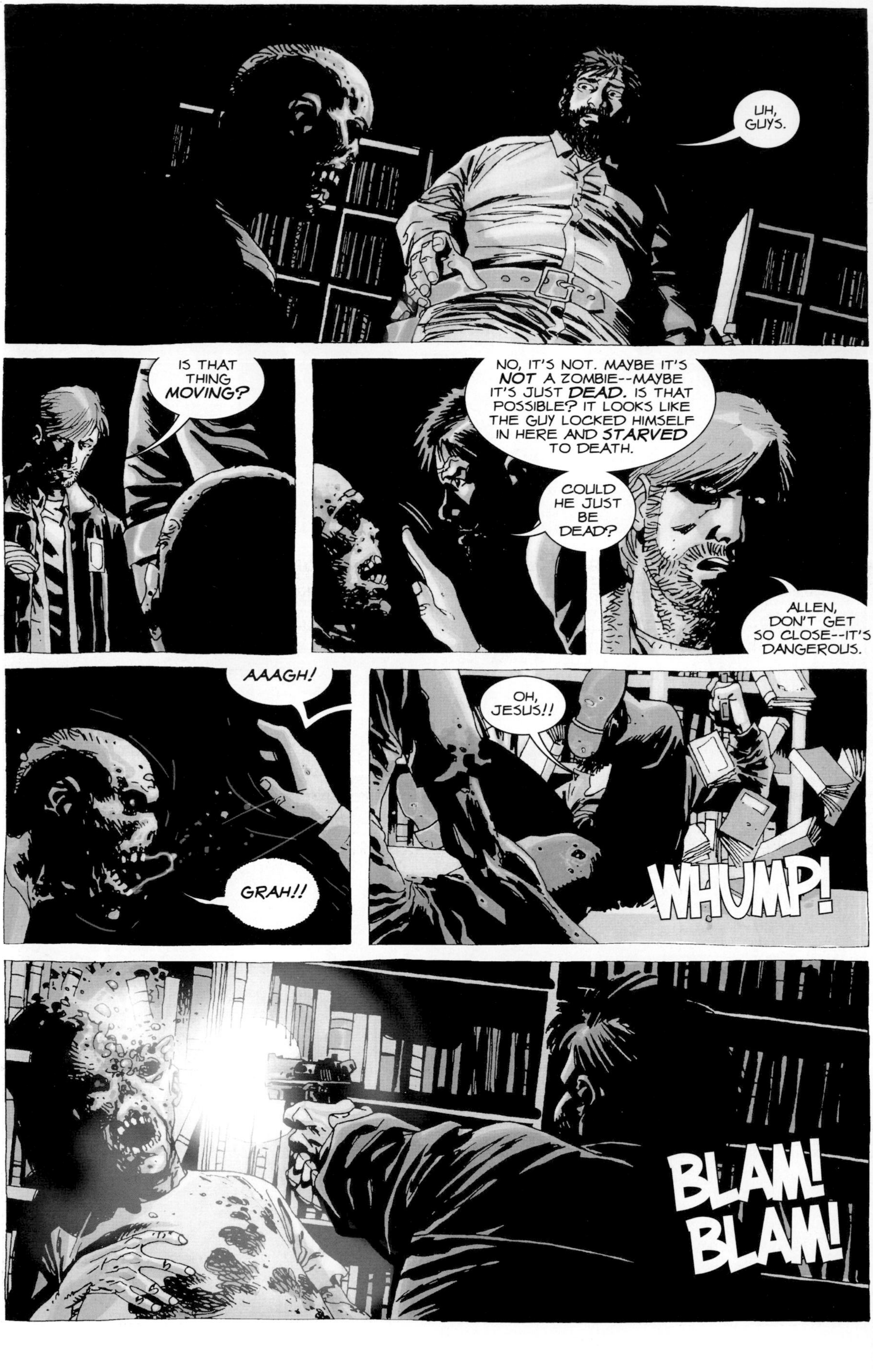
UH, GUYS.
IS THAT THING MOVING?
NO, IT'S NOT. MAYBE IT'S NOT A ZOMBIE--MAYBE IT'S JUST DEAD. IS THAT POSSIBLE? IT LOOKS LIKE THE GUY LOCKED HIMSELF IN HERE AND STARVED TO DEATH.
COULD HE JUST BE DEAD?
ALLEN, DON'T GET SO CLOSE--IT'S DANGEROUS.
AAAGH!
GRAH!!
OH, JESUS!!
WHUMP!
BLAM! BLAM!

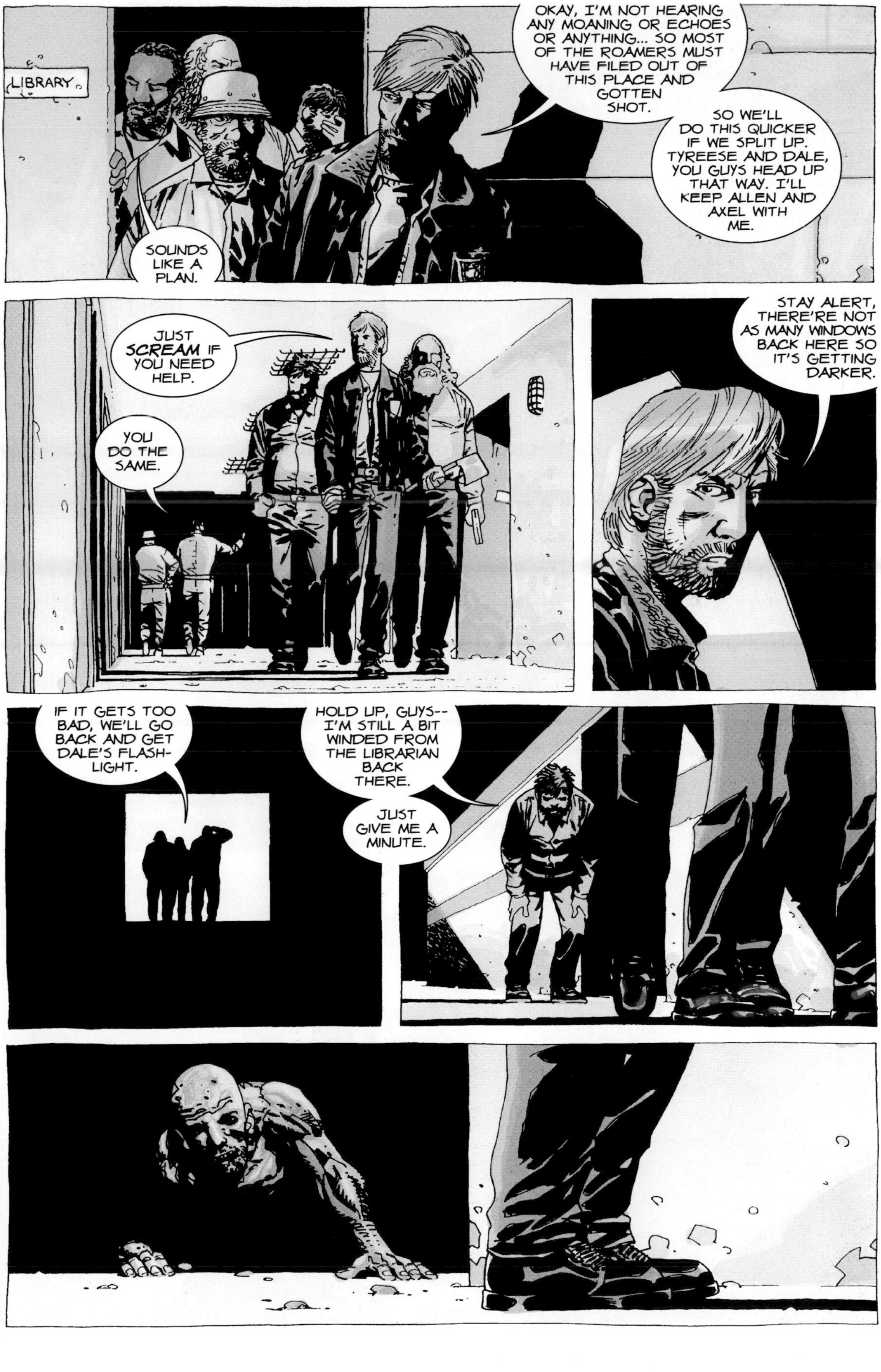
LIBRARY
OKAY, I'M NOT HEARING ANY MOANING OR ECHOES OR ANYTHING... SO MOST OF THE ROAMERS MUST HAVE FILED OUT OF THIS PLACE AND GOTTEN SHOT.
SO WE'LL DO THIS QUICKER IF WE SPLIT UP. TYREESE AND DALE, YOU GUYS HEAD UP THAT WAY. I'LL KEEP ALLEN AND AXEL WITH ME.
SOUNDS LIKE A PLAN.
JUST SCREAM IF YOU NEED HELP.
YOU DO THE SAME.
STAY ALERT, THERE'RE NOT AS MANY WINDOWS BACK HERE SO IT'S GETTING DARKER.
IF IT GETS TOO BAD, WE'LL GO BACK AND GET DALE'S FLASH-LIGHT.
HOLD UP, GUYS-- I'M STILL A BIT WINDED FROM THE LIBRARIAN BACK THERE.
JUST GIVE ME A MINUTE.

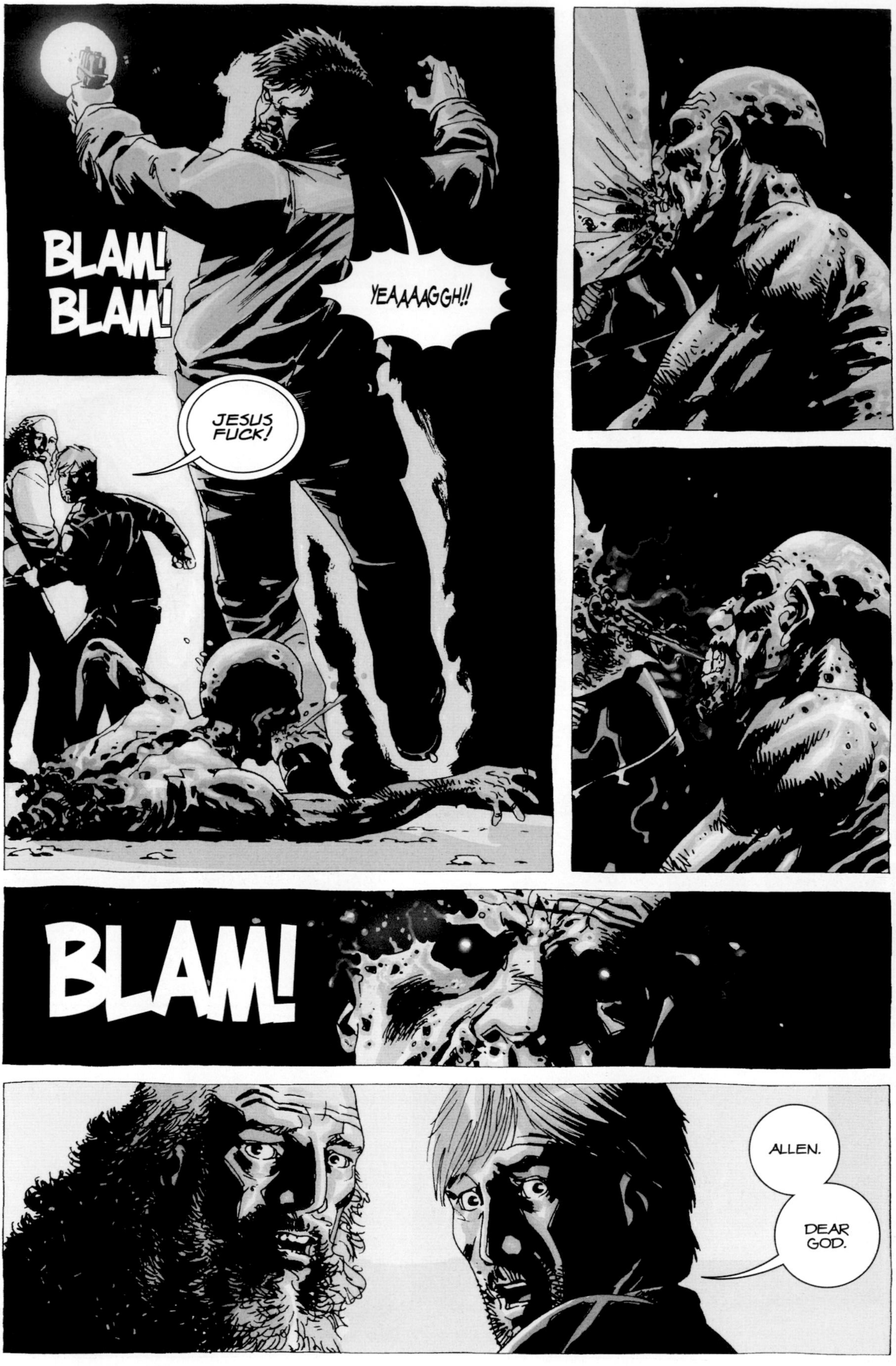
BLAM! BLAM!
YEAAAAGGH!!
JESUS FUCK!
BLAM!
ALLEN.
DEAR GOD.

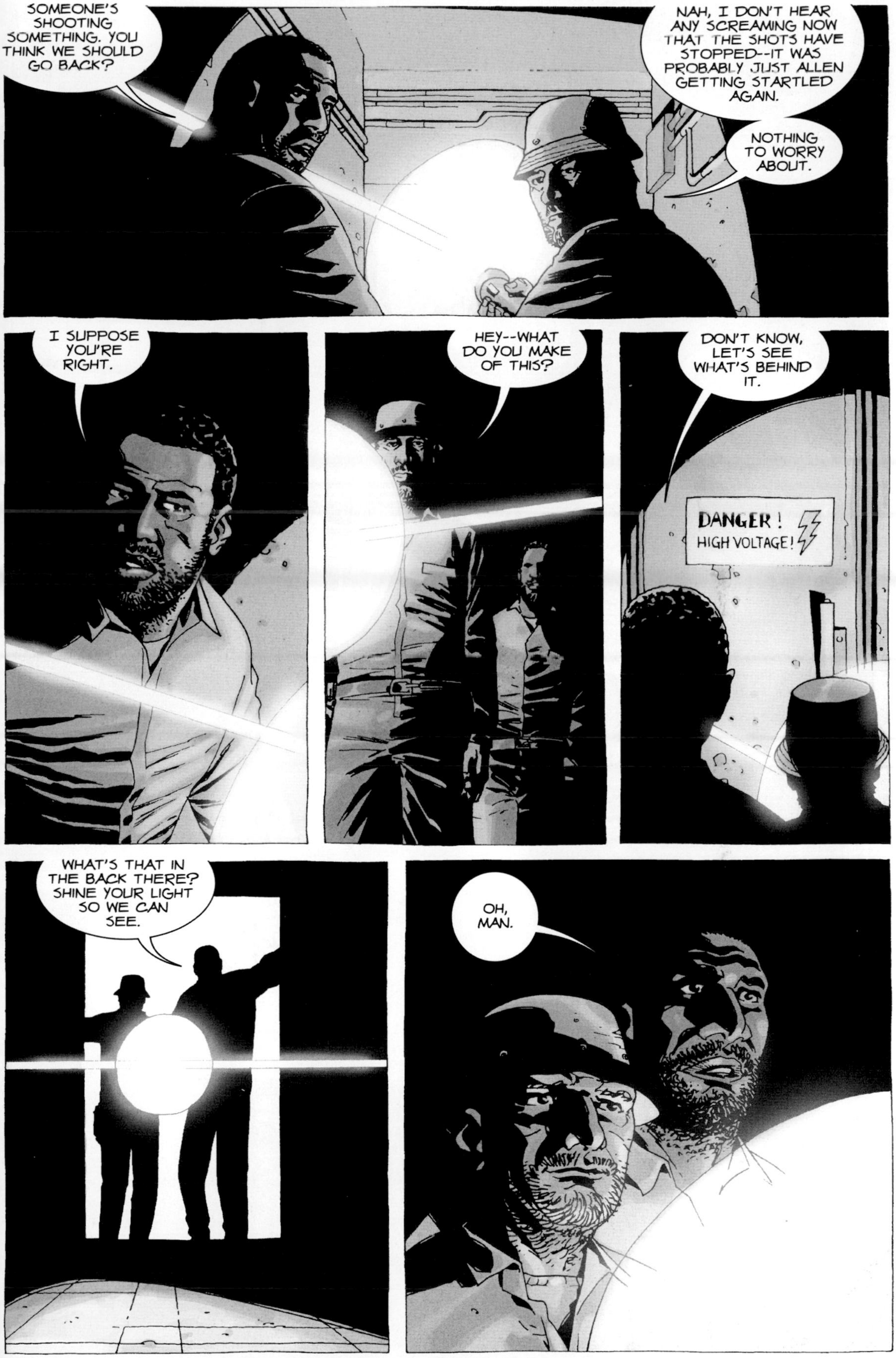
SOMEONE'S SHOOTING SOMETHING. YOU THINK WE SHOULD GO BACK?
NAH, I DON'T HEAR ANY SCREAMING NOW THAT THE SHOTS HAVE STOPPED--IT WAS PROBABLY JUST ALLEN GETTING STARTLED AGAIN.
NOTHING TO WORRY ABOUT.
I SUPPOSE YOU'RE RIGHT.
HEY--WHAT DO YOU MAKE OF THIS?
DON'T KNOW, LET'S SEE WHAT'S BEHIND IT.
DANGER ! HIGH VOLTAGE !
WHAT'S THAT IN THE BACK THERE? SHINE YOUR LIGHT SO WE CAN SEE.
OH, MAN.

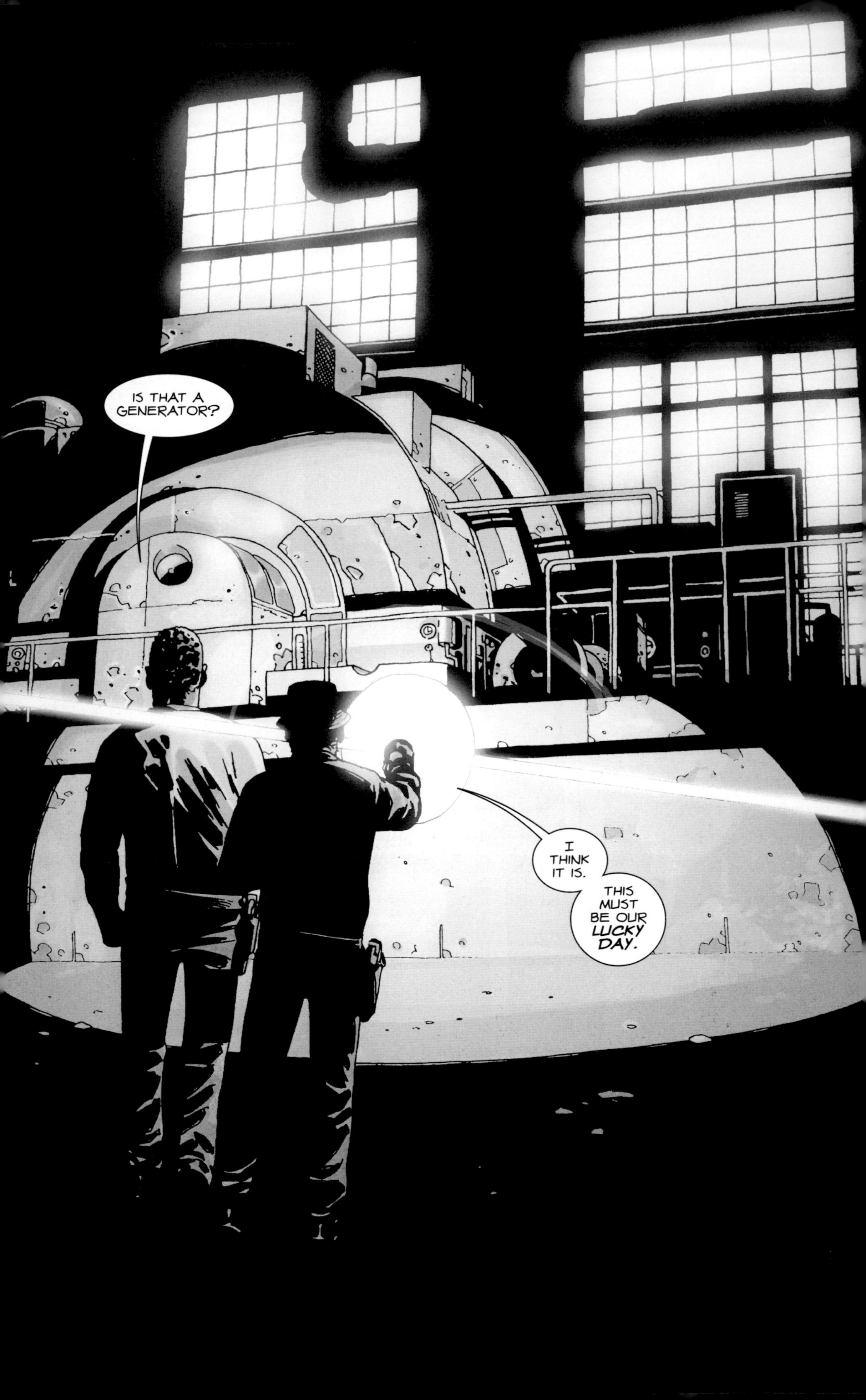

IS THAT A GENERATOR?
I THINK IT IS.
THIS MUST BE OUR LUCKY DAY.

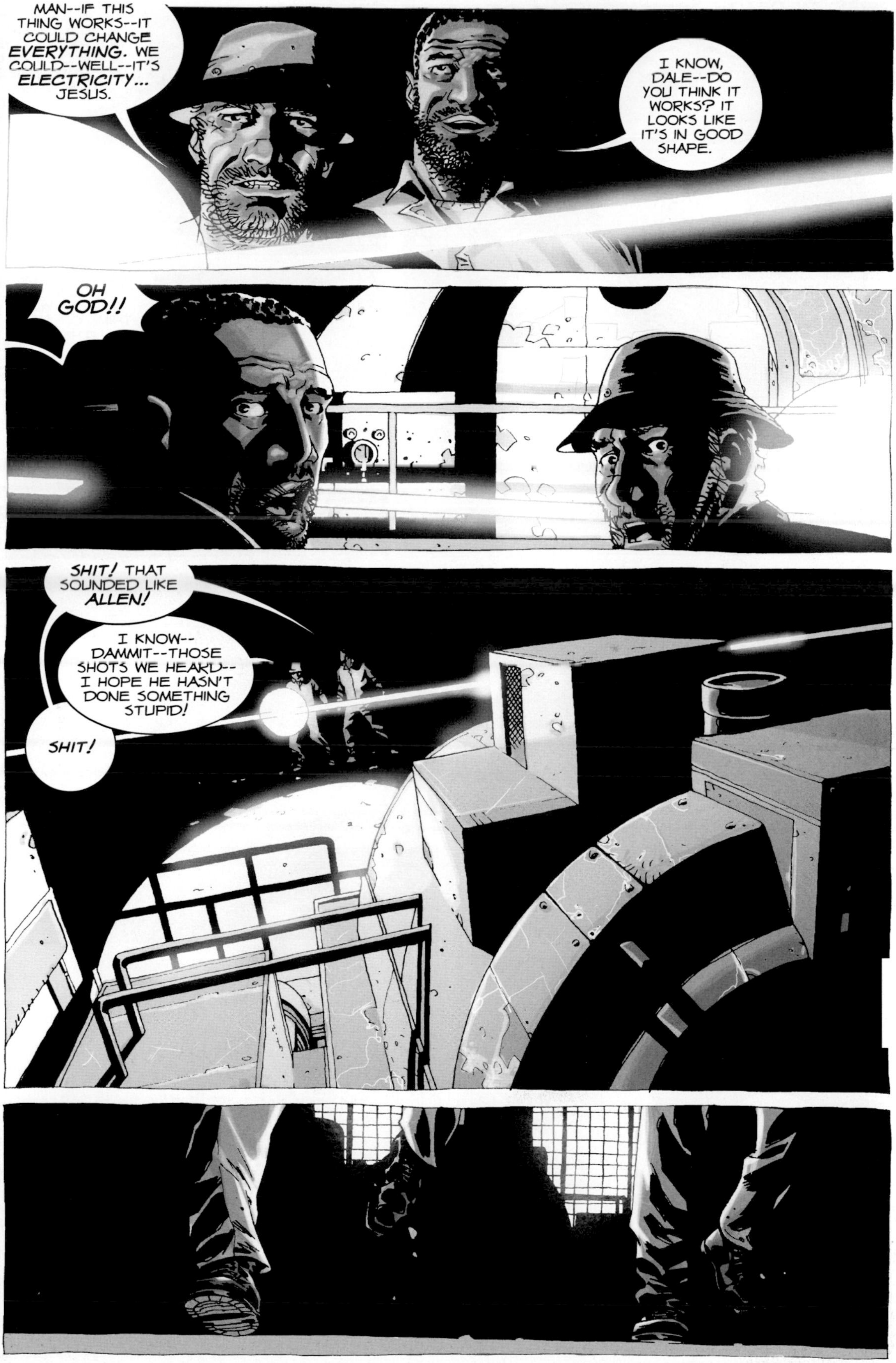
MAN--IF THIS THING WORKS--IT COULD CHANGE EVERYTHING. WE COULD--WELL--IT'S ELECTRICITY... JESUS.
I KNOW, DALE--DO YOU THINK IT WORKS? IT LOOKS LIKE IT'S IN GOOD SHAPE.
OH GOD!!
SHIT! THAT SOUNDED LIKE ALLEN!
I KNOW-- DAMMIT--THOSE SHOTS WE HEARD-- I HOPE HE HASN'T DONE SOMETHING STUPID!
SHIT!

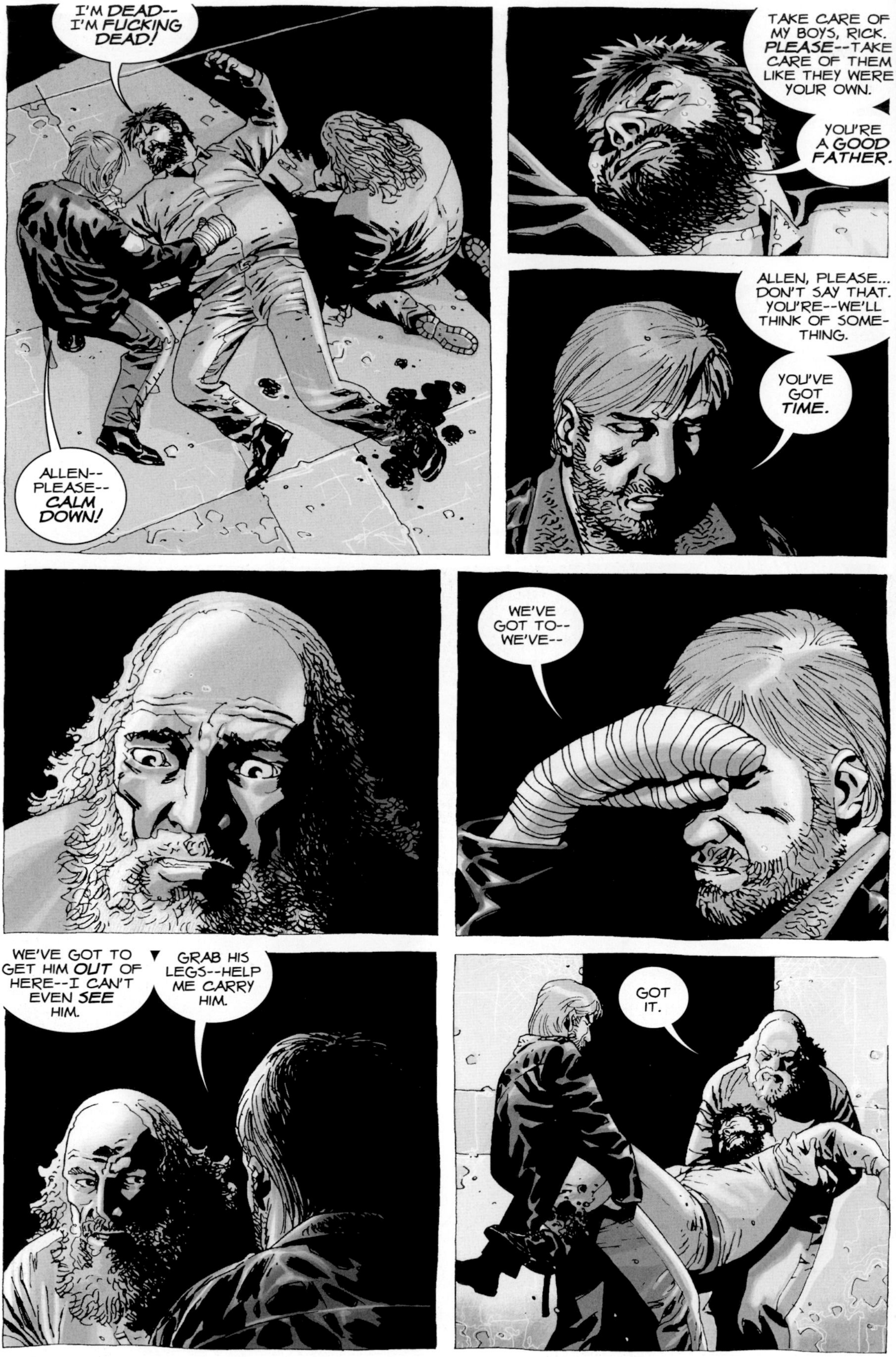
I'M DEAD--
I'M FUCKING DEAD!
ALLEN--
PLEASE--
CALM DOWN!
TAKE CARE OF MY BOYS, RICK. PLEASE--TAKE CARE OF THEM LIKE THEY WERE YOUR OWN.
YOU'RE A GOOD FATHER.
ALLEN, PLEASE... DON'T SAY THAT. YOU'RE--WE'LL THINK OF SOMETHING.
YOU'VE GOT TIME.
WE'VE GOT TO--
WE'VE--
WE'VE GOT TO GET HIM OUT OF HERE--I CAN'T EVEN SEE HIM.
GRAB HIS LEGS--HELP ME CARRY HIM.
GOT IT.

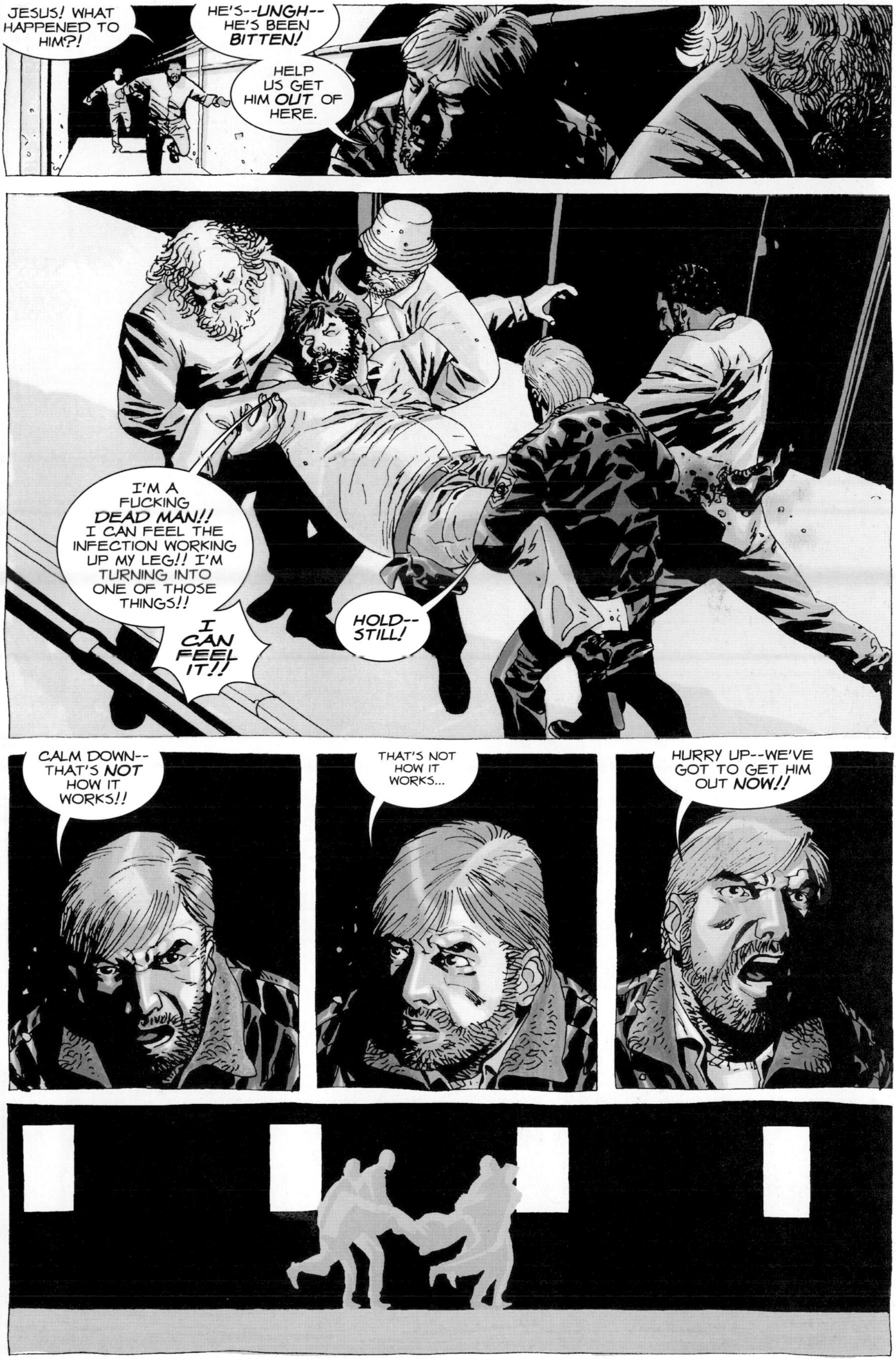
JESUS! WHAT HAPPENED TO HIM?!
HE'S--UNGH-- HE'S BEEN BITTEN!
HELP US GET HIM OUT OF HERE.
I'M A FUCKING DEAD MAN!! I CAN FEEL THE INFECTION WORKING UP MY LEG!! I'M TURNING INTO ONE OF THOSE THINGS!!
I CAN FEEL IT!!
HOLD-- STILL!
CALM DOWN-- THAT'S NOT HOW IT WORKS!!
THAT'S NOT HOW IT WORKS...
HURRY UP--WE'VE GOT TO GET HIM OUT NOW!!

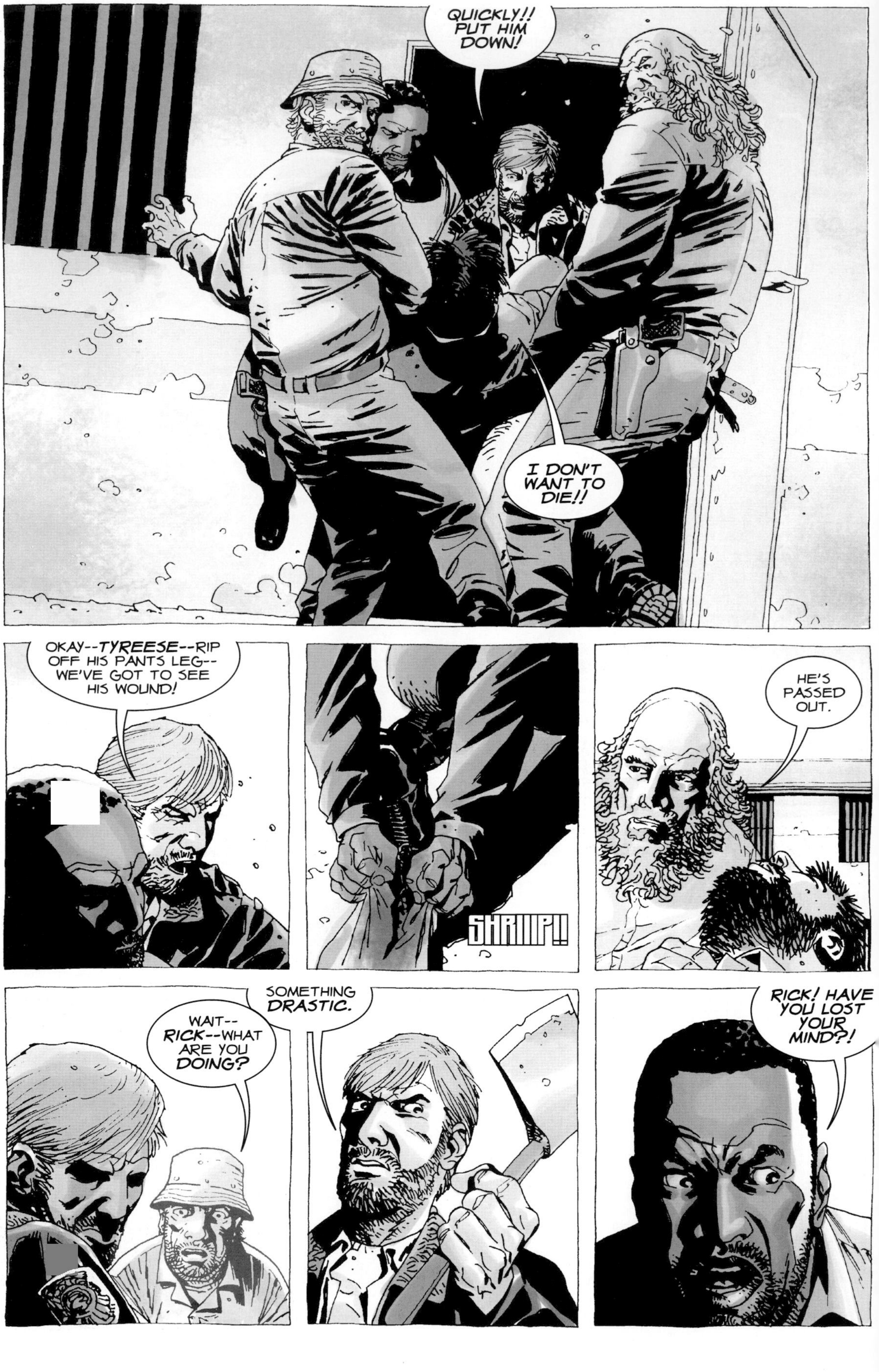
QUICKLY!! PUT HIM DOWN!
I DON'T WANT TO DIE!!
OKAY--TYREESE--RIP OFF HIS PANTS LEG-- WE'VE GOT TO SEE HIS WOUND!
SHRIIIP!!
HE'S PASSED OUT.
WAIT-- RICK--WHAT ARE YOU DOING?
SOMETHING DRASTIC.
RICK! HAVE YOU LOST YOUR MIND?!

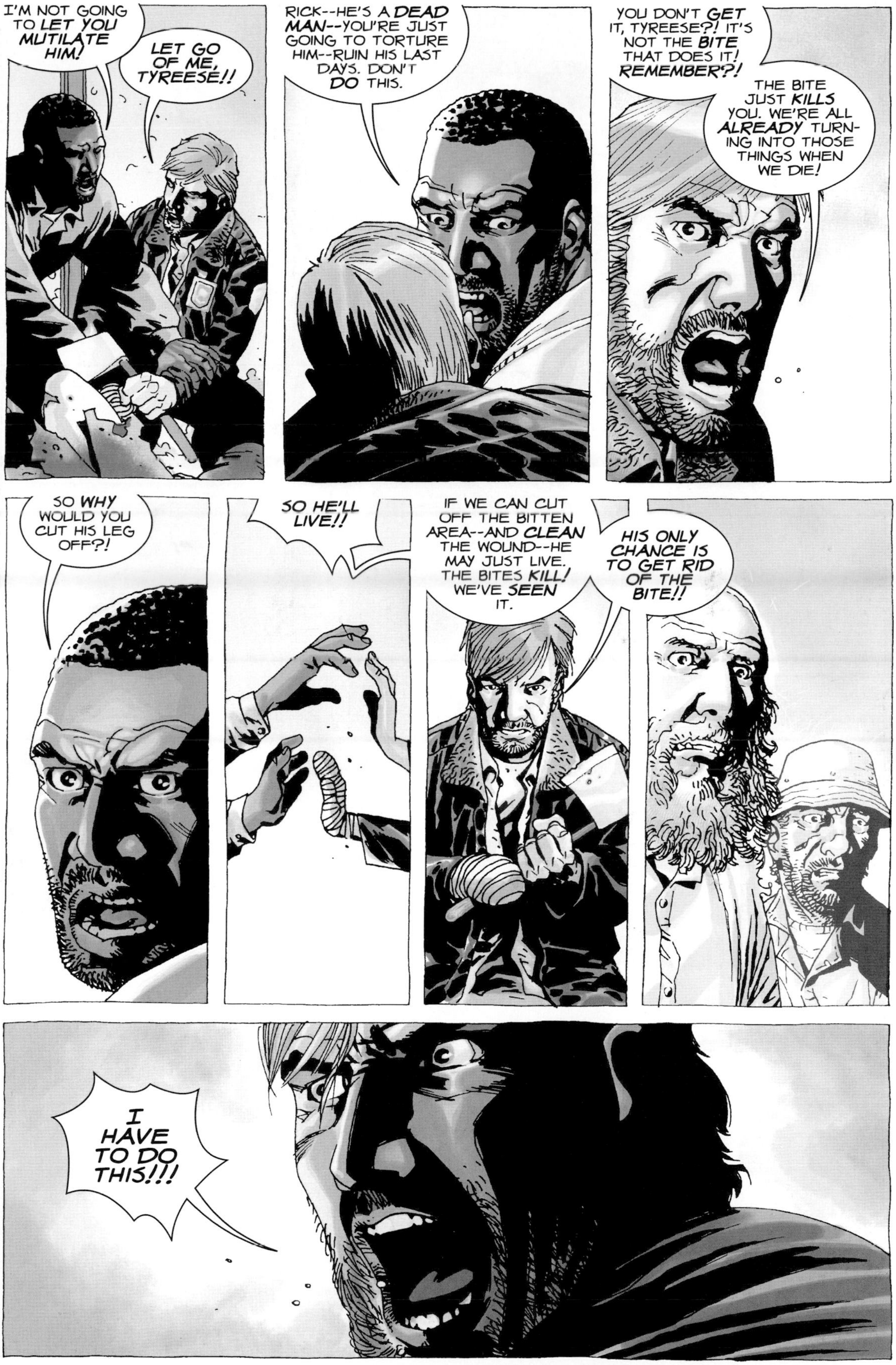
I'M NOT GOING TO LET YOU MUTILATE HIM!
LET GO OF ME, TYREESE!!
RICK--HE'S A DEAD MAN--YOU'RE JUST GOING TO TORTURE HIM--RUIN HIS LAST DAYS. DON'T DO THIS.
YOU DON'T GET IT, TYREESE?! IT'S NOT THE BITE THAT DOES IT! REMEMBER?!
THE BITE JUST KILLS YOU. WE'RE ALL ALREADY TURNING INTO THOSE THINGS WHEN WE DIE!
SO WHY WOULD YOU CUT HIS LEG OFF?!
SO HE'LL LIVE!!
IF WE CAN CUT OFF THE BITTEN AREA--AND CLEAN THE WOUND--HE MAY JUST LIVE. THE BITES KILL! WE'VE SEEN IT.
HIS ONLY CHANCE IS TO GET RID OF THE BITE!!
I HAVE TO DO THIS!!!

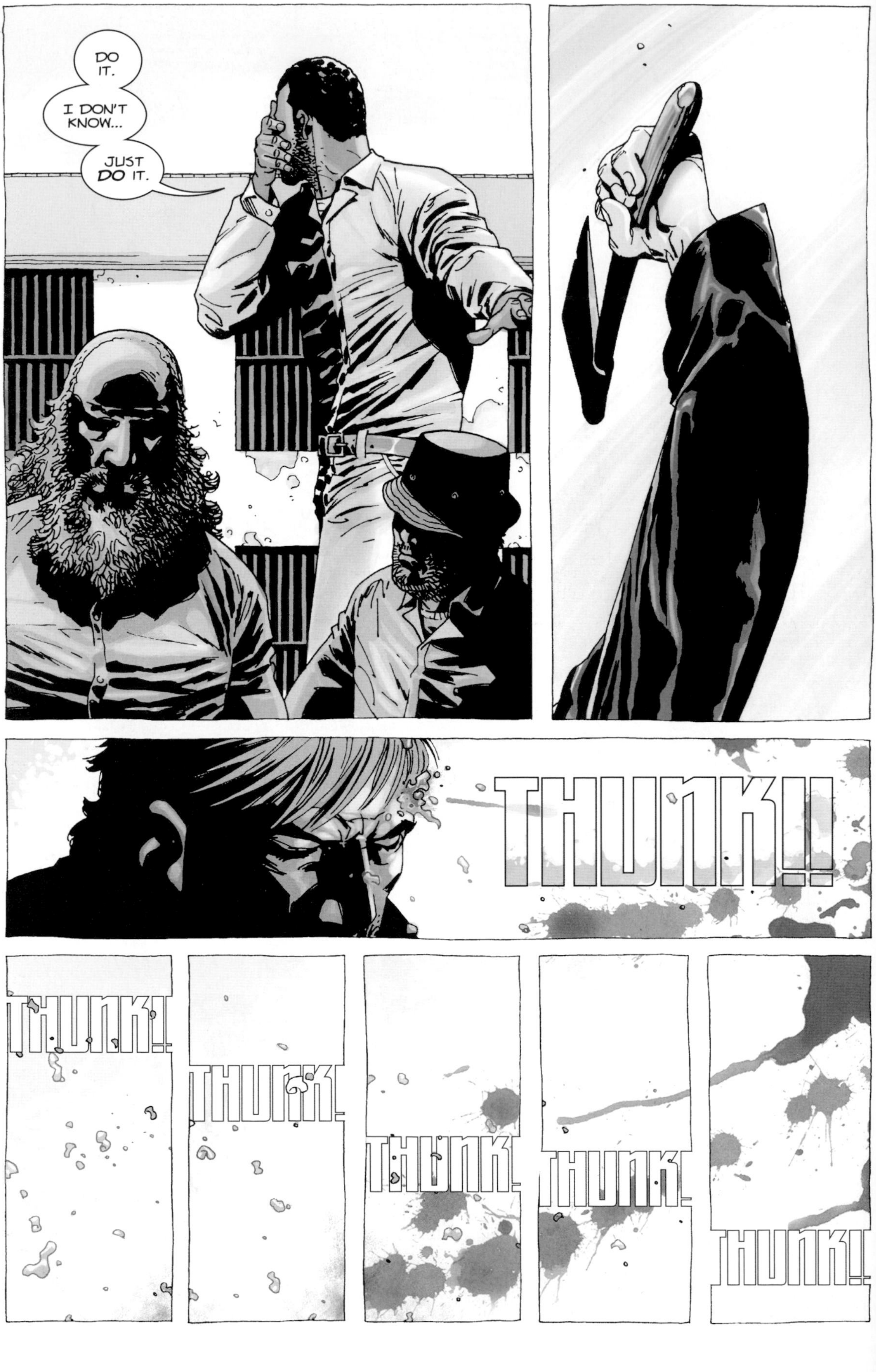

DO IT.
I DON'T KNOW...
JUST DO IT.
THUNK!!
THUNK!!
THUNK!
THUNK!
THUNK!
THUNK!!

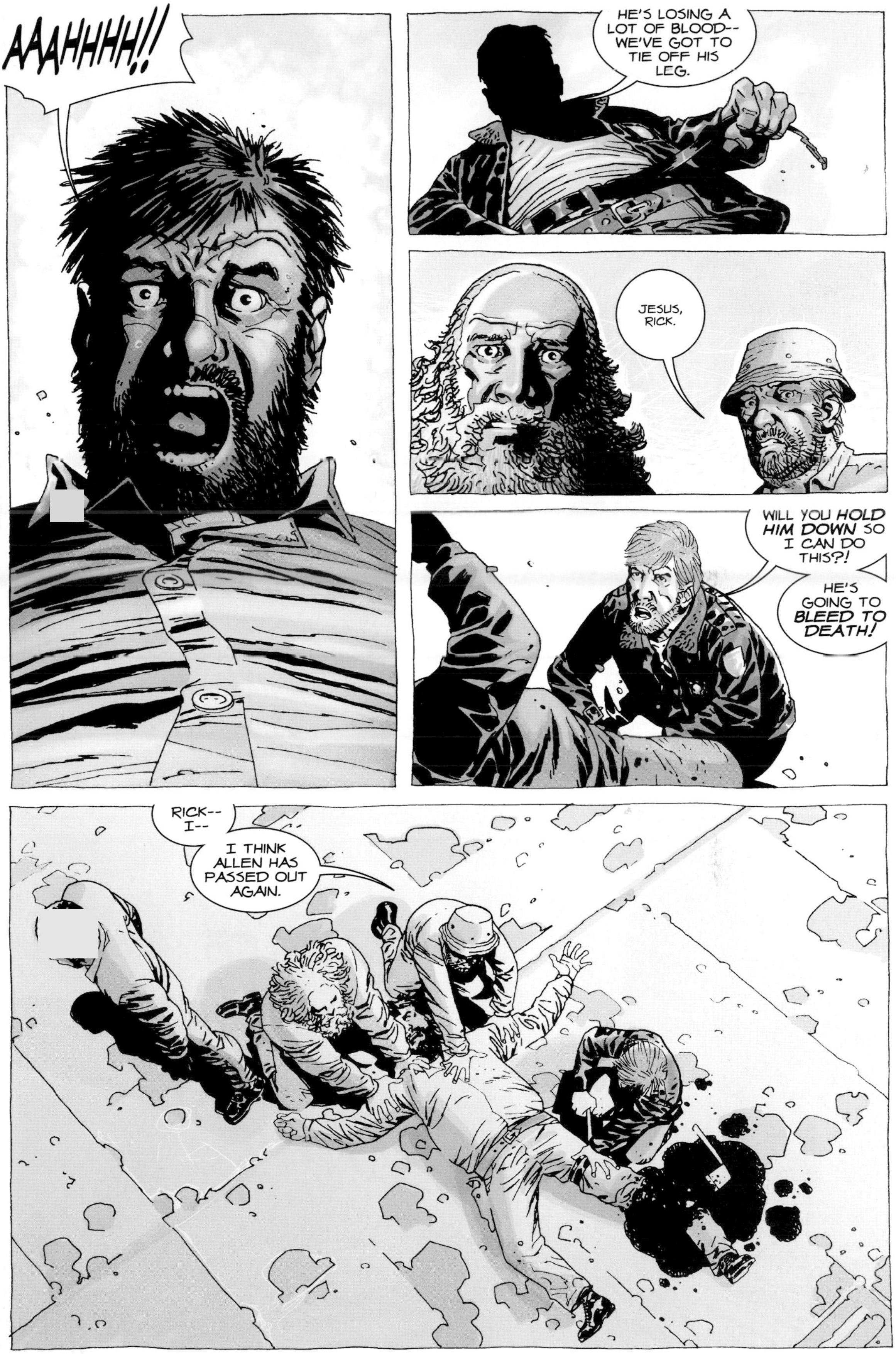

AAAHHHH!!
HE'S LOSING A LOT OF BLOOD-- WE'VE GOT TO TIE OFF HIS LEG.
JESUS, RICK.
WILL YOU HOLD HIM DOWN SO I CAN DO THIS?!
HE'S GOING TO BLEED TO DEATH!
RICK-- I--
I THINK ALLEN HAS PASSED OUT AGAIN.

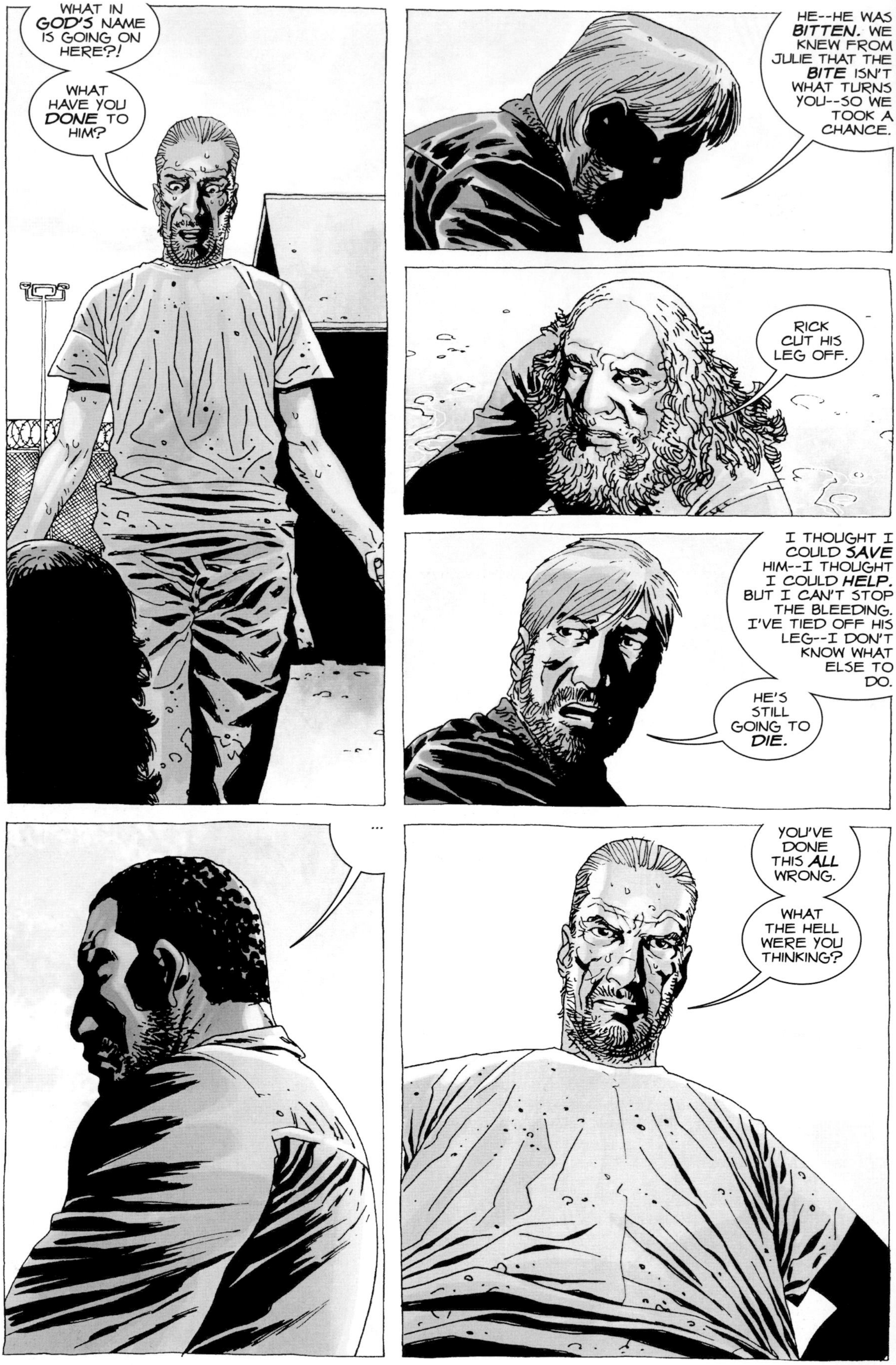
WHAT IN GOD'S NAME IS GOING ON HERE?!
WHAT HAVE YOU DONE TO HIM?
HE--HE WAS BITTEN. WE KNEW FROM JULIE THAT THE BITE ISN'T WHAT TURNS YOU--SO WE TOOK A CHANCE.
RICK CUT HIS LEG OFF.
I THOUGHT I COULD SAVE HIM--I THOUGHT I COULD HELP. BUT I CAN'T STOP THE BLEEDING. I'VE TIED OFF HIS LEG--I DON'T KNOW WHAT ELSE TO DO.
HE'S STILL GOING TO DIE.
...
YOU'VE DONE THIS ALL WRONG.
WHAT THE HELL WERE YOU THINKING?

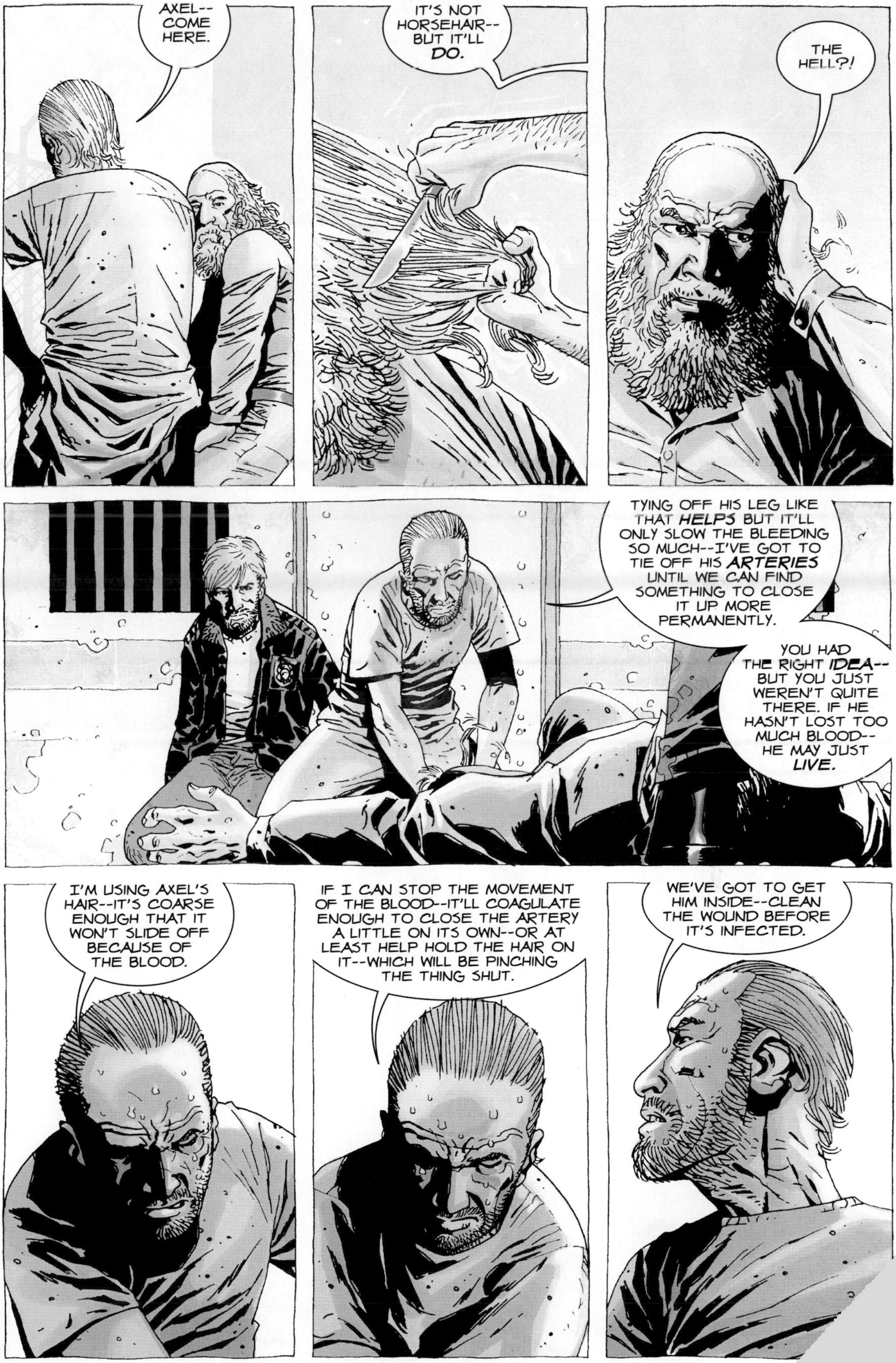
AXEL-- COME HERE.
IT'S NOT HORSEHAIR-- BUT IT'LL DO.
THE HELL?!
TYING OFF HIS LEG LIKE THAT HELPS BUT IT'LL ONLY SLOW THE BLEEDING SO MUCH--I'VE GOT TO TIE OFF HIS ARTERIES UNTIL WE CAN FIND SOMETHING TO CLOSE IT UP MORE PERMANENTLY.
YOU HAD THE RIGHT IDEA-- BUT YOU JUST WEREN'T QUITE THERE. IF HE HASN'T LOST TOO MUCH BLOOD-- HE MAY JUST LIVE.
I'M USING AXEL'S HAIR--IT'S COARSE ENOUGH THAT IT WON'T SLIDE OFF BECAUSE OF THE BLOOD.
IF I CAN STOP THE MOVEMENT OF THE BLOOD--IT'LL COAGULATE ENOUGH TO CLOSE THE ARTERY A LITTLE ON ITS OWN--OR AT LEAST HELP HOLD THE HAIR ON IT--WHICH WILL BE PINCHING THE THING SHUT.
WE'VE GOT TO GET HIM INSIDE--CLEAN THE WOUND BEFORE IT'S INFECTED.

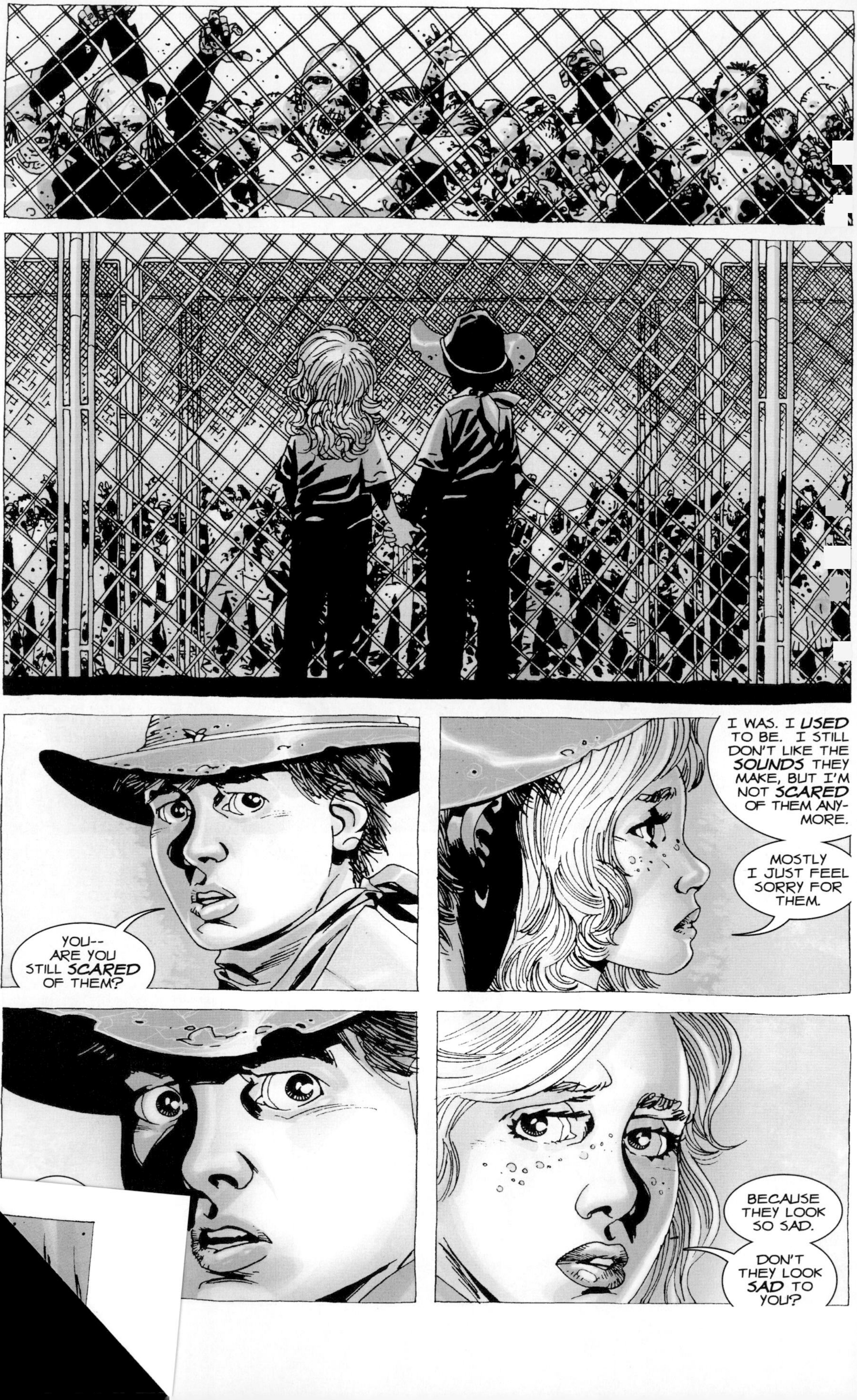
YOU-- ARE YOU STILL SCARED OF THEM?
I WAS. I USED TO BE. I STILL DON'T LIKE THE SOUNDS THEY MAKE, BUT I'M NOT SCARED OF THEM ANY-MORE.
MOSTLY I JUST FEEL SORRY FOR THEM.
BECAUSE THEY LOOK SO SAD.
DON'T THEY LOOK SAD TO YOU?

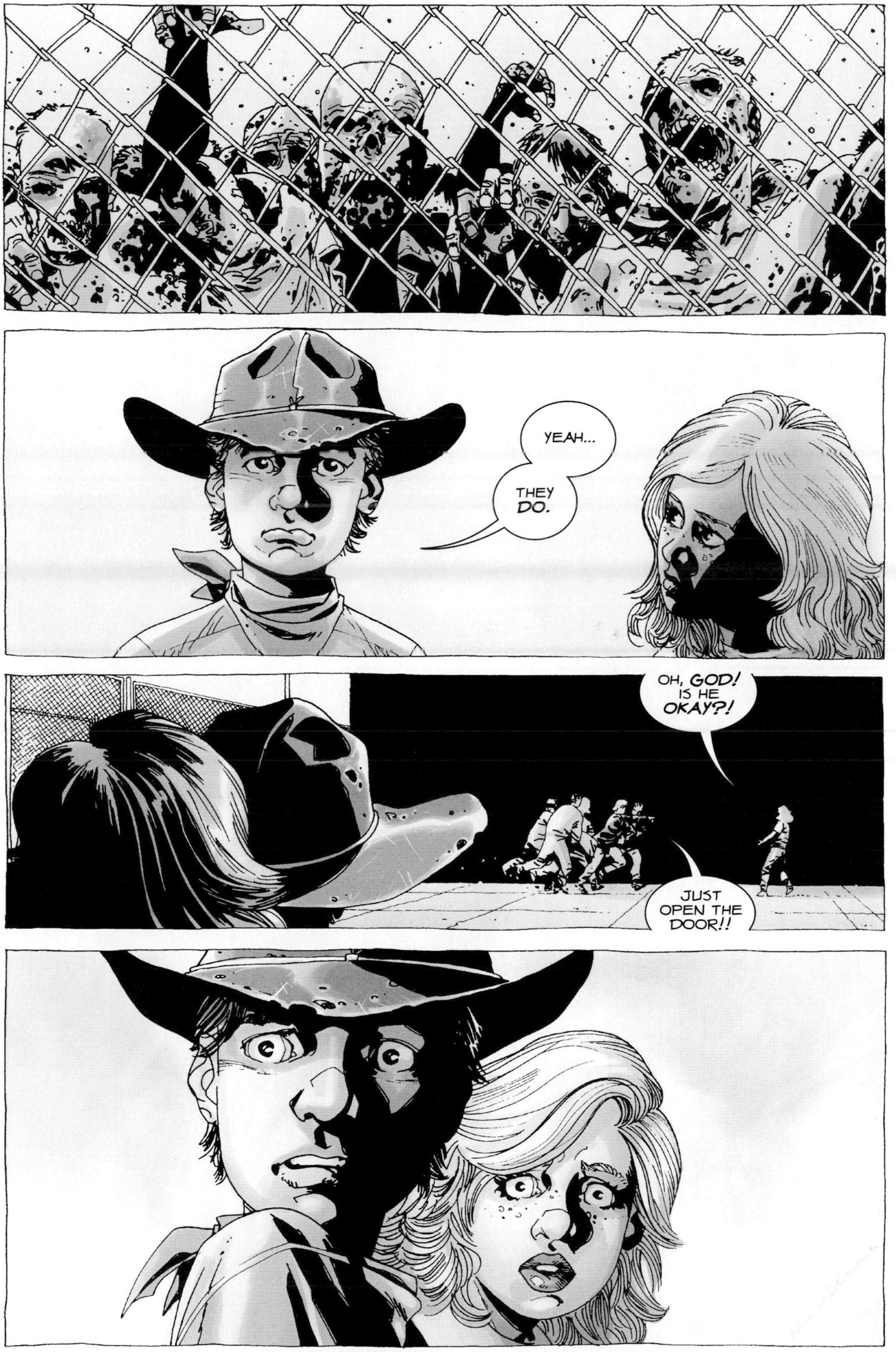
YEAH...
THEY DO.
OH, GOD! IS HE OKAY?!
JUST OPEN THE DOOR!!

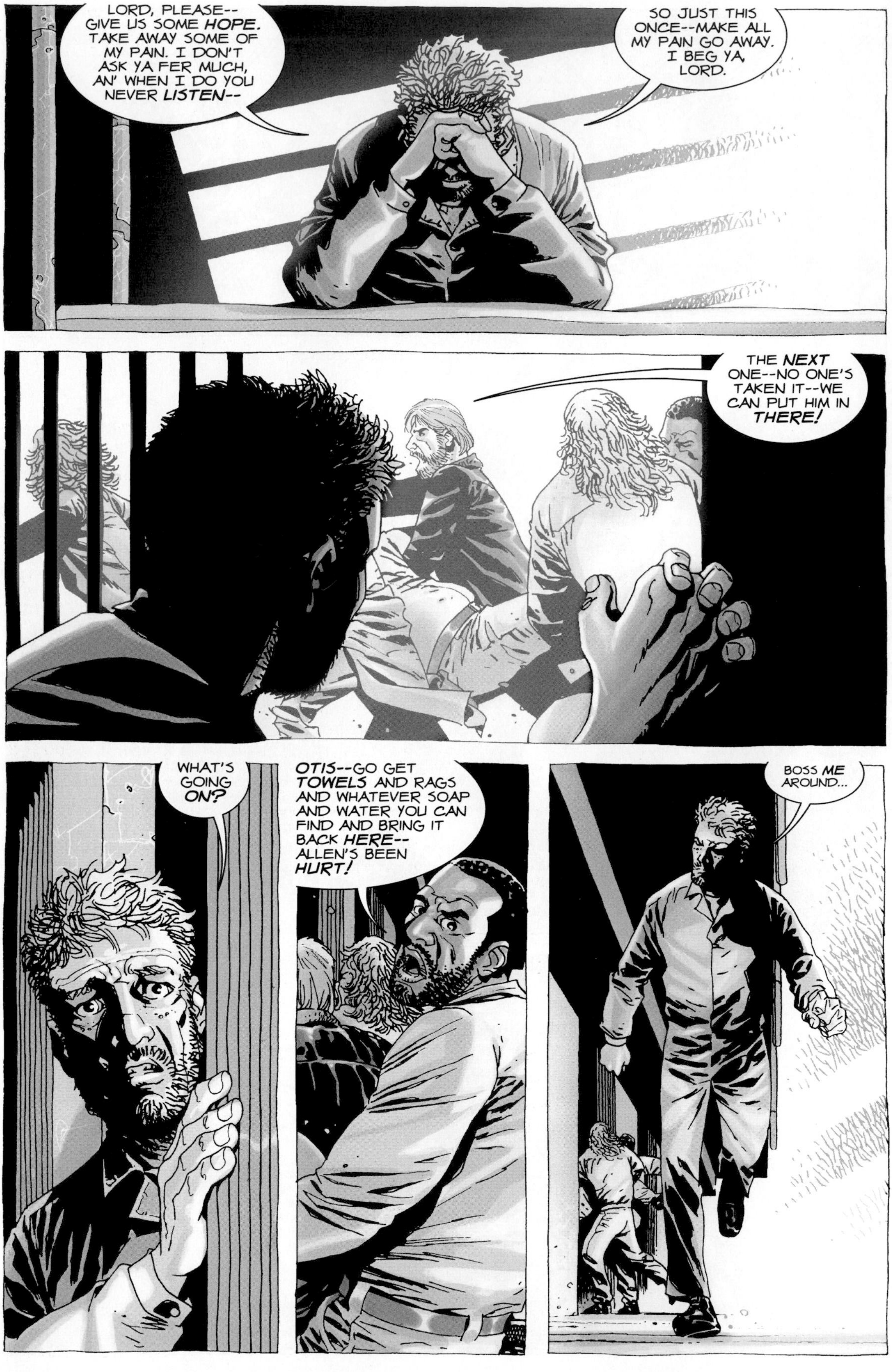
LORD, PLEASE-- GIVE US SOME HOPE. TAKE AWAY SOME OF MY PAIN. I DON'T ASK YA FER MUCH, AN' WHEN I DO YOU NEVER LISTEN--
SO JUST THIS ONCE--MAKE ALL MY PAIN GO AWAY. I BEG YA, LORD.
THE NEXT ONE--NO ONE'S TAKEN IT--WE CAN PUT HIM IN THERE!
WHAT'S GOING ON?
OTIS--GO GET TOWELS AND RAGS AND WHATEVER SOAP AND WATER YOU CAN FIND AND BRING IT BACK HERE-- ALLEN'S BEEN HURT!
BOSS ME AROUND...

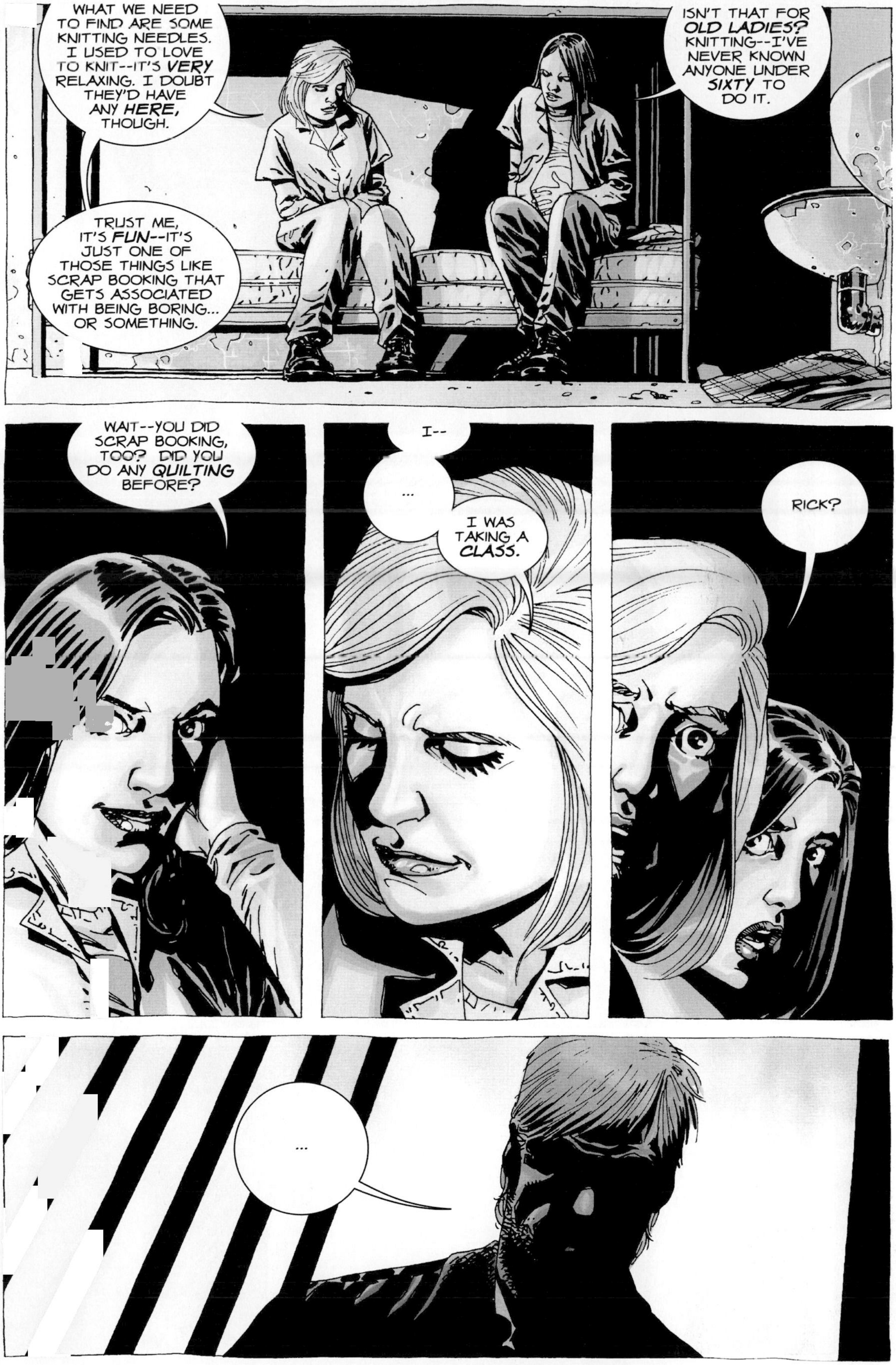
WHAT WE NEED TO FIND ARE SOME KNITTING NEEDLES. I USED TO LOVE TO KNIT--IT'S VERY RELAXING. I DOUBT THEY'D HAVE ANY HERE, THOUGH.
ISN'T THAT FOR OLD LADIES? KNITTING--I'VE NEVER KNOWN ANYONE UNDER SIXTY TO DO IT.
TRUST ME, IT'S FUN--IT'S JUST ONE OF THOSE THINGS LIKE SCRAP BOOKING THAT GETS ASSOCIATED WITH BEING BORING... OR SOMETHING.
WAIT--YOU DID SCRAP BOOKING, TOO? DID YOU DO ANY QUILTING BEFORE?
I--
...
I WAS TAKING A CLASS.
RICK?
...

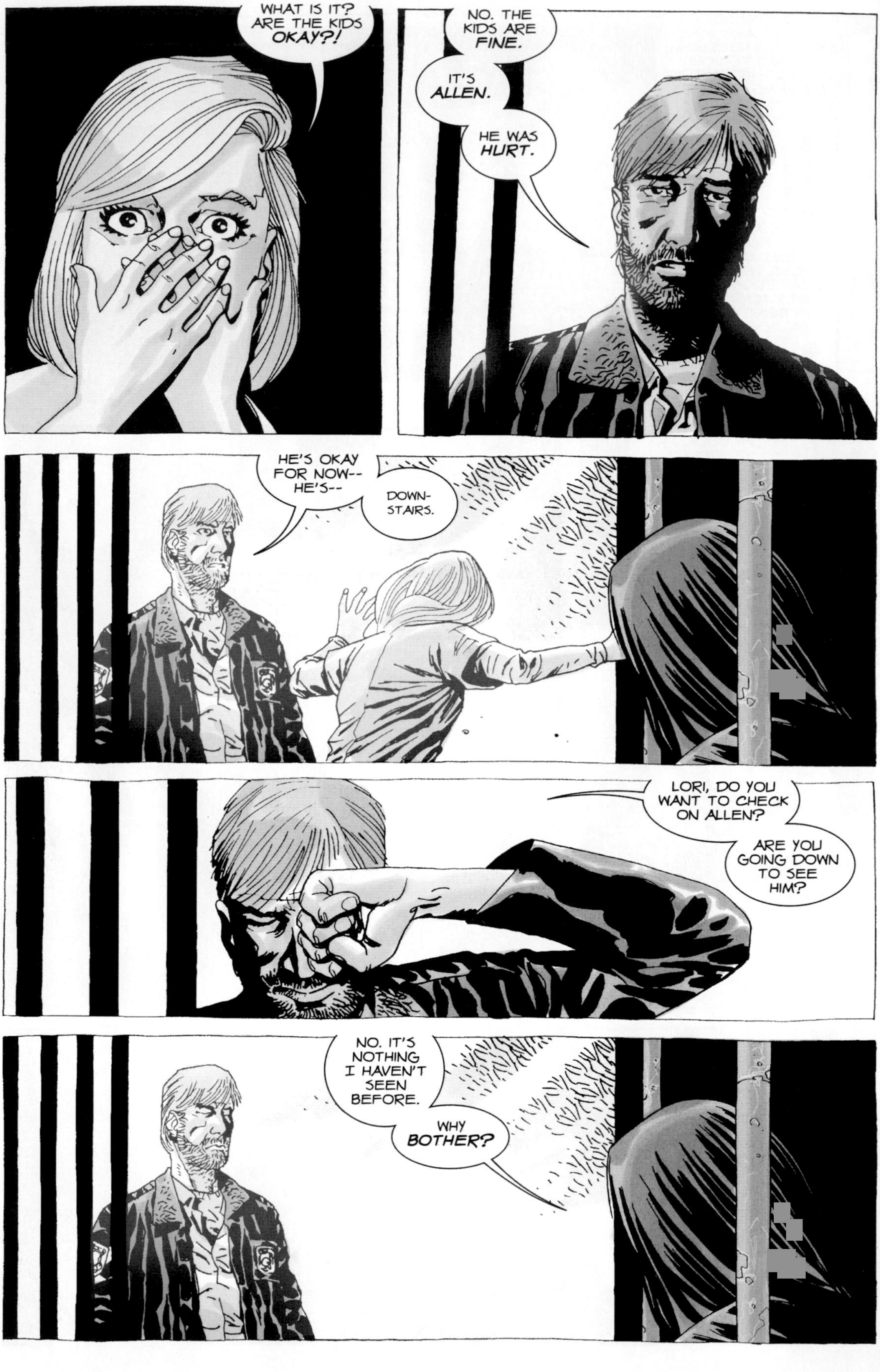
WHAT IS IT? ARE THE KIDS OKAY?!
NO. THE KIDS ARE FINE.
IT'S ALLEN.
HE WAS HURT.
HE'S OKAY FOR NOW-- HE'S--
DOWN-STAIRS.
LORI, DO YOU WANT TO CHECK ON ALLEN?
ARE YOU GOING DOWN TO SEE HIM?
NO. IT'S NOTHING I HAVEN'T SEEN BEFORE.
WHY BOTHER?

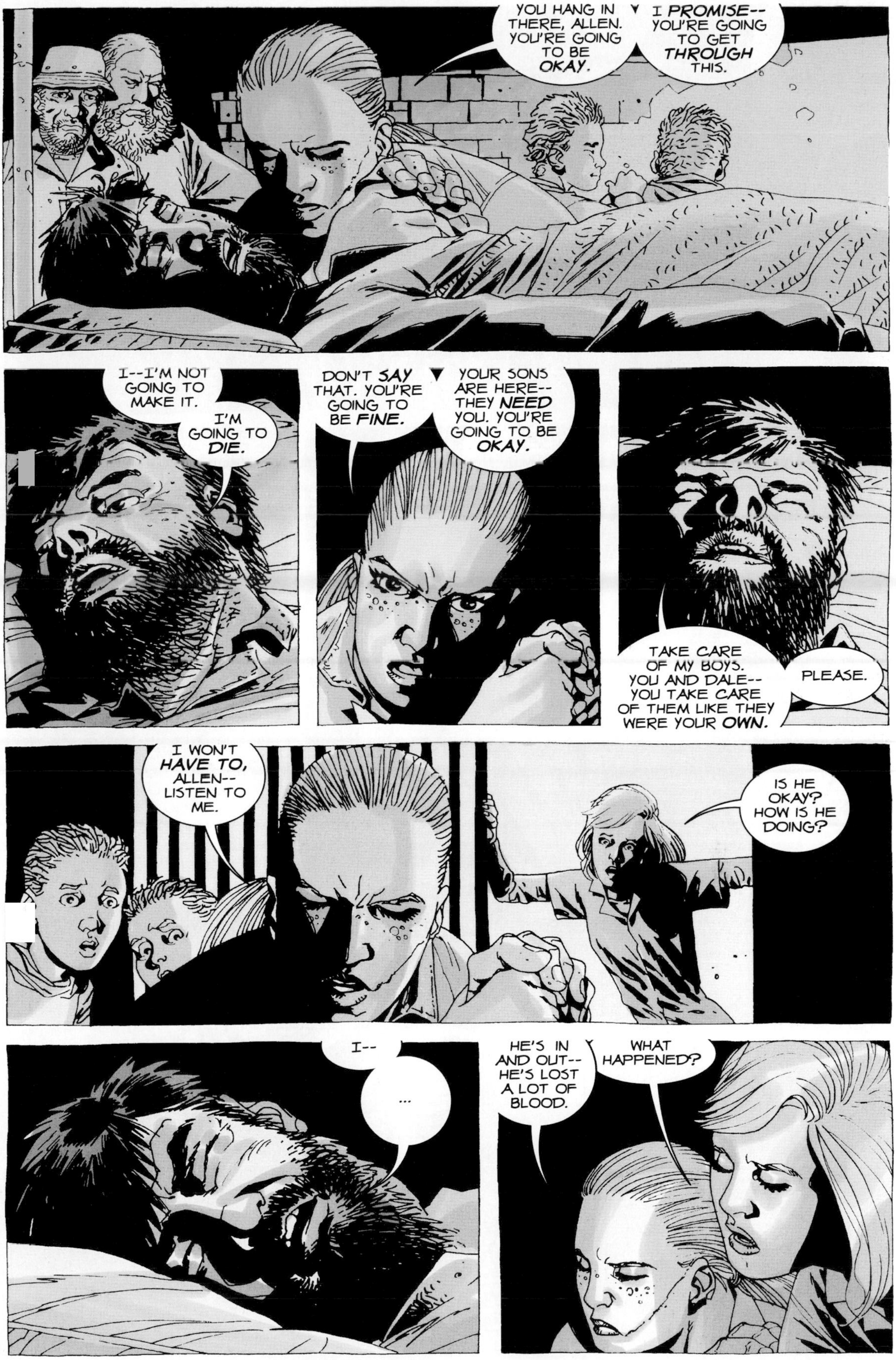
YOU HANG IN THERE, ALLEN. YOU'RE GOING TO BE OKAY.
I PROMISE-- YOU'RE GOING TO GET THROUGH THIS.
I--I'M NOT GOING TO MAKE IT.
I'M GOING TO DIE.
DON'T SAY THAT. YOU'RE GOING TO BE FINE.
YOUR SONS ARE HERE-- THEY NEED YOU. YOU'RE GOING TO BE OKAY.
TAKE CARE OF MY BOYS. YOU AND DALE-- YOU TAKE CARE OF THEM LIKE THEY WERE YOUR OWN.
PLEASE.
I WON'T HAVE TO, ALLEN-- LISTEN TO ME.
IS HE OKAY? HOW IS HE DOING?
I--
...
HE'S IN AND OUT-- HE'S LOST A LOT OF BLOOD.
WHAT HAPPENED?

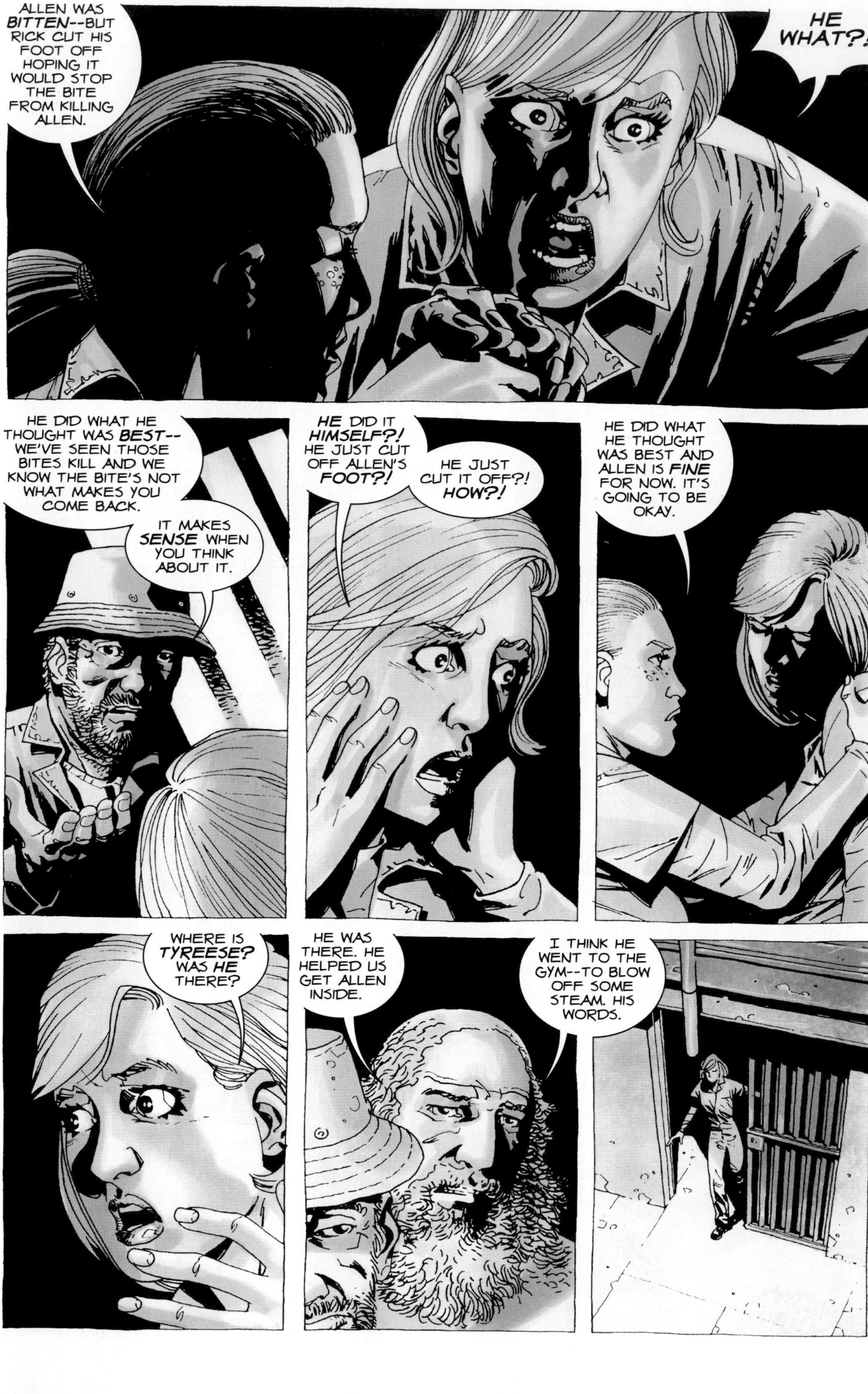
ALLEN WAS BITTEN--BUT RICK CUT HIS FOOT OFF HOPING IT WOULD STOP THE BITE FROM KILLING ALLEN.
HE WHAT?!
HE DID WHAT HE THOUGHT WAS BEST-- WE'VE SEEN THOSE BITES KILL AND WE KNOW THE BITE'S NOT WHAT MAKES YOU COME BACK.
IT MAKES SENSE WHEN YOU THINK ABOUT IT.
HE DID IT HIMSELF?! HE JUST CUT OFF ALLEN'S FOOT?!
HE JUST CUT IT OFF?! HOW?!
HE DID WHAT HE THOUGHT WAS BEST AND ALLEN IS FINE FOR NOW. IT'S GOING TO BE OKAY.
WHERE IS TYREESE? WAS HE THERE?
HE WAS THERE. HE HELPED US GET ALLEN INSIDE.
I THINK HE WENT TO THE GYM--TO BLOW OFF SOME STEAM. HIS WORDS.

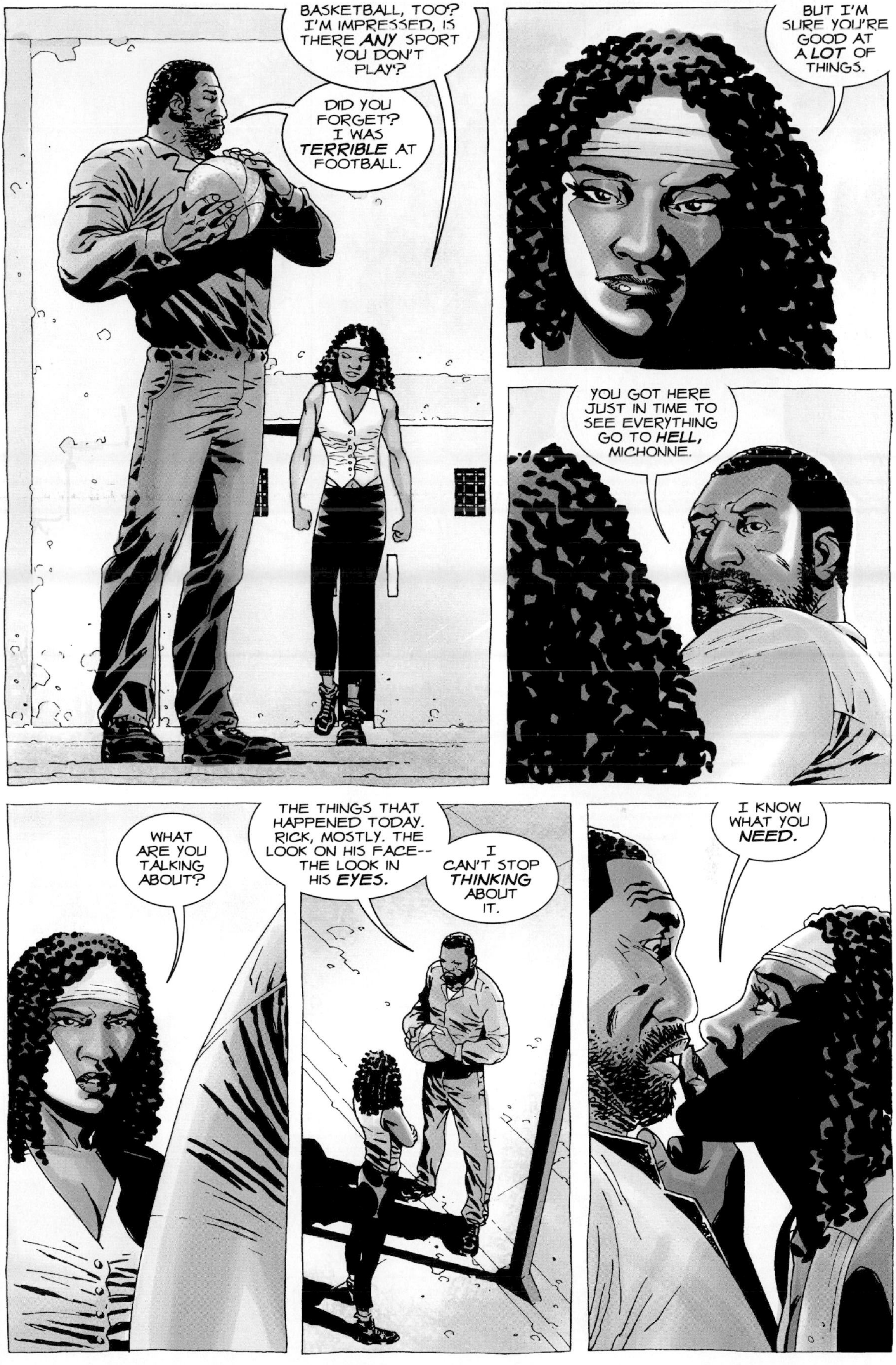
BASKETBALL, TOO? I'M IMPRESSED, IS THERE ANY SPORT YOU DON'T PLAY?
DID YOU FORGET? I WAS TERRIBLE AT FOOTBALL.
BUT I'M SURE YOU'RE GOOD AT A LOT OF THINGS.
YOU GOT HERE JUST IN TIME TO SEE EVERYTHING GO TO HELL, MICHONNE.
WHAT ARE YOU TALKING ABOUT?
THE THINGS THAT HAPPENED TODAY. RICK, MOSTLY. THE LOOK ON HIS FACE-- THE LOOK IN HIS EYES.
I CAN'T STOP THINKING ABOUT IT.
I KNOW WHAT YOU NEED.

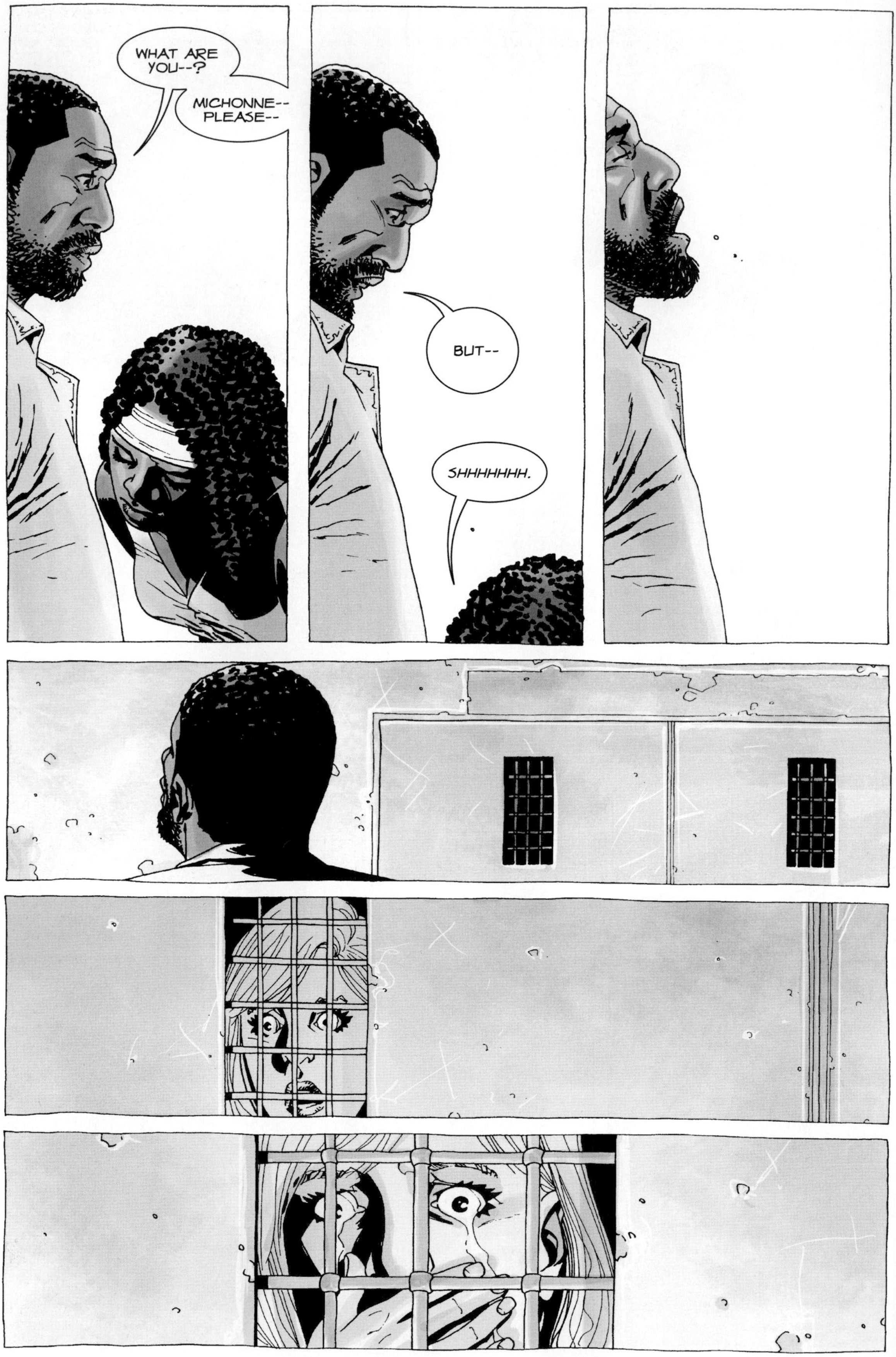
WHAT ARE YOU--?
MICHONNE-- PLEASE--
BUT--
SHHHHHHH.

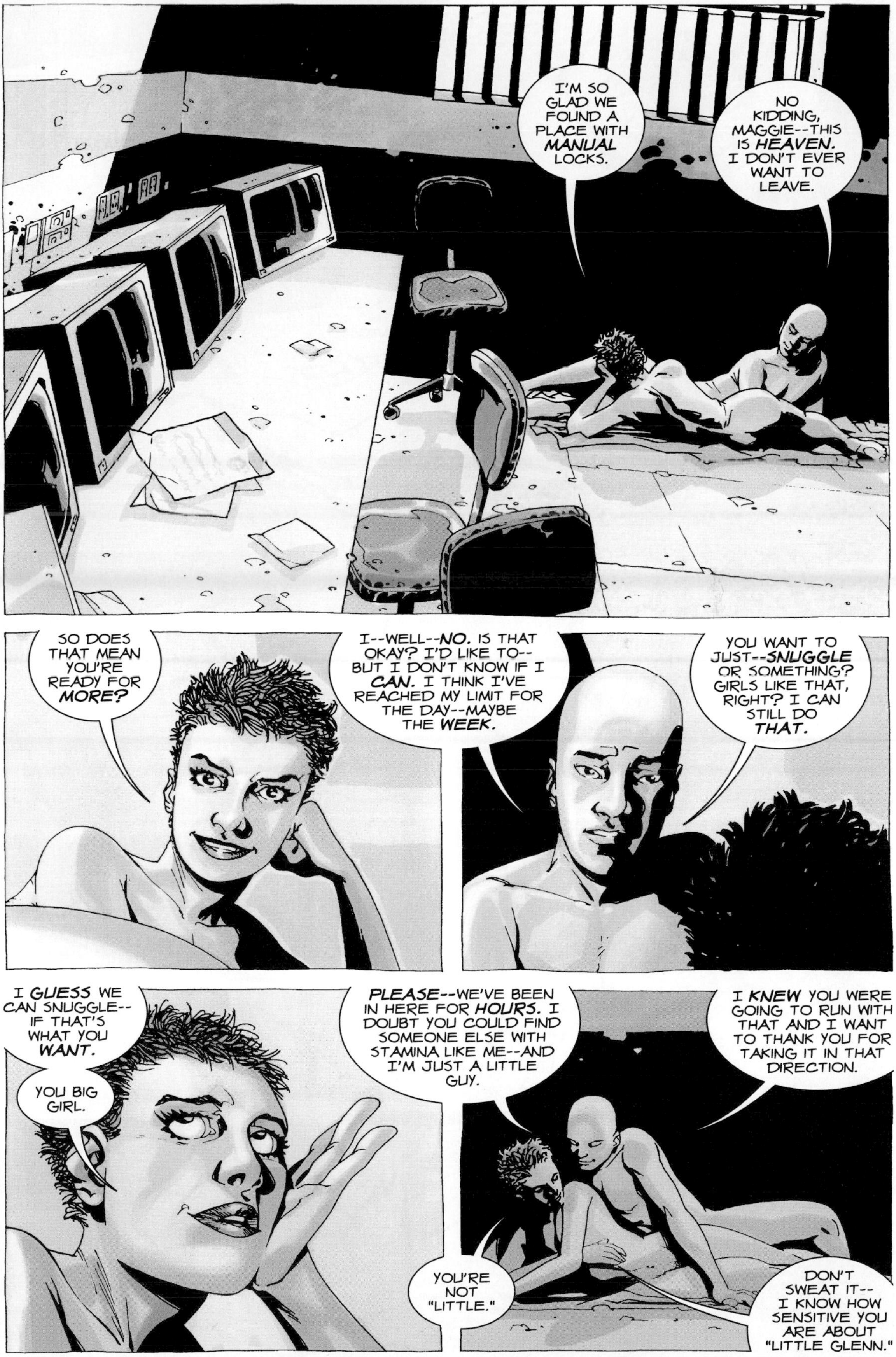
I'M SO GLAD WE FOUND A PLACE WITH MANUAL LOCKS.
NO KIDDING, MAGGIE--THIS IS HEAVEN. I DON'T EVER WANT TO LEAVE.
SO DOES THAT MEAN YOU'RE READY FOR MORE?
I--WELL--NO. IS THAT OKAY? I'D LIKE TO--BUT I DON'T KNOW IF I CAN. I THINK I'VE REACHED MY LIMIT FOR THE DAY--MAYBE THE WEEK.
YOU WANT TO JUST--SNUGGLE OR SOMETHING? GIRLS LIKE THAT, RIGHT? I CAN STILL DO THAT.
I GUESS WE CAN SNUGGLE--IF THAT'S WHAT YOU WANT.
YOU BIG GIRL.
PLEASE--WE'VE BEEN IN HERE FOR HOURS. I DOUBT YOU COULD FIND SOMEONE ELSE WITH STAMINA LIKE ME--AND I'M JUST A LITTLE GUY.
I KNEW YOU WERE GOING TO RUN WITH THAT AND I WANT TO THANK YOU FOR TAKING IT IN THAT DIRECTION.
YOU'RE NOT "LITTLE."
DON'T SWEAT IT--I KNOW HOW SENSITIVE YOU ARE ABOUT "LITTLE GLENN."

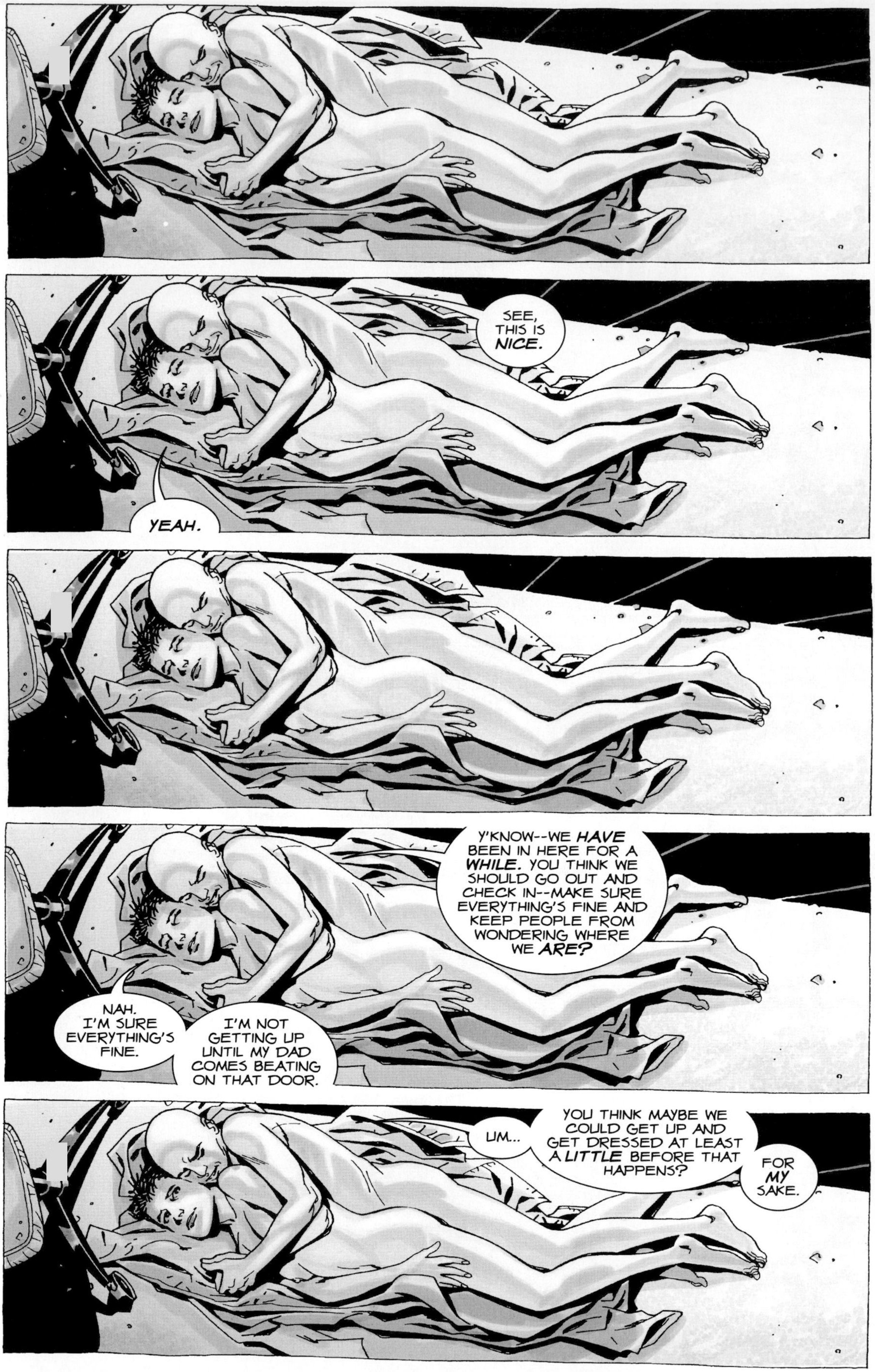
SEE, THIS IS NICE.
YEAH.
Y'KNOW--WE HAVE BEEN IN HERE FOR A WHILE. YOU THINK WE SHOULD GO OUT AND CHECK IN--MAKE SURE EVERYTHING'S FINE AND KEEP PEOPLE FROM WONDERING WHERE WE ARE?
NAH. I'M SURE EVERYTHING'S FINE.
I'M NOT GETTING UP UNTIL MY DAD COMES BEATING ON THAT DOOR.
UM...
YOU THINK MAYBE WE COULD GET UP AND GET DRESSED AT LEAST A LITTLE BEFORE THAT HAPPENS?
FOR MY SAKE.

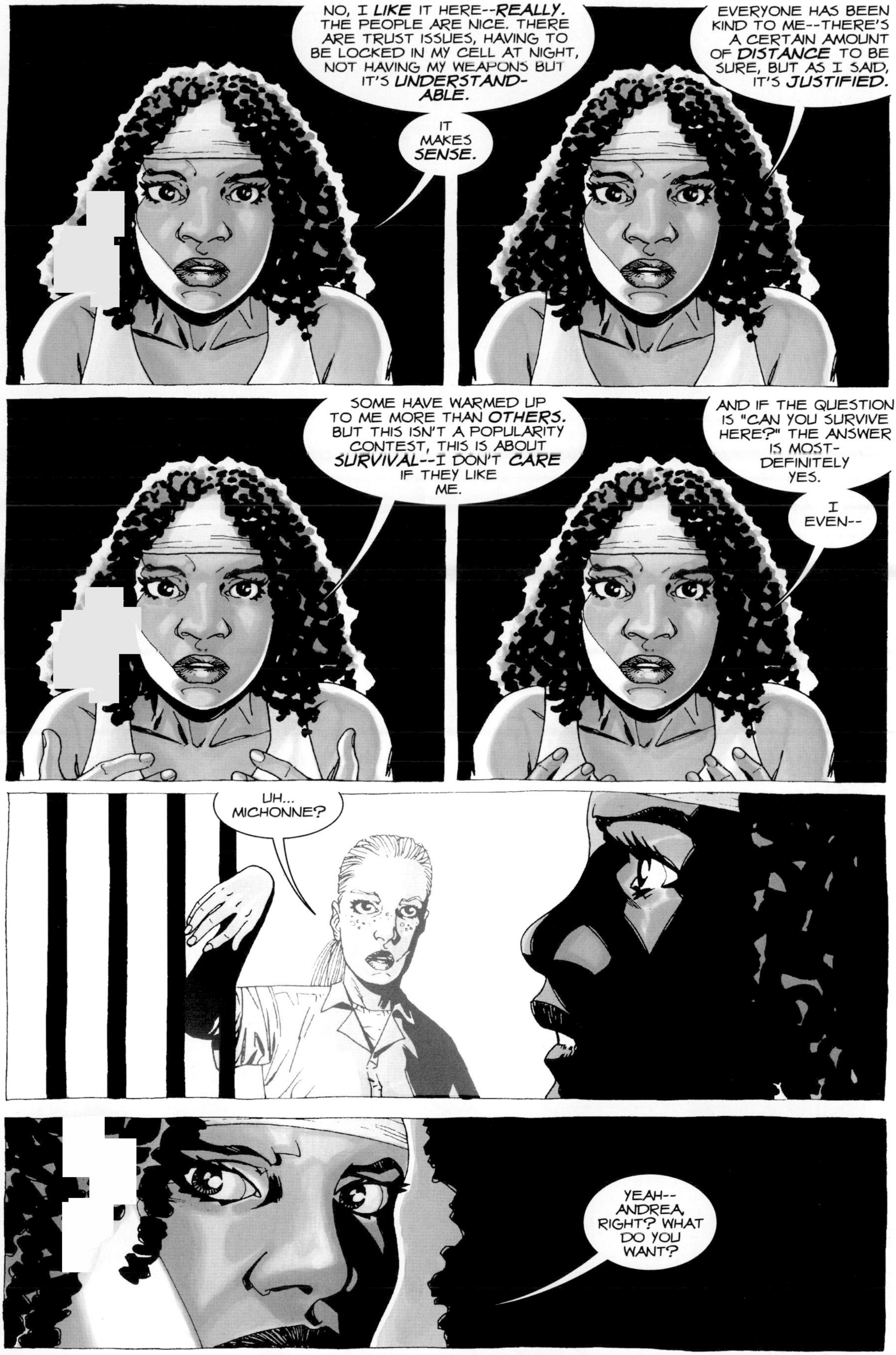
NO, I LIKE IT HERE--REALLY. THE PEOPLE ARE NICE. THERE ARE TRUST ISSUES, HAVING TO BE LOCKED IN MY CELL AT NIGHT, NOT HAVING MY WEAPONS BUT IT'S UNDERSTANDABLE.
IT MAKES SENSE.
EVERYONE HAS BEEN KIND TO ME--THERE'S A CERTAIN AMOUNT OF DISTANCE TO BE SURE, BUT AS I SAID, IT'S JUSTIFIED.
SOME HAVE WARMED UP TO ME MORE THAN OTHERS. BUT THIS ISN'T A POPULARITY CONTEST, THIS IS ABOUT SURVIVAL--I DON'T CARE IF THEY LIKE ME.
AND IF THE QUESTION IS "CAN YOU SURVIVE HERE?" THE ANSWER IS MOST-DEFINITELY YES.
I EVEN--
UH... MICHONNE?
YEAH--ANDREA, RIGHT? WHAT DO YOU WANT?

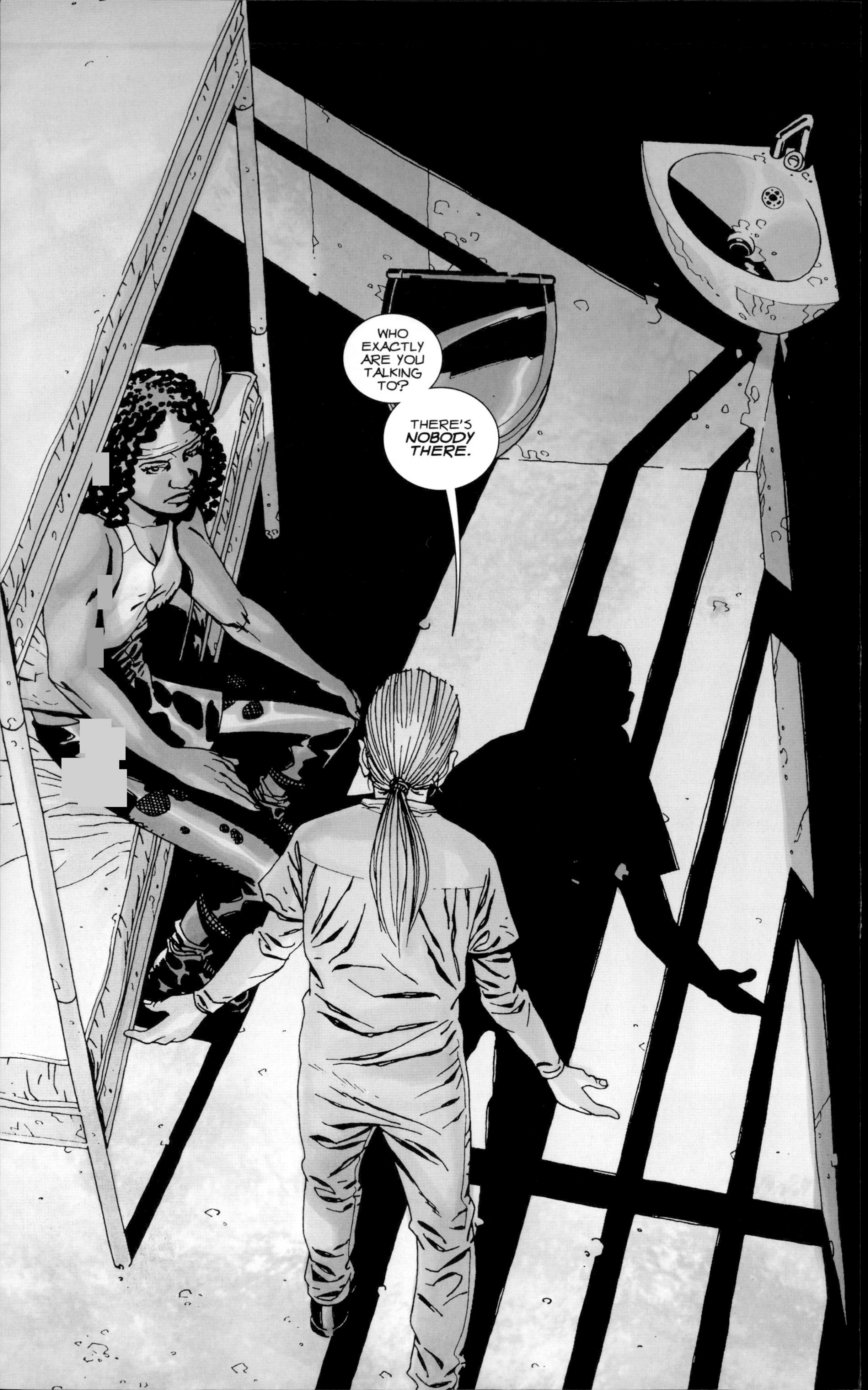
WHO EXACTLY ARE YOU TALKING TO?
THERE'S *NOBODY THERE.*

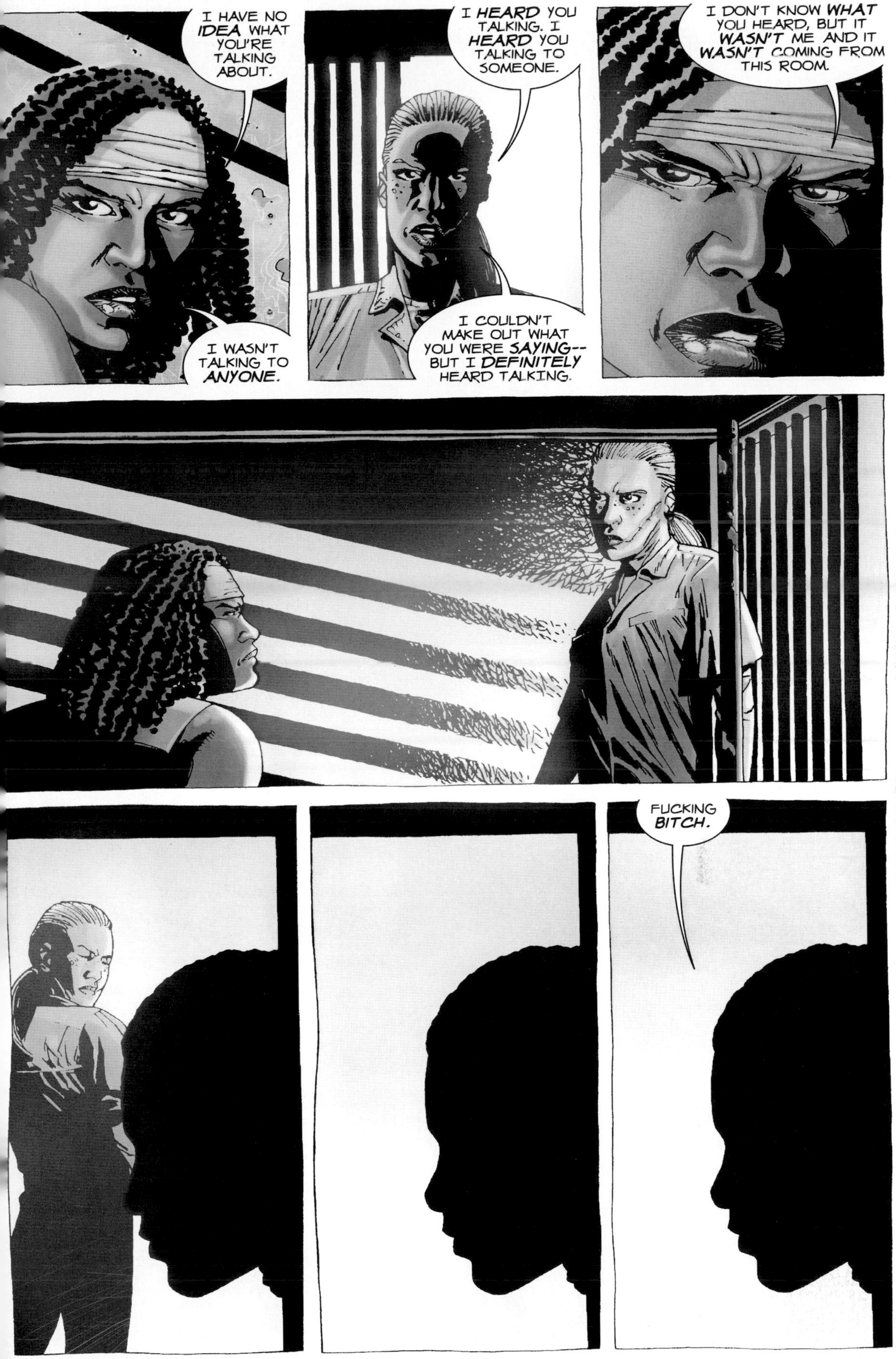
I HAVE NO IDEA WHAT YOU'RE TALKING ABOUT.
I WASN'T TALKING TO ANYONE.
I HEARD YOU TALKING. I HEARD YOU TALKING TO SOMEONE.
I COULDN'T MAKE OUT WHAT YOU WERE SAYING-- BUT I DEFINITELY HEARD TALKING.
I DON'T KNOW WHAT YOU HEARD, BUT IT WASN'T ME AND IT WASN'T COMING FROM THIS ROOM.
FUCKING BITCH.

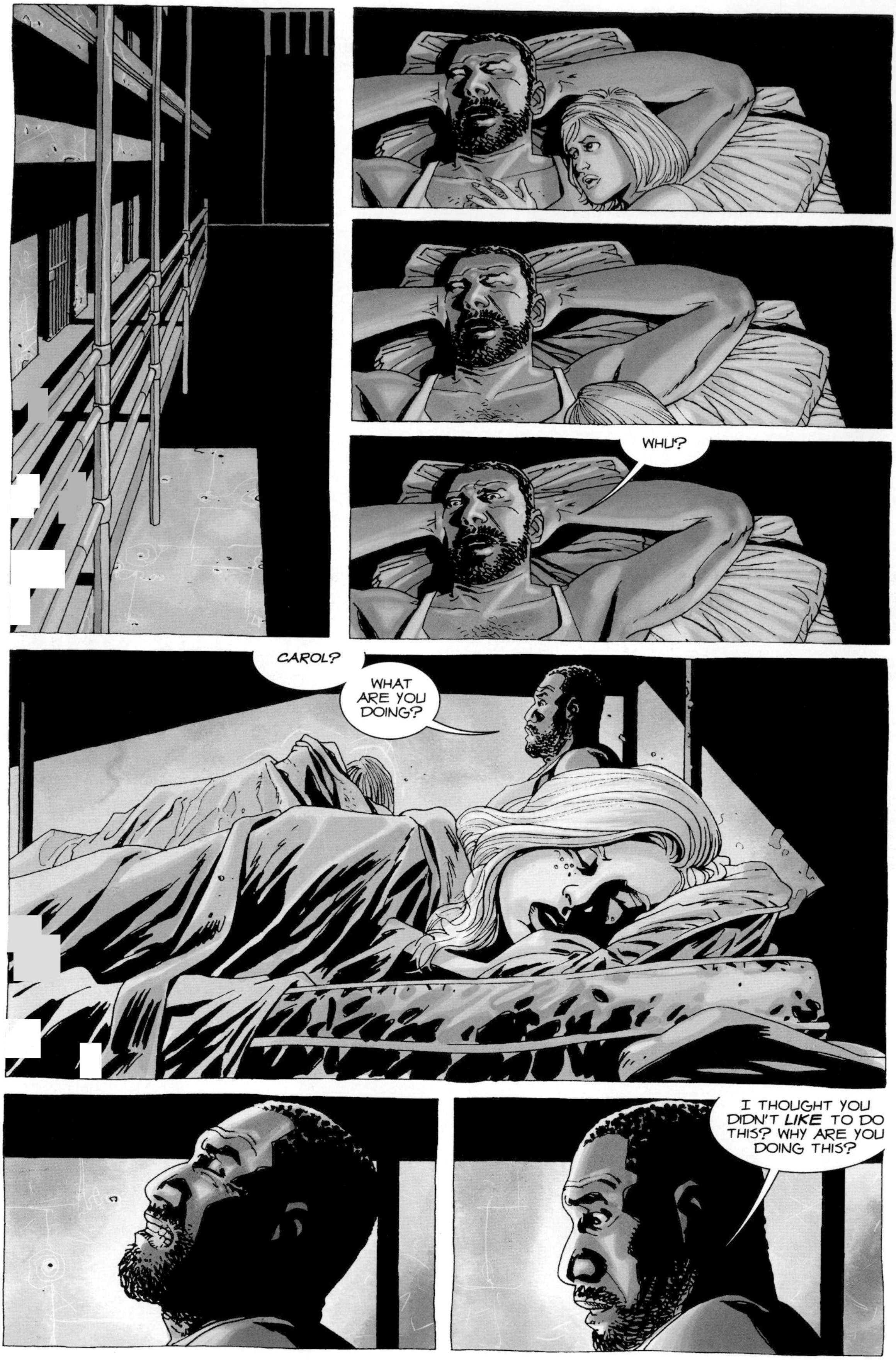
WHU?
CAROL?
WHAT ARE YOU DOING?
I THOUGHT YOU DIDN'T LIKE TO DO THIS? WHY ARE YOU DOING THIS?

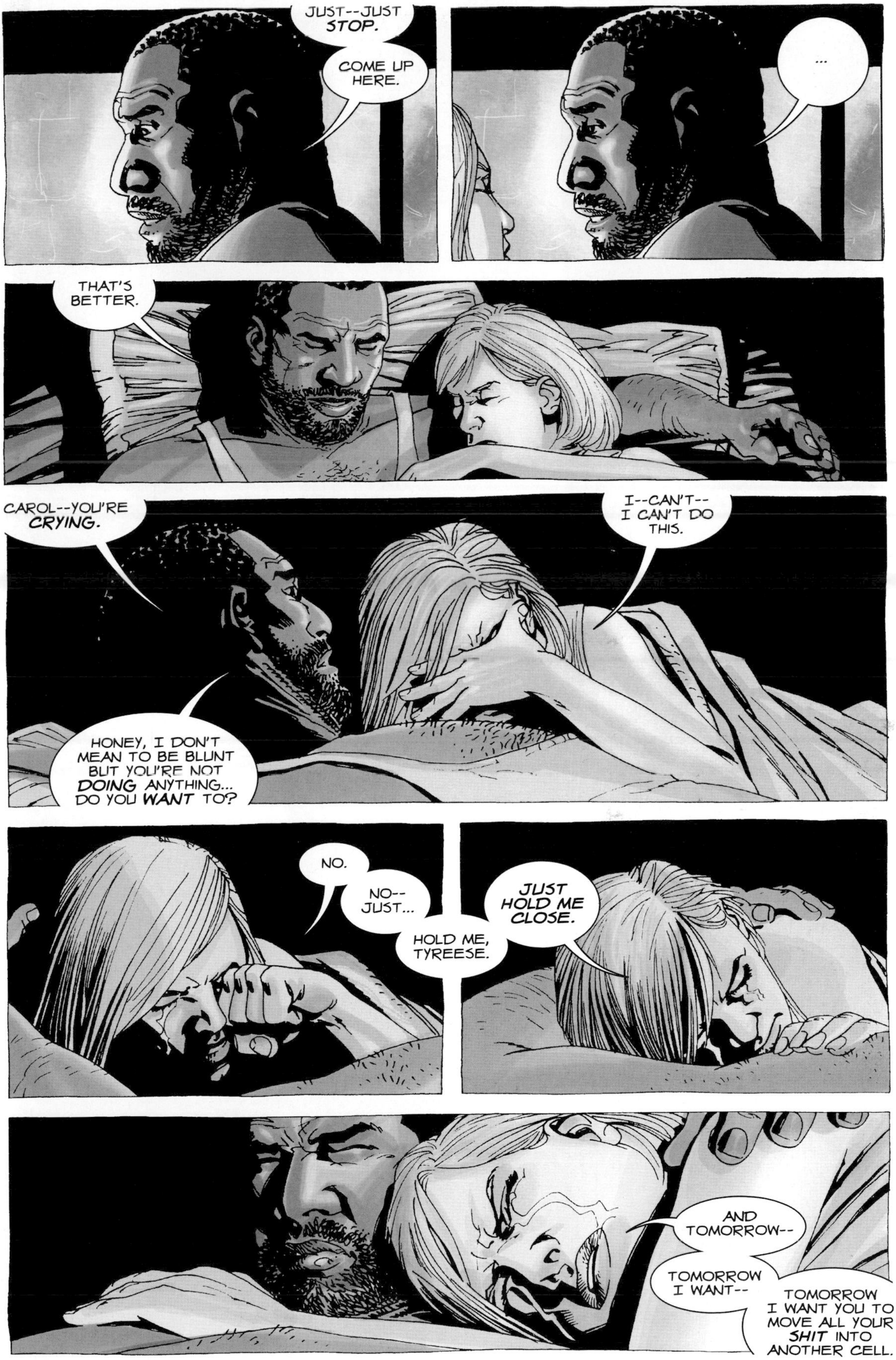
JUST--JUST STOP.
COME UP HERE.
...
THAT'S BETTER.
CAROL--YOU'RE CRYING.
I--CAN'T-- I CAN'T DO THIS.
HONEY, I DON'T MEAN TO BE BLUNT BUT YOU'RE NOT DOING ANYTHING... DO YOU WANT TO?
NO.
NO-- JUST...
HOLD ME, TYREESE.
JUST HOLD ME CLOSE.
AND TOMORROW--
TOMORROW I WANT--
TOMORROW I WANT YOU TO MOVE ALL YOUR SHIT INTO ANOTHER CELL.

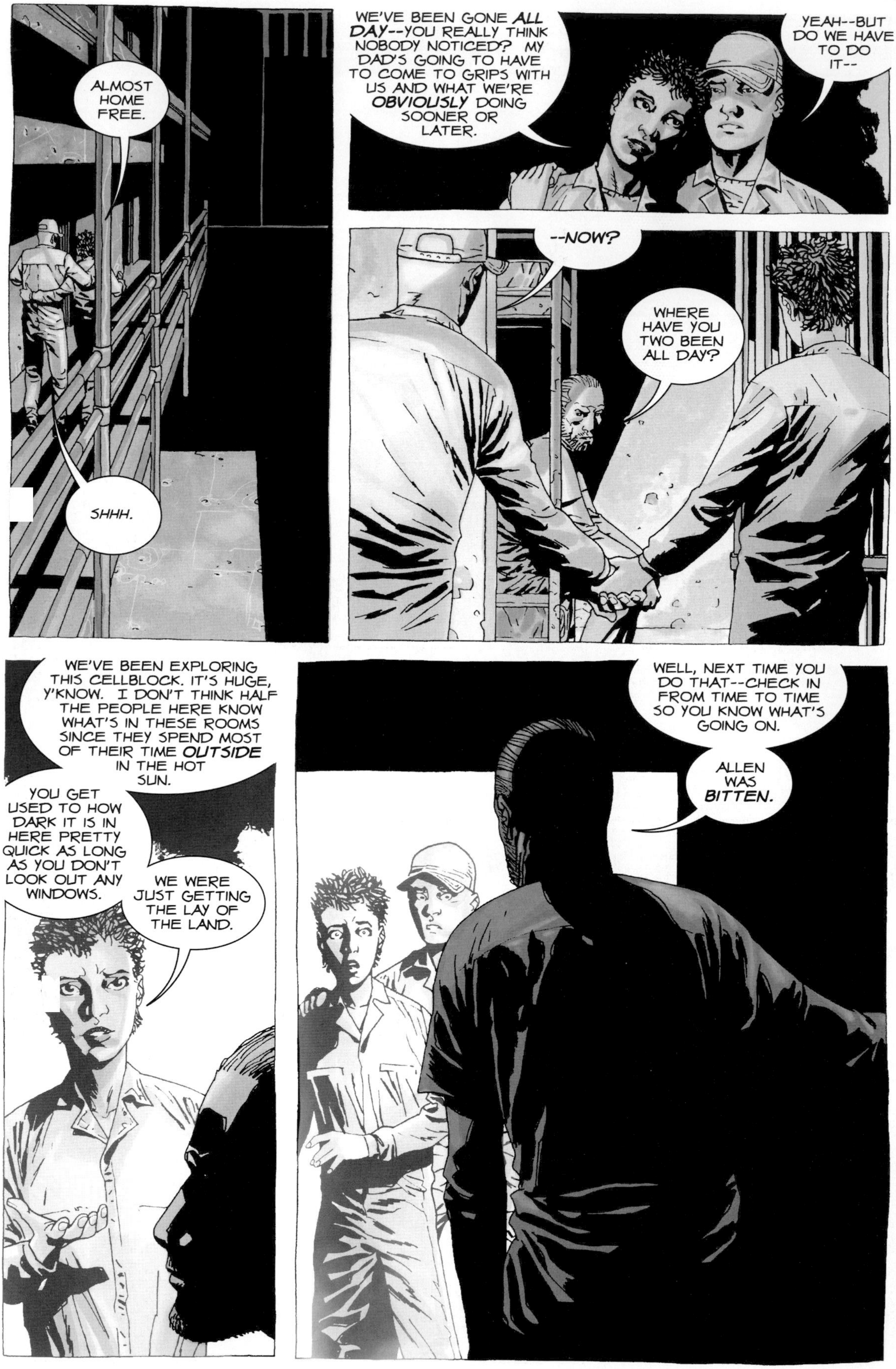
ALMOST HOME FREE.
SHHH.
WE'VE BEEN GONE ALL DAY--YOU REALLY THINK NOBODY NOTICED? MY DAD'S GOING TO HAVE TO COME TO GRIPS WITH US AND WHAT WE'RE OBVIOUSLY DOING SOONER OR LATER.
YEAH--BUT DO WE HAVE TO DO IT--
--NOW?
WHERE HAVE YOU TWO BEEN ALL DAY?
WE'VE BEEN EXPLORING THIS CELLBLOCK. IT'S HUGE, Y'KNOW. I DON'T THINK HALF THE PEOPLE HERE KNOW WHAT'S IN THESE ROOMS SINCE THEY SPEND MOST OF THEIR TIME OUTSIDE IN THE HOT SUN.
YOU GET USED TO HOW DARK IT IS IN HERE PRETTY QUICK AS LONG AS YOU DON'T LOOK OUT ANY WINDOWS.
WE WERE JUST GETTING THE LAY OF THE LAND.
WELL, NEXT TIME YOU DO THAT--CHECK IN FROM TIME TO TIME SO YOU KNOW WHAT'S GOING ON.
ALLEN WAS BITTEN.

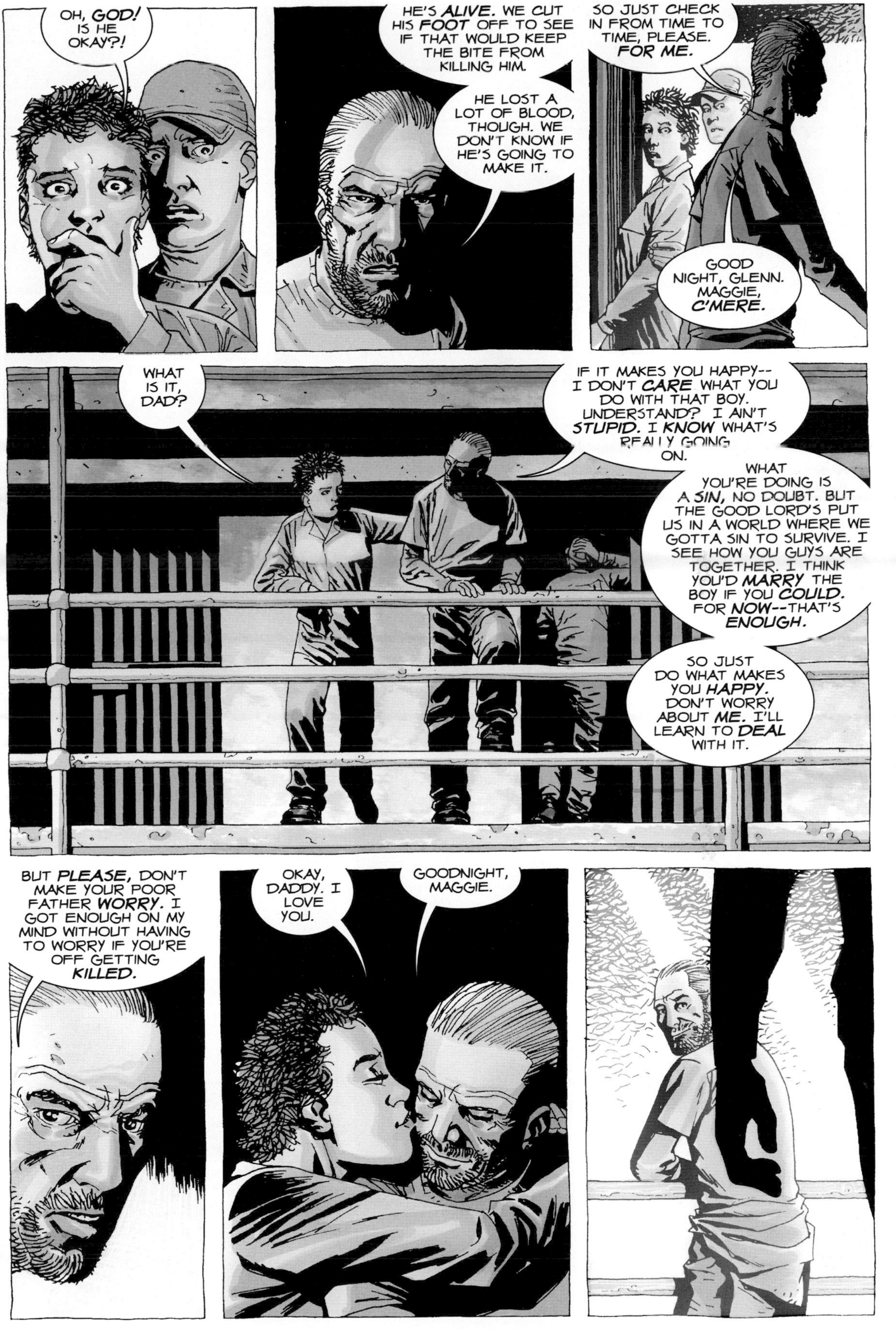
OH, GOD! IS HE OKAY?!
HE'S ALIVE. WE CUT HIS FOOT OFF TO SEE IF THAT WOULD KEEP THE BITE FROM KILLING HIM.
HE LOST A LOT OF BLOOD, THOUGH. WE DON'T KNOW IF HE'S GOING TO MAKE IT.
SO JUST CHECK IN FROM TIME TO TIME, PLEASE. FOR ME.
GOOD NIGHT, GLENN. MAGGIE, C'MERE.
WHAT IS IT, DAD?
IF IT MAKES YOU HAPPY-- I DON'T CARE WHAT YOU DO WITH THAT BOY. UNDERSTAND? I AIN'T STUPID. I KNOW WHAT'S REALLY GOING ON.
WHAT YOU'RE DOING IS A SIN, NO DOUBT. BUT THE GOOD LORD'S PUT US IN A WORLD WHERE WE GOTTA SIN TO SURVIVE. I SEE HOW YOU GUYS ARE TOGETHER. I THINK YOU'D MARRY THE BOY IF YOU COULD. FOR NOW--THAT'S ENOUGH.
SO JUST DO WHAT MAKES YOU HAPPY. DON'T WORRY ABOUT ME. I'LL LEARN TO DEAL WITH IT.
BUT PLEASE, DON'T MAKE YOUR POOR FATHER WORRY. I GOT ENOUGH ON MY MIND WITHOUT HAVING TO WORRY IF YOU'RE OFF GETTING KILLED.
OKAY, DADDY. I LOVE YOU.
GOODNIGHT, MAGGIE.

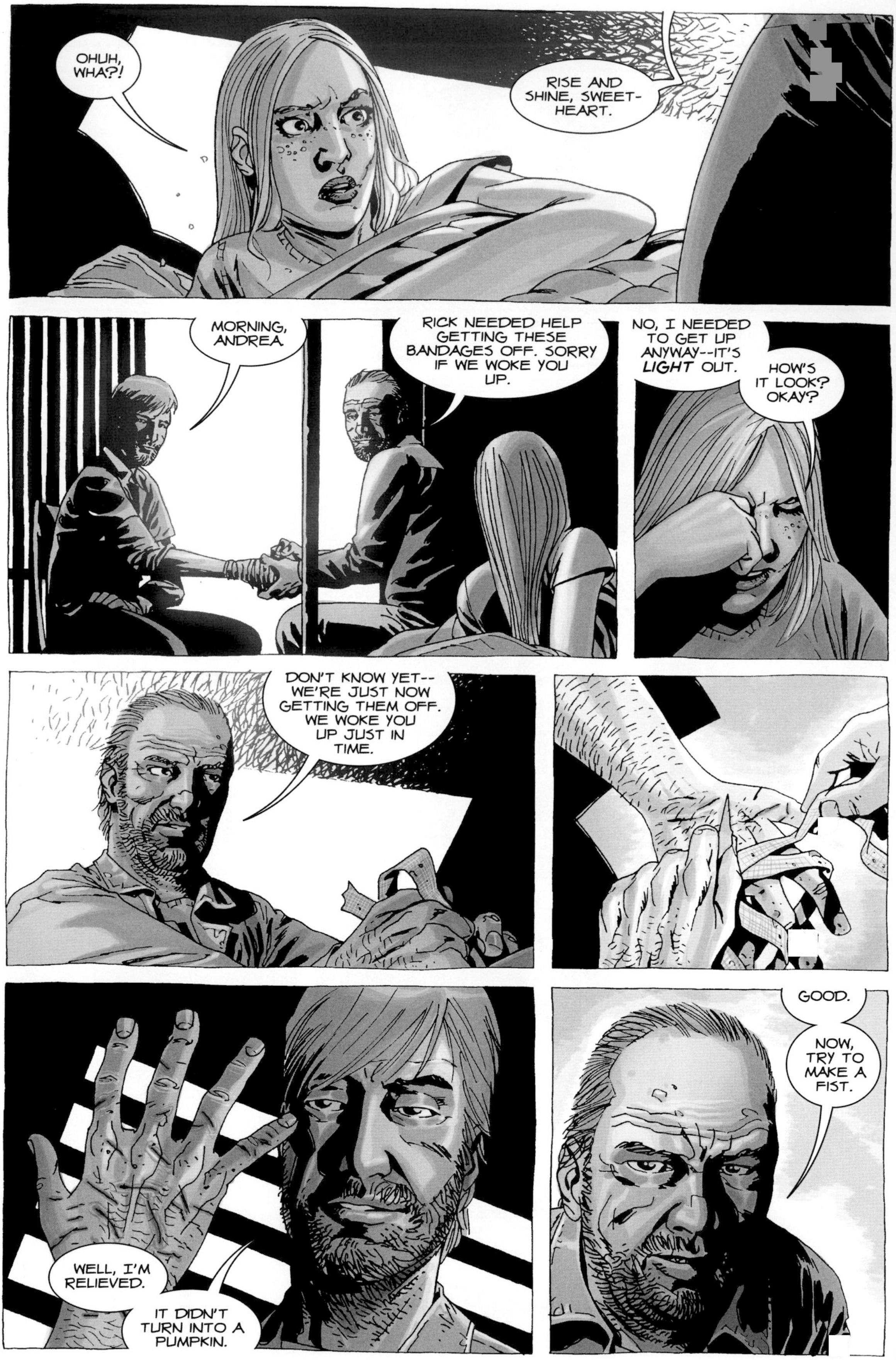
OHUH, WHA?!
RISE AND SHINE, SWEET-HEART.
MORNING, ANDREA.
RICK NEEDED HELP GETTING THESE BANDAGES OFF. SORRY IF WE WOKE YOU UP.
NO, I NEEDED TO GET UP ANYWAY--IT'S LIGHT OUT.
HOW'S IT LOOK? OKAY?
DON'T KNOW YET-- WE'RE JUST NOW GETTING THEM OFF. WE WOKE YOU UP JUST IN TIME.
WELL, I'M RELIEVED.
IT DIDN'T TURN INTO A PUMPKIN.
GOOD.
NOW, TRY TO MAKE A FIST.

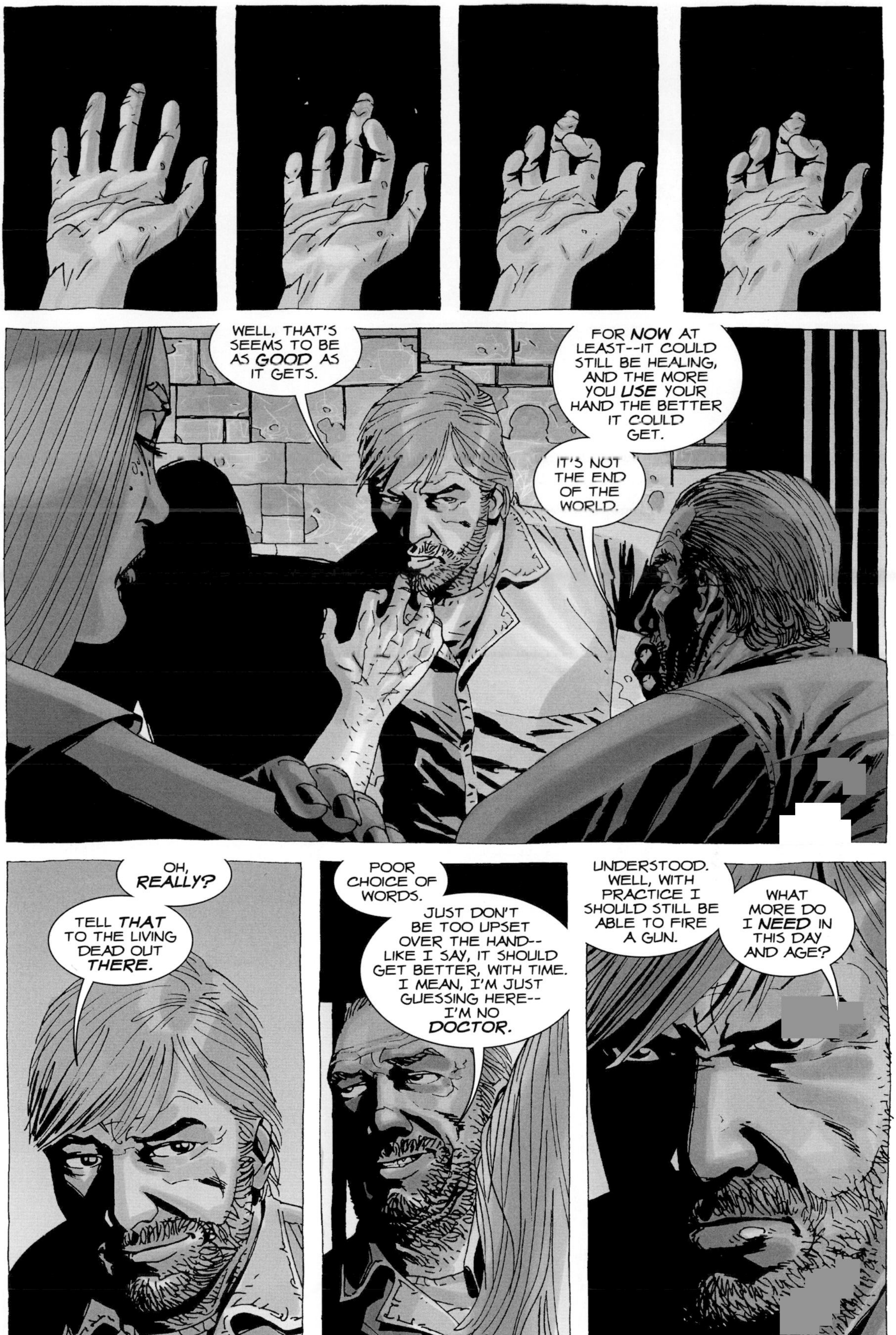
WELL, THAT'S SEEMS TO BE AS GOOD AS IT GETS.
FOR NOW AT LEAST--IT COULD STILL BE HEALING, AND THE MORE YOU USE YOUR HAND THE BETTER IT COULD GET.
IT'S NOT THE END OF THE WORLD.
OH, REALLY?
TELL THAT TO THE LIVING DEAD OUT THERE.
POOR CHOICE OF WORDS.
JUST DON'T BE TOO UPSET OVER THE HAND-- LIKE I SAY, IT SHOULD GET BETTER, WITH TIME. I MEAN, I'M JUST GUESSING HERE-- I'M NO DOCTOR.
UNDERSTOOD. WELL, WITH PRACTICE I SHOULD STILL BE ABLE TO FIRE A GUN.
WHAT MORE DO I NEED IN THIS DAY AND AGE?

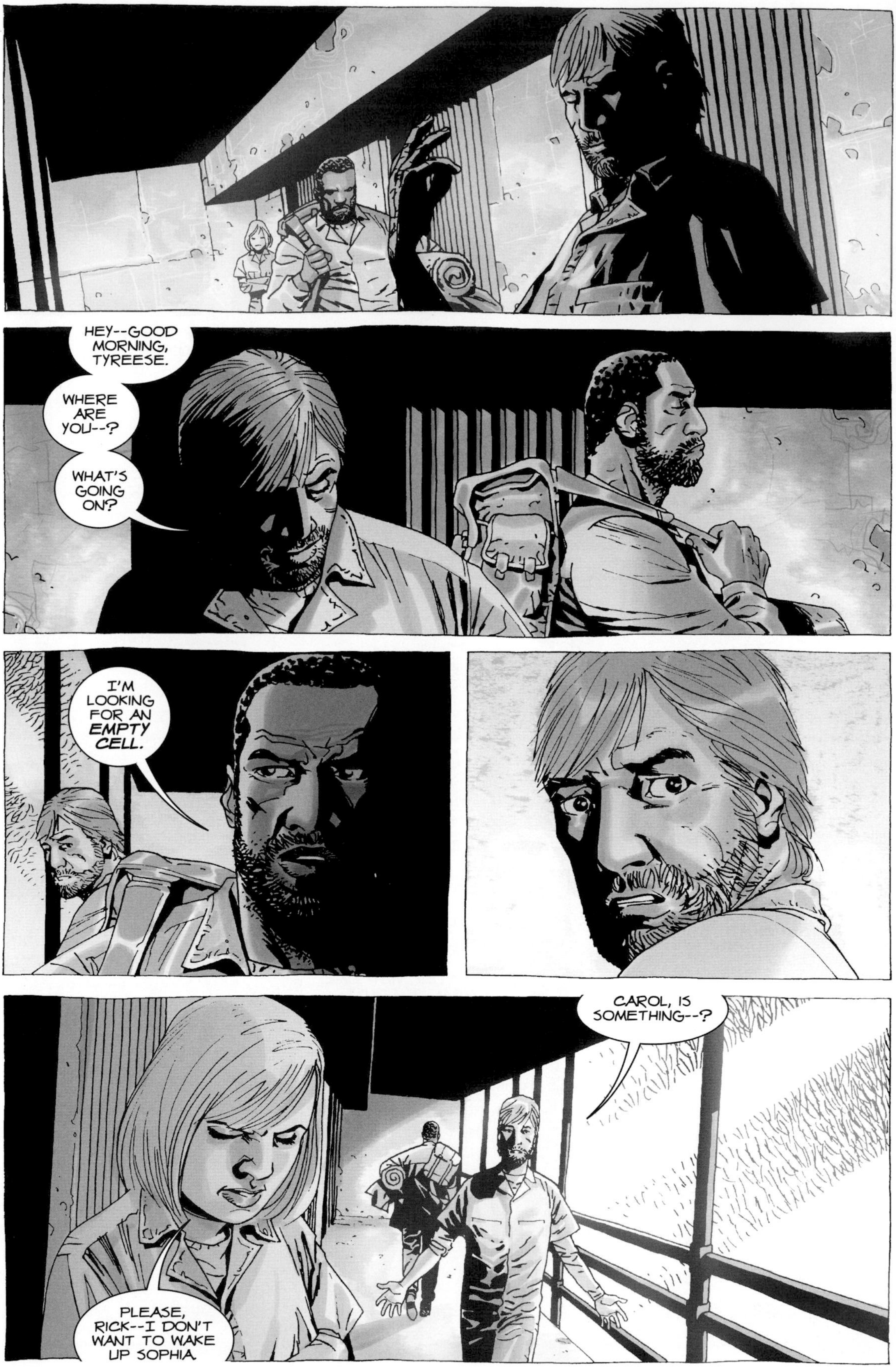
HEY--GOOD MORNING, TYREESE.
WHERE ARE YOU--?
WHAT'S GOING ON?
I'M LOOKING FOR AN EMPTY CELL.
CAROL, IS SOMETHING--?
PLEASE, RICK--I DON'T WANT TO WAKE UP SOPHIA.

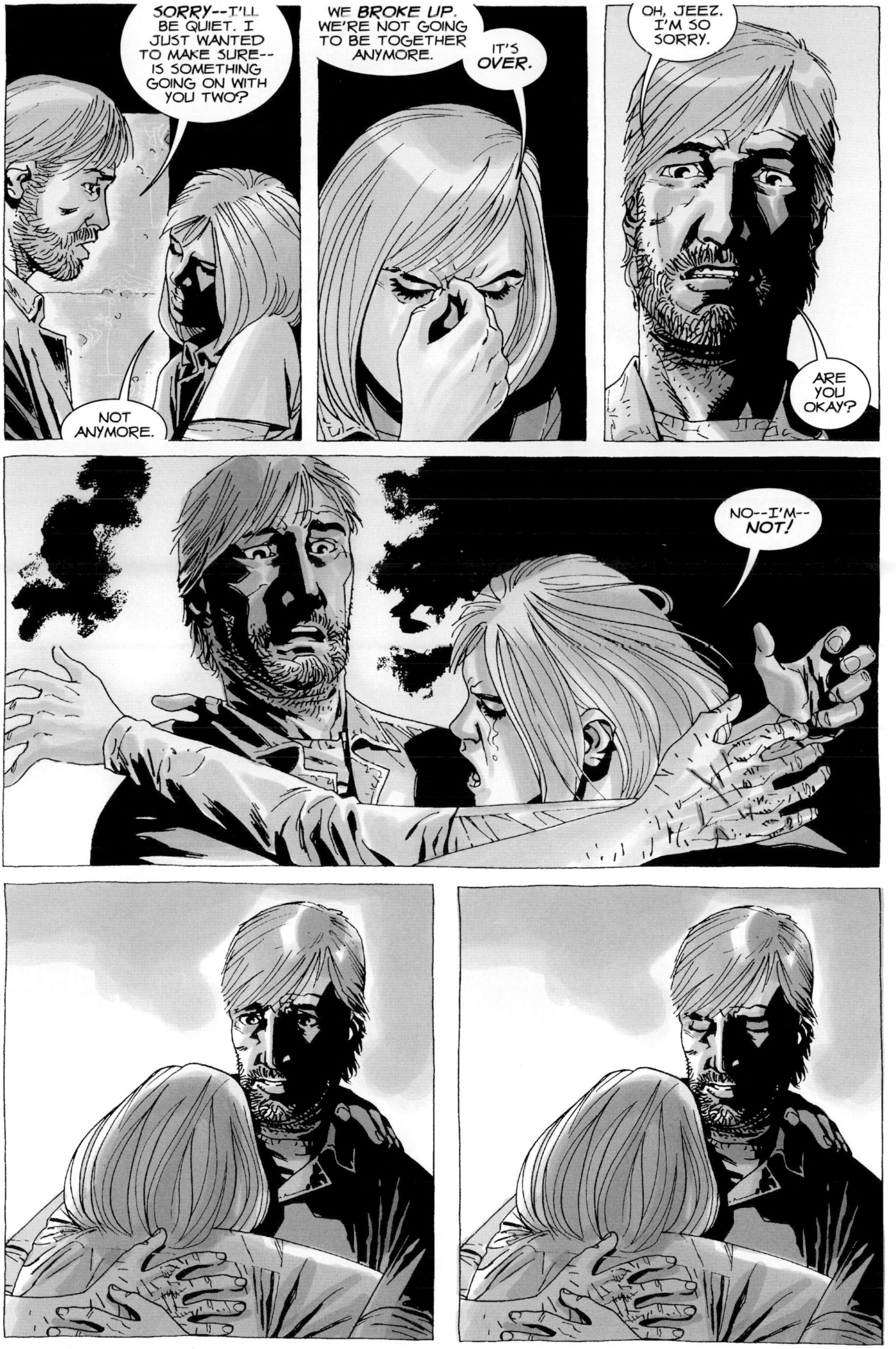
SORRY--I'LL BE QUIET. I JUST WANTED TO MAKE SURE-- IS SOMETHING GOING ON WITH YOU TWO?
NOT ANYMORE.
WE BROKE UP. WE'RE NOT GOING TO BE TOGETHER ANYMORE.
IT'S OVER.
OH, JEEZ. I'M SO SORRY.
ARE YOU OKAY?
NO--I'M--NOT!

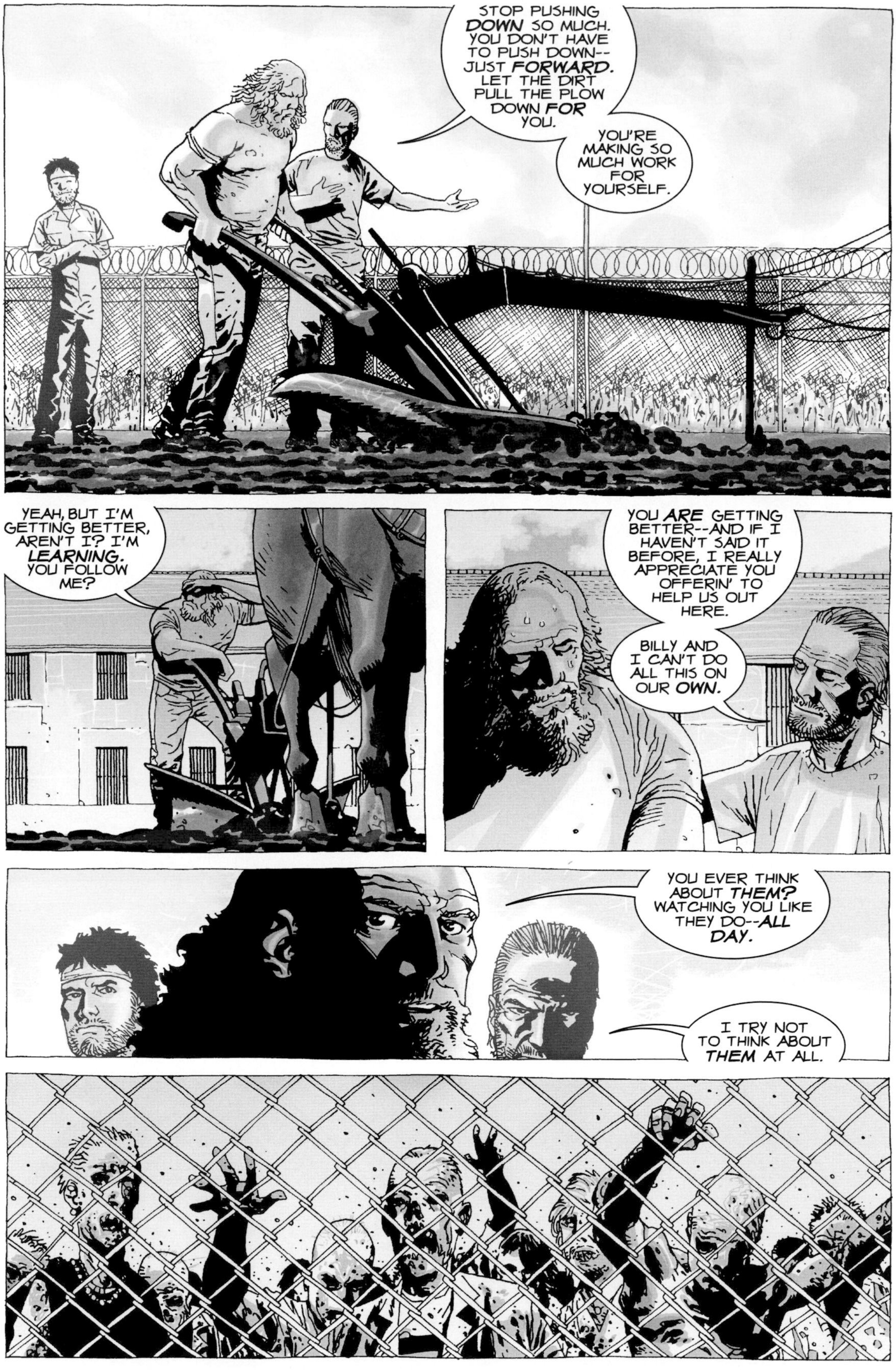
STOP PUSHING DOWN SO MUCH. YOU DON'T HAVE TO PUSH DOWN-- JUST FORWARD. LET THE DIRT PULL THE PLOW DOWN FOR YOU.
YOU'RE MAKING SO MUCH WORK FOR YOURSELF.
YEAH, BUT I'M GETTING BETTER, AREN'T I? I'M LEARNING. YOU FOLLOW ME?
YOU ARE GETTING BETTER--AND IF I HAVEN'T SAID IT BEFORE, I REALLY APPRECIATE YOU OFFERIN' TO HELP US OUT HERE.
BILLY AND I CAN'T DO ALL THIS ON OUR OWN.
YOU EVER THINK ABOUT THEM? WATCHING YOU LIKE THEY DO--ALL DAY.
I TRY NOT TO THINK ABOUT THEM AT ALL.

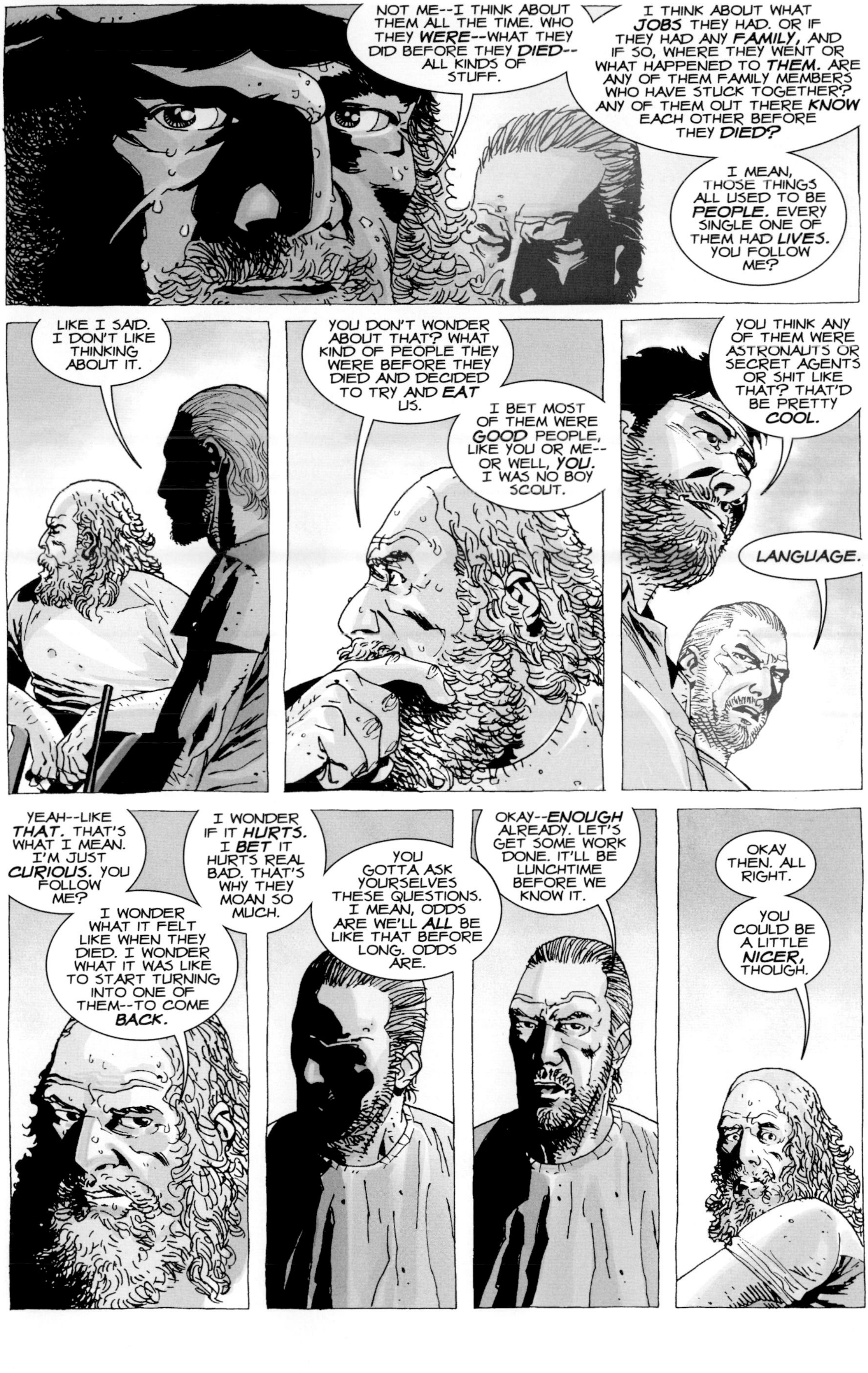
NOT ME--I THINK ABOUT THEM ALL THE TIME. WHO THEY WERE--WHAT THEY DID BEFORE THEY DIED--ALL KINDS OF STUFF.
I THINK ABOUT WHAT JOBS THEY HAD. OR IF THEY HAD ANY FAMILY, AND IF SO, WHERE THEY WENT OR WHAT HAPPENED TO THEM. ARE ANY OF THEM FAMILY MEMBERS WHO HAVE STUCK TOGETHER? ANY OF THEM OUT THERE KNOW EACH OTHER BEFORE THEY DIED?
I MEAN, THOSE THINGS ALL USED TO BE PEOPLE. EVERY SINGLE ONE OF THEM HAD LIVES. YOU FOLLOW ME?
LIKE I SAID. I DON'T LIKE THINKING ABOUT IT.
YOU DON'T WONDER ABOUT THAT? WHAT KIND OF PEOPLE THEY WERE BEFORE THEY DIED AND DECIDED TO TRY AND EAT US.
I BET MOST OF THEM WERE GOOD PEOPLE, LIKE YOU OR ME--OR WELL, YOU. I WAS NO BOY SCOUT.
YOU THINK ANY OF THEM WERE ASTRONAUTS OR SECRET AGENTS OR SHIT LIKE THAT? THAT'D BE PRETTY COOL.
LANGUAGE.
YEAH--LIKE THAT. THAT'S WHAT I MEAN. I'M JUST CURIOUS. YOU FOLLOW ME?
I WONDER WHAT IT FELT LIKE WHEN THEY DIED. I WONDER WHAT IT WAS LIKE TO START TURNING INTO ONE OF THEM--TO COME BACK.
I WONDER IF IT HURTS. I BET IT HURTS REAL BAD. THAT'S WHY THEY MOAN SO MUCH.
YOU GOTTA ASK YOURSELVES THESE QUESTIONS. I MEAN, ODDS ARE WE'LL ALL BE LIKE THAT BEFORE LONG. ODDS ARE.
OKAY--ENOUGH ALREADY. LET'S GET SOME WORK DONE. IT'LL BE LUNCHTIME BEFORE WE KNOW IT.
OKAY THEN. ALL RIGHT.
YOU COULD BE A LITTLE NICER, THOUGH.

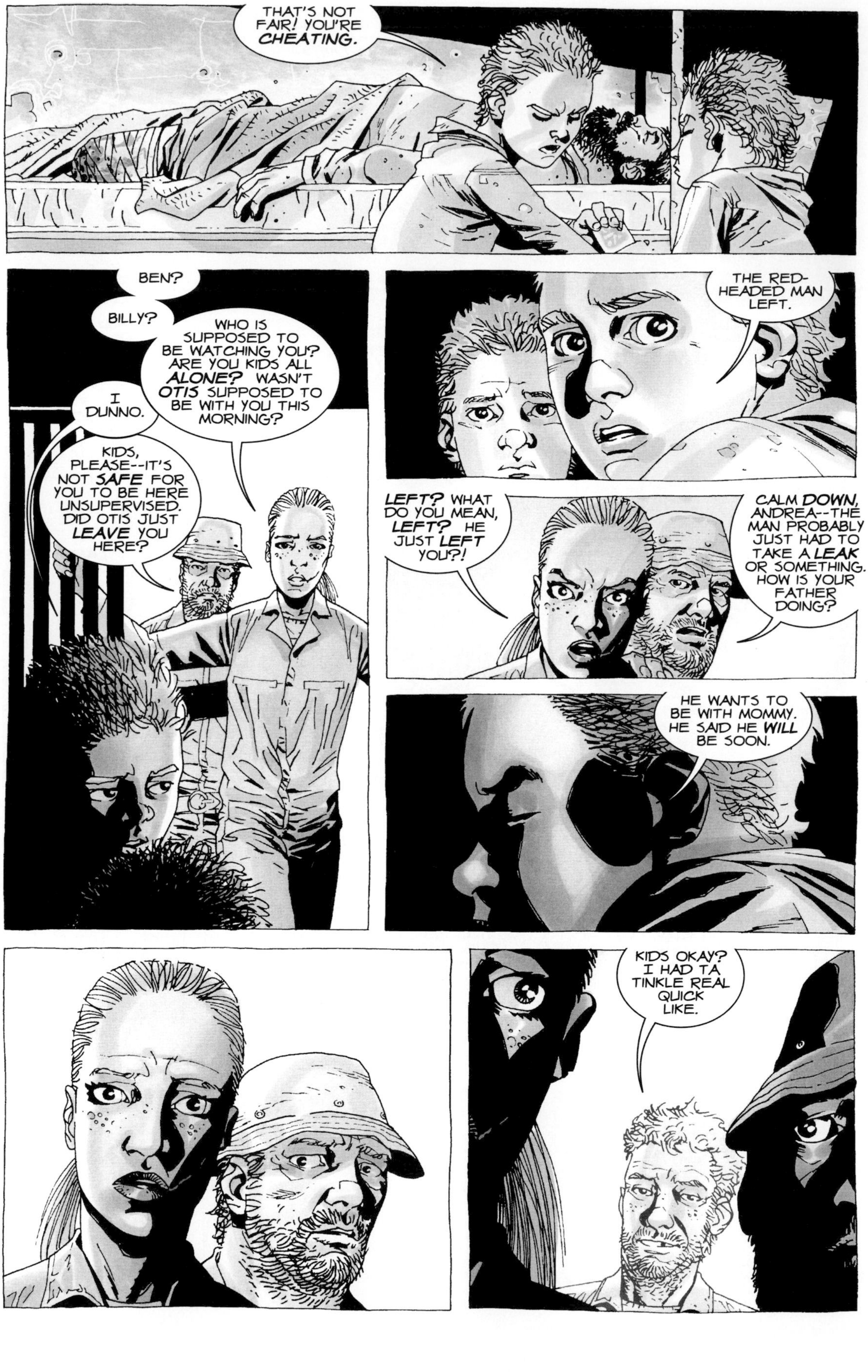
THAT'S NOT FAIR! YOU'RE CHEATING.
BEN?
BILLY?
WHO IS SUPPOSED TO BE WATCHING YOU? ARE YOU KIDS ALL ALONE? WASN'T OTIS SUPPOSED TO BE WITH YOU THIS MORNING?
I DUNNO.
KIDS, PLEASE--IT'S NOT SAFE FOR YOU TO BE HERE UNSUPERVISED. DID OTIS JUST LEAVE YOU HERE?
THE RED-HEADED MAN LEFT.
LEFT? WHAT DO YOU MEAN, LEFT? HE JUST LEFT YOU?!
CALM DOWN, ANDREA--THE MAN PROBABLY JUST HAD TO TAKE A LEAK OR SOMETHING. HOW IS YOUR FATHER DOING?
HE WANTS TO BE WITH MOMMY. HE SAID HE WILL BE SOON.
KIDS OKAY? I HAD TA TINKLE REAL QUICK LIKE.

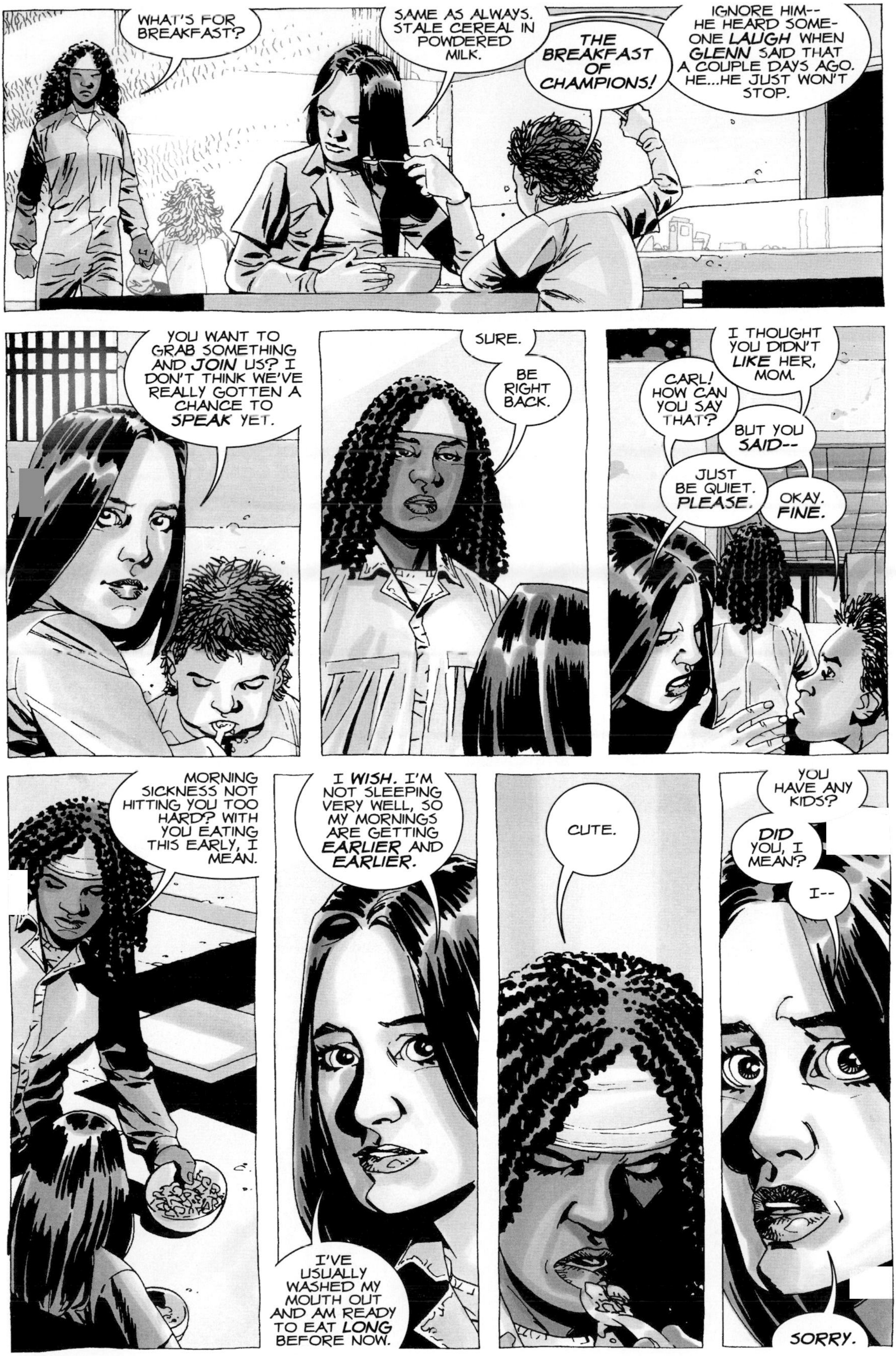
WHAT'S FOR BREAKFAST?
SAME AS ALWAYS. STALE CEREAL IN POWDERED MILK.
THE BREAKFAST OF CHAMPIONS!
IGNORE HIM-- HE HEARD SOME-ONE LAUGH WHEN GLENN SAID THAT A COUPLE DAYS AGO. HE...HE JUST WON'T STOP.
YOU WANT TO GRAB SOMETHING AND JOIN US? I DON'T THINK WE'VE REALLY GOTTEN A CHANCE TO SPEAK YET.
SURE.
BE RIGHT BACK.
I THOUGHT YOU DIDN'T LIKE HER, MOM.
CARL! HOW CAN YOU SAY THAT?
BUT YOU SAID--
JUST BE QUIET. PLEASE.
OKAY. FINE.
MORNING SICKNESS NOT HITTING YOU TOO HARD? WITH YOU EATING THIS EARLY, I MEAN.
I WISH. I'M NOT SLEEPING VERY WELL, SO MY MORNINGS ARE GETTING EARLIER AND EARLIER.
I'VE USUALLY WASHED MY MOUTH OUT AND AM READY TO EAT LONG BEFORE NOW.
CUTE.
YOU HAVE ANY KIDS?
DID YOU, I MEAN?
I--
SORRY.

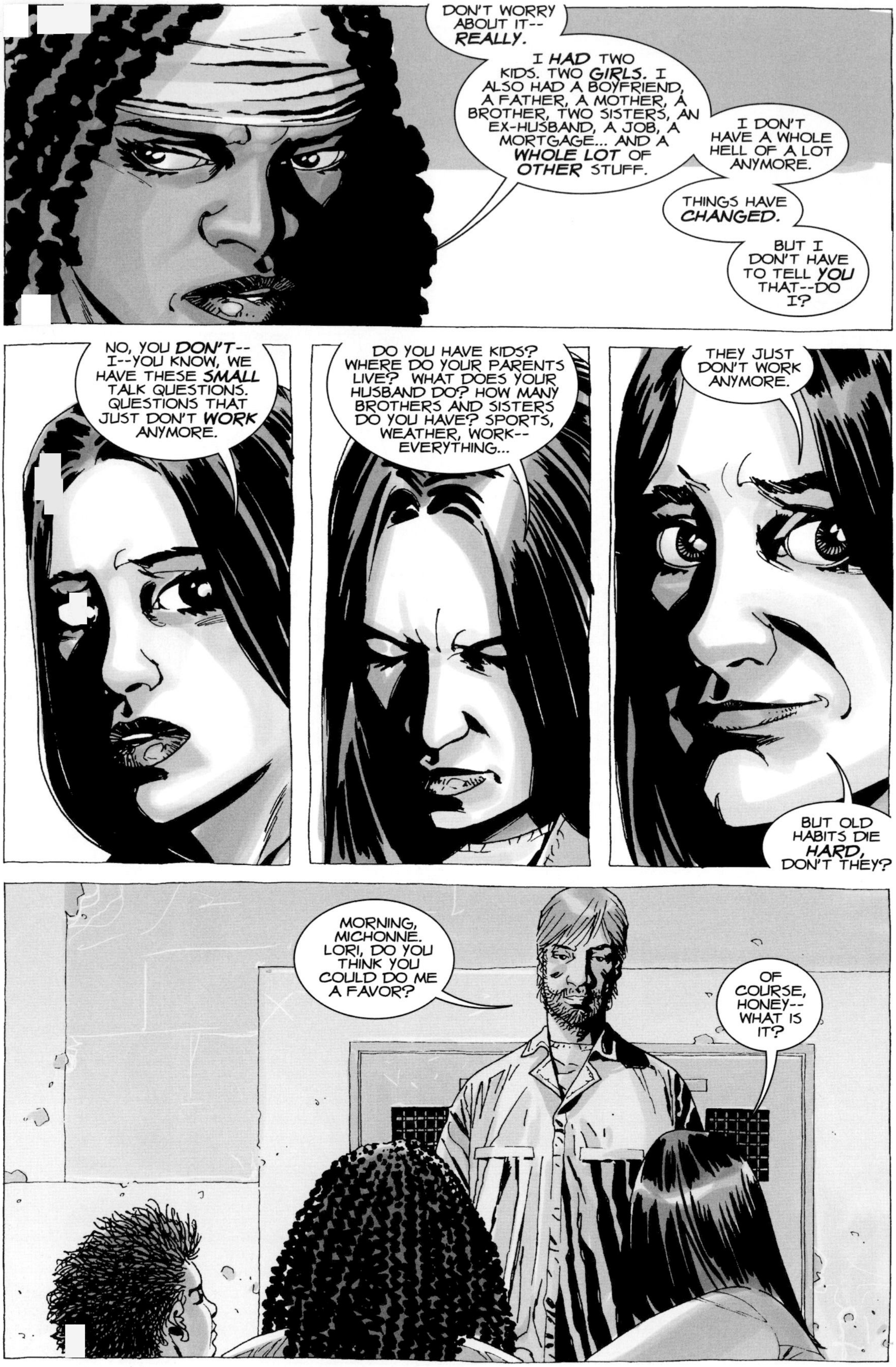

DON'T WORRY ABOUT IT-- REALLY.
I HAD TWO KIDS. TWO GIRLS. I ALSO HAD A BOYFRIEND, A FATHER, A MOTHER, A BROTHER, TWO SISTERS, AN EX-HUSBAND, A JOB, A MORTGAGE... AND A WHOLE LOT OF OTHER STUFF.
I DON'T HAVE A WHOLE HELL OF A LOT ANYMORE.
THINGS HAVE CHANGED.
BUT I DON'T HAVE TO TELL YOU THAT--DO I?
NO, YOU DON'T-- I--YOU KNOW, WE HAVE THESE SMALL TALK QUESTIONS. QUESTIONS THAT JUST DON'T WORK ANYMORE.
DO YOU HAVE KIDS? WHERE DO YOUR PARENTS LIVE? WHAT DOES YOUR HUSBAND DO? HOW MANY BROTHERS AND SISTERS DO YOU HAVE? SPORTS, WEATHER, WORK-- EVERYTHING...
THEY JUST DON'T WORK ANYMORE.
BUT OLD HABITS DIE HARD, DON'T THEY?
MORNING, MICHONNE. LORI, DO YOU THINK YOU COULD DO ME A FAVOR?
OF COURSE, HONEY-- WHAT IS IT?

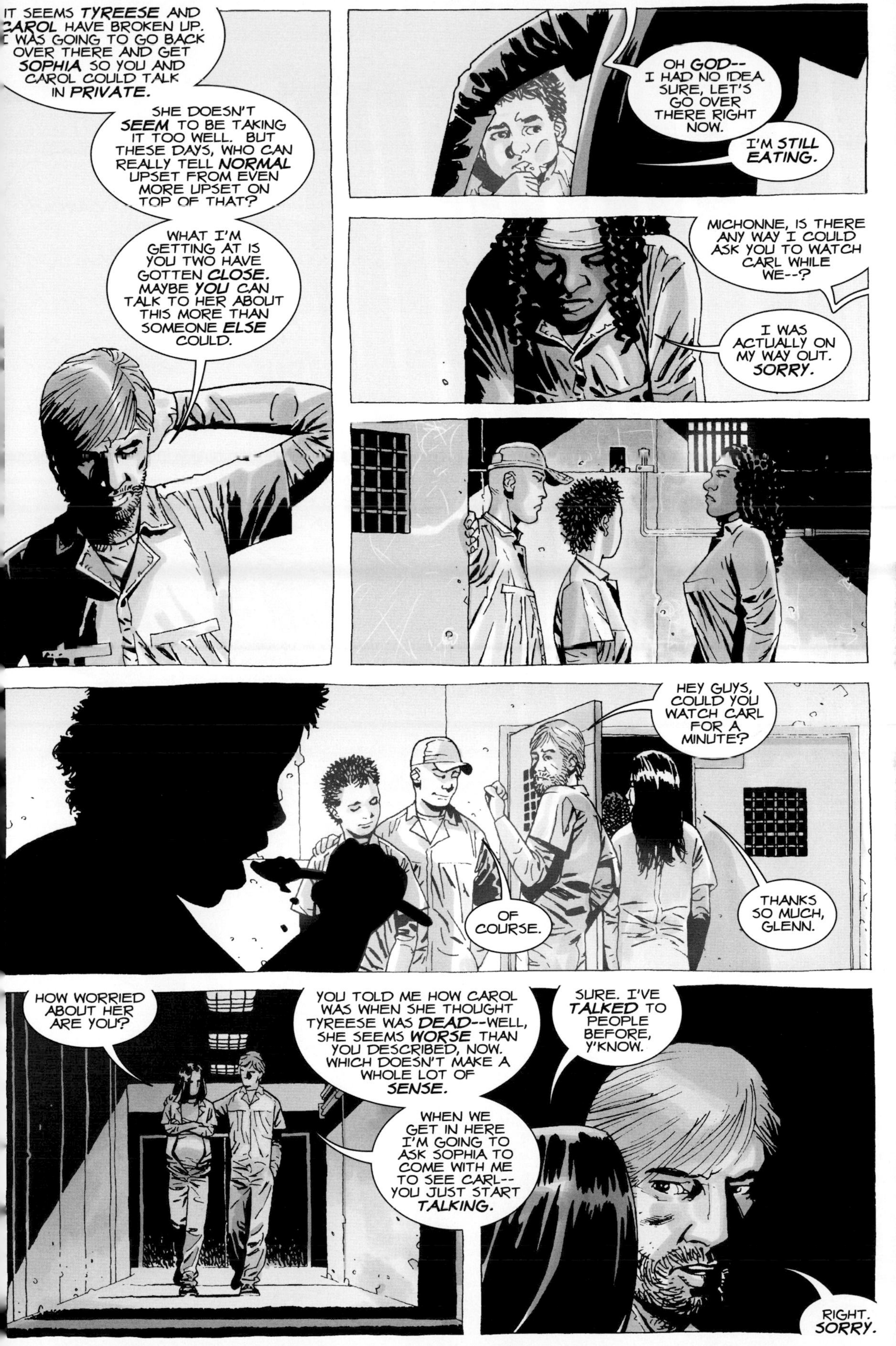
IT SEEMS TYREESE AND CAROL HAVE BROKEN UP. I WAS GOING TO GO BACK OVER THERE AND GET SOPHIA SO YOU AND CAROL COULD TALK IN PRIVATE.
SHE DOESN'T SEEM TO BE TAKING IT TOO WELL. BUT THESE DAYS, WHO CAN REALLY TELL NORMAL UPSET FROM EVEN MORE UPSET ON TOP OF THAT?
WHAT I'M GETTING AT IS YOU TWO HAVE GOTTEN CLOSE. MAYBE YOU CAN TALK TO HER ABOUT THIS MORE THAN SOMEONE ELSE COULD.
OH GOD-- I HAD NO IDEA. SURE, LET'S GO OVER THERE RIGHT NOW.
I'M STILL EATING.
MICHONNE, IS THERE ANY WAY I COULD ASK YOU TO WATCH CARL WHILE WE--?
I WAS ACTUALLY ON MY WAY OUT. SORRY.
HEY GUYS, COULD YOU WATCH CARL FOR A MINUTE?
OF COURSE.
THANKS SO MUCH, GLENN.
HOW WORRIED ABOUT HER ARE YOU?
YOU TOLD ME HOW CAROL WAS WHEN SHE THOUGHT TYREESE WAS DEAD--WELL, SHE SEEMS WORSE THAN YOU DESCRIBED, NOW. WHICH DOESN'T MAKE A WHOLE LOT OF SENSE.
WHEN WE GET IN HERE I'M GOING TO ASK SOPHIA TO COME WITH ME TO SEE CARL-- YOU JUST START TALKING.
SURE. I'VE TALKED TO PEOPLE BEFORE, Y'KNOW.
RIGHT. SORRY.

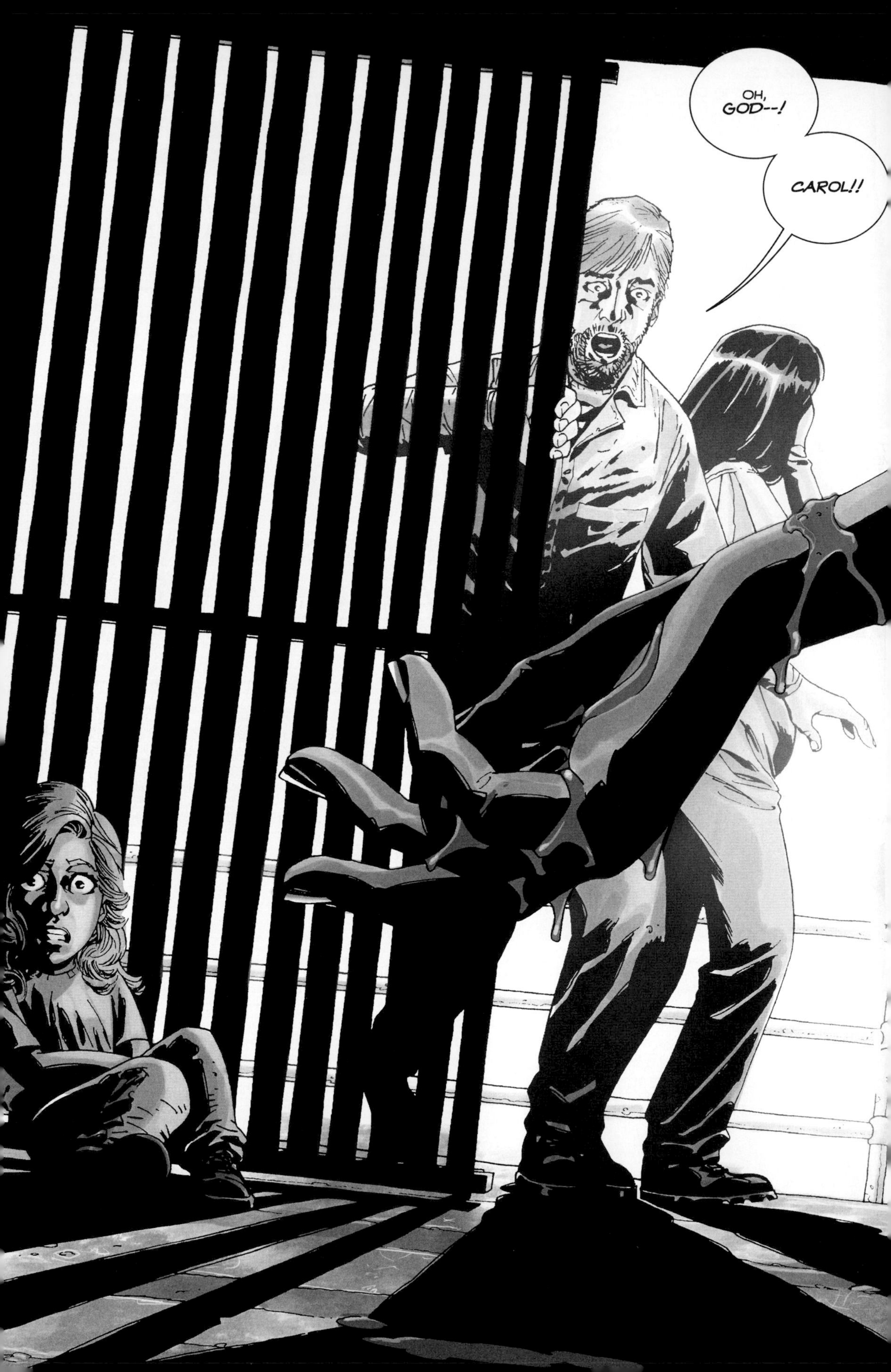
OH, GOD--!
CAROL!!

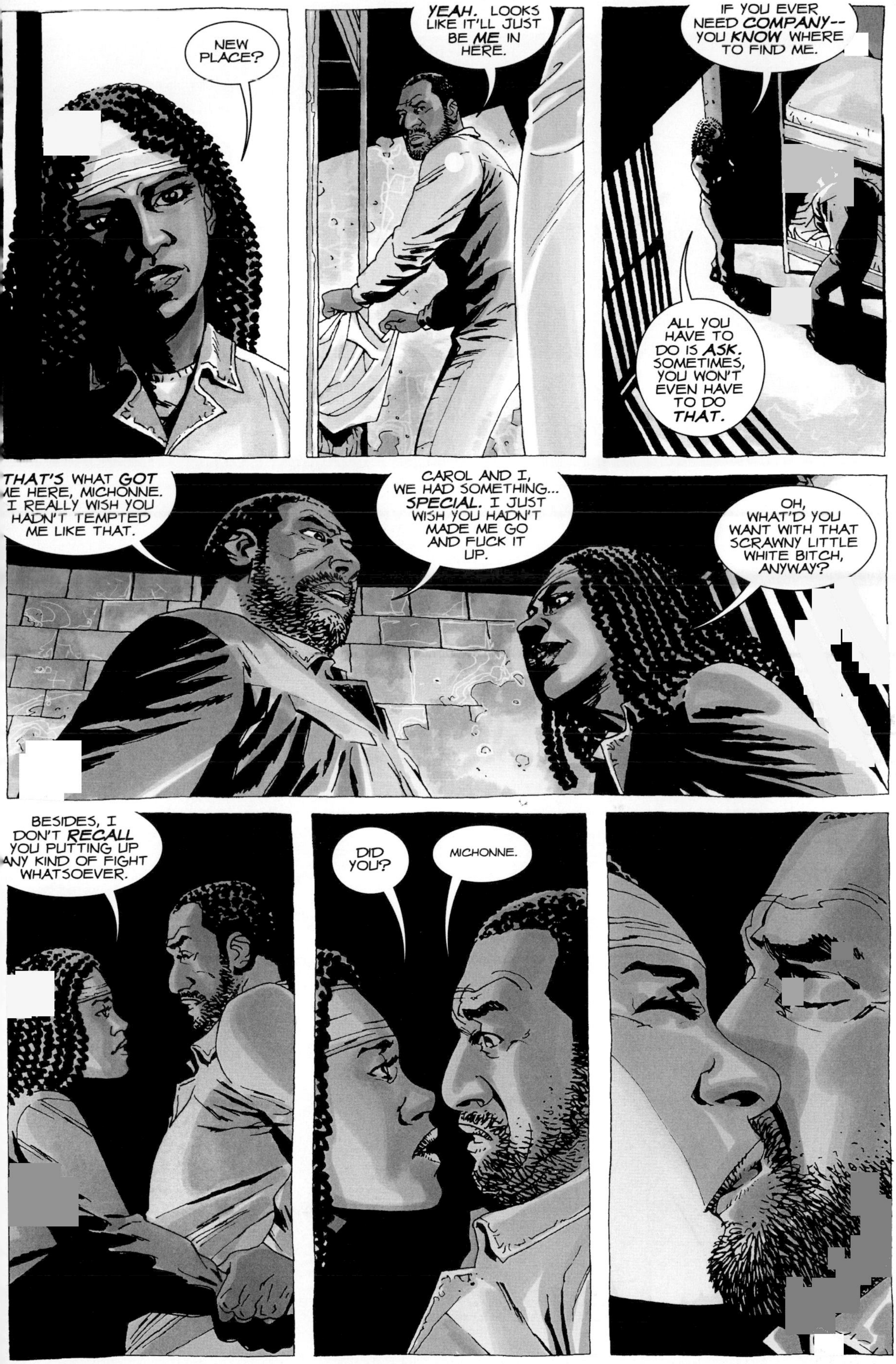
NEW PLACE?
YEAH. LOOKS LIKE IT'LL JUST BE ME IN HERE.
IF YOU EVER NEED COMPANY-- YOU KNOW WHERE TO FIND ME.
ALL YOU HAVE TO DO IS ASK. SOMETIMES, YOU WON'T EVEN HAVE TO DO THAT.
THAT'S WHAT GOT ME HERE, MICHONNE. I REALLY WISH YOU HADN'T TEMPTED ME LIKE THAT.
CAROL AND I, WE HAD SOMETHING... SPECIAL. I JUST WISH YOU HADN'T MADE ME GO AND FUCK IT UP.
OH, WHAT'D YOU WANT WITH THAT SCRAWNY LITTLE WHITE BITCH, ANYWAY?
BESIDES, I DON'T RECALL YOU PUTTING UP ANY KIND OF FIGHT WHATSOEVER.
DID YOU?
MICHONNE.

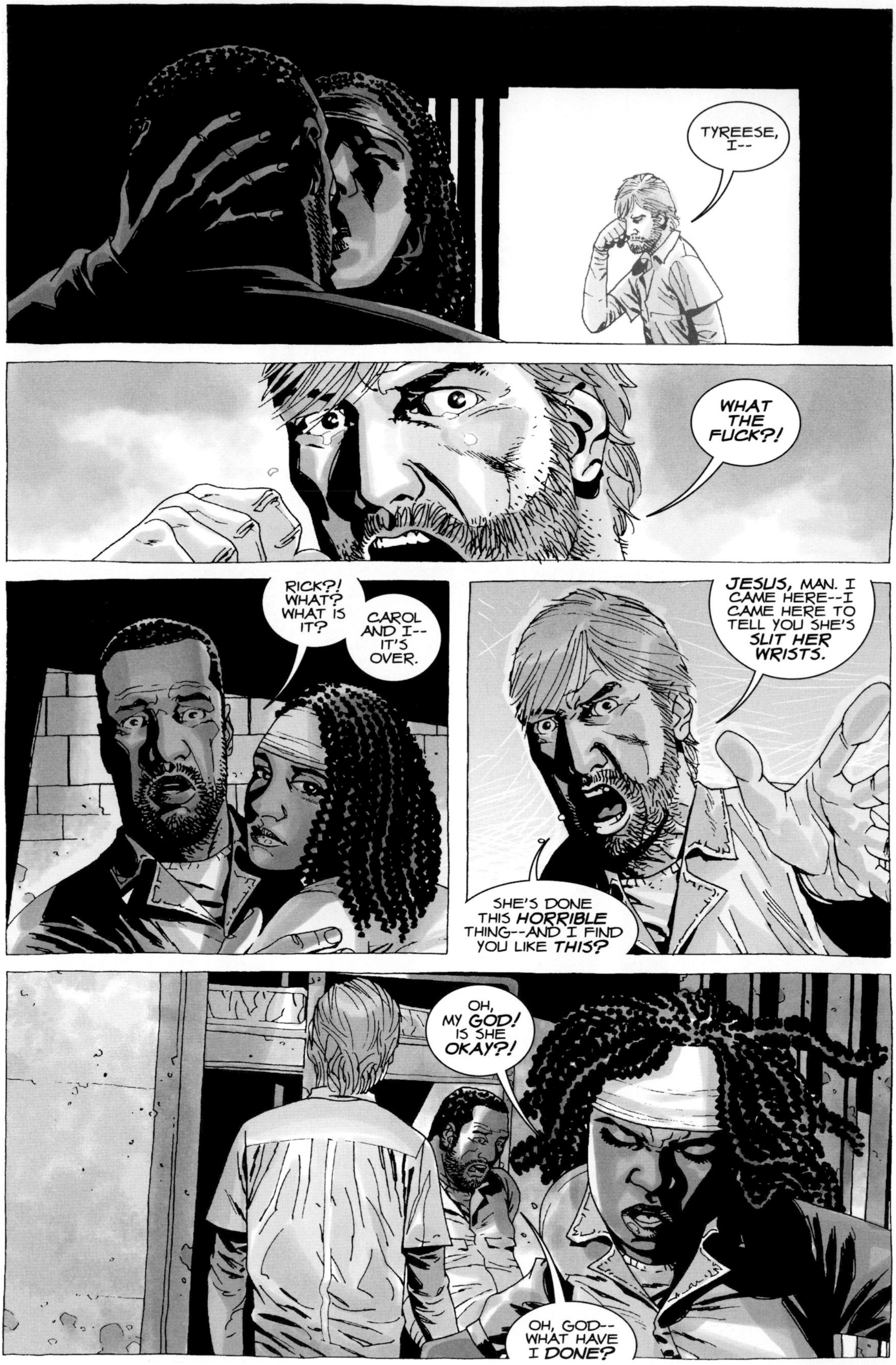
TYREESE, I--
WHAT THE FUCK?!
RICK?! WHAT? WHAT IS IT?
CAROL AND I-- IT'S OVER.
JESUS, MAN. I CAME HERE--I CAME HERE TO TELL YOU SHE'S SLIT HER WRISTS.
SHE'S DONE THIS HORRIBLE THING--AND I FIND YOU LIKE THIS?
OH, MY GOD! IS SHE OKAY?!
OH, GOD-- WHAT HAVE I DONE?

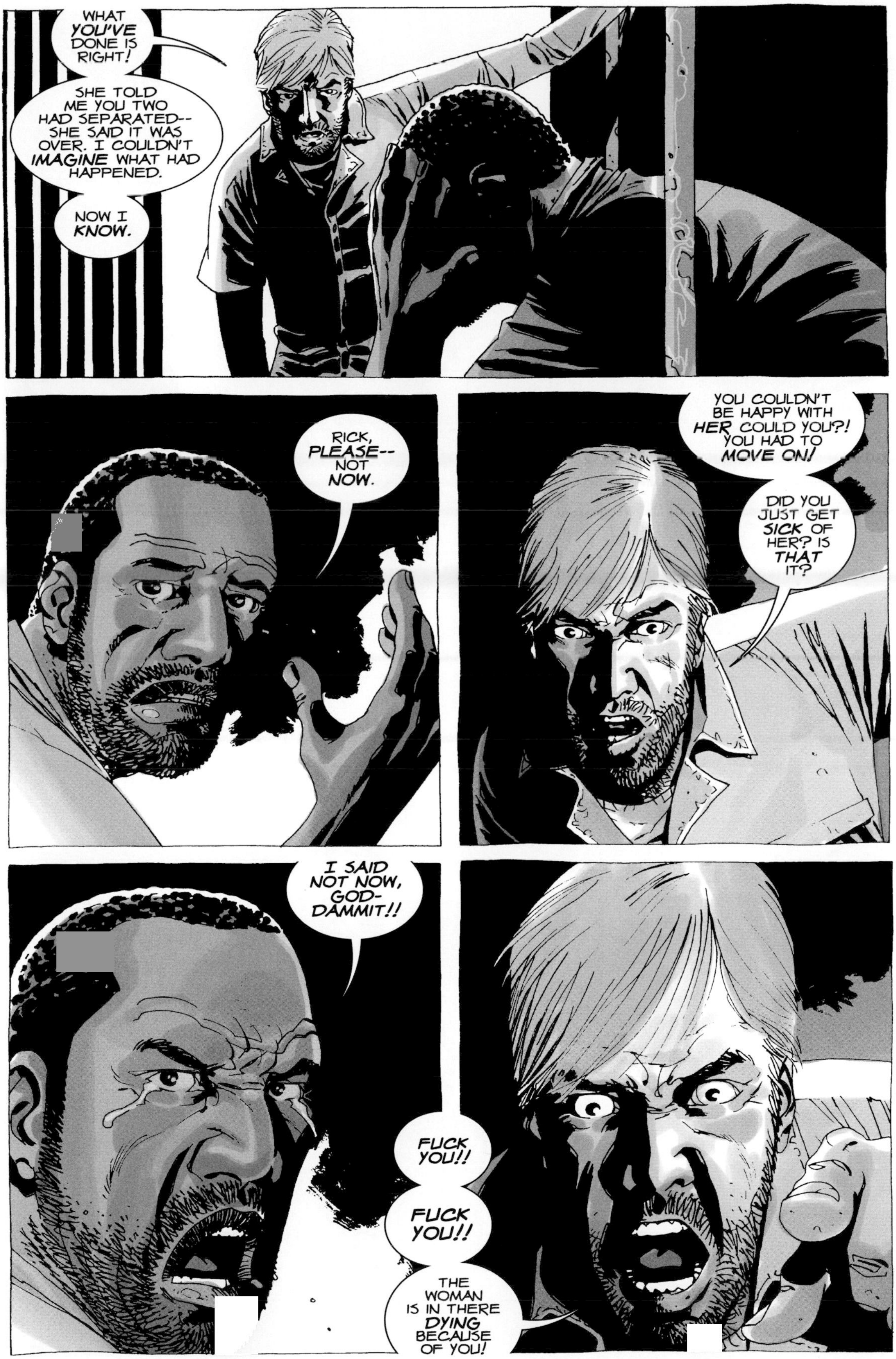
WHAT YOU'VE DONE IS RIGHT!
SHE TOLD ME YOU TWO HAD SEPARATED-- SHE SAID IT WAS OVER. I COULDN'T IMAGINE WHAT HAD HAPPENED.
NOW I KNOW.
RICK, PLEASE-- NOT NOW.
YOU COULDN'T BE HAPPY WITH HER COULD YOU?! YOU HAD TO MOVE ON!
DID YOU JUST GET SICK OF HER? IS THAT IT?
I SAID NOT NOW, GOD-DAMMIT!!
FUCK YOU!!
FUCK YOU!!
THE WOMAN IS IN THERE DYING BECAUSE OF YOU!

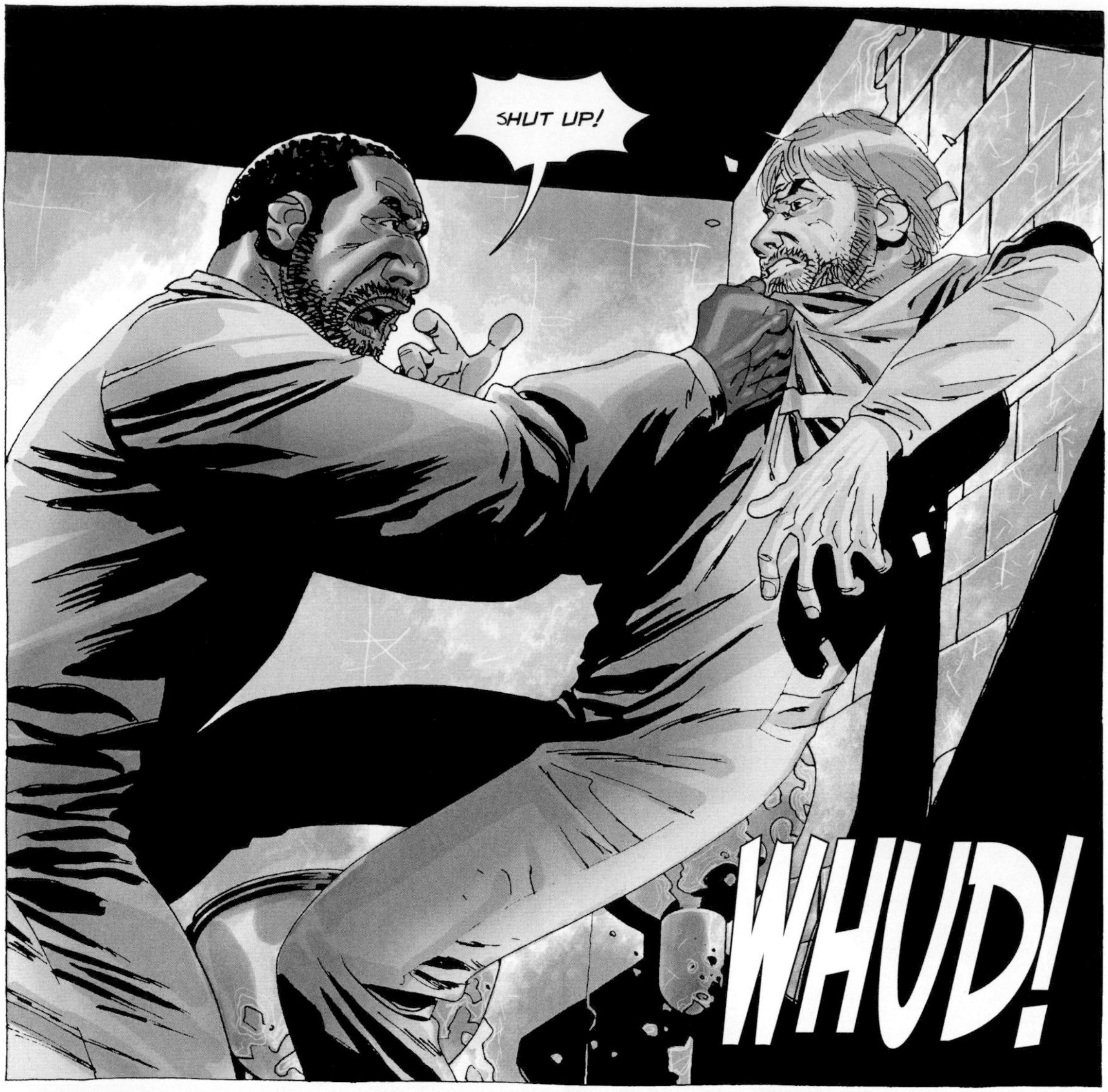
SHUT UP!
WHUD!

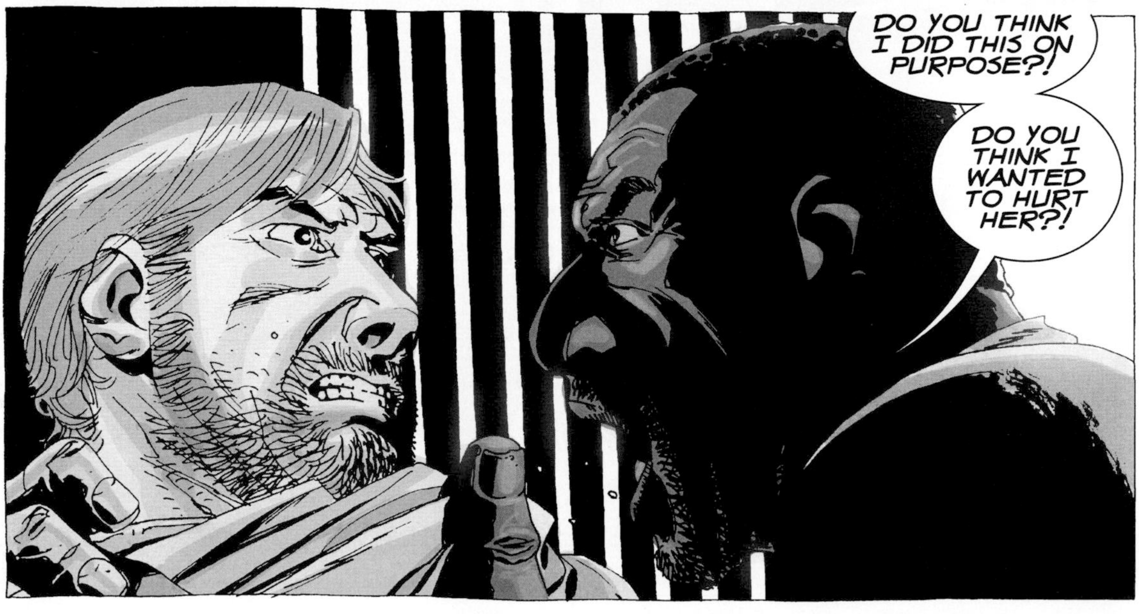
DO YOU THINK I DID THIS ON PURPOSE?!
DO YOU THINK I WANTED TO HURT HER?!

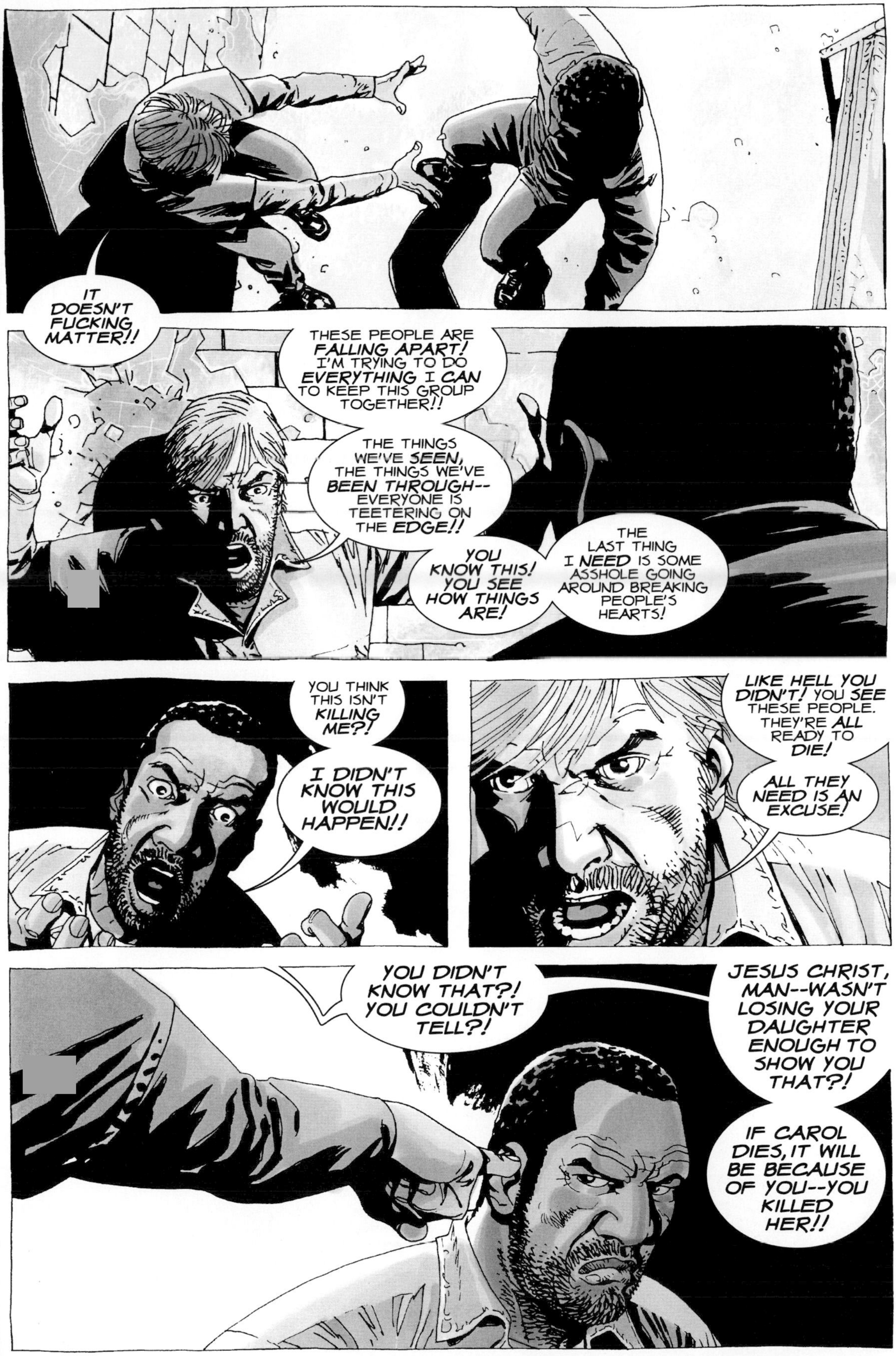
IT DOESN'T FUCKING MATTER!!
THESE PEOPLE ARE FALLING APART! I'M TRYING TO DO EVERYTHING I CAN TO KEEP THIS GROUP TOGETHER!!
THE THINGS WE'VE SEEN, THE THINGS WE'VE BEEN THROUGH-- EVERYONE IS TEETERING ON THE EDGE!!
YOU KNOW THIS! YOU SEE HOW THINGS ARE!
THE LAST THING I NEED IS SOME ASSHOLE GOING AROUND BREAKING PEOPLE'S HEARTS!
YOU THINK THIS ISN'T KILLING ME?!
I DIDN'T KNOW THIS WOULD HAPPEN!!
LIKE HELL YOU DIDN'T! YOU SEE THESE PEOPLE. THEY'RE ALL READY TO DIE!
ALL THEY NEED IS AN EXCUSE!
YOU DIDN'T KNOW THAT?! YOU COULDN'T TELL?!
JESUS CHRIST, MAN--WASN'T LOSING YOUR DAUGHTER ENOUGH TO SHOW YOU THAT?!
IF CAROL DIES, IT WILL BE BECAUSE OF YOU--YOU KILLED HER!!

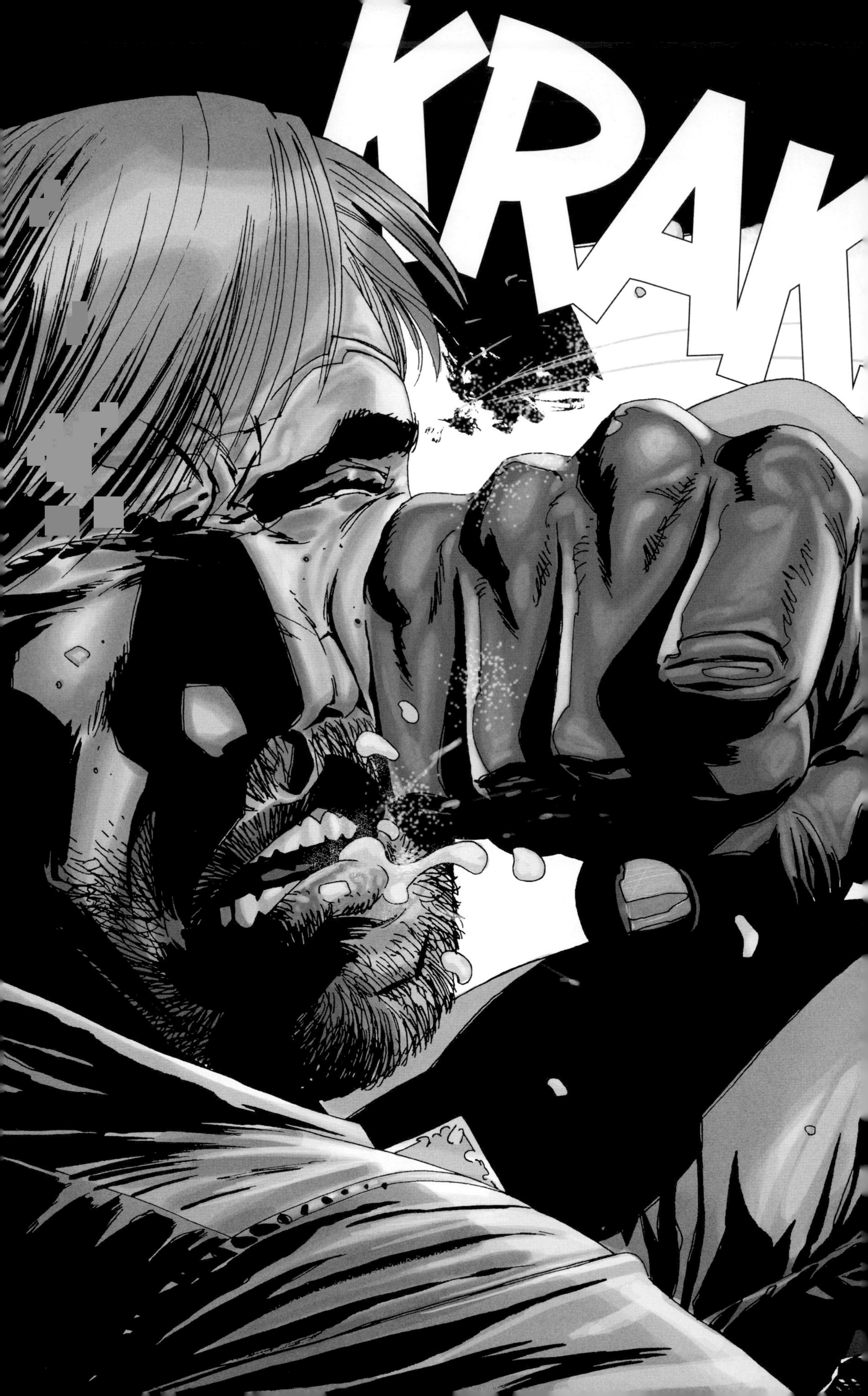
KRAA

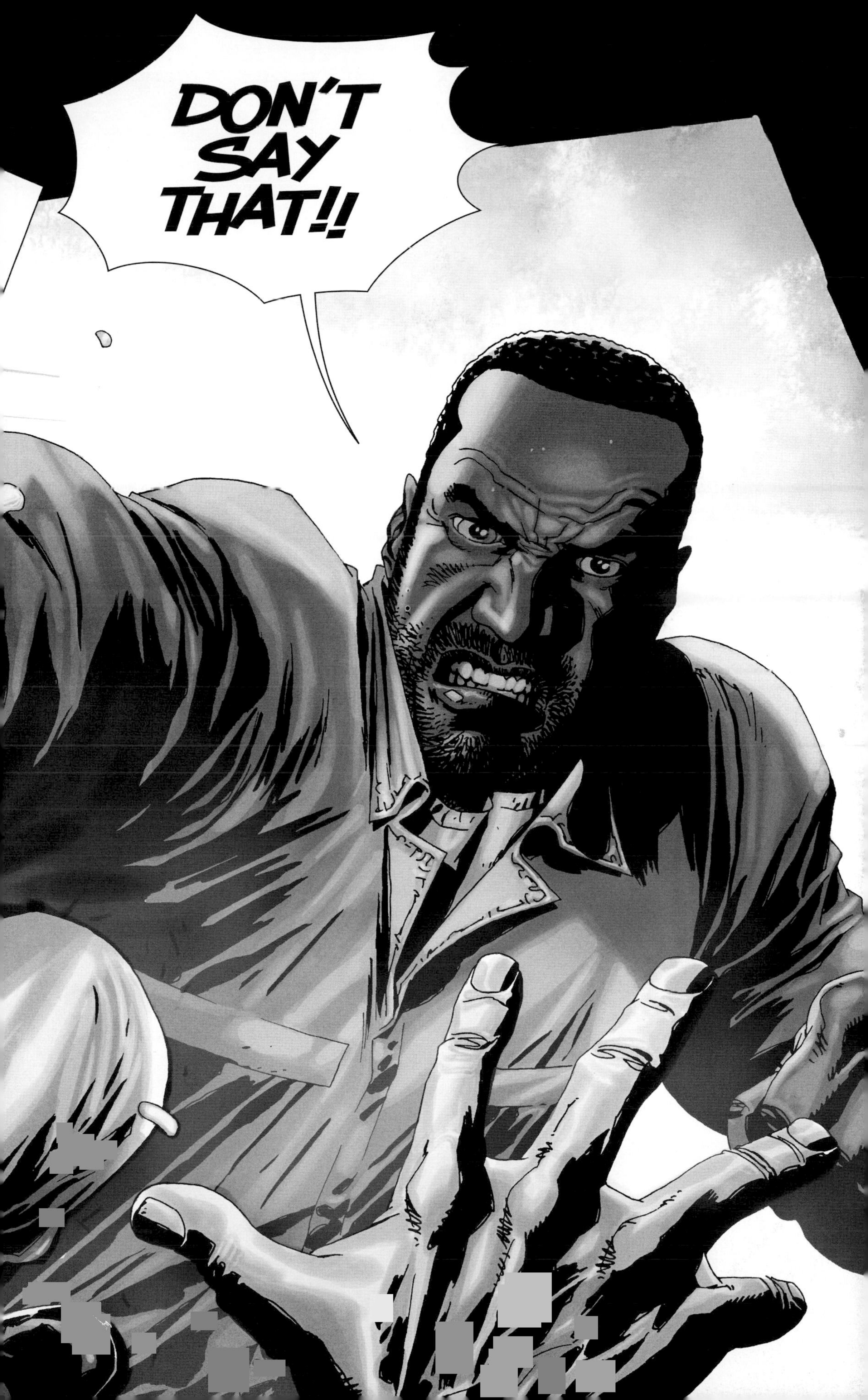
DON'T SAY THAT!!

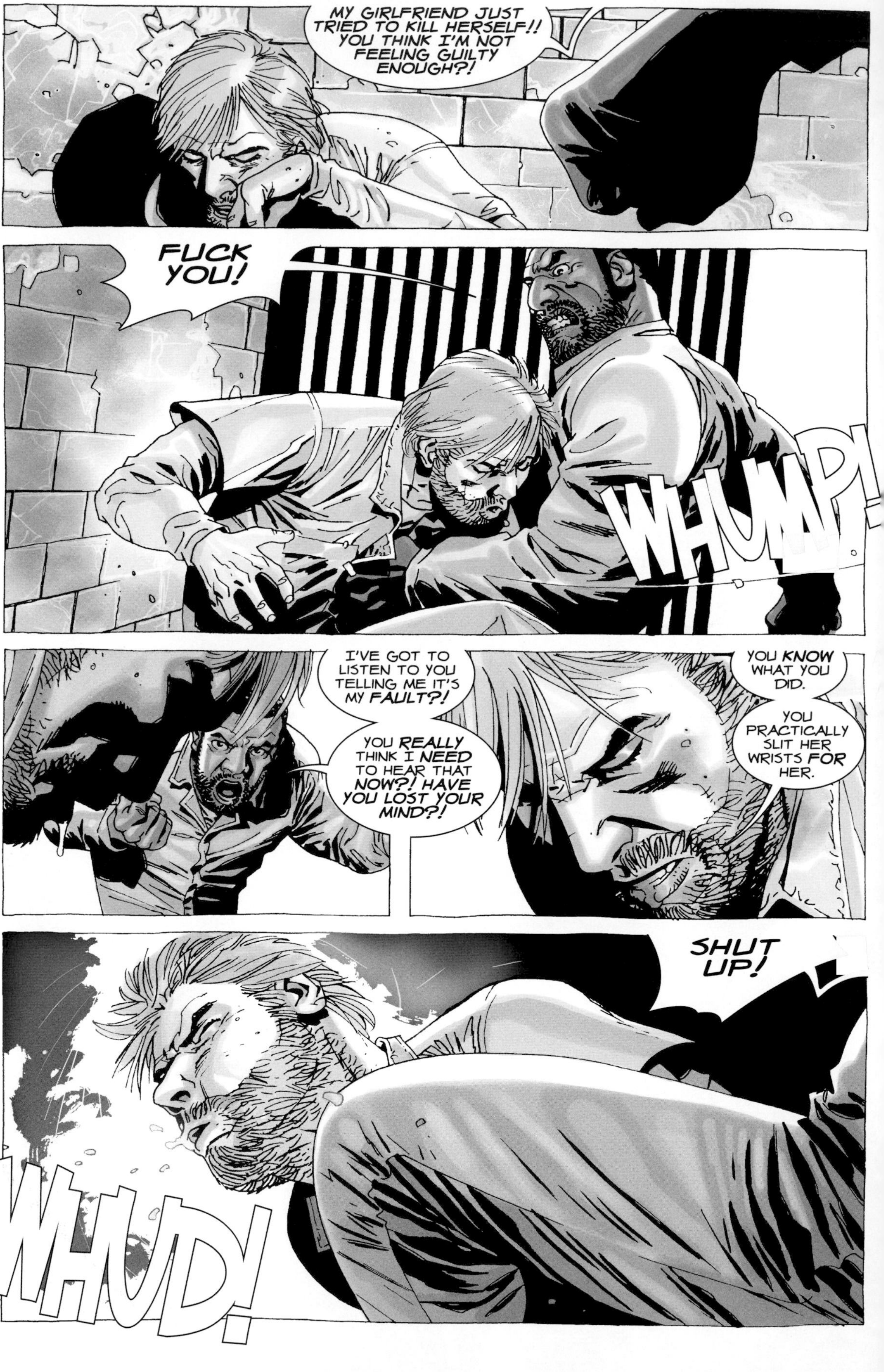
MY GIRLFRIEND JUST TRIED TO KILL HERSELF!! YOU THINK I'M NOT FEELING GUILTY ENOUGH?!
FUCK YOU!
WHUMP!
I'VE GOT TO LISTEN TO YOU TELLING ME IT'S MY FAULT?!
YOU REALLY THINK I NEED TO HEAR THAT NOW?! HAVE YOU LOST YOUR MIND?!
YOU KNOW WHAT YOU DID.
YOU PRACTICALLY SLIT HER WRISTS FOR HER.
SHUT UP!
WHUD!

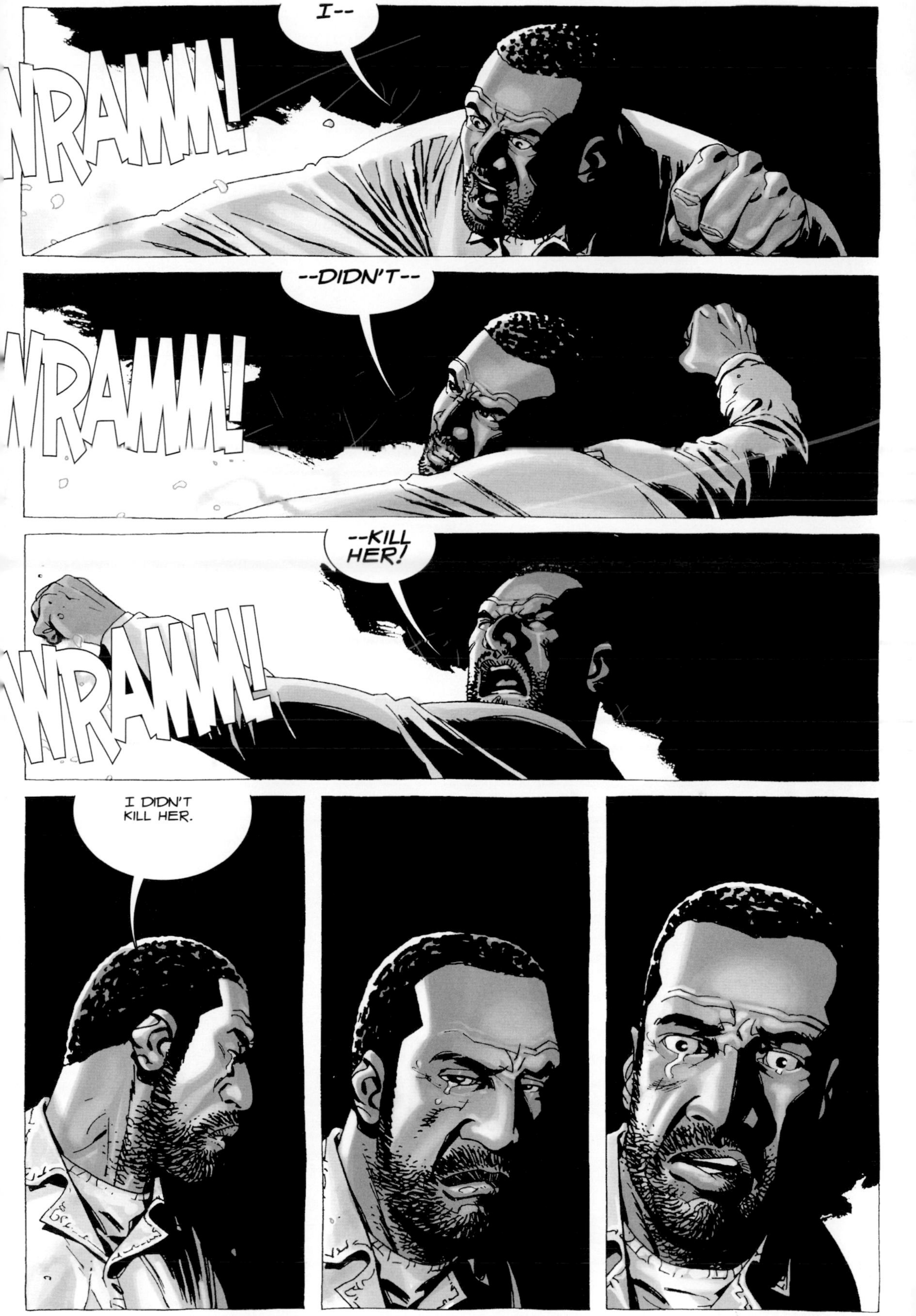
I--
WRAMM!
--DIDN'T--
WRAMM!
--KILL HER!
WRAMM!
I DIDN'T KILL HER.

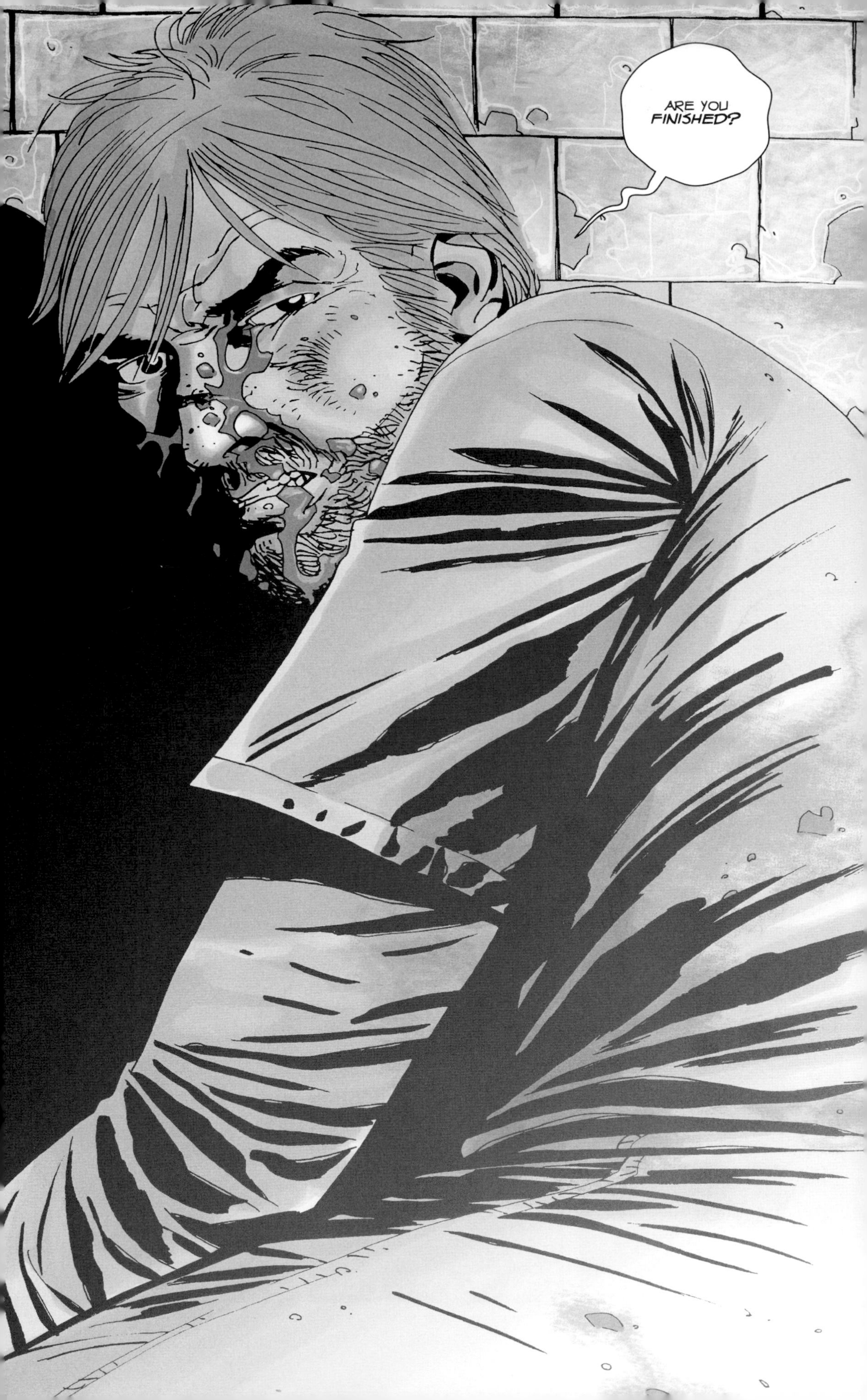
ARE YOU FINISHED?

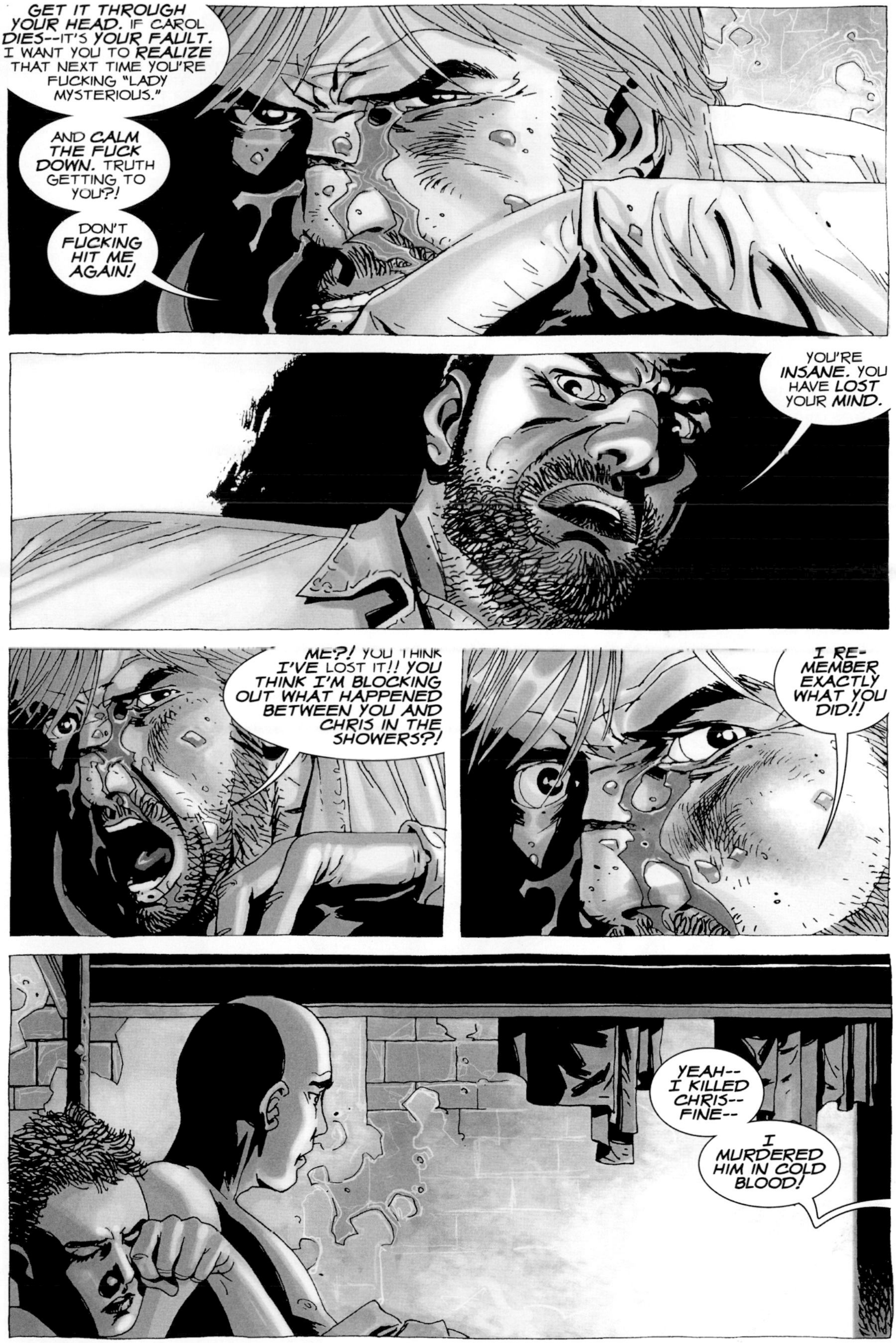
GET IT THROUGH YOUR HEAD. IF CAROL DIES--IT'S YOUR FAULT. I WANT YOU TO REALIZE THAT NEXT TIME YOU'RE FUCKING "LADY MYSTERIOUS."
AND CALM THE FUCK DOWN. TRUTH GETTING TO YOU?!
DON'T FUCKING HIT ME AGAIN!
YOU'RE INSANE. YOU HAVE LOST YOUR MIND.
ME?! YOU THINK I'VE LOST IT!! YOU THINK I'M BLOCKING OUT WHAT HAPPENED BETWEEN YOU AND CHRIS IN THE SHOWERS?!
I RE-MEMBER EXACTLY WHAT YOU DID!!
YEAH-- I KILLED CHRIS-- FINE--
I MURDERED HIM IN COLD BLOOD!

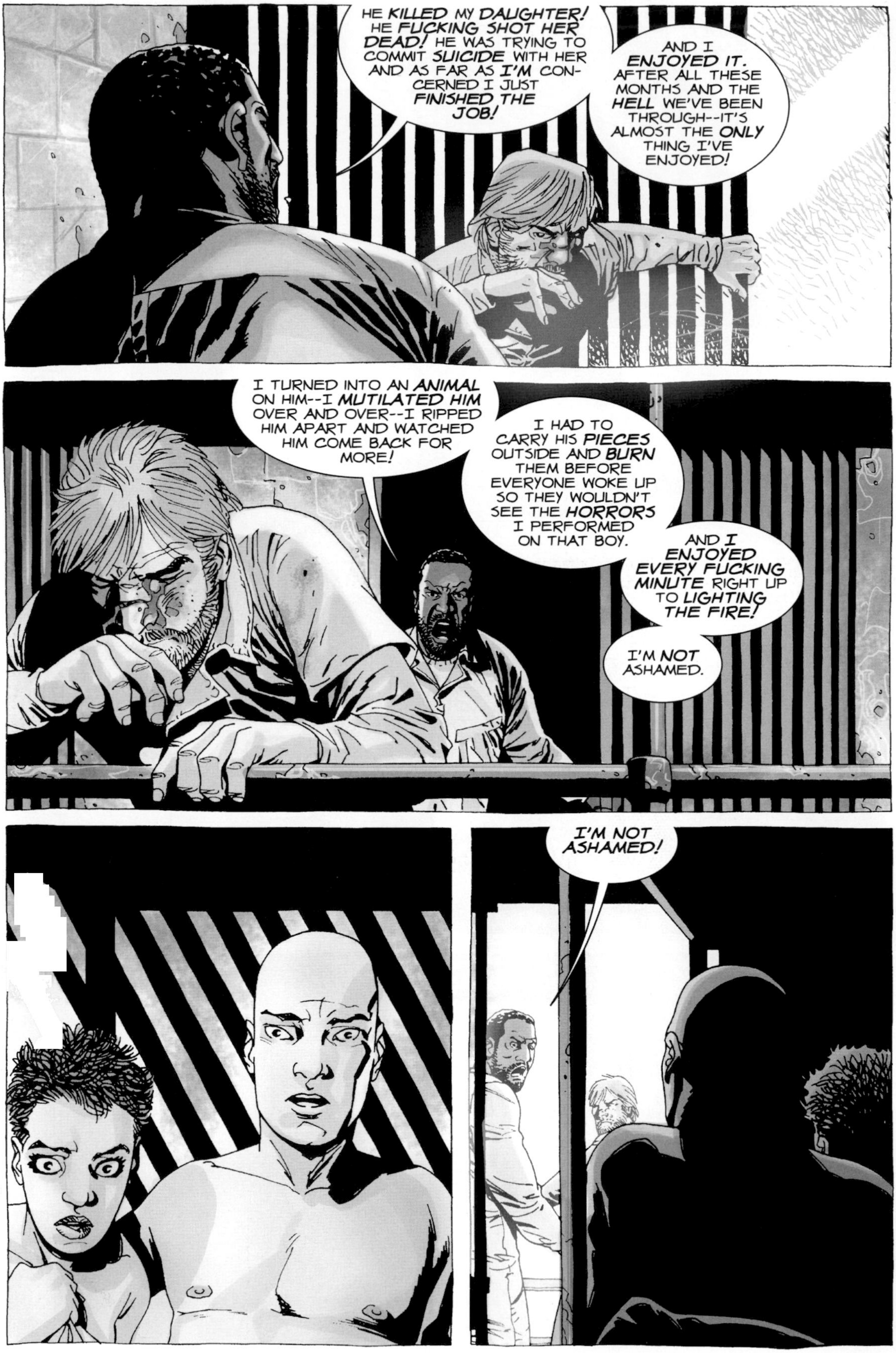
HE KILLED MY DAUGHTER! HE FUCKING SHOT HER DEAD! HE WAS TRYING TO COMMIT SUICIDE WITH HER AND AS FAR AS I'M CONCERNED I JUST FINISHED THE JOB!
AND I ENJOYED IT. AFTER ALL THESE MONTHS AND THE HELL WE'VE BEEN THROUGH--IT'S ALMOST THE ONLY THING I'VE ENJOYED!
I TURNED INTO AN ANIMAL ON HIM--I MUTILATED HIM OVER AND OVER--I RIPPED HIM APART AND WATCHED HIM COME BACK FOR MORE!
I HAD TO CARRY HIS PIECES OUTSIDE AND BURN THEM BEFORE EVERYONE WOKE UP SO THEY WOULDN'T SEE THE HORRORS I PERFORMED ON THAT BOY.
AND I ENJOYED EVERY FUCKING MINUTE RIGHT UP TO LIGHTING THE FIRE!
I'M NOT ASHAMED.
I'M NOT ASHAMED!

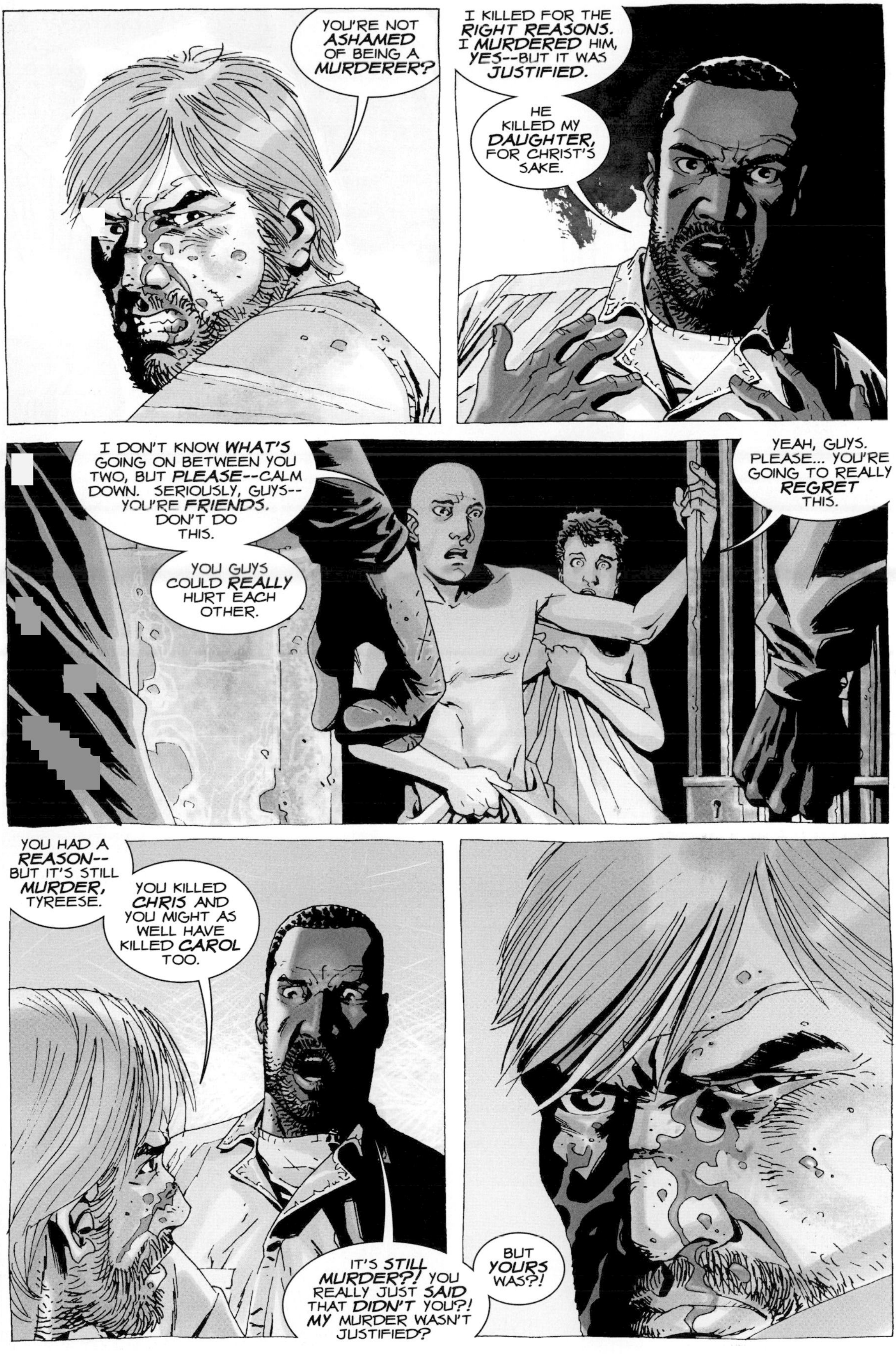
YOU'RE NOT ASHAMED OF BEING A MURDERER?
I KILLED FOR THE RIGHT REASONS. I MURDERED HIM, YES--BUT IT WAS JUSTIFIED.
HE KILLED MY DAUGHTER, FOR CHRIST'S SAKE.
I DON'T KNOW WHAT'S GOING ON BETWEEN YOU TWO, BUT PLEASE--CALM DOWN. SERIOUSLY, GUYS-- YOU'RE FRIENDS. DON'T DO THIS.
YOU GUYS COULD REALLY HURT EACH OTHER.
YEAH, GUYS. PLEASE... YOU'RE GOING TO REALLY REGRET THIS.
YOU HAD A REASON-- BUT IT'S STILL MURDER, TYREESE.
YOU KILLED CHRIS AND YOU MIGHT AS WELL HAVE KILLED CAROL TOO.
IT'S STILL MURDER?! YOU REALLY JUST SAID THAT DIDN'T YOU?! MY MURDER WASN'T JUSTIFIED?
BUT YOURS WAS?!

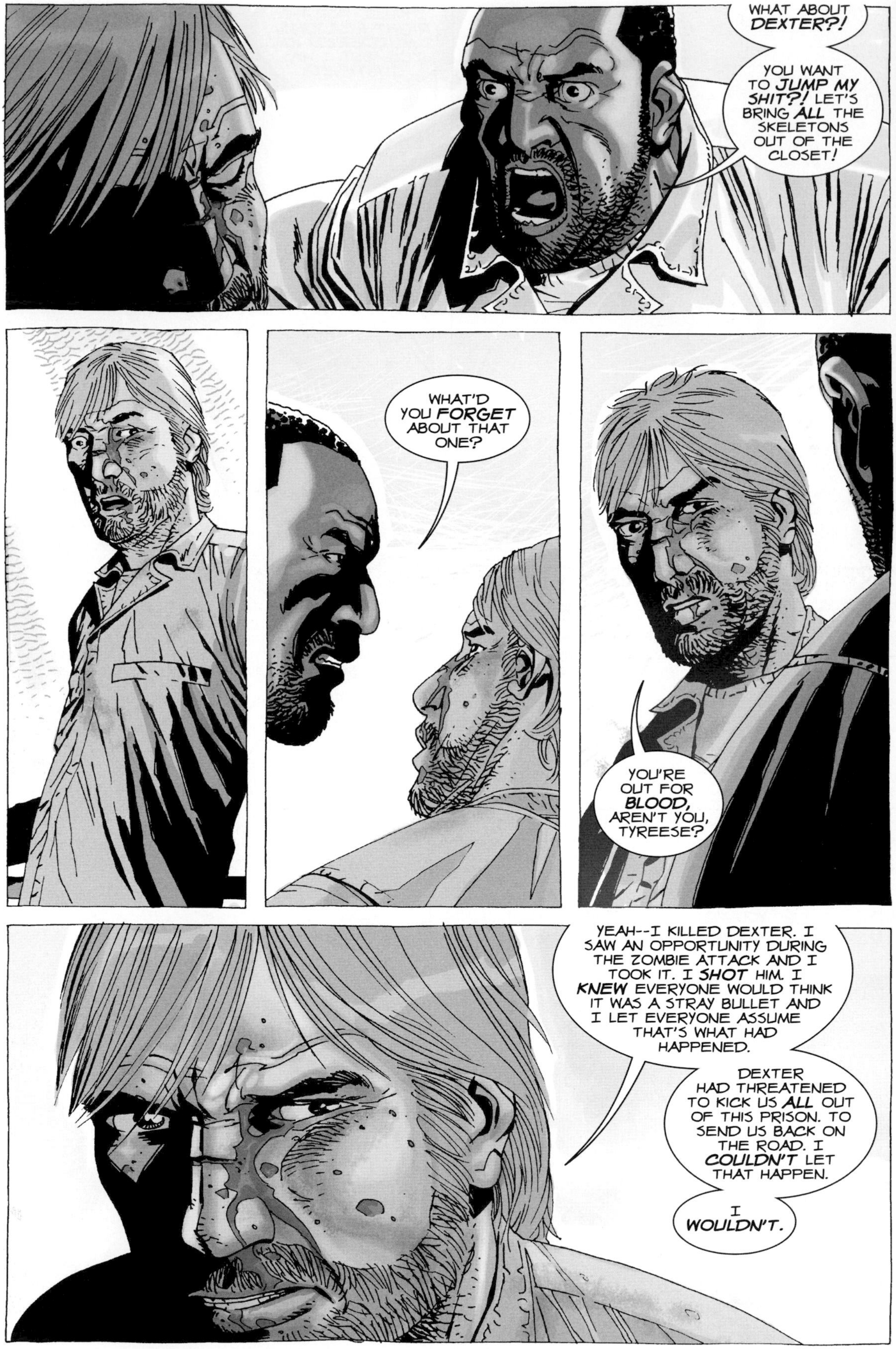
WHAT ABOUT DEXTER?!
YOU WANT TO JUMP MY SHIT?! LET'S BRING ALL THE SKELETONS OUT OF THE CLOSET!
WHAT'D YOU FORGET ABOUT THAT ONE?
YOU'RE OUT FOR BLOOD, AREN'T YOU, TYREESE?
YEAH--I KILLED DEXTER. I SAW AN OPPORTUNITY DURING THE ZOMBIE ATTACK AND I TOOK IT. I SHOT HIM. I KNEW EVERYONE WOULD THINK IT WAS A STRAY BULLET AND I LET EVERYONE ASSUME THAT'S WHAT HAD HAPPENED.
DEXTER HAD THREATENED TO KICK US ALL OUT OF THIS PRISON. TO SEND US BACK ON THE ROAD. I COULDN'T LET THAT HAPPEN.
I WOULDN'T.

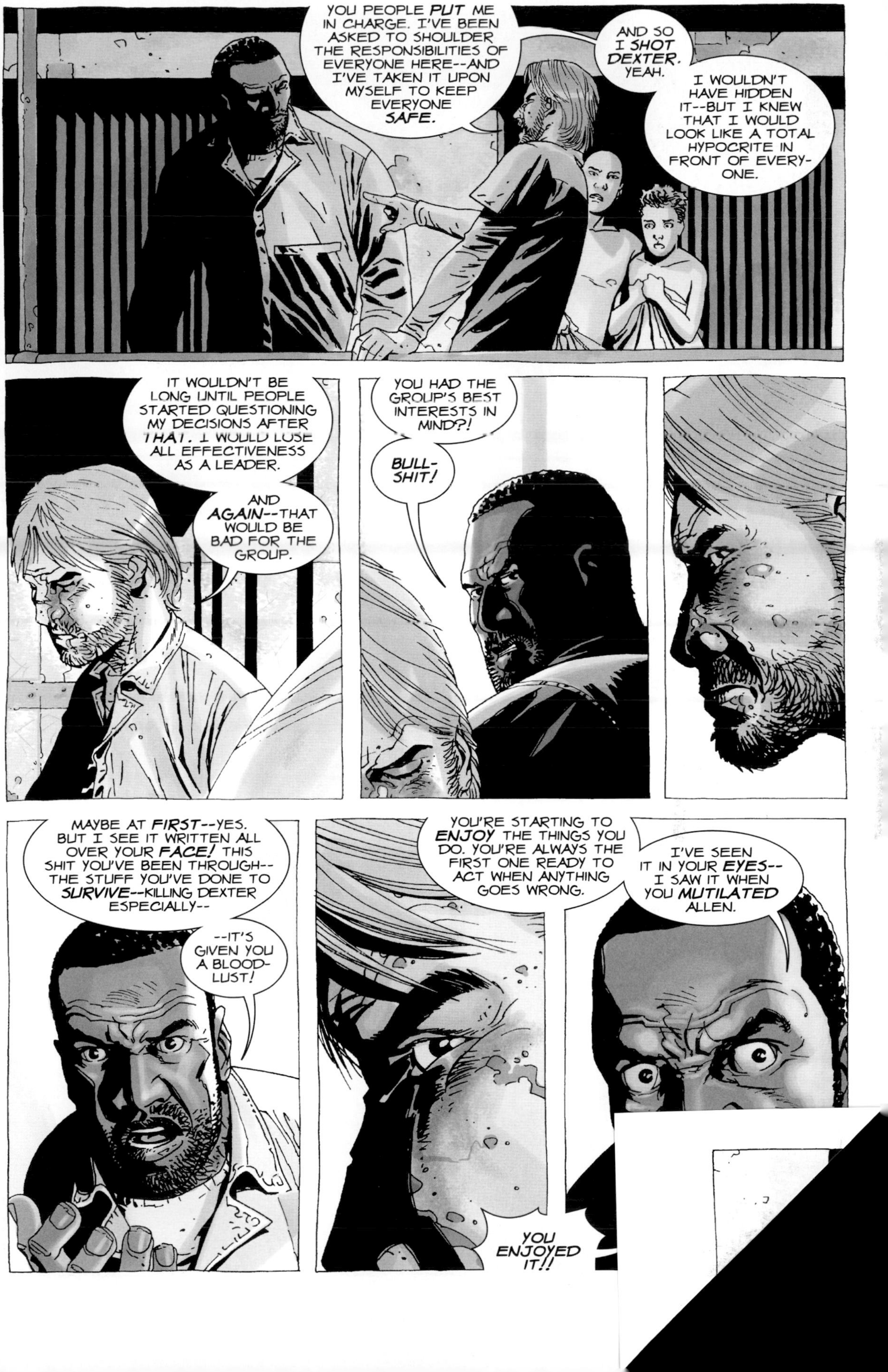
YOU PEOPLE PUT ME IN CHARGE. I'VE BEEN ASKED TO SHOULDER THE RESPONSIBILITIES OF EVERYONE HERE--AND I'VE TAKEN IT UPON MYSELF TO KEEP EVERYONE SAFE.
AND SO I SHOT DEXTER. YEAH.
I WOULDN'T HAVE HIDDEN IT--BUT I KNEW THAT I WOULD LOOK LIKE A TOTAL HYPOCRITE IN FRONT OF EVERY-ONE.
IT WOULDN'T BE LONG UNTIL PEOPLE STARTED QUESTIONING MY DECISIONS AFTER THAT. I WOULD LOSE ALL EFFECTIVENESS AS A LEADER.
AND AGAIN--THAT WOULD BE BAD FOR THE GROUP.
YOU HAD THE GROUP'S BEST INTERESTS IN MIND?!
BULL-SHIT!
MAYBE AT FIRST--YES. BUT I SEE IT WRITTEN ALL OVER YOUR FACE! THIS SHIT YOU'VE BEEN THROUGH--THE STUFF YOU'VE DONE TO SURVIVE--KILLING DEXTER ESPECIALLY--
--IT'S GIVEN YOU A BLOOD-LUST!
YOU'RE STARTING TO ENJOY THE THINGS YOU DO. YOU'RE ALWAYS THE FIRST ONE READY TO ACT WHEN ANYTHING GOES WRONG.
I'VE SEEN IT IN YOUR EYES--I SAW IT WHEN YOU MUTILATED ALLEN.
YOU ENJOYED IT!!

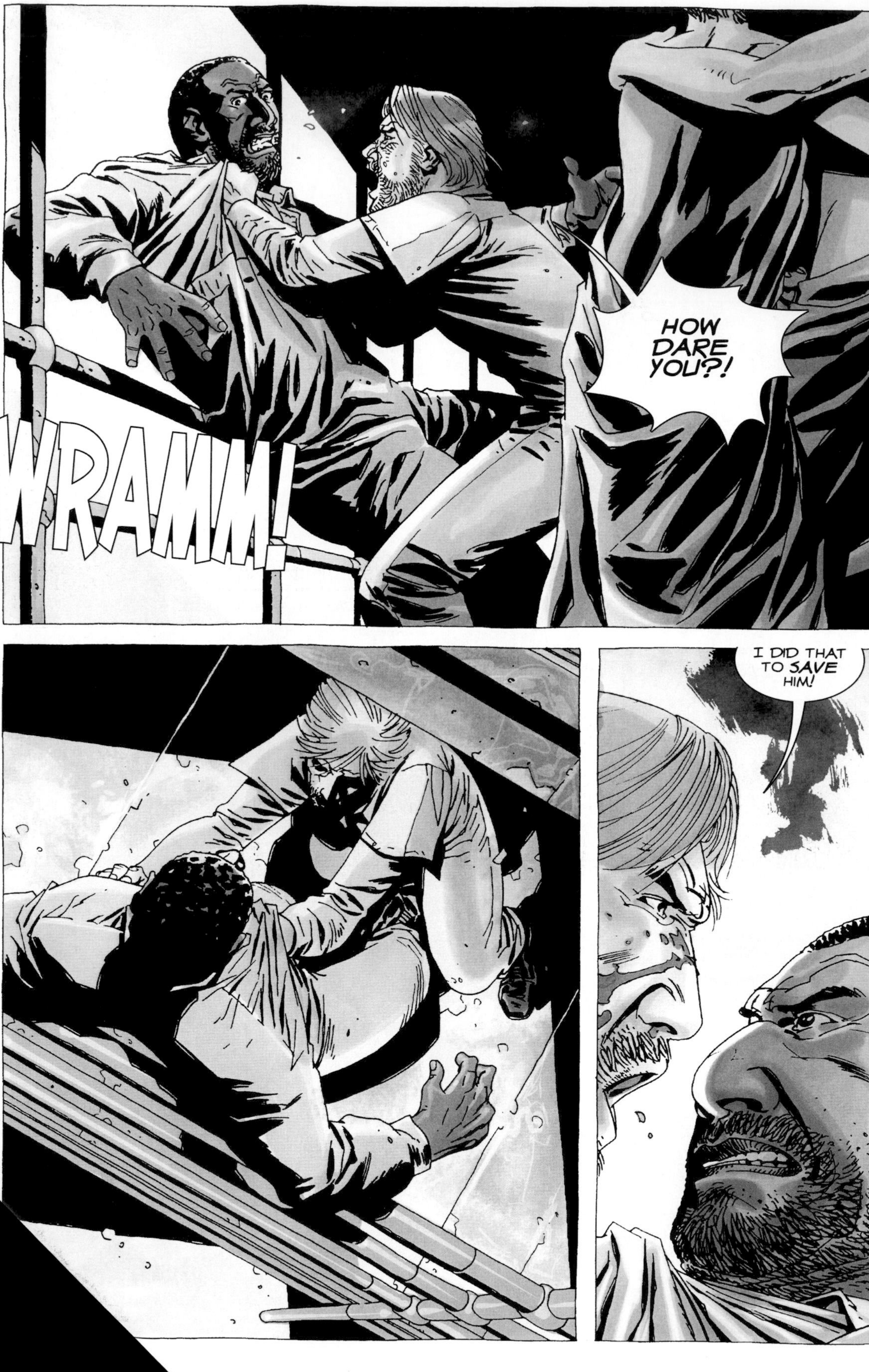
HOW DARE YOU?!
WRAMM!
I DID THAT TO SAVE HIM!

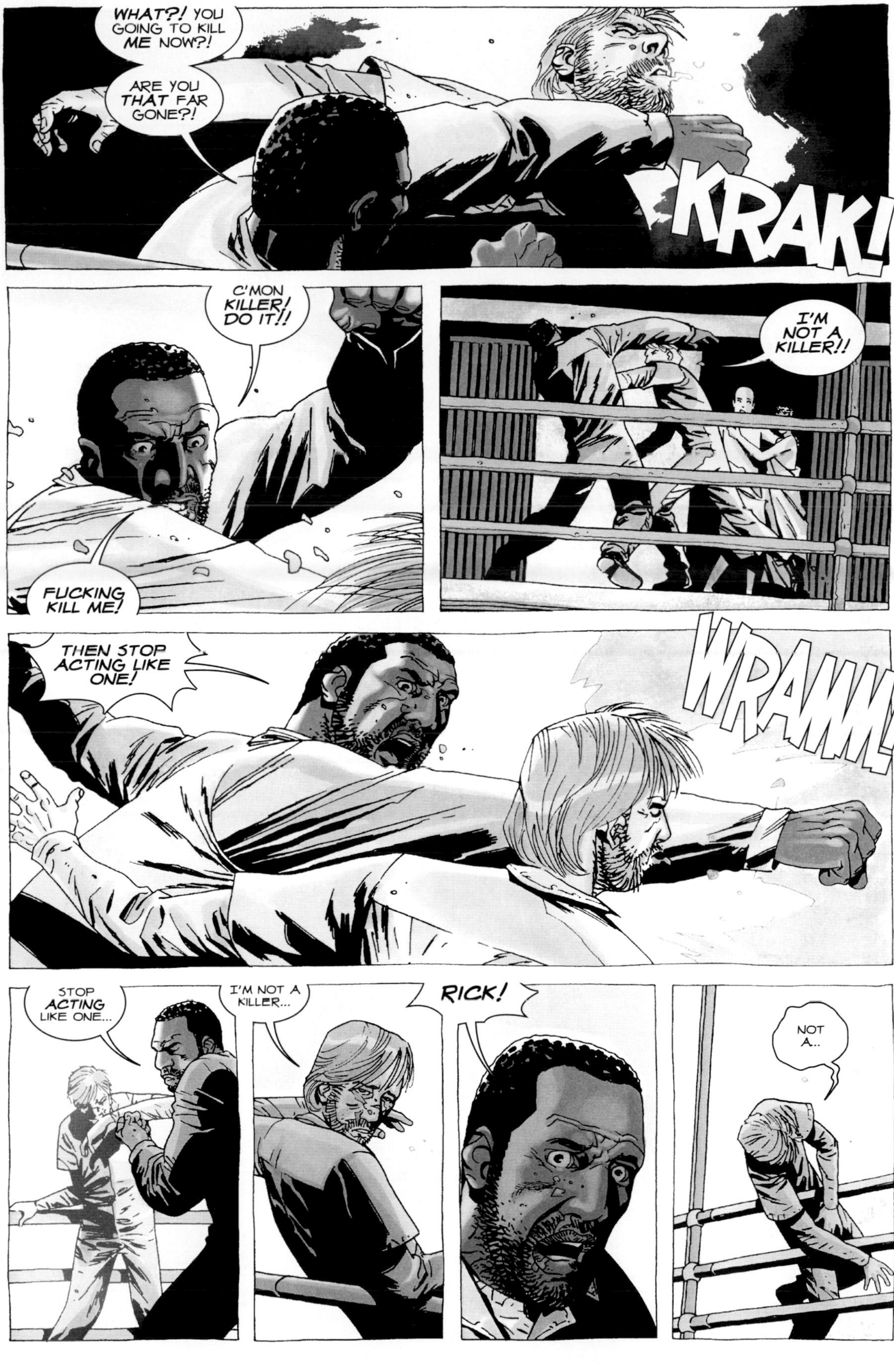

WHAT?! YOU GOING TO KILL ME NOW?!
ARE YOU THAT FAR GONE?!
KRAK!
C'MON KILLER! DO IT!!
FUCKING KILL ME!
I'M NOT A KILLER!!
THEN STOP ACTING LIKE ONE!
WRAMM!
STOP ACTING LIKE ONE...
I'M NOT A KILLER...
RICK!
NOT A...

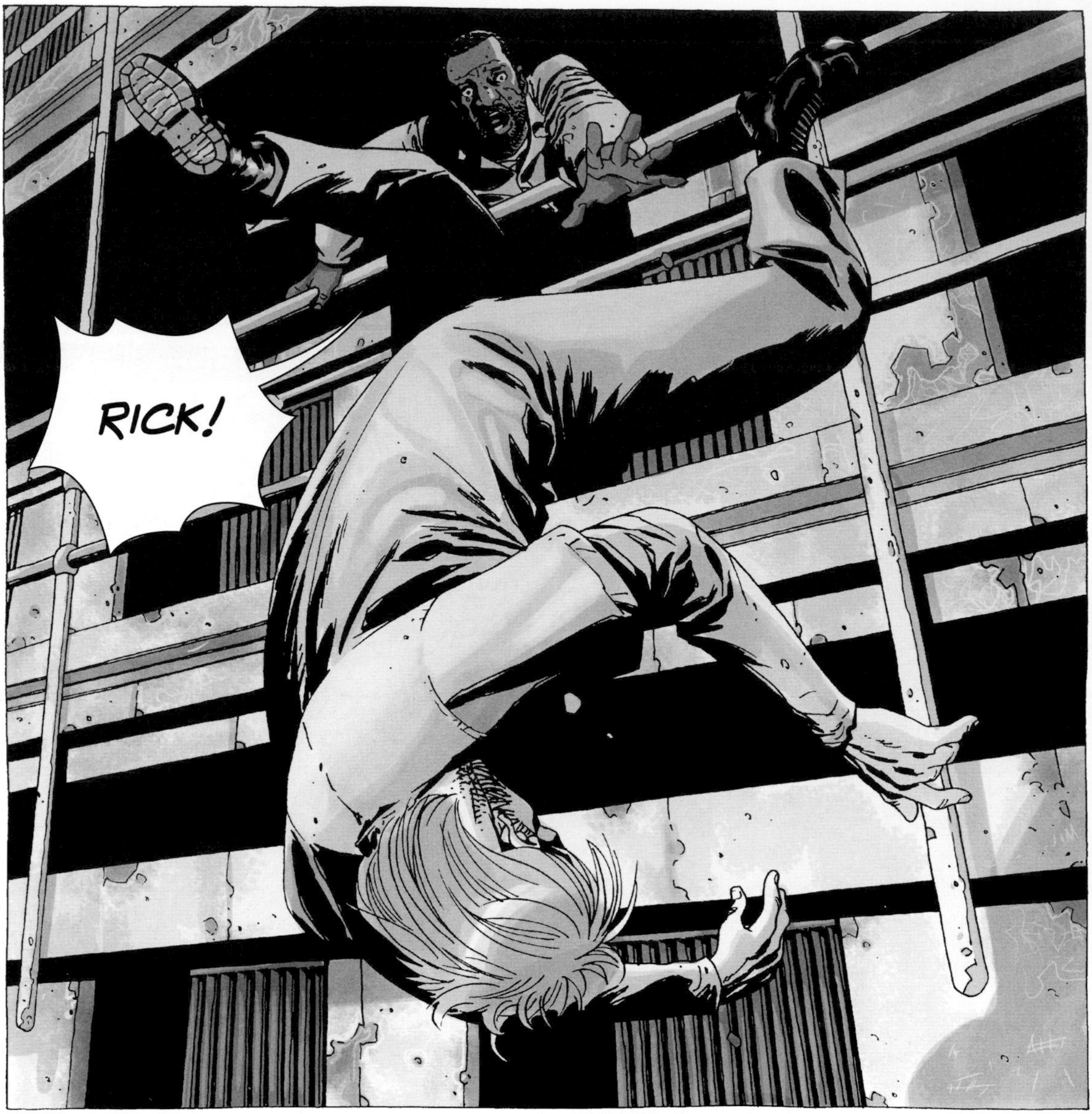
RICK!

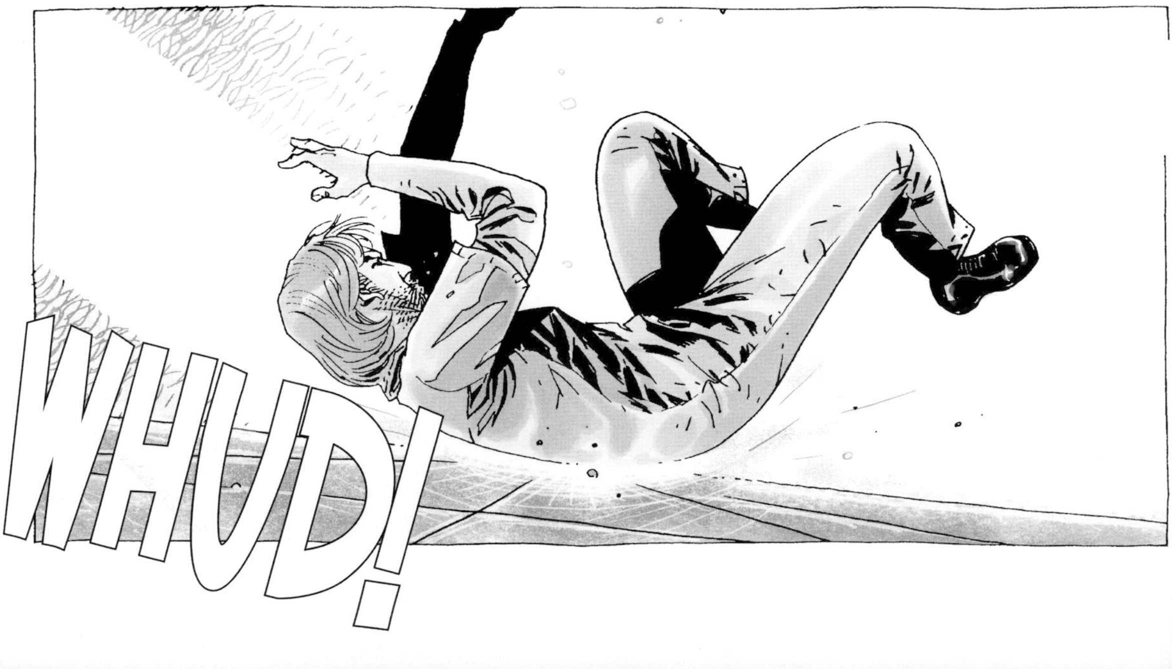
WHUD!

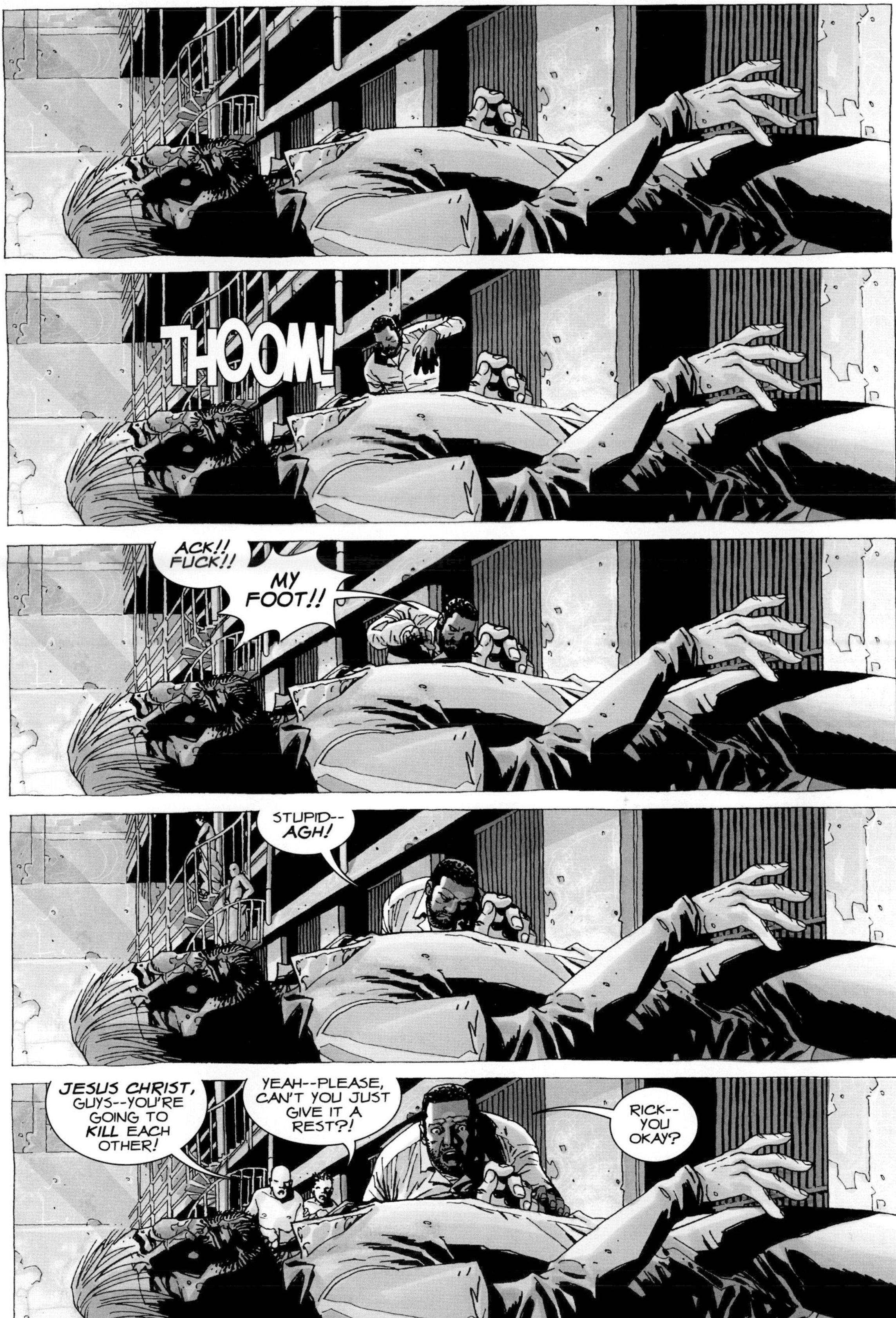
THOOM!
ACK!! FUCK!!
MY FOOT!!
STUPID-- AGH!
JESUS CHRIST, GUYS--YOU'RE GOING TO KILL EACH OTHER!
YEAH--PLEASE, CAN'T YOU JUST GIVE IT A REST?!
RICK-- YOU OKAY?

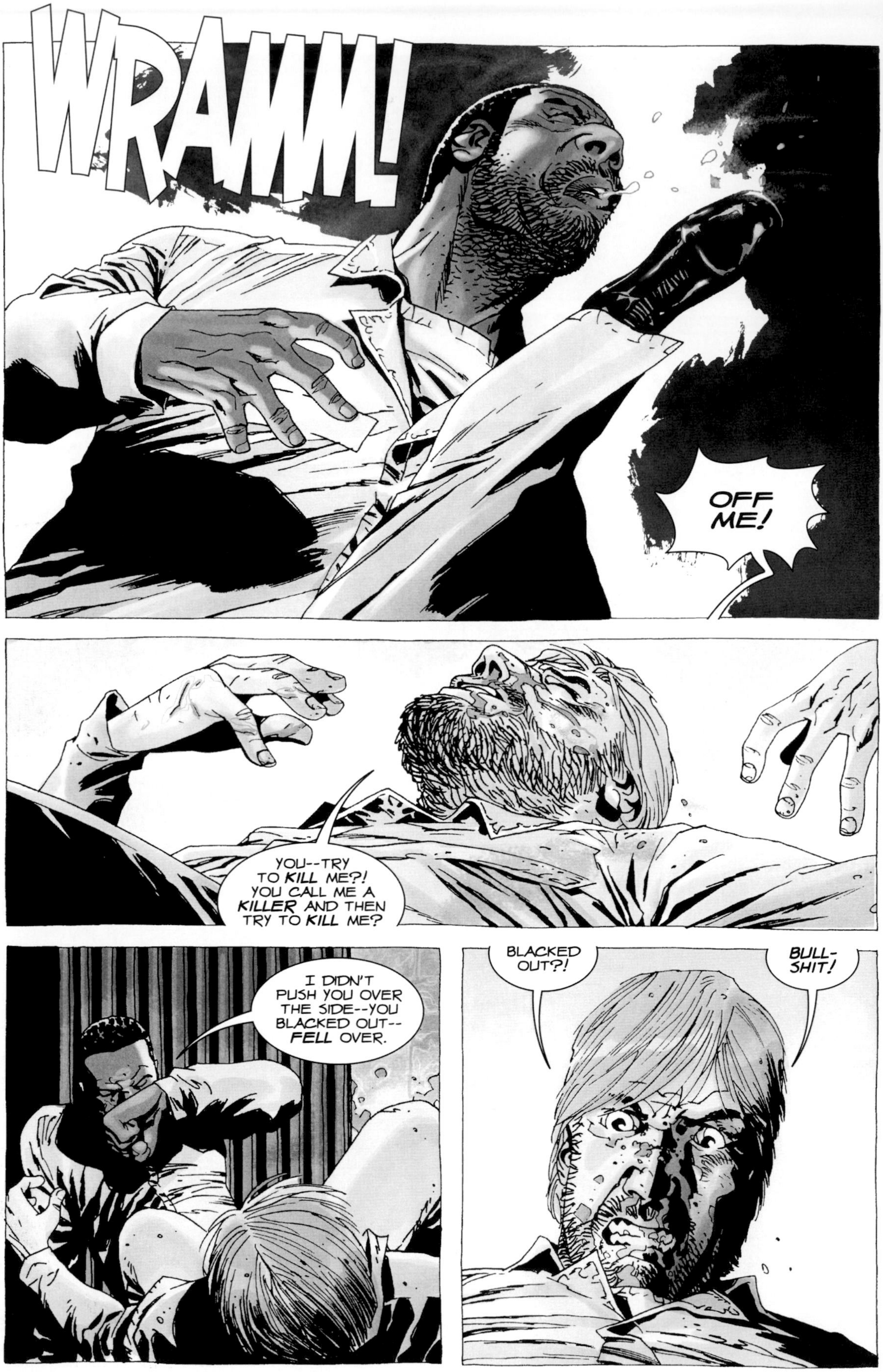
WRAMM!
OFF ME!
YOU--TRY TO KILL ME?! YOU CALL ME A KILLER AND THEN TRY TO KILL ME?
I DIDN'T PUSH YOU OVER THE SIDE--YOU BLACKED OUT-- FELL OVER.
BLACKED OUT?!
BULL-SHIT!

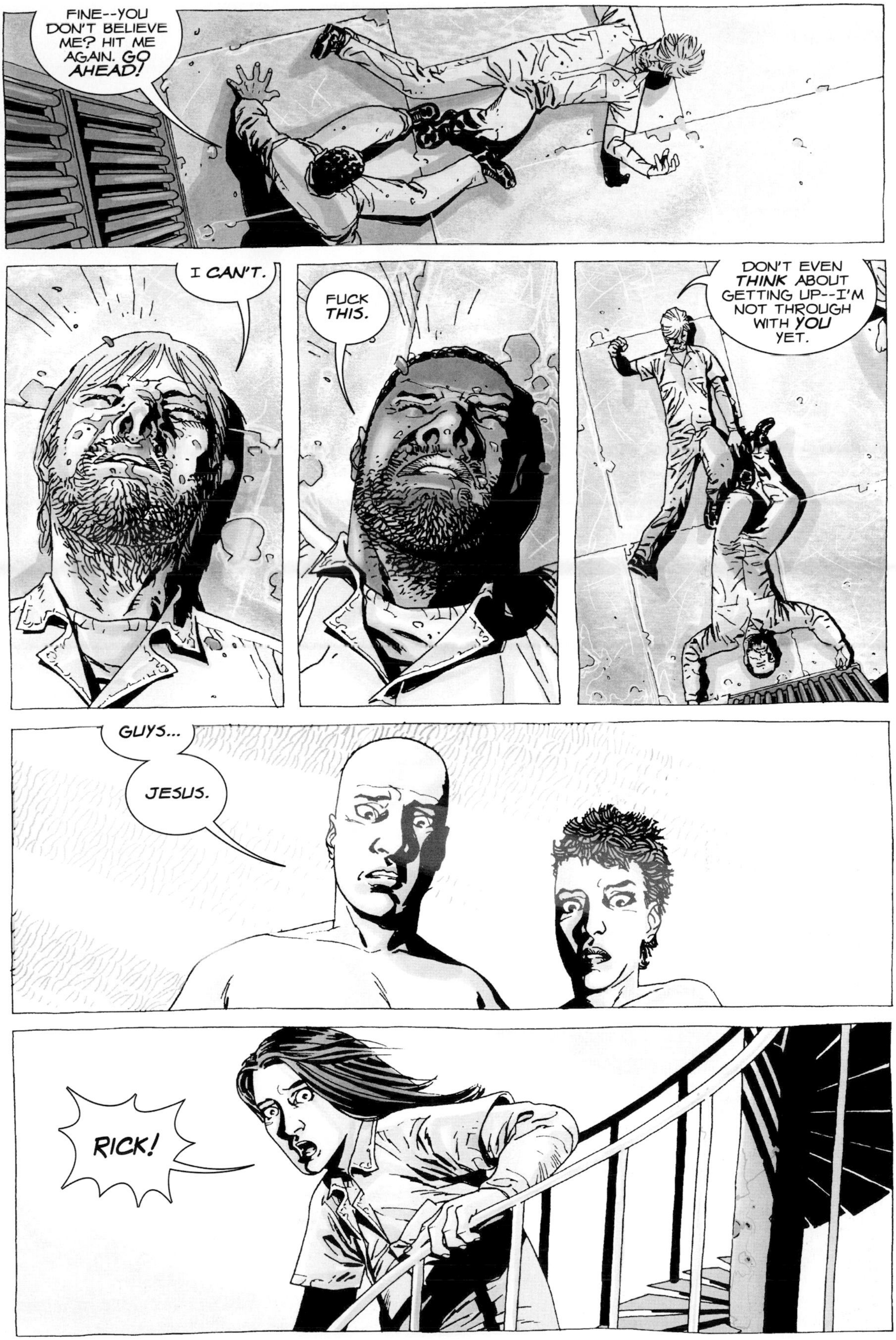
FINE--YOU DON'T BELIEVE ME? HIT ME AGAIN. GO AHEAD!
I CAN'T.
FUCK THIS.
DON'T EVEN THINK ABOUT GETTING UP--I'M NOT THROUGH WITH YOU YET.
GUYS...
JESUS.
RICK!

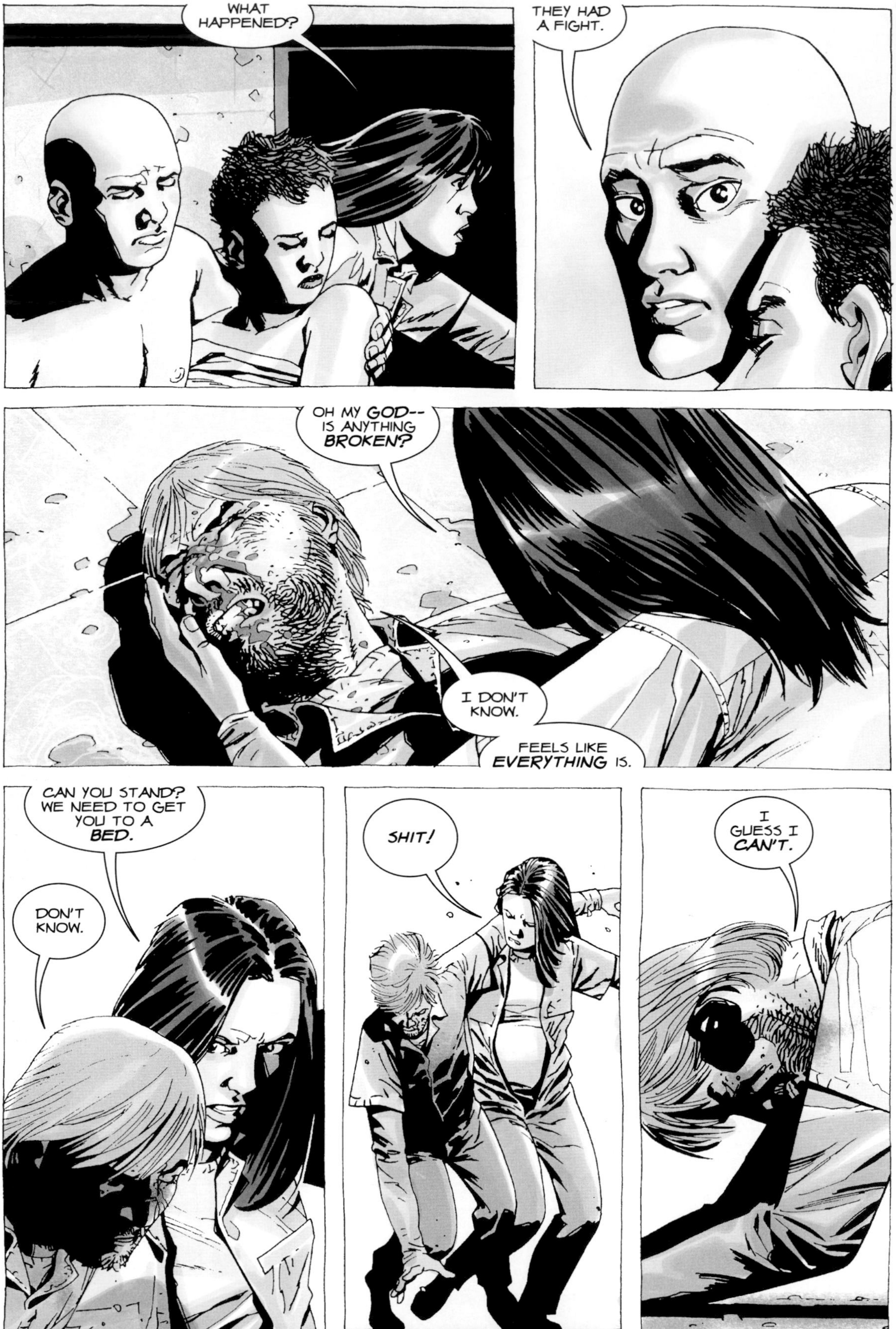
WHAT HAPPENED?
THEY HAD A FIGHT.
OH MY GOD-- IS ANYTHING BROKEN?
I DON'T KNOW.
FEELS LIKE EVERYTHING IS.
CAN YOU STAND? WE NEED TO GET YOU TO A BED.
DON'T KNOW.
SHIT!
I GUESS I CAN'T.

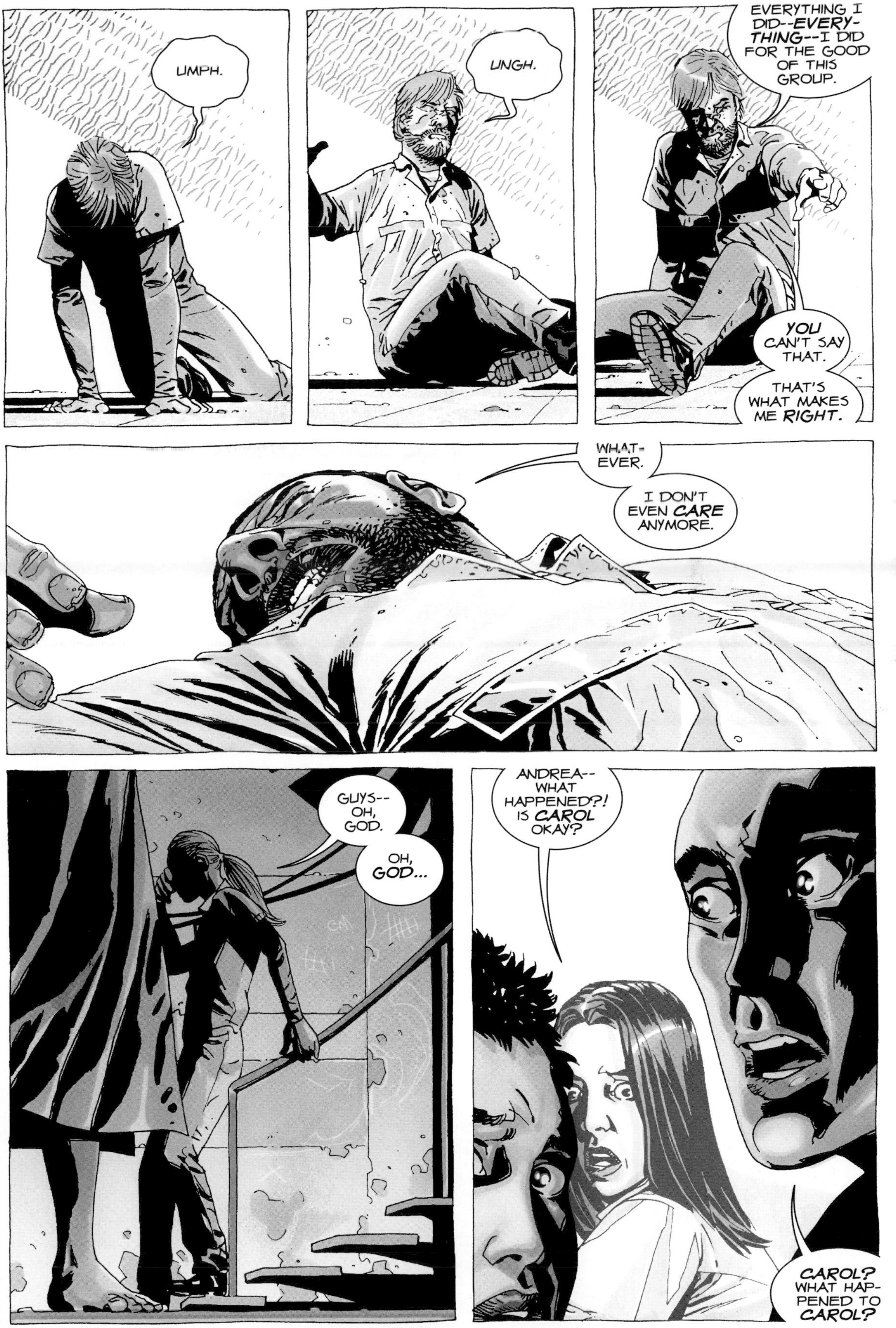
UMPH.
UNGH.
EVERYTHING I DID--EVERY-THING--I DID FOR THE GOOD OF THIS GROUP.
YOU CAN'T SAY THAT.
THAT'S WHAT MAKES ME RIGHT.
WHAT-EVER.
I DON'T EVEN CARE ANYMORE.
GUYS--OH, GOD.
OH, GOD...
ANDREA--WHAT HAPPENED?! IS CAROL OKAY?
CAROL? WHAT HAP-PENED TO CAROL?

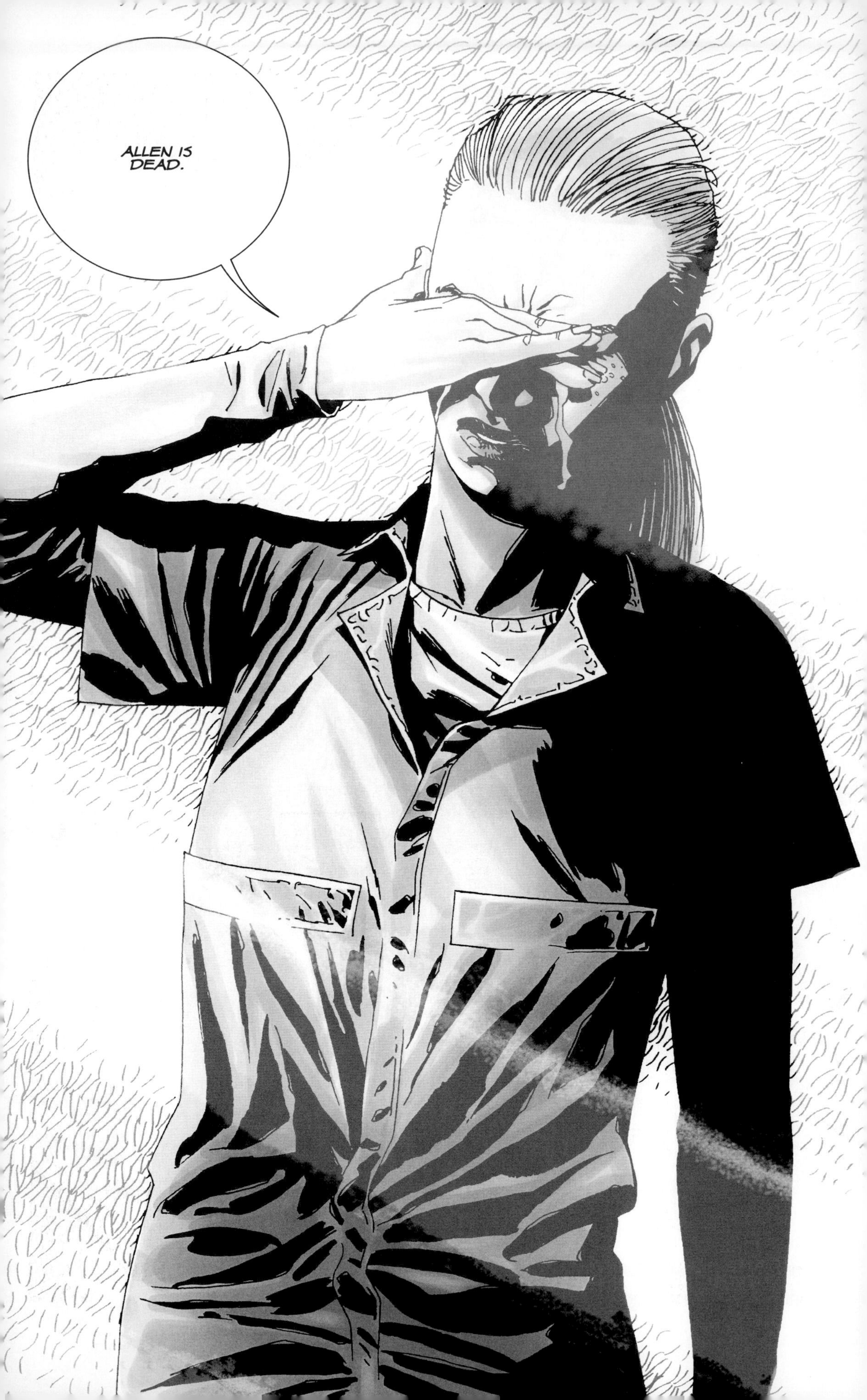
ALLEN IS DEAD.

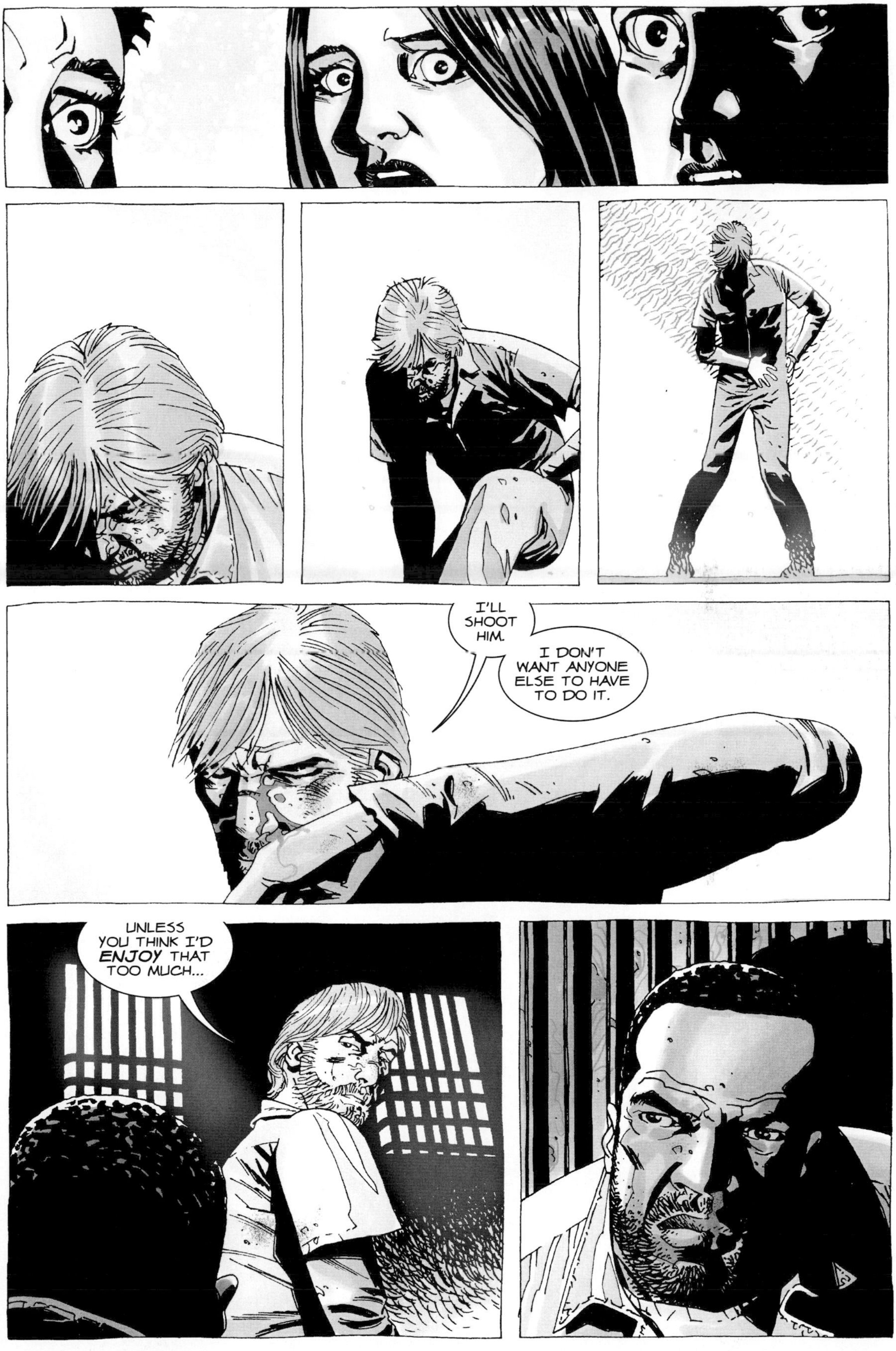
I'LL SHOOT HIM.
I DON'T WANT ANYONE ELSE TO HAVE TO DO IT.
UNLESS YOU THINK I'D ENJOY THAT TOO MUCH...

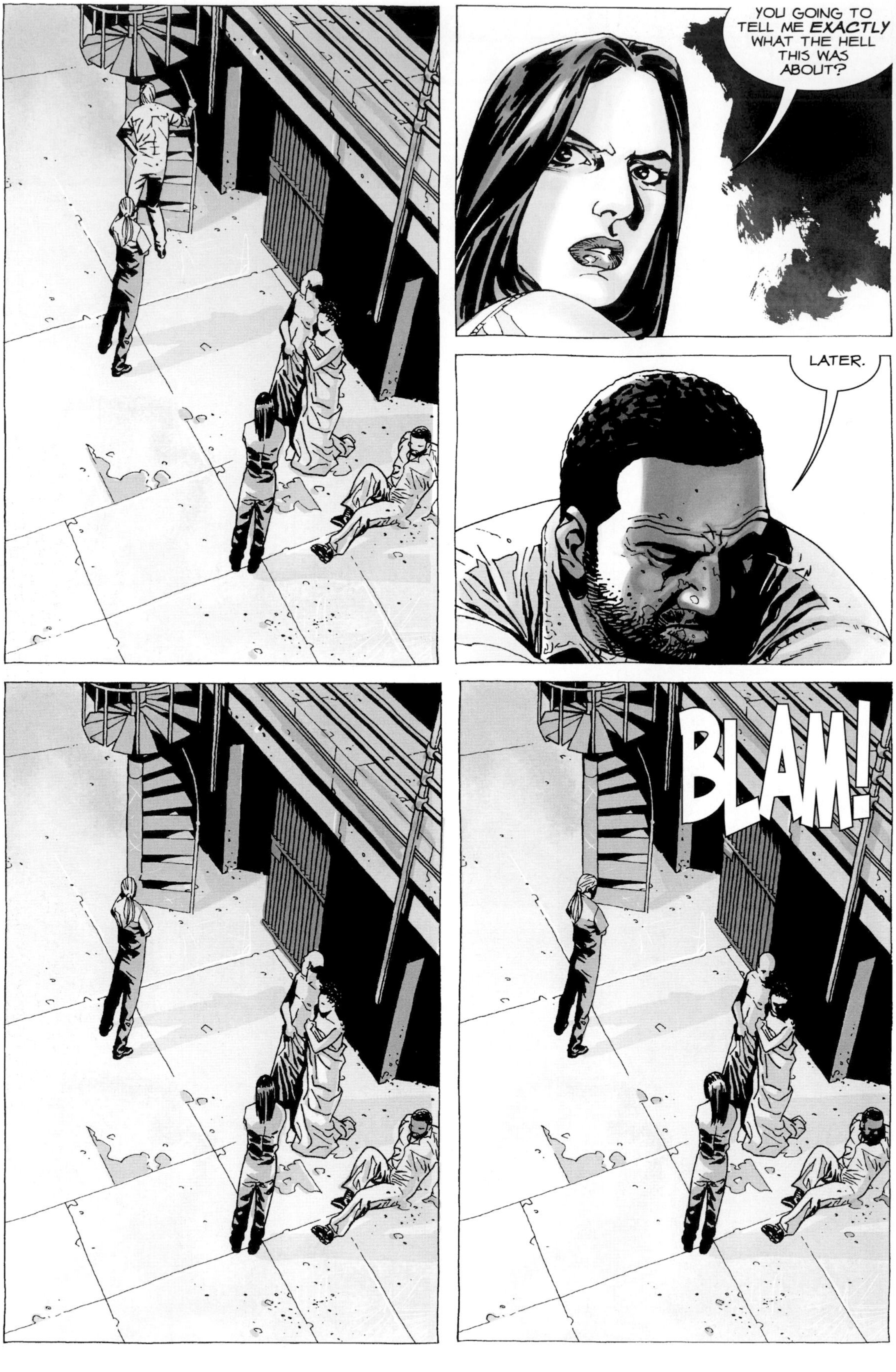
YOU GOING TO TELL ME EXACTLY WHAT THE HELL THIS WAS ABOUT?
LATER.
BLAM!

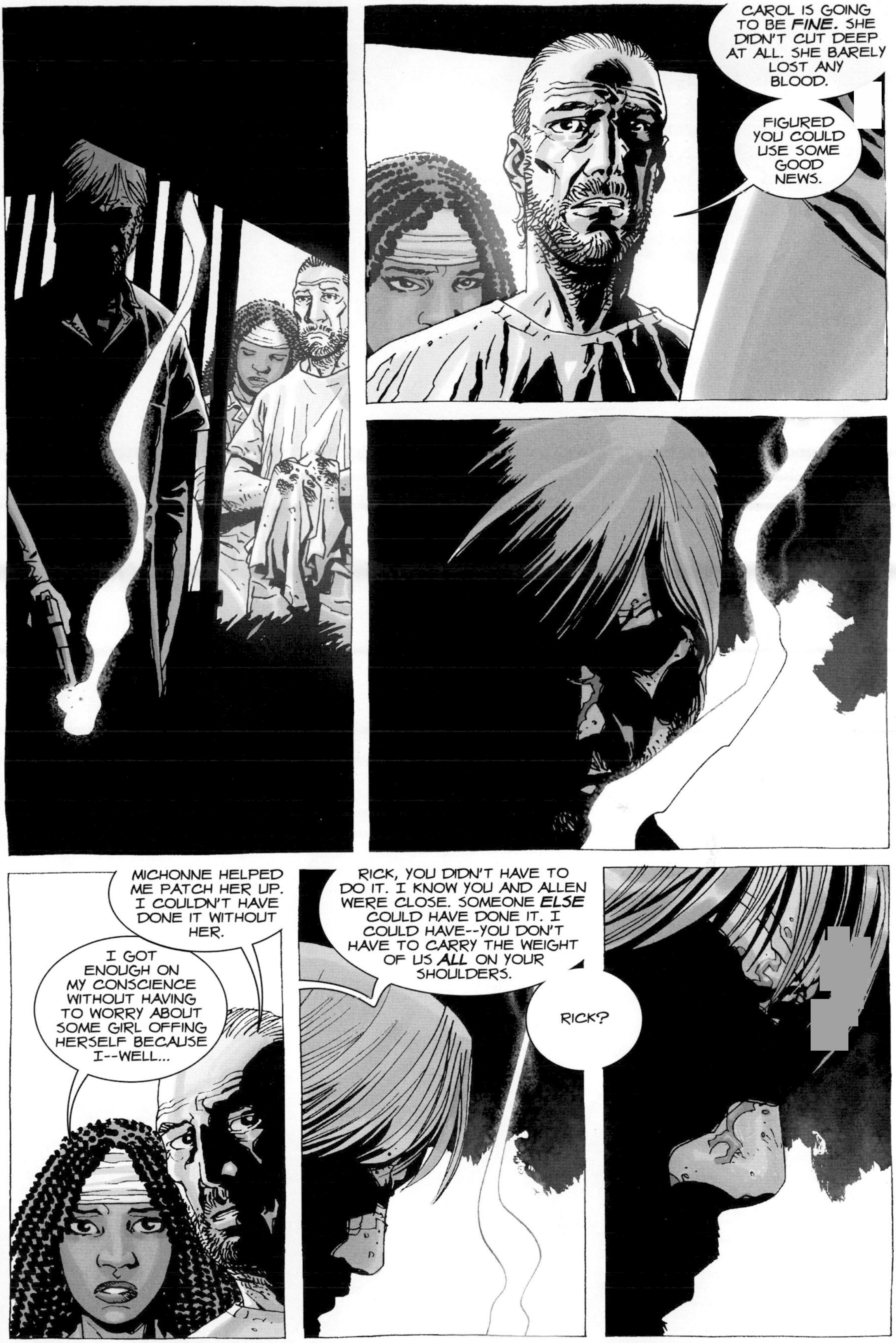
CAROL IS GOING TO BE FINE. SHE DIDN'T CUT DEEP AT ALL. SHE BARELY LOST ANY BLOOD.
FIGURED YOU COULD USE SOME GOOD NEWS.
MICHONNE HELPED ME PATCH HER UP. I COULDN'T HAVE DONE IT WITHOUT HER.
I GOT ENOUGH ON MY CONSCIENCE WITHOUT HAVING TO WORRY ABOUT SOME GIRL OFFING HERSELF BECAUSE I--WELL...
RICK, YOU DIDN'T HAVE TO DO IT. I KNOW YOU AND ALLEN WERE CLOSE. SOMEONE ELSE COULD HAVE DONE IT. I COULD HAVE--YOU DON'T HAVE TO CARRY THE WEIGHT OF US ALL ON YOUR SHOULDERS.
RICK?

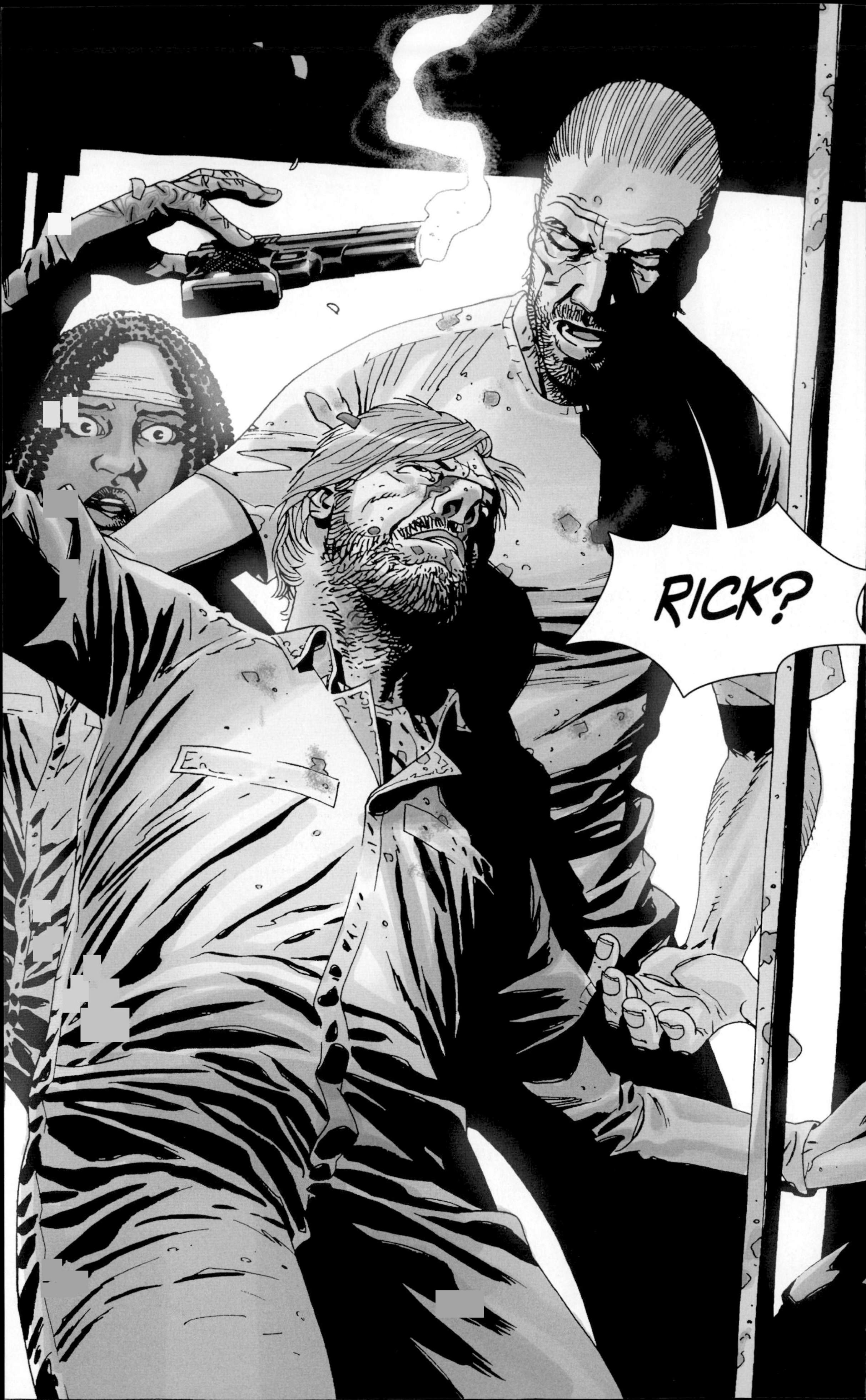
RICK?

RICK?

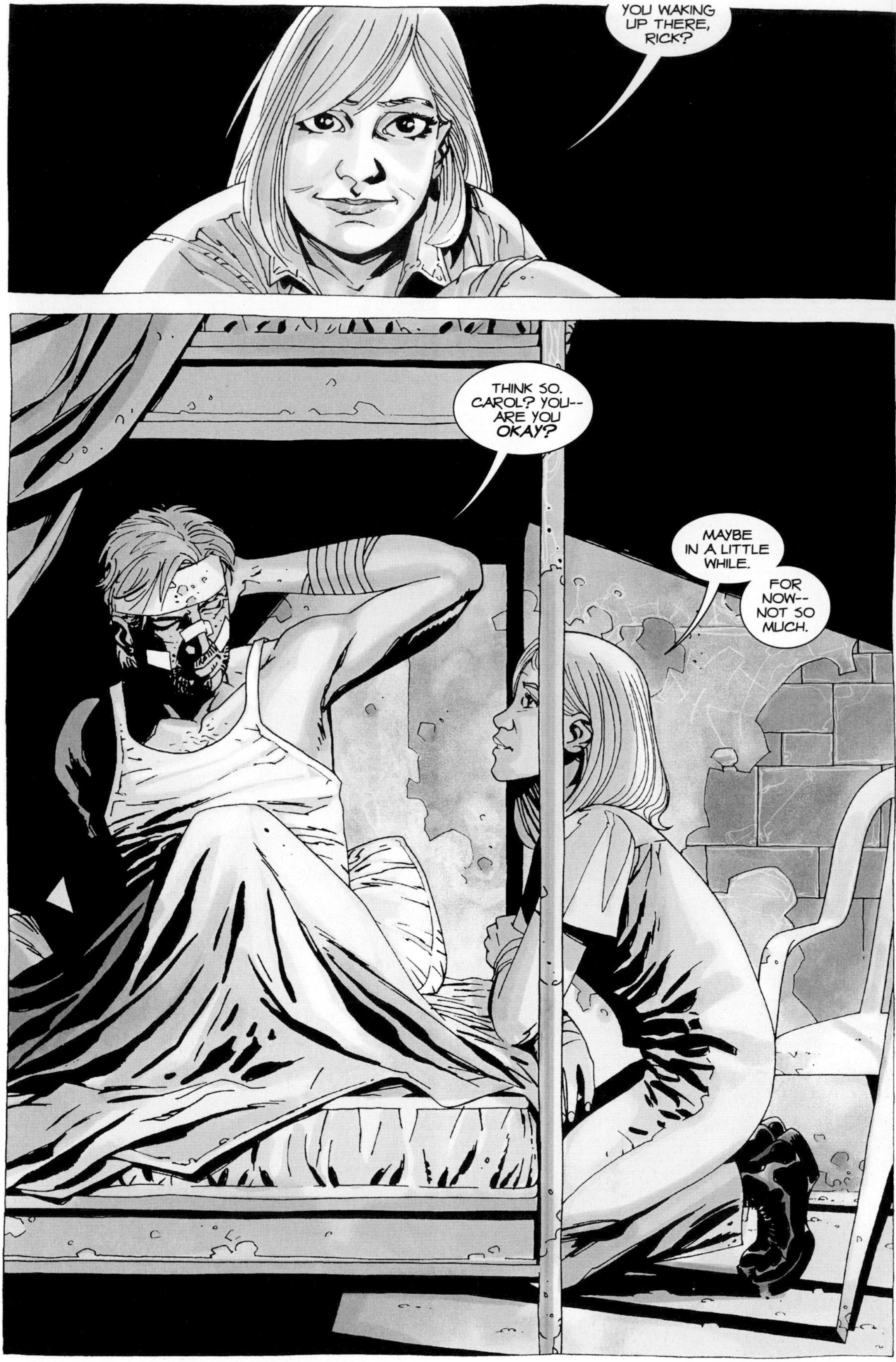
YOU WAKING UP THERE, RICK?
THINK SO. CAROL? YOU-- ARE YOU OKAY?
MAYBE IN A LITTLE WHILE.
FOR NOW-- NOT SO MUCH.

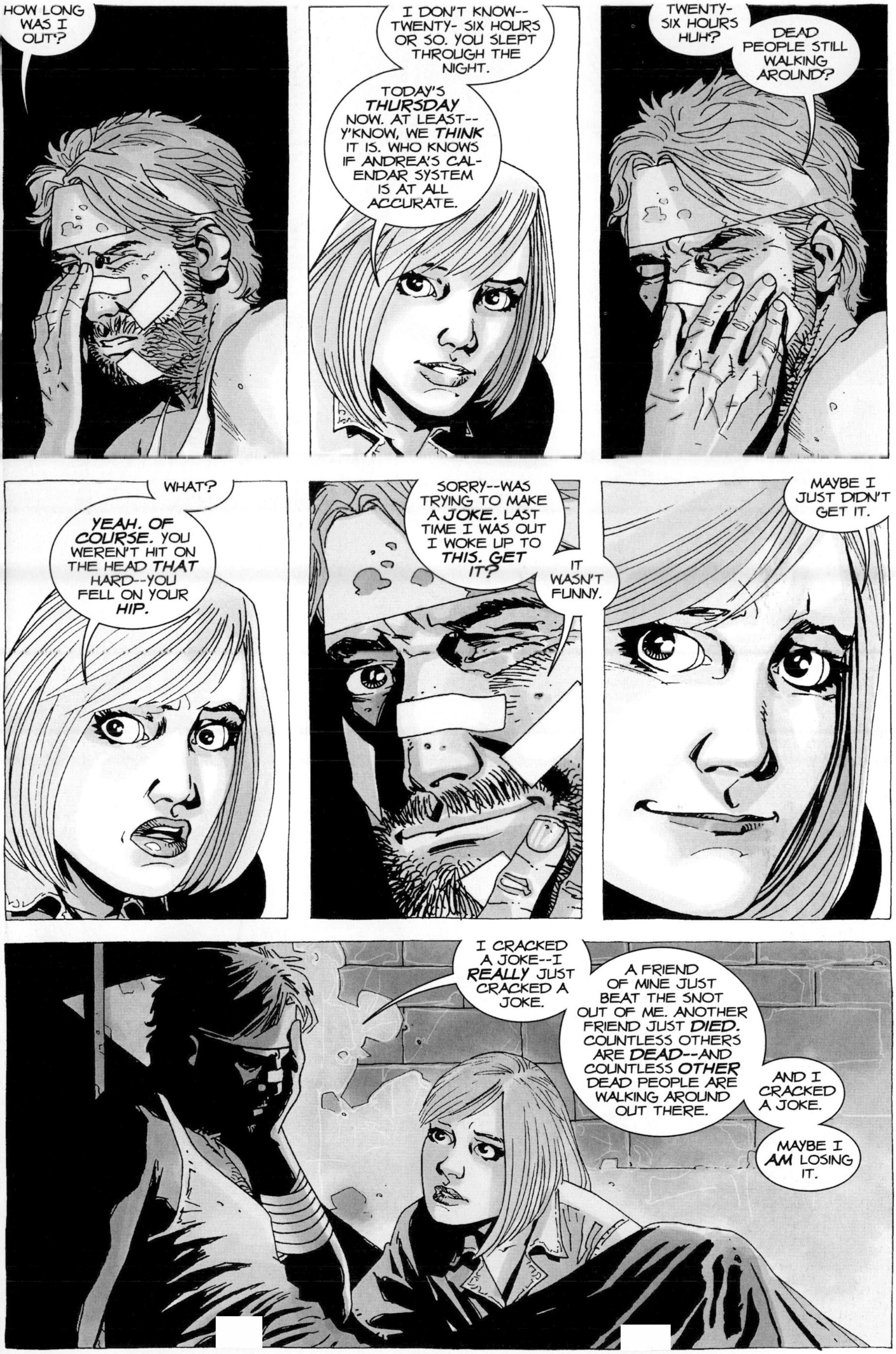
HOW LONG WAS I OUT?
I DON'T KNOW-- TWENTY- SIX HOURS OR SO. YOU SLEPT THROUGH THE NIGHT.
TODAY'S THURSDAY NOW. AT LEAST-- Y'KNOW, WE THINK IT IS. WHO KNOWS IF ANDREA'S CAL- ENDAR SYSTEM IS AT ALL ACCURATE.
TWENTY- SIX HOURS HUH?
DEAD PEOPLE STILL WALKING AROUND?
WHAT?
YEAH. OF COURSE. YOU WEREN'T HIT ON THE HEAD THAT HARD--YOU FELL ON YOUR HIP.
SORRY--WAS TRYING TO MAKE A JOKE. LAST TIME I WAS OUT I WOKE UP TO THIS. GET IT?
IT WASN'T FUNNY.
MAYBE I JUST DIDN'T GET IT.
I CRACKED A JOKE--I REALLY JUST CRACKED A JOKE.
A FRIEND OF MINE JUST BEAT THE SNOT OUT OF ME. ANOTHER FRIEND JUST DIED. COUNTLESS OTHERS ARE DEAD--AND COUNTLESS OTHER DEAD PEOPLE ARE WALKING AROUND OUT THERE.
AND I CRACKED A JOKE.
MAYBE I AM LOSING IT.

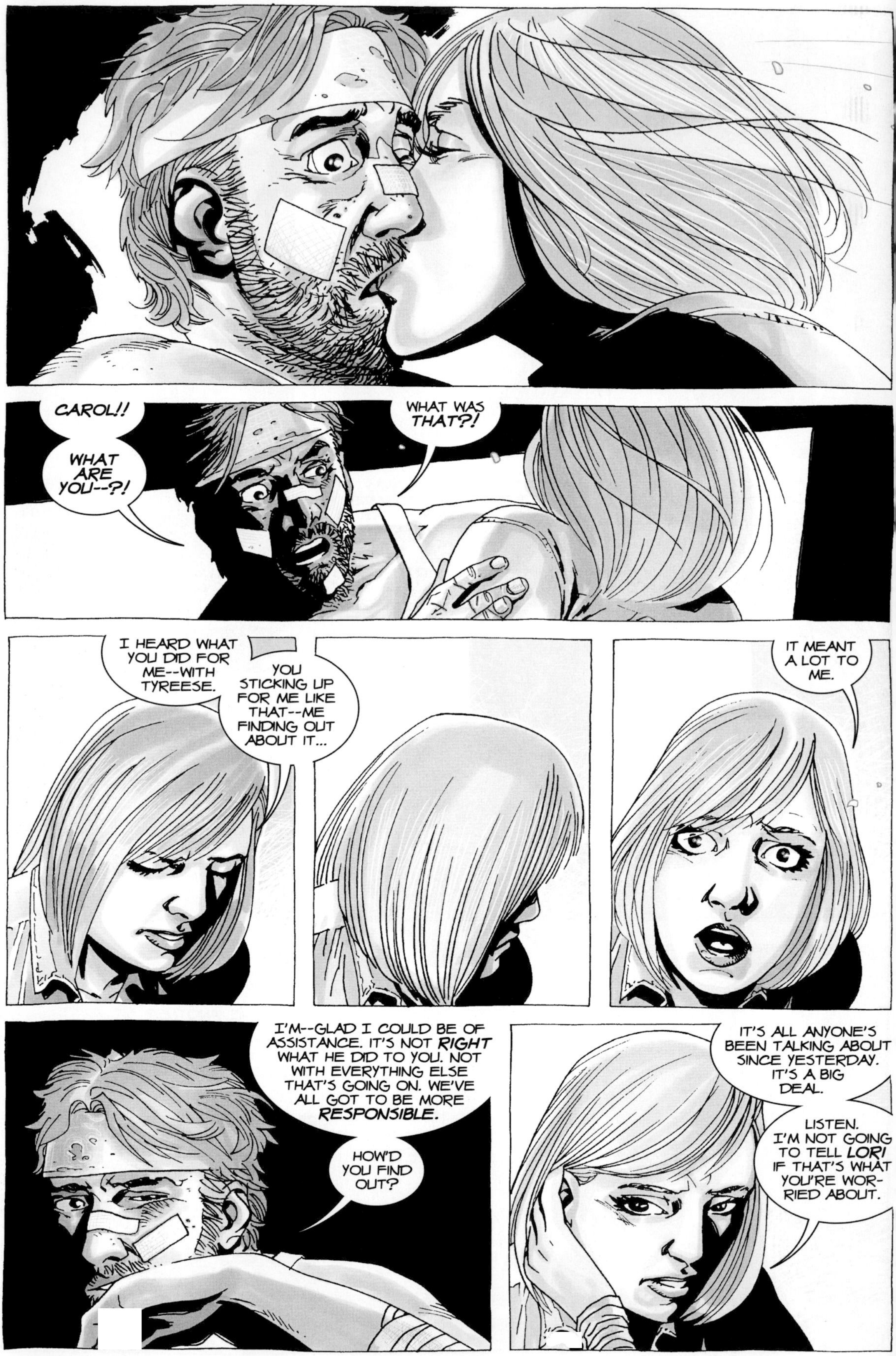
CAROL!!
WHAT ARE YOU--?!
WHAT WAS THAT?!
I HEARD WHAT YOU DID FOR ME--WITH TYREESE.
YOU STICKING UP FOR ME LIKE THAT--ME FINDING OUT ABOUT IT...
IT MEANT A LOT TO ME.
I'M--GLAD I COULD BE OF ASSISTANCE. IT'S NOT RIGHT WHAT HE DID TO YOU. NOT WITH EVERYTHING ELSE THAT'S GOING ON. WE'VE ALL GOT TO BE MORE RESPONSIBLE.
HOW'D YOU FIND OUT?
IT'S ALL ANYONE'S BEEN TALKING ABOUT SINCE YESTERDAY. IT'S A BIG DEAL.
LISTEN. I'M NOT GOING TO TELL LORI IF THAT'S WHAT YOU'RE WORRIED ABOUT.

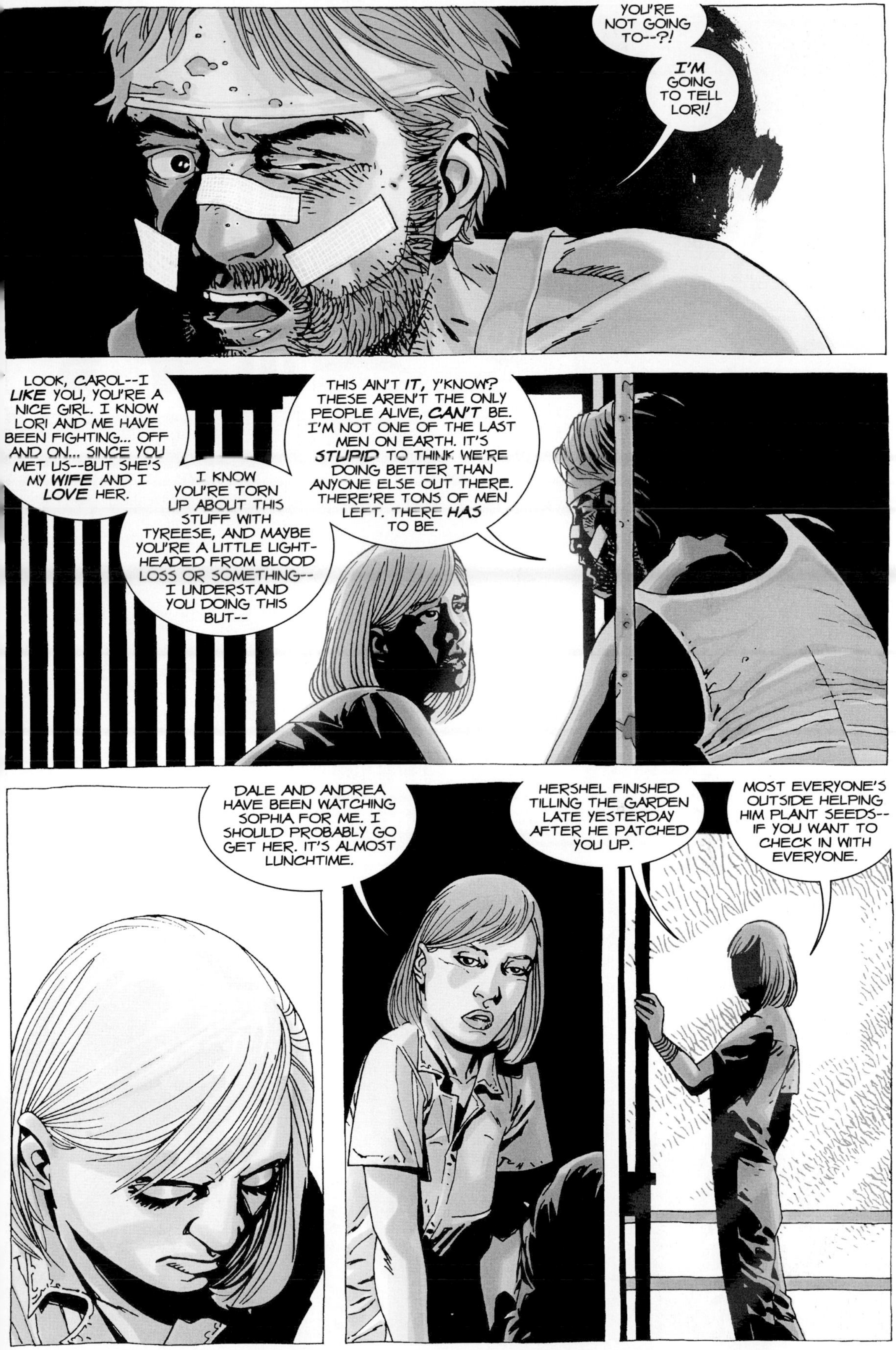
YOU'RE NOT GOING TO--?!
I'M GOING TO TELL LORI!
LOOK, CAROL--I LIKE YOU, YOU'RE A NICE GIRL. I KNOW LORI AND ME HAVE BEEN FIGHTING... OFF AND ON... SINCE YOU MET US--BUT SHE'S MY WIFE AND I LOVE HER.
I KNOW YOU'RE TORN UP ABOUT THIS STUFF WITH TYREESE, AND MAYBE YOU'RE A LITTLE LIGHT-HEADED FROM BLOOD LOSS OR SOMETHING-- I UNDERSTAND YOU DOING THIS BUT--
THIS AIN'T IT, Y'KNOW? THESE AREN'T THE ONLY PEOPLE ALIVE, CAN'T BE. I'M NOT ONE OF THE LAST MEN ON EARTH. IT'S STUPID TO THINK WE'RE DOING BETTER THAN ANYONE ELSE OUT THERE. THERE'RE TONS OF MEN LEFT. THERE HAS TO BE.
DALE AND ANDREA HAVE BEEN WATCHING SOPHIA FOR ME. I SHOULD PROBABLY GO GET HER. IT'S ALMOST LUNCHTIME.
HERSHEL FINISHED TILLING THE GARDEN LATE YESTERDAY AFTER HE PATCHED YOU UP.
MOST EVERYONE'S OUTSIDE HELPING HIM PLANT SEEDS-- IF YOU WANT TO CHECK IN WITH EVERYONE.

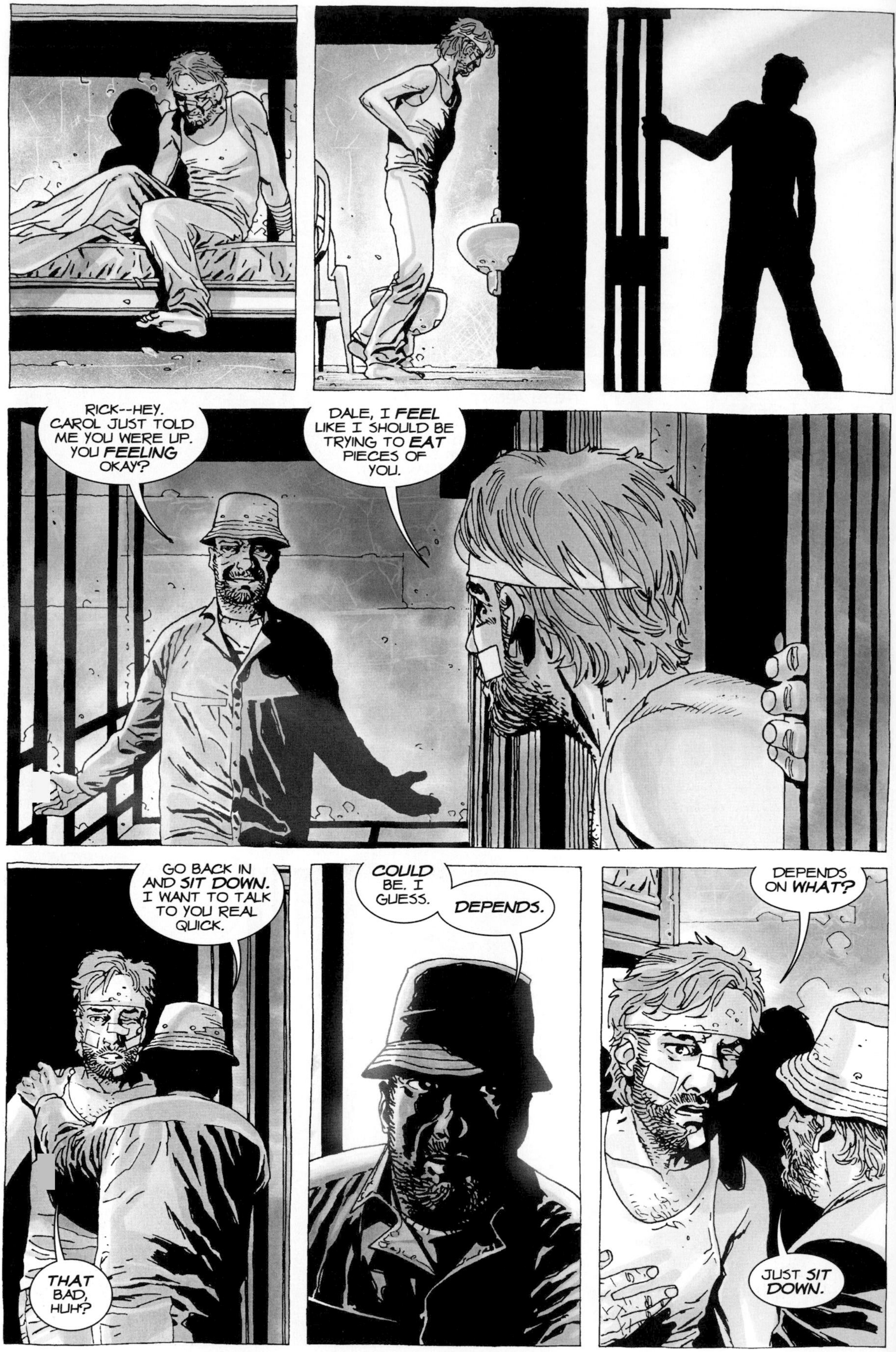
RICK--HEY. CAROL JUST TOLD ME YOU WERE UP. YOU FEELING OKAY?
DALE, I FEEL LIKE I SHOULD BE TRYING TO EAT PIECES OF YOU.
GO BACK IN AND SIT DOWN. I WANT TO TALK TO YOU REAL QUICK.
THAT BAD, HUH?
COULD BE. I GUESS.
DEPENDS.
DEPENDS ON WHAT?
JUST SIT DOWN.

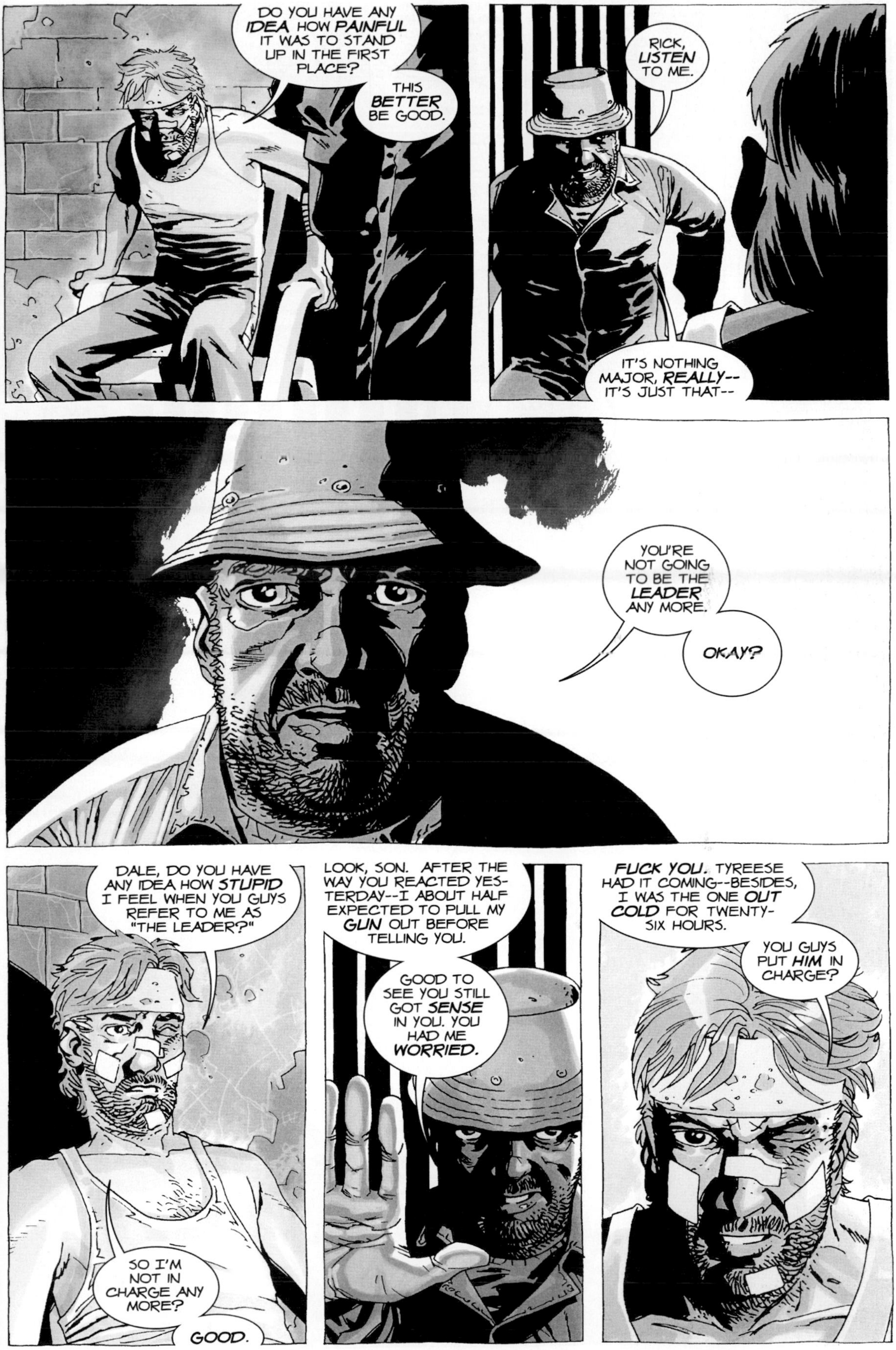
DO YOU HAVE ANY IDEA HOW PAINFUL IT WAS TO STAND UP IN THE FIRST PLACE?
THIS BETTER BE GOOD.
RICK, LISTEN TO ME.
IT'S NOTHING MAJOR, REALLY-- IT'S JUST THAT--
YOU'RE NOT GOING TO BE THE LEADER ANY MORE.
OKAY?
DALE, DO YOU HAVE ANY IDEA HOW STUPID I FEEL WHEN YOU GUYS REFER TO ME AS "THE LEADER?"
SO I'M NOT IN CHARGE ANY MORE?
GOOD.
LOOK, SON. AFTER THE WAY YOU REACTED YES-TERDAY--I ABOUT HALF EXPECTED TO PULL MY GUN OUT BEFORE TELLING YOU.
GOOD TO SEE YOU STILL GOT SENSE IN YOU. YOU HAD ME WORRIED.
FUCK YOU. TYREESE HAD IT COMING--BESIDES, I WAS THE ONE OUT COLD FOR TWENTY-SIX HOURS.
YOU GUYS PUT HIM IN CHARGE?

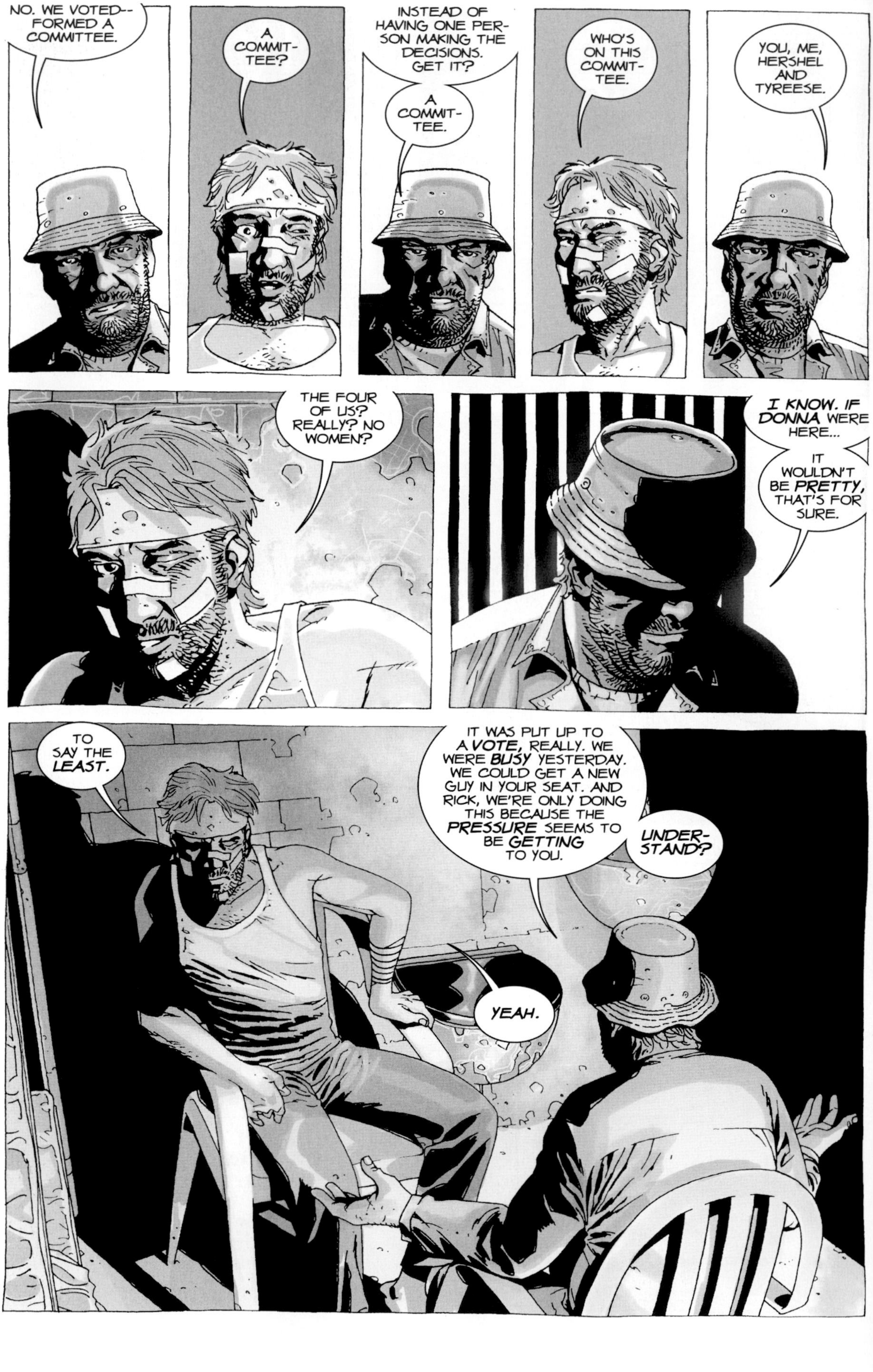

NO. WE VOTED-- FORMED A COMMITTEE.
A COMMITTEE?
INSTEAD OF HAVING ONE PERSON MAKING THE DECISIONS. GET IT?
A COMMITTEE.
WHO'S ON THIS COMMITTEE.
YOU, ME, HERSHEL AND TYREESE.
THE FOUR OF US? REALLY? NO WOMEN?
I KNOW. IF DONNA WERE HERE...
IT WOULDN'T BE PRETTY, THAT'S FOR SURE.
TO SAY THE LEAST.
IT WAS PUT UP TO A VOTE, REALLY. WE WERE BUSY YESTERDAY. WE COULD GET A NEW GUY IN YOUR SEAT. AND RICK, WE'RE ONLY DOING THIS BECAUSE THE PRESSURE SEEMS TO BE GETTING TO YOU.
UNDERSTAND?
YEAH.

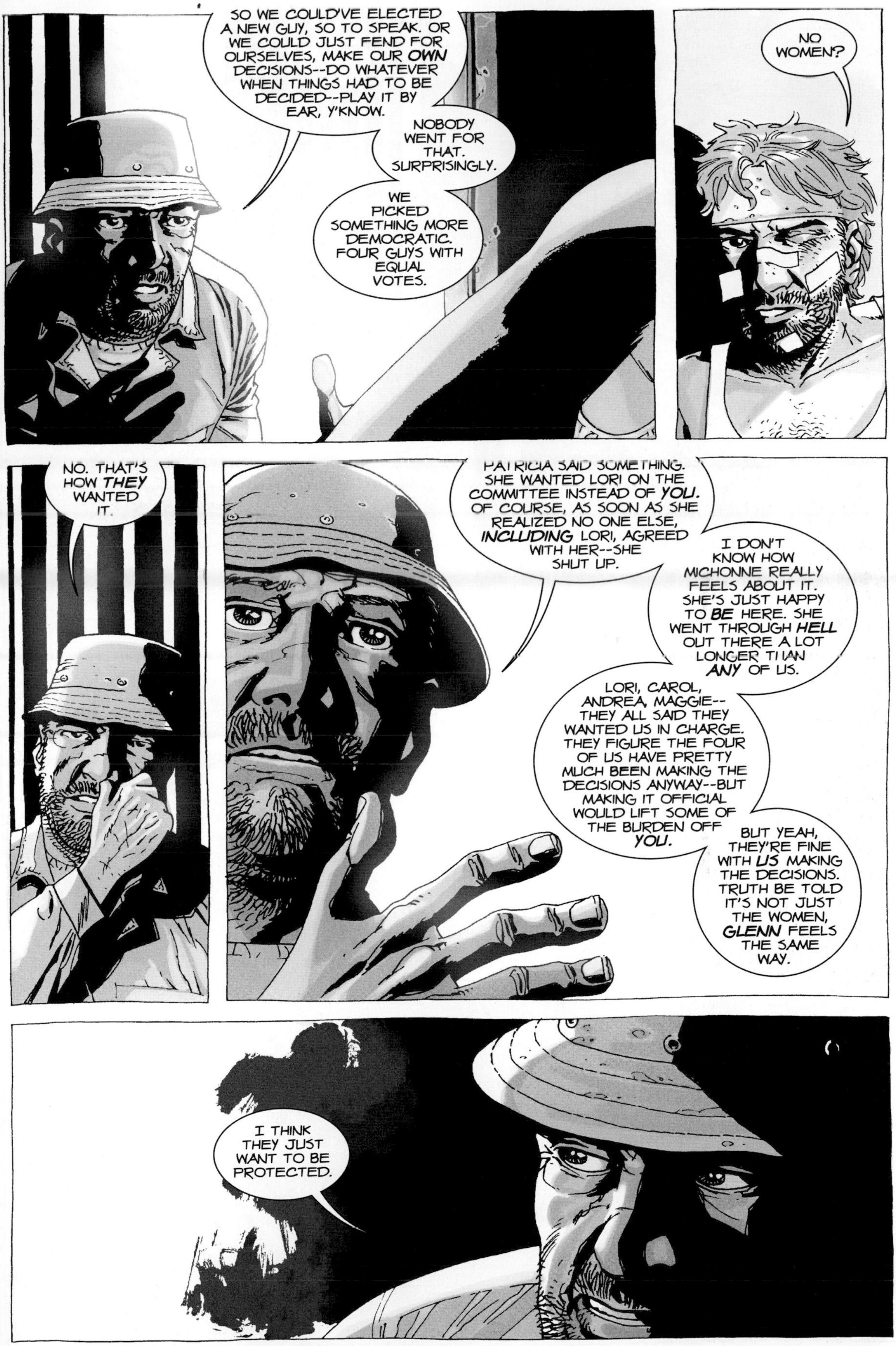
SO WE COULD'VE ELECTED A NEW GUY, SO TO SPEAK. OR WE COULD JUST FEND FOR OURSELVES, MAKE OUR OWN DECISIONS--DO WHATEVER WHEN THINGS HAD TO BE DECIDED--PLAY IT BY EAR, Y'KNOW.
NOBODY WENT FOR THAT. SURPRISINGLY.
WE PICKED SOMETHING MORE DEMOCRATIC. FOUR GUYS WITH EQUAL VOTES.
NO WOMEN?
NO. THAT'S HOW THEY WANTED IT.
PATRICIA SAID SOMETHING. SHE WANTED LORI ON THE COMMITTEE INSTEAD OF YOU. OF COURSE, AS SOON AS SHE REALIZED NO ONE ELSE, INCLUDING LORI, AGREED WITH HER--SHE SHUT UP.
I DON'T KNOW HOW MICHONNE REALLY FEELS ABOUT IT. SHE'S JUST HAPPY TO BE HERE. SHE WENT THROUGH HELL OUT THERE A LOT LONGER THAN ANY OF US.
LORI, CAROL, ANDREA, MAGGIE-- THEY ALL SAID THEY WANTED US IN CHARGE. THEY FIGURE THE FOUR OF US HAVE PRETTY MUCH BEEN MAKING THE DECISIONS ANYWAY--BUT MAKING IT OFFICIAL WOULD LIFT SOME OF THE BURDEN OFF YOU.
BUT YEAH, THEY'RE FINE WITH US MAKING THE DECISIONS. TRUTH BE TOLD IT'S NOT JUST THE WOMEN, GLENN FEELS THE SAME WAY.
I THINK THEY JUST WANT TO BE PROTECTED.

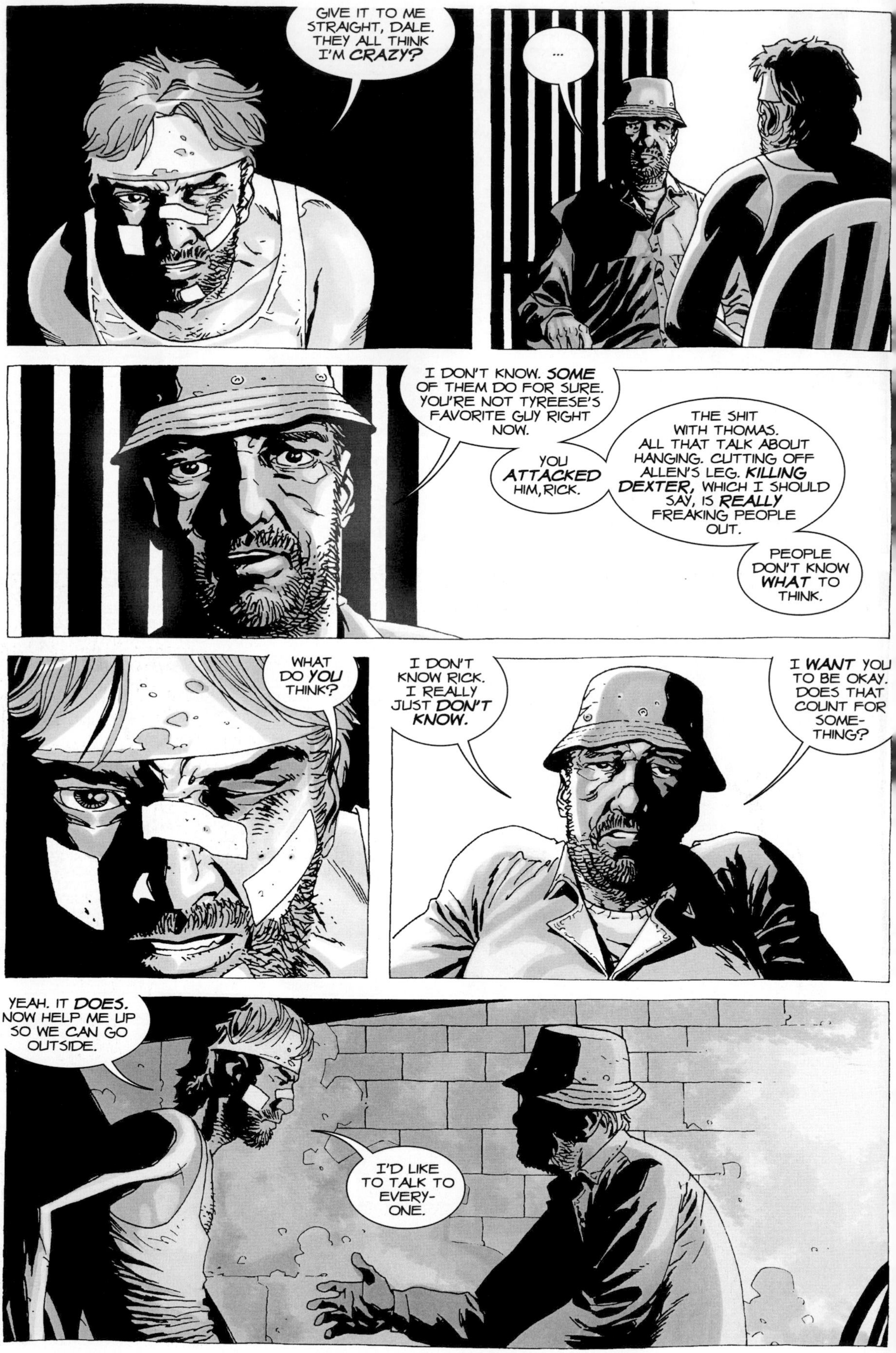
GIVE IT TO ME STRAIGHT, DALE. THEY ALL THINK I'M CRAZY?
...
I DON'T KNOW. SOME OF THEM DO FOR SURE. YOU'RE NOT TYREESE'S FAVORITE GUY RIGHT NOW.
YOU ATTACKED HIM, RICK.
THE SHIT WITH THOMAS. ALL THAT TALK ABOUT HANGING. CUTTING OFF ALLEN'S LEG. KILLING DEXTER, WHICH I SHOULD SAY, IS REALLY FREAKING PEOPLE OUT.
PEOPLE DON'T KNOW WHAT TO THINK.
WHAT DO YOU THINK?
I DON'T KNOW RICK. I REALLY JUST DON'T KNOW.
I WANT YOU TO BE OKAY. DOES THAT COUNT FOR SOME-THING?
YEAH. IT DOES. NOW HELP ME UP SO WE CAN GO OUTSIDE.
I'D LIKE TO TALK TO EVERY-ONE.

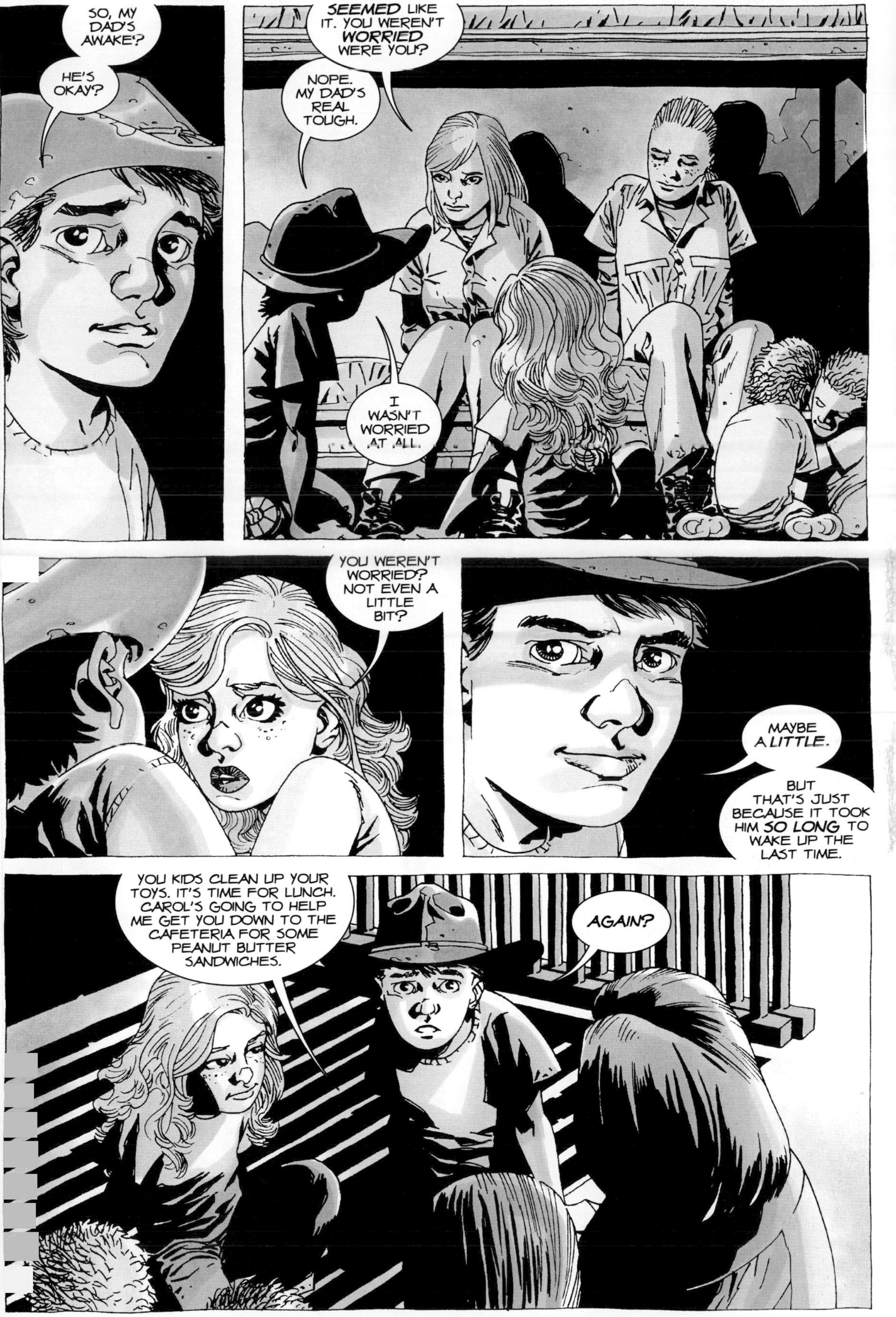
SO, MY DAD'S AWAKE?
HE'S OKAY?
SEEMED LIKE IT. YOU WEREN'T WORRIED WERE YOU?
NOPE. MY DAD'S REAL TOUGH.
I WASN'T WORRIED AT ALL.
YOU WEREN'T WORRIED? NOT EVEN A LITTLE BIT?
MAYBE A LITTLE.
BUT THAT'S JUST BECAUSE IT TOOK HIM SO LONG TO WAKE UP THE LAST TIME.
YOU KIDS CLEAN UP YOUR TOYS. IT'S TIME FOR LUNCH. CAROL'S GOING TO HELP ME GET YOU DOWN TO THE CAFETERIA FOR SOME PEANUT BUTTER SANDWICHES.
AGAIN?

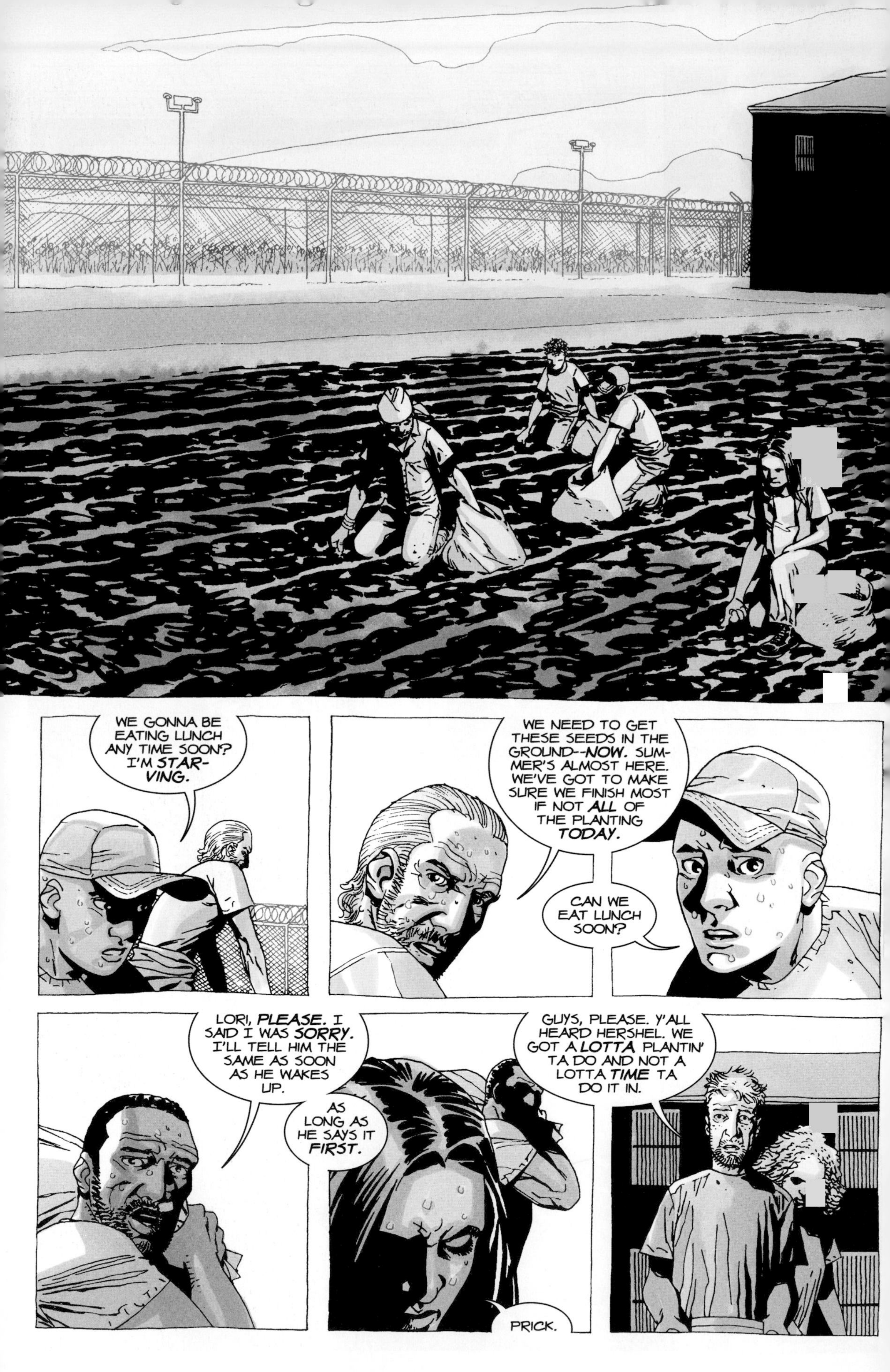
WE GONNA BE EATING LUNCH ANY TIME SOON? I'M STAR-VING.
WE NEED TO GET THESE SEEDS IN THE GROUND--NOW. SUMMER'S ALMOST HERE. WE'VE GOT TO MAKE SURE WE FINISH MOST IF NOT ALL OF THE PLANTING TODAY.
CAN WE EAT LUNCH SOON?
LORI, PLEASE. I SAID I WAS SORRY. I'LL TELL HIM THE SAME AS SOON AS HE WAKES UP.
AS LONG AS HE SAYS IT FIRST.
PRICK.
GUYS, PLEASE. Y'ALL HEARD HERSHEL. WE GOT A LOTTA PLANTIN' TA DO AND NOT A LOTTA TIME TA DO IT IN.

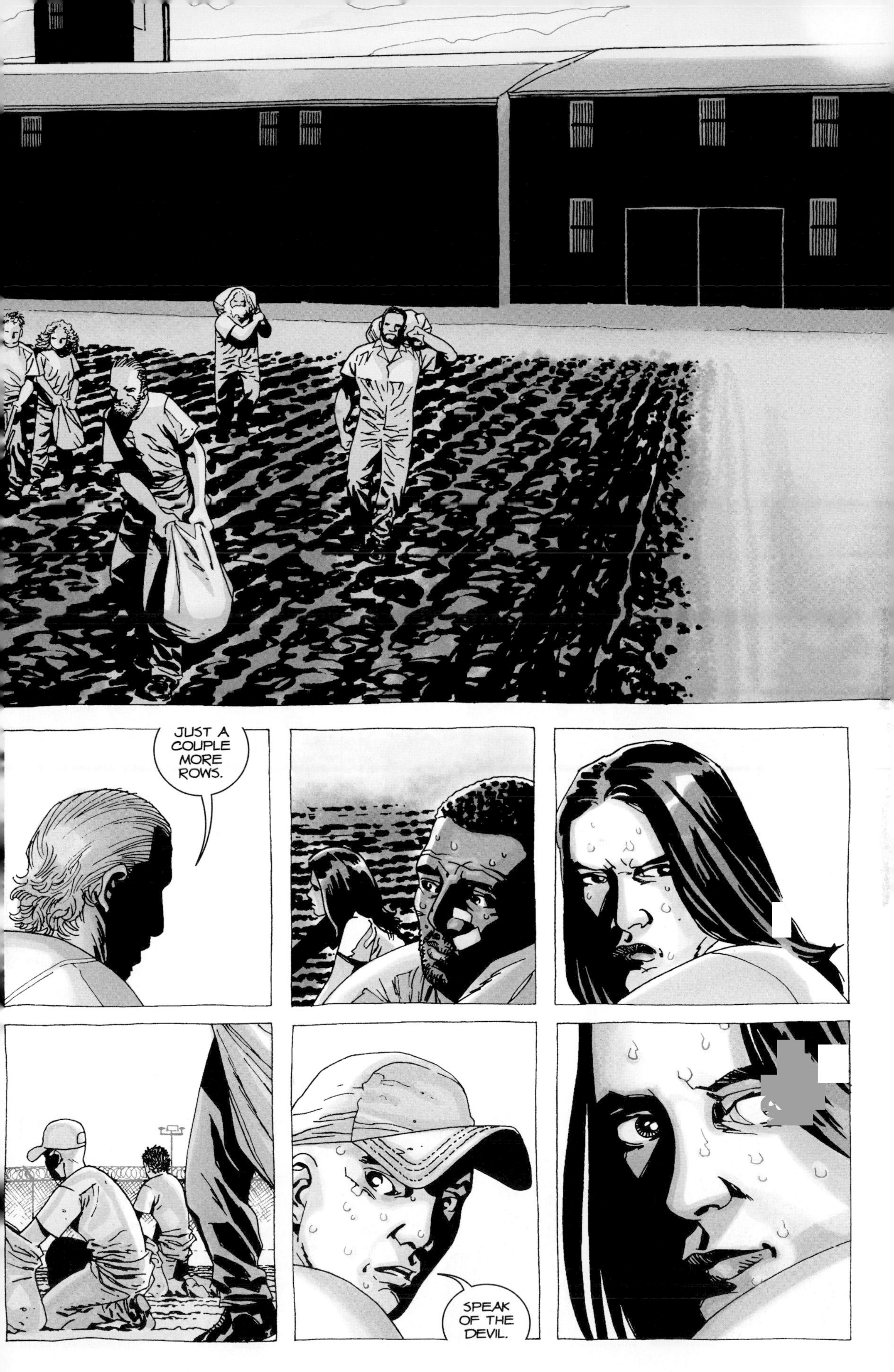
JUST A COUPLE MORE ROWS.
SPEAK OF THE DEVIL.

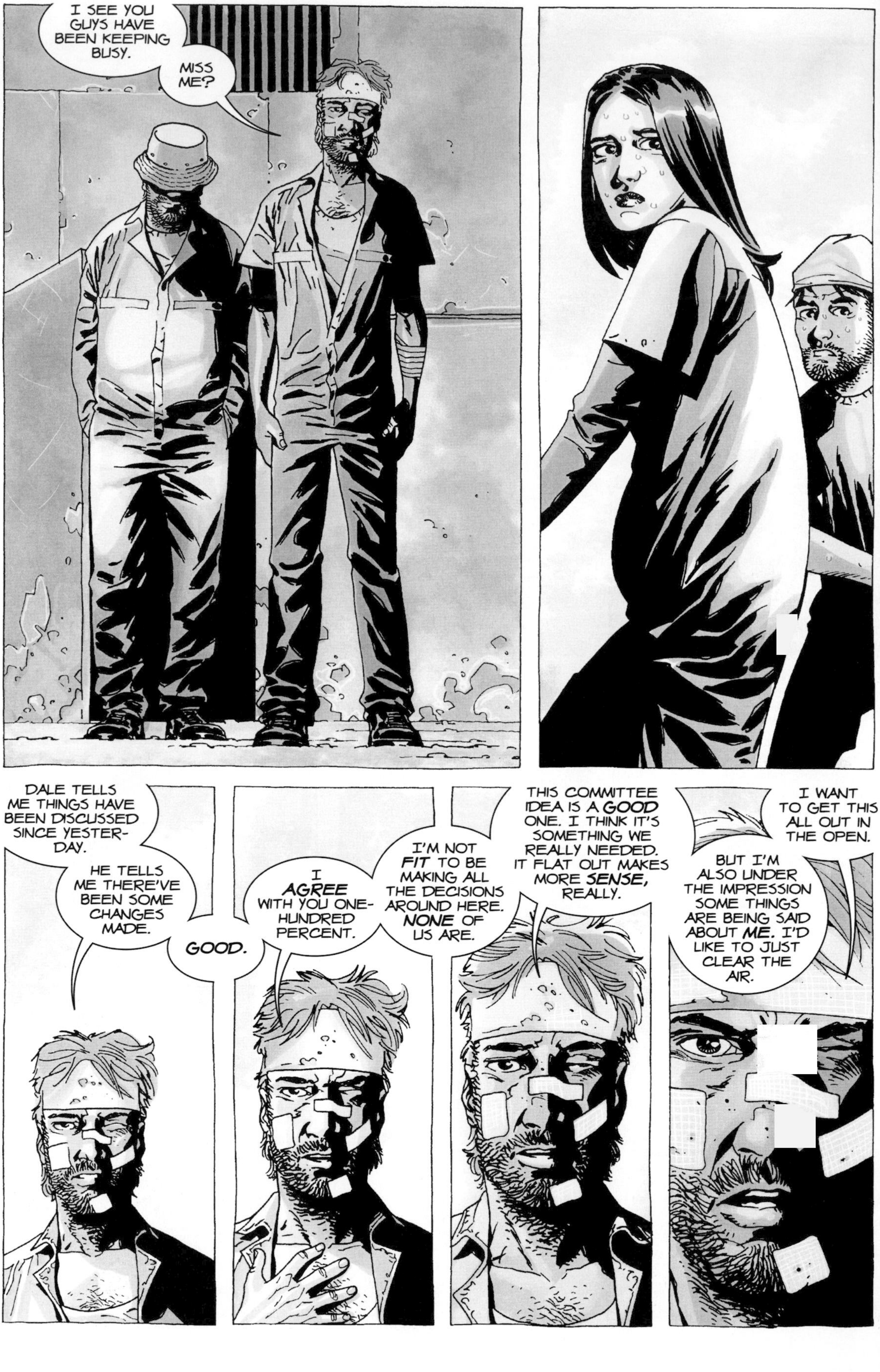
I SEE YOU GUYS HAVE BEEN KEEPING BUSY.
MISS ME?
DALE TELLS ME THINGS HAVE BEEN DISCUSSED SINCE YESTER-DAY.
HE TELLS ME THERE'VE BEEN SOME CHANGES MADE.
GOOD.
I AGREE WITH YOU ONE-HUNDRED PERCENT.
I'M NOT FIT TO BE MAKING ALL THE DECISIONS AROUND HERE. NONE OF US ARE.
THIS COMMITTEE IDEA IS A GOOD ONE. I THINK IT'S SOMETHING WE REALLY NEEDED. IT FLAT OUT MAKES MORE SENSE, REALLY.
I WANT TO GET THIS ALL OUT IN THE OPEN.
BUT I'M ALSO UNDER THE IMPRESSION SOME THINGS ARE BEING SAID ABOUT ME. I'D LIKE TO JUST CLEAR THE AIR.

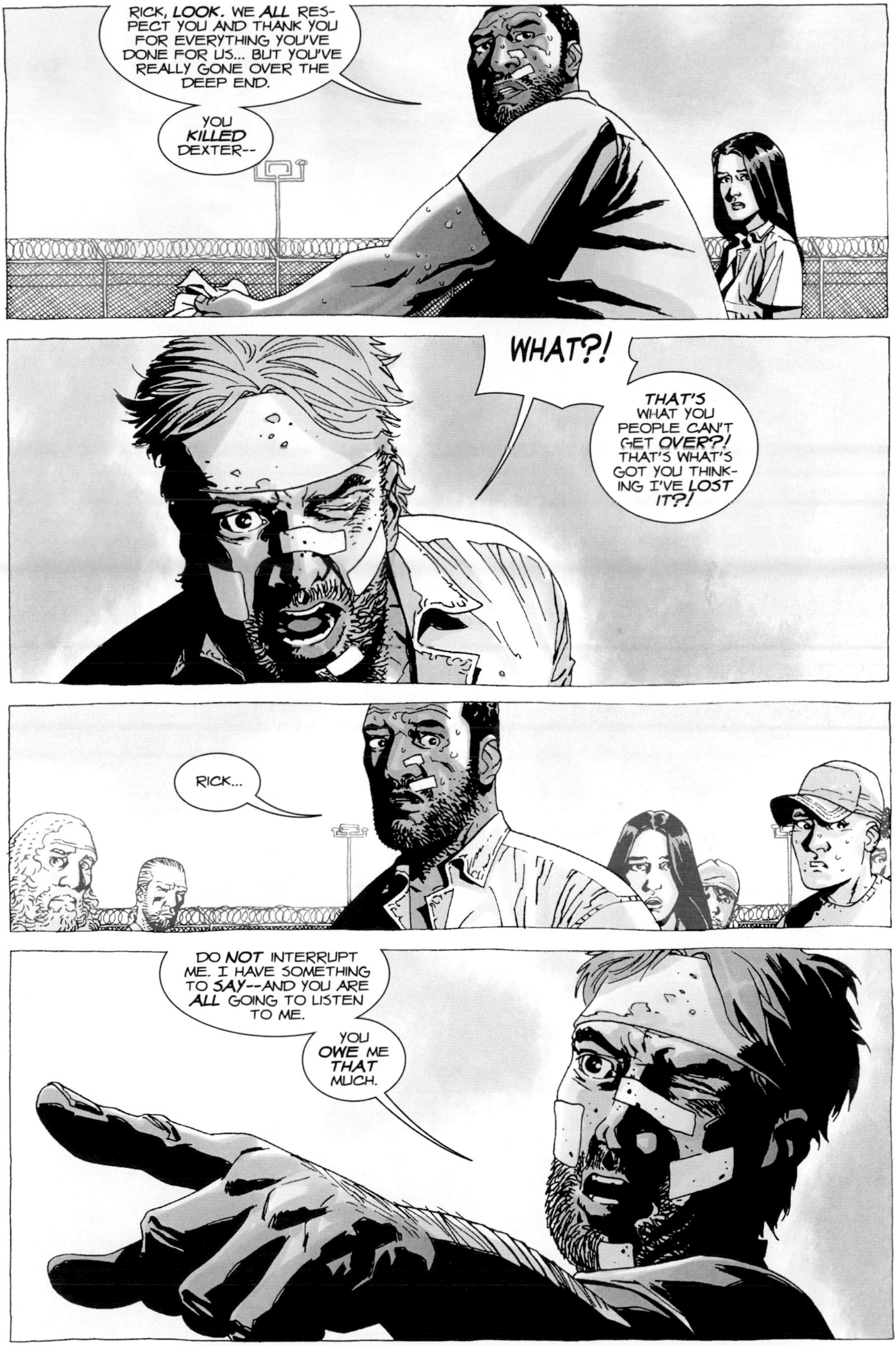
RICK, LOOK. WE ALL RESPECT YOU AND THANK YOU FOR EVERYTHING YOU'VE DONE FOR US... BUT YOU'VE REALLY GONE OVER THE DEEP END.
YOU KILLED DEXTER--
WHAT?!
THAT'S WHAT YOU PEOPLE CAN'T GET OVER?! THAT'S WHAT'S GOT YOU THINKING I'VE LOST IT?!
RICK...
DO NOT INTERRUPT ME. I HAVE SOMETHING TO SAY--AND YOU ARE ALL GOING TO LISTEN TO ME.
YOU OWE ME THAT MUCH.

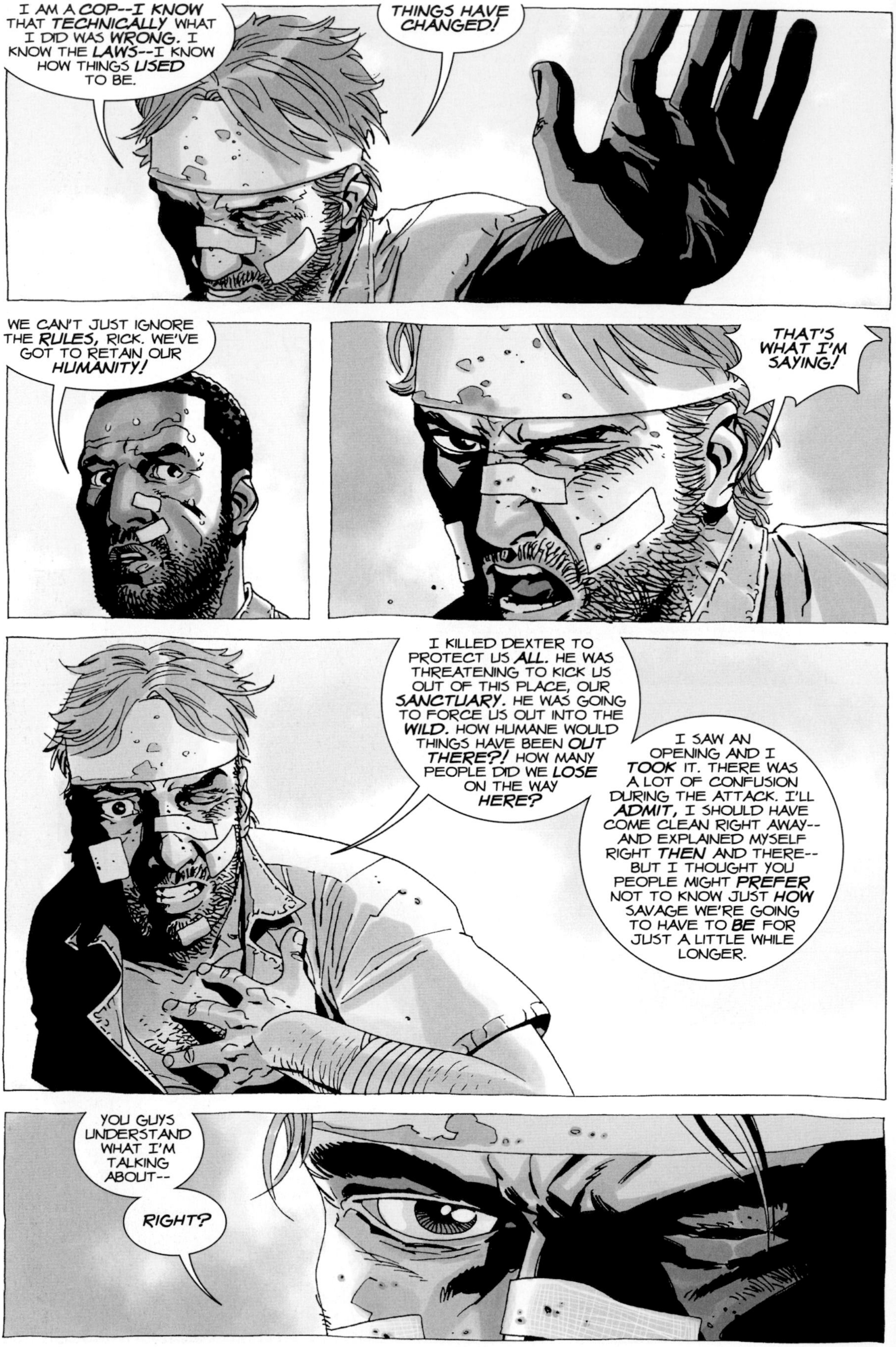
I AM A COP--I KNOW THAT TECHNICALLY WHAT I DID WAS WRONG. I KNOW THE LAWS--I KNOW HOW THINGS USED TO BE.
THINGS HAVE CHANGED!
WE CAN'T JUST IGNORE THE RULES, RICK. WE'VE GOT TO RETAIN OUR HUMANITY!
THAT'S WHAT I'M SAYING!
I KILLED DEXTER TO PROTECT US ALL. HE WAS THREATENING TO KICK US OUT OF THIS PLACE, OUR SANCTUARY. HE WAS GOING TO FORCE US OUT INTO THE WILD. HOW HUMANE WOULD THINGS HAVE BEEN OUT THERE?! HOW MANY PEOPLE DID WE LOSE ON THE WAY HERE?
I SAW AN OPENING AND I TOOK IT. THERE WAS A LOT OF CONFUSION DURING THE ATTACK. I'LL ADMIT, I SHOULD HAVE COME CLEAN RIGHT AWAY--AND EXPLAINED MYSELF RIGHT THEN AND THERE--BUT I THOUGHT YOU PEOPLE MIGHT PREFER NOT TO KNOW JUST HOW SAVAGE WE'RE GOING TO HAVE TO BE FOR JUST A LITTLE WHILE LONGER.
YOU GUYS UNDERSTAND WHAT I'M TALKING ABOUT--
RIGHT?

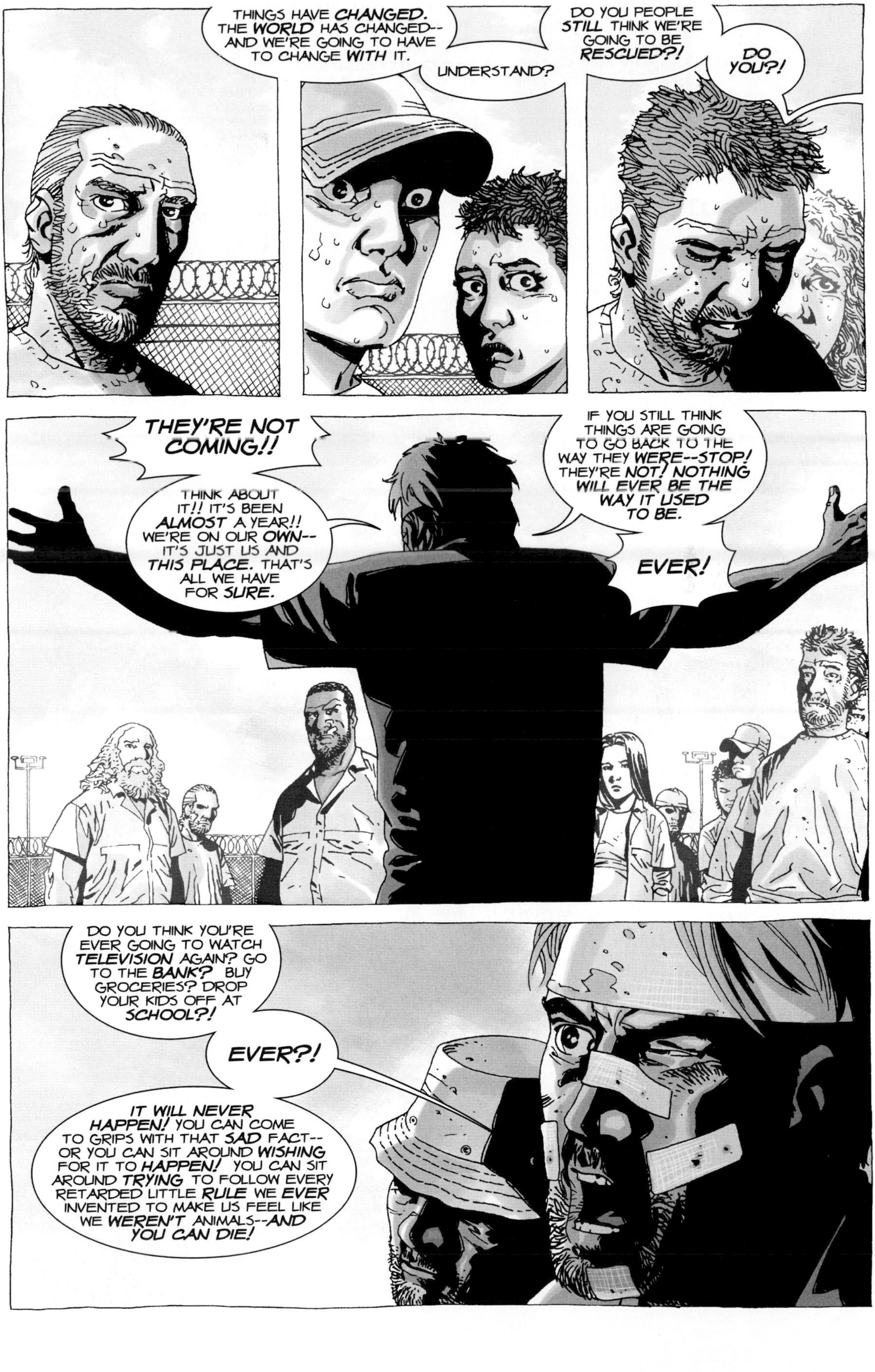
THINGS HAVE CHANGED. THE WORLD HAS CHANGED-- AND WE'RE GOING TO HAVE TO CHANGE WITH IT.
UNDERSTAND?
DO YOU PEOPLE STILL THINK WE'RE GOING TO BE RESCUED?!
DO YOU?!
THEY'RE NOT COMING!!
THINK ABOUT IT!! IT'S BEEN ALMOST A YEAR!! WE'RE ON OUR OWN-- IT'S JUST US AND THIS PLACE. THAT'S ALL WE HAVE FOR SURE.
IF YOU STILL THINK THINGS ARE GOING TO GO BACK TO THE WAY THEY WERE--STOP! THEY'RE NOT! NOTHING WILL EVER BE THE WAY IT USED TO BE.
EVER!
DO YOU THINK YOU'RE EVER GOING TO WATCH TELEVISION AGAIN? GO TO THE BANK? BUY GROCERIES? DROP YOUR KIDS OFF AT SCHOOL?!
EVER?!
IT WILL NEVER HAPPEN! YOU CAN COME TO GRIPS WITH THAT SAD FACT-- OR YOU CAN SIT AROUND WISHING FOR IT TO HAPPEN! YOU CAN SIT AROUND TRYING TO FOLLOW EVERY RETARDED LITTLE RULE WE EVER INVENTED TO MAKE US FEEL LIKE WE WEREN'T ANIMALS--AND YOU CAN DIE!

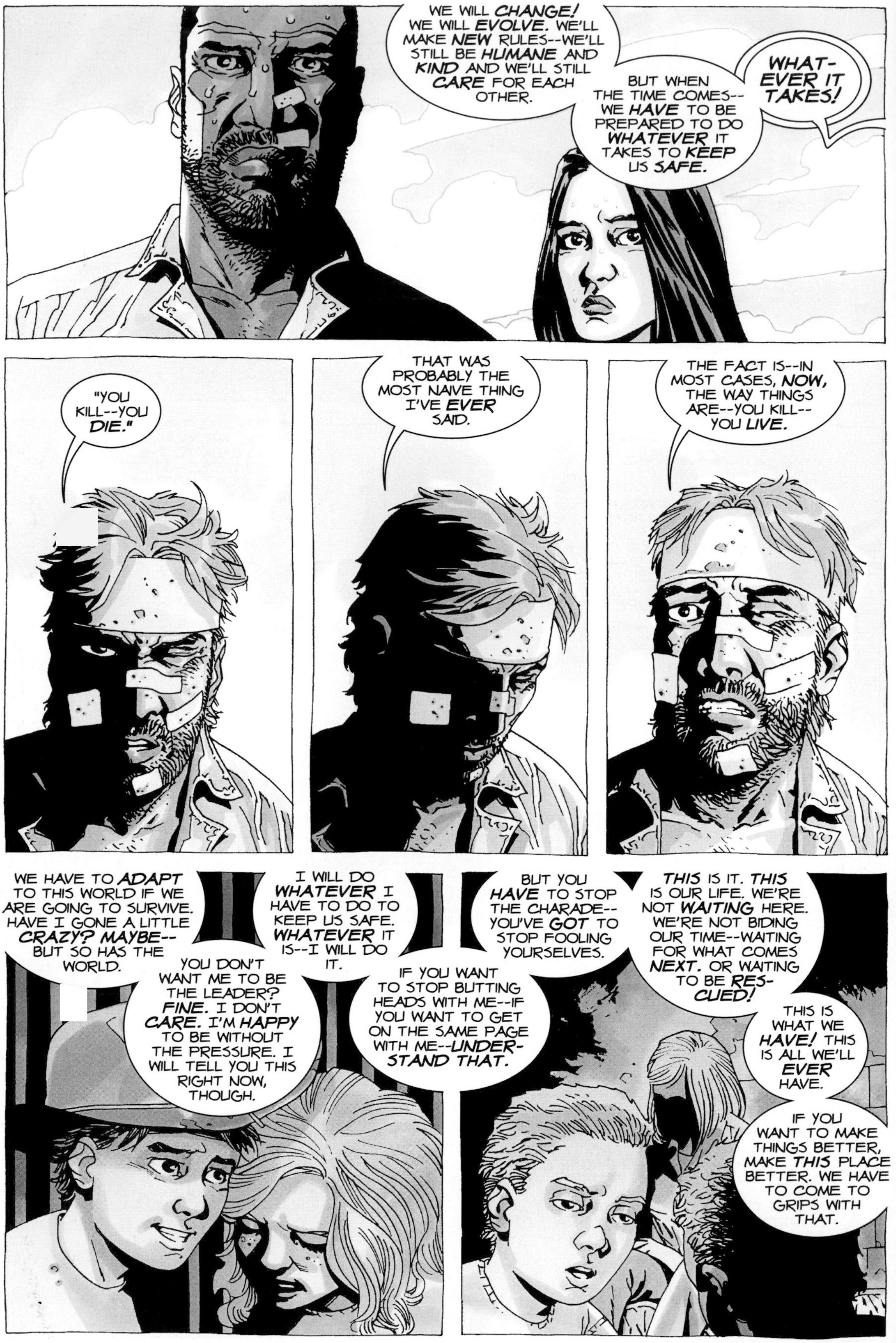
WE WILL CHANGE! WE WILL EVOLVE. WE'LL MAKE NEW RULES--WE'LL STILL BE HUMANE AND KIND AND WE'LL STILL CARE FOR EACH OTHER.
BUT WHEN THE TIME COMES--WE HAVE TO BE PREPARED TO DO WHATEVER IT TAKES TO KEEP US SAFE.
WHAT-EVER IT TAKES!
"YOU KILL--YOU DIE."
THAT WAS PROBABLY THE MOST NAIVE THING I'VE EVER SAID.
THE FACT IS--IN MOST CASES, NOW, THE WAY THINGS ARE--YOU KILL--YOU LIVE.
WE HAVE TO ADAPT TO THIS WORLD IF WE ARE GOING TO SURVIVE. HAVE I GONE A LITTLE CRAZY? MAYBE--BUT SO HAS THE WORLD.
YOU DON'T WANT ME TO BE THE LEADER? FINE. I DON'T CARE. I'M HAPPY TO BE WITHOUT THE PRESSURE. I WILL TELL YOU THIS RIGHT NOW, THOUGH.
I WILL DO WHATEVER I HAVE TO DO TO KEEP US SAFE. WHATEVER IT IS--I WILL DO IT.
IF YOU WANT TO STOP BUTTING HEADS WITH ME--IF YOU WANT TO GET ON THE SAME PAGE WITH ME--UNDER-STAND THAT.
BUT YOU HAVE TO STOP THE CHARADE--YOU'VE GOT TO STOP FOOLING YOURSELVES.
THIS IS IT. THIS IS OUR LIFE. WE'RE NOT WAITING HERE. WE'RE NOT BIDING OUR TIME--WAITING FOR WHAT COMES NEXT. OR WAITING TO BE RES-CUED!
THIS IS WHAT WE HAVE! THIS IS ALL WE'LL EVER HAVE.
IF YOU WANT TO MAKE THINGS BETTER, MAKE THIS PLACE BETTER. WE HAVE TO COME TO GRIPS WITH THAT.

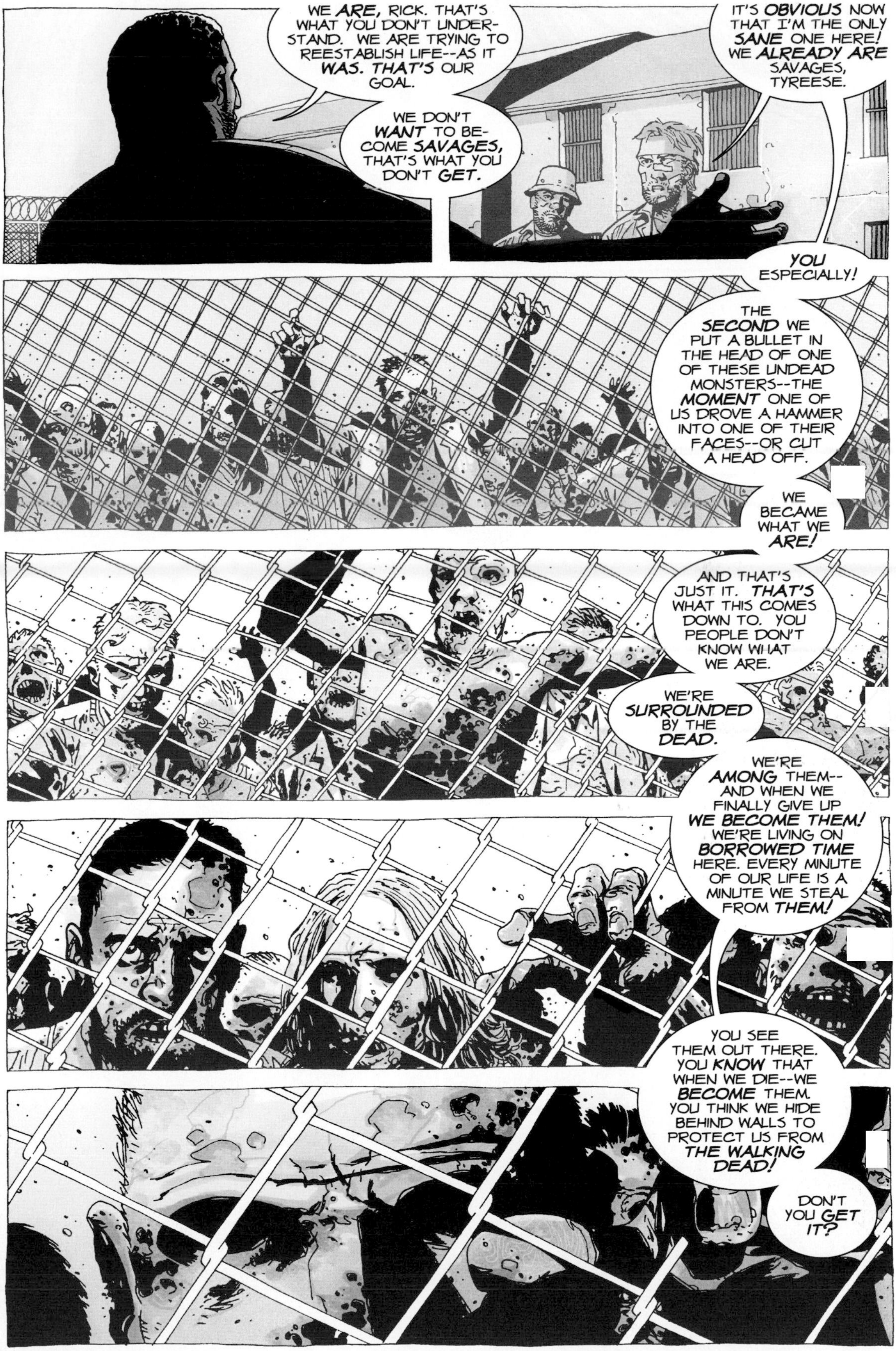
WE ARE, RICK. THAT'S WHAT YOU DON'T UNDER-STAND. WE ARE TRYING TO REESTABLISH LIFE--AS IT WAS. THAT'S OUR GOAL.
WE DON'T WANT TO BE-COME SAVAGES, THAT'S WHAT YOU DON'T GET.
IT'S OBVIOUS NOW THAT I'M THE ONLY SANE ONE HERE! WE ALREADY ARE SAVAGES, TYREESE.
YOU ESPECIALLY!
THE SECOND WE PUT A BULLET IN THE HEAD OF ONE OF THESE UNDEAD MONSTERS--THE MOMENT ONE OF US DROVE A HAMMER INTO ONE OF THEIR FACES--OR CUT A HEAD OFF.
WE BECAME WHAT WE ARE!
AND THAT'S JUST IT. THAT'S WHAT THIS COMES DOWN TO. YOU PEOPLE DON'T KNOW WHAT WE ARE.
WE'RE SURROUNDED BY THE DEAD.
WE'RE AMONG THEM--AND WHEN WE FINALLY GIVE UP WE BECOME THEM! WE'RE LIVING ON BORROWED TIME HERE. EVERY MINUTE OF OUR LIFE IS A MINUTE WE STEAL FROM THEM!
YOU SEE THEM OUT THERE. YOU KNOW THAT WHEN WE DIE--WE BECOME THEM. YOU THINK WE HIDE BEHIND WALLS TO PROTECT US FROM THE WALKING DEAD!
DON'T YOU GET IT?

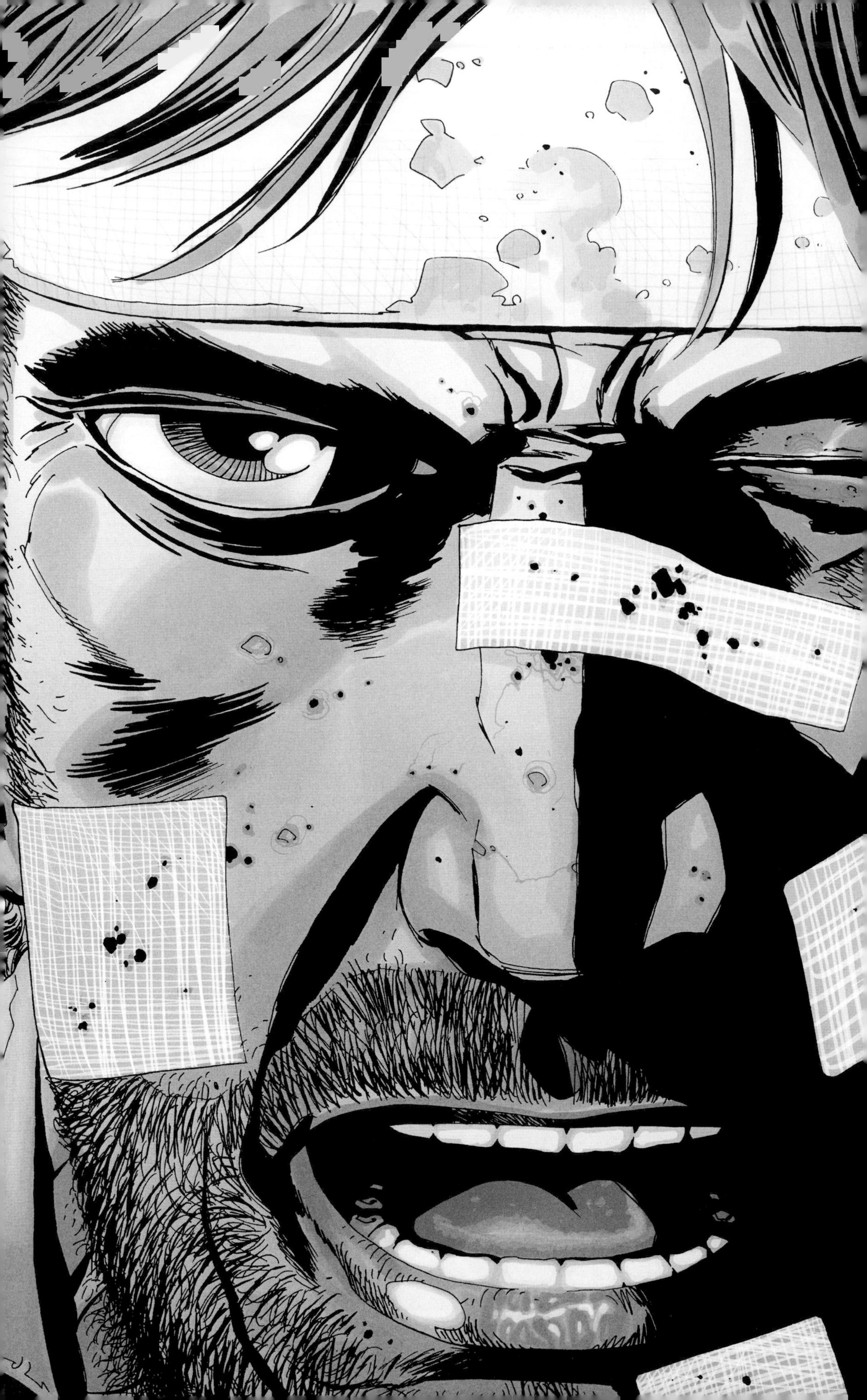

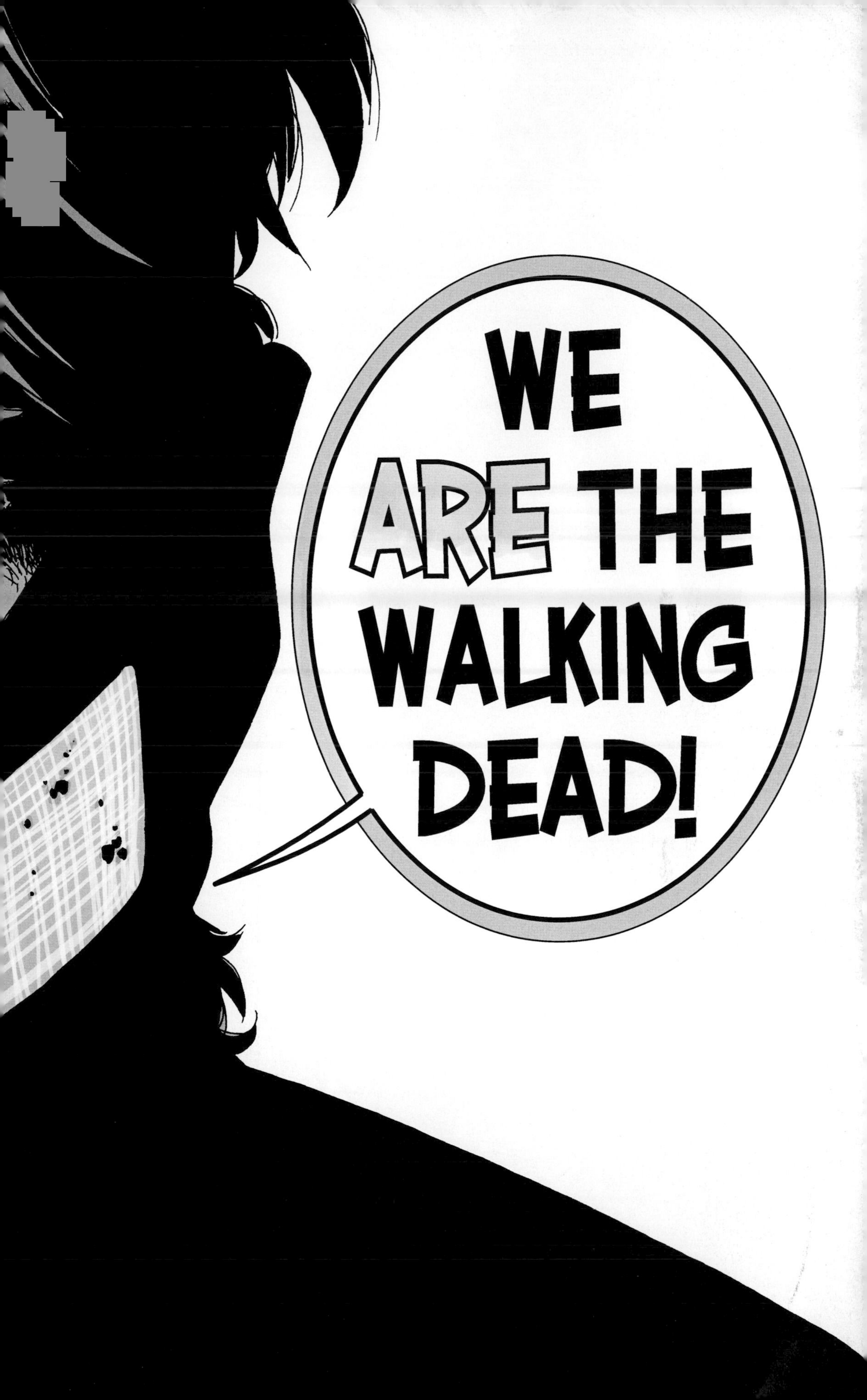
WE ARE THE WALKING DEAD!

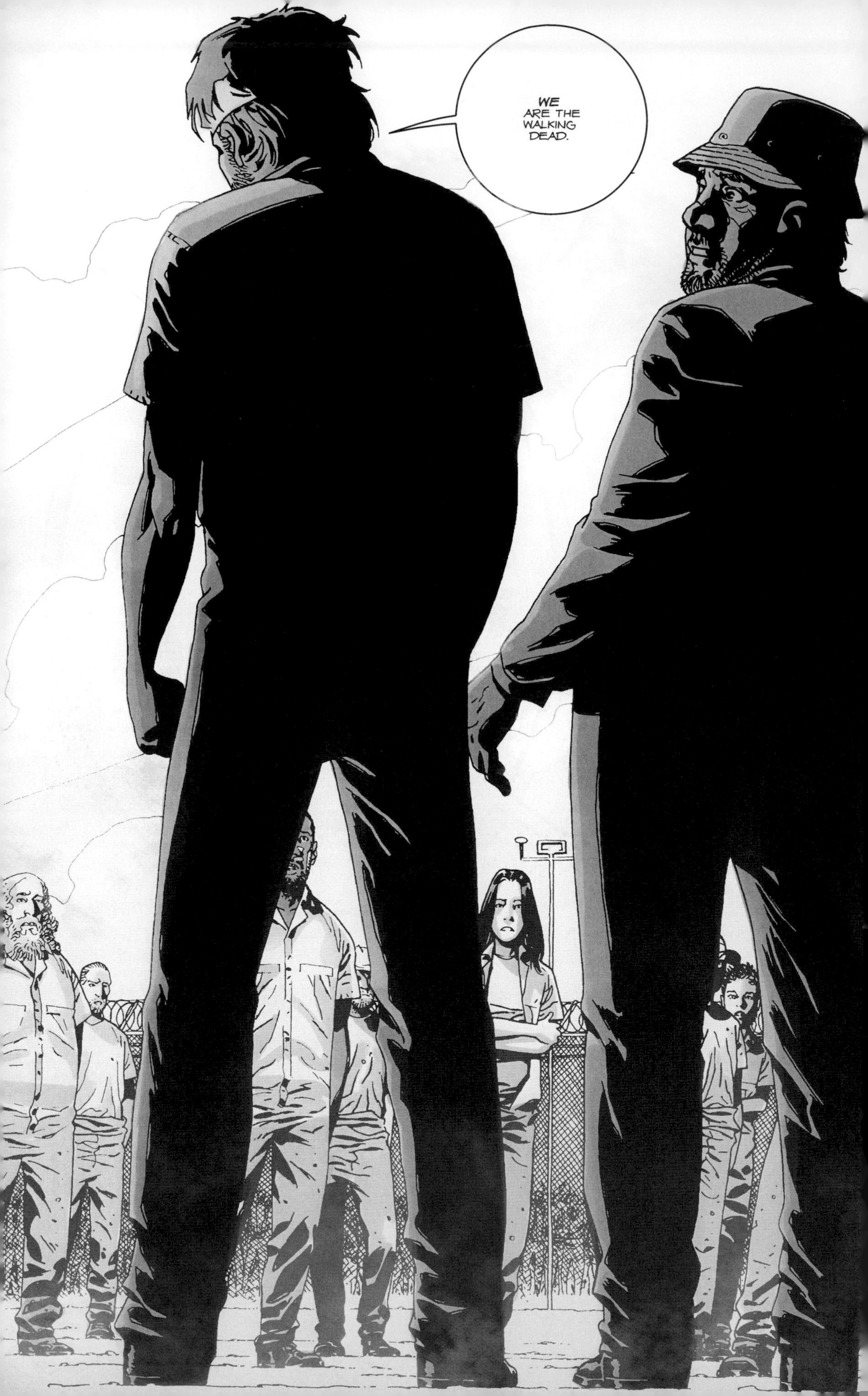
WE ARE THE WALKING DEAD.

TO BE CONTINUED...

MORE GREAT BOOKS FROM
ROBERT KIRKMAN & IMAGE COMICS!

BRIT
VOLUME THREE: FUBAR
THE ASTOUNDING
WOLF-MAN
VOLUME ONE
HAUNT
CAPES
PUNCHING THE CLOCK
INVINCIBLE
ULTIMATE COLLECTION
5
THE OFFICIAL HANDBOOK OF THE
INVINCIBLE
UNIVERSE

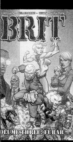

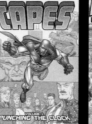

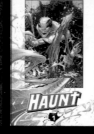

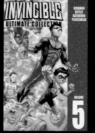

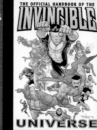

THE ASTOUNDING WOLF-MAN

VOL. 1[redacted]P
ISBN[redacted]978-1-58240-862-0
$14.99
VOL. 2[redacted]P
ISBN[redacted]978-1-60706-007-9
$14.99
VOL. 3[redacted]P
ISBN[redacted]978-1-60706-111-3
$16.99

BATTLE POPE

VOL. 1: GENESIS TP
ISBN: 978-1-58240-572-8
$14.99
VOL. 2: MAYHEM TP
ISBN: 978-1-58240-529-2
$12.99
VOL. 3[redacted]PILLOW TALK TP
ISBN[redacted]978-1-58240-677-0
$12.99
VOL. 4: WRATH OF GOD TP
ISBN: 978-1-58240-751-7
$9.99

BRIT

VOL. 1: OLD SOLDIER TP
ISBN: 978-1-58240-678-7
$14.99
VOL. 2[redacted]AWOL
ISBN[redacted]978-1-58240-864-4
$14.99
VOL. 3[redacted]UBAR
ISBN[redacted]978-1-60706-061-1
$16.99

CAPES

VOL. 1[redacted]PUNCHING THE CLOCK TP
ISBN[redacted]978-1-58240-756-2
$17.99

HAUNT

VOL. 1 TP
ISBN: 978-1-60706-154-0
$9.99

INVINCIBLE

VOL. 1: FAMILY MATTERS TP
ISBN: 978-1-58240-711-1
$12.99
VOL. 2: EIGHT IS ENOUGH TP
ISBN: 978-1-58240-347-2
$12.99
VOL. 3: PERFECT STRANGERS TP
ISBN: 978-1-58240-793-7
$12.99
VOL. 4: HEAD OF THE CLASS TP
ISBN: 978-1-58240-440-2
$14.95
VOL. 5: THE FACTS OF LIFE TP
ISBN: 978-1-58240-554-4
$14.99
VOL. 6: A DIFFERENT WORLD TP
ISBN: 978-1-58240-579-7
$14.99
VOL. 7: THREE'S COMPANY TP
ISBN: 978-1-58240-656-5
$14.99
VOL. 8: MY FAVORITE MARTIAN TP
ISBN: 978-1-58240-683-1
$14.99
VOL. 9: OUT OF THIS WORLD TP
ISBN: 978-1-58240-827-9
$14.99
VOL. 10: WHO'S THE BOSS TP
ISBN: 978-1-60706-013-0
$16.99
VOL. 11: HAPPY DAYS TP
ISBN: 978-1-60706-062-8
$16.99
VOL. 12: STILL STANDING TP
ISBN: 978-1-60706-166-3
$16.99
ULTIMATE COLLECTION, VOL. 1 HC
ISBN 978-1-58240-500-1
$34.95
ULTIMATE COLLECTION, VOL. 2 HC
ISBN: 978-1-58240-594-0
$34.99
ULTIMATE COLLECTION, VOL. 3 HC
ISBN: 978-1-58240-763-0
$34.99
ULTIMATE COLLECTION, VOL. 4 HC
ISBN: 978-1-58240-989-4
$34.99
ULTIMATE COLLECTION, VOL. 5 HC
ISBN: 978-1-60706-116-8
$34.99
THE OFFICIAL HANDBOOK OF THE INVINCIBLE UNIVERSE TP
ISBN: 978-1-58240-831-6
$12.99
THE COMPLETE INVINCIBLE LIBRARY, VOL. 1 HC
ISBN: 978-1-58240-718-0
$125.00
THE COMPLETE INVINCIBLE LIBRARY, VOL. 2 HC
ISBN: 978-1-60706-112-0
$125.00

THE WALKING DEAD

VOL. 1: DAYS GONE BYE TP
ISBN: 978-1-58240-672-5
$9.99
VOL. 2: MILES BEHIND US TP
ISBN: 978-1-58240-413-4
$14.99
VOL. 3: SAFETY BEHIND BARS TP
ISBN: 978-1-58240-487-5
$14.99
VOL. 4: THE HEART'S DESIRE TP
ISBN: 978-1-58240-530-8
$14.99
VOL. 5: THE BEST DEFENSE TP
ISBN: 978-1-58240-612-1
$14.99
VOL. 6: THIS SORROWFUL LIFE TP
ISBN: 978-1-58240-684-8
$14.99
VOL. 7: THE CALM BEFORE TP
ISBN: 978-1-58240-828-6
$14.99
VOL. 8: MADE TO SUFFER TP
ISBN: 978-1-58240-883-5
$14.99
VOL. 9: HERE WE REMAIN TP
ISBN: 978-1-60706-022-2
$14.99
VOL. 10: THE ROAD AHEAD TP
ISBN: 978-1-60706-075-8
$14.99
VOL. 11: FEAR THE HUNTERS TP
ISBN: 978-1-60706-181-6
$14.99
BOOK ONE HC
ISBN: 978-1-58240-619-0
$29.99
BOOK TWO HC
ISBN: 978-1-58240-698-5
$29.99
BOOK THREE HC
ISBN: 978-1-58240-825-5
$29.99
BOOK FOUR HC
ISBN: 978-1-60706-000-0
$29.99
BOOK FIVE HC
ISBN: 978-1-60706-171-7
$29.99
THE WALKING DEAD DELUXE HARDCOVER, VOL. 2
ISBN: 978-1-60706-029-7
$100.00

REAPER

GRAPHIC NOVEL
ISBN: 978-1-58240-354-2
$6.95

TECH JACKET

VOL. 1: THE BOY FROM EARTH TP
ISBN: 978-1-58240-771-5
$14.99

TALES OF THE REALM

HARDCOVER
ISBN: 978-1-58240-426-0
$34.95
TRADE PAPERBACK
ISBN: 978-1-58240-394-6
$14.95

BRIT
VOLUME ONE: OLD SOLDIER
REAPER
Battle POPE
Wrath of God
THE COMPLETE
INVINCIBLE
LIBRARY: VOLUME TWO
INVINCIBLE
HAPPY DAYS
TECH JACKET
THE BOY FROM EARTH

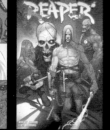

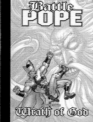

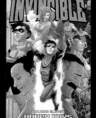

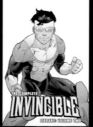

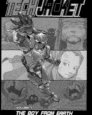

TO FIND YOUR NEAREST COMIC BOOK STORE, CALL:
1-888-COMIC-BOOK